# Lions & Love: King Of Clubs

Sistar Sunra

<h1 style="text-align: center">Copyrights Of The Song Titles Used</h1>

**To Pimp a Butterfly** is the third studio album by American rapper Kendrick Lamar. It was released on March 15, 2015, by Top Dawg Entertainment, Aftermath Entertainment and Interscope Records.

**Good Kid, M.A.A.D City** (stylized as **good kid, m.A.A.d city**) is the second studio album by American rapper Kendrick Lamar. It was released on October 22, 2012, through Top Dawg Entertainment, Aftermath Entertainment and Interscope Records.

**Untitled Unmastered** (stylized as **untitled unmastered.**) is a compilation album by American rapper Kendrick Lamar. It was released on March 4, 2016,[1] by Top Dawg Entertainment, Aftermath Entertainment and Interscope Records. The Act and Titles of the Chapters are Song Titles from these three albums.

King of Clubs also uses song titles from this artist as act and chapter titles. Along with **Damn** (stylized as **DAMN.**) is the fourth studio album by American rapper Kendrick Lamar. It was released on April 14, 2017, through Top Dawg Entertainment, Aftermath Entertainment and Interscope Records.

The soundtrack for the 2018 American superhero film Black Panther, based on the Marvel Comics character of the same name and produced by Marvel Studios, consists of an original score composed by Ludwig Göransson and original songs performed by Kendrick Lamar.

# Table of Contents

# Dedication

This one is dedicated to all my sons out there trying to fit into society while finding themselves. In the end…You always have a choice in everything you do…Remember this…You are loved. Do well to live your life in a true and real manner then run from who you indeed are.

The ideal male image was never invented by you, so their mold will not fit. I pray that you reinvent yourselves painted in the colors that make shut eyes see the light of your beautiful souls. It is your life to live and your soul that will lead you to happiness. No one can define bliss for you. It is a unique experience meant to be held for each and every one of you.

Who you are deep down inside, hidden in the shadow, cannot stay in darkness for long. A part of each of you loves the light, and the abyss cannot contain what was meant to shine brightly. It is with the discovery of self-love that your love for others grows more luminous. Do not fear the dark, for it will reveal the way toward sunshine where you will know peace.

Make no comparisons of yourself toward anyone else. Your experience based on your unique gifts to this world will make it more beautiful when you live in your light. Ase, my lovelies….

# Acknowledgment

All Praises to the Most-High: Living Inspiration, My Family, Love, Musicians with words in their spirit reaching the minds of us all, and that spark of Divine the Healing Optimism contacting us all...The art of storytelling is born when the mind and heart recognize another soul and struggle in the human form connected to their own.

Light Workers, Numerologists, Tarot Readers, Starseeds, Ancestors...The underestimated, overlooked, and doubtful overthinkers that see everything with a unique perspective....My Mirrors...Eye see you in me.

The Universoul Family, mankind, womankind, and those told they are too immature...Yes, You too. This Classroom we call Earth is intriguing because of your contribution! I pray that each of you discovers what makes you shine and never stop illuminating your own paths.

# About the Author

The author is a growing student of life, mother, daughter, aunt, and an optimistic lover of progressive thinking. An enigmatic, imaginative, and intuitive weaver of dreams born and raised in rural East Texas.

Her journey led her to write early in life when personal pain trying to discover the meaning of her own existence became too much to bear alone. She began to use many genres of music to inspire her storytelling. Though her views and opinions may contradict what society deems acceptable by usual standards. She only wishes to make it all make sense using scenarios considered taboo.

Sistar Sun RA seeks to entertain, nurture, and connect the minds and hearts of her readers. She means to find hope in hopeless situations and bring humor to the topics people take too seriously, using her imagination birthing lions and setting them free in the jungles of our thoughts.

King of Clubs is the second installment of the Lions Series, continuing the Queen of Hearts storyline. Introducing more vivid characters tying the original lions together with love, loyalty, lessons, and eventually leading all toward divine healing.

# ACT ONE

DAMN, BLACK HIPPY!

# Chapter One: Feel/Vice City

**Lionel Eugene Dunn**

The night Mami delivered Amani, I was tripping after Hakim bailed on me. He told me that I was a part of *THE PACT* to help save Mandisa, but he didn't need my help other than just trusting him. I was terrified when Dr. King surfaced. When I saw Mandisa's change in behavior around her father, it made me want to swing on his ass. His blue eyes had this callous stare locked on her the moment we walked into the room. If it was not for Cyrus getting Amani to wake up, that motherfucker probably would have flipped out. He didn't want us there, and he didn't fancy Cyrus touching Amani. I saw that shit. But Mami kept him listening to her.

She softened him up until he realized other motherfuckers could take better care of her. I think he understood Mami was serious about the divorce shit when she insisted Mandisa go to school. Dr. King really didn't want her to leave at all. He had a lock on her hand in the seat. Mandisa looked like she had been beaten by the man. Her eyes were down or on her mother and sister the entire time. She acknowledged us walking in after Cyrus woke up Amani. But she would not look at me! I think that if Mandisa said a word to either of us before he said it was okay, he would have gone off right there.

When I'm terrified like that, I shut the fuck up, wanna fight, or else…I'll start to cry. Nobody knew what to do but Hakim and Mami. That became obvious from the moment we learned Dr. King was here in Longview. Hakim suddenly snapped into his Master Manipulator Mode. That shit makes me nervous after the shit that happened when they made *The Contract*. When Hakim is stressed like this, he turns into a mean, crazy, and evil nigga. The last few months that he's been around more, I've started to see the shit Cyrus and Kaliah were talking about.

I fell back with the insults because the more I went for him, the sadder he became. He wasn't furious at me. He was so depressed that he attacked me, striving to get angry, but it wouldn't work, so he'd leave. He was pissed at me the time I called Mandisa a bitch. If Cyrus hadn't held my brother until I apologized, Hakim would have treated me like an op, straight traitor. I could see it in his eyes. They were enormous and bloodshot the moment he locked his sight on me.

You're gonna think I'm fucking with your heads when I say this shit…But I started to hear a motherfucker screaming at me. Not Hakim, another voice I've never heard before…it was so loud it scared the shit out of me!

When Hakim tried to run into the highway and kill himself…I had an asthma attack! I couldn't breathe. I fell to the floor, trying to get to my inhaler in his bag. I gave up when I saw Mandisa attempting to stop him. Cyrus saw it happening and tried to help before he made a run to stop Hakim. I was more worried about my brother!

He was gonna do that shit if Mandisa broke up with him. I know that Hakim is crazy now...well…he's always been weird. But I kept pushing him until he was so sad he wanted to die again. Cyrus told me that Hakim tried to kill himself many times after we fought, and I never knew. It fucked me up.

But being nice to Hakim still feels off because he talks like he doesn't respect anyone when he is SCARED. He said some shit that made me start to think back. A lot of niggas are afraid of my brother, and they will not fuck with any of us because of that shit. I know that 'Pretty Tony' Guccione, the owner of Gucci's, can't stand Cyrus, but he's terrified to turn him away because of Hakim. Cyrus knows better than to press his luck, and that's why he's always moving around. We club everywhere we can get in, and when you have money…You know that nigga Tony isn't going to turn down Cyrus spending his paper as long as Hakim is around him. We went to Gucci's with Mandisa once, we all had to fight when Tony tried to come at her, and Hakim said that was the last time for them.

***

I'm with my boy, so I'm not trippin' on these niggas. Lester Woods will pop a nigga if he doesn't want to catch hands. Best believe if any of these niggas test Les, Lionel is gonna fuck them up. He's really like my big brother. Lester always seems to know when I'm alone and afraid. He comes and finds me no matter where I may be and tries to cheer me up. It never fails. The moment Hakim bails on me when I'm scared, Lester Woods calls or comes by.

Lester was my best friend, Jamire's big brother, who was always around the hood. Les was a pimp. Yeah, really, but not the kind that *Sweets* and Ace were back in the gap. See, Lester is a bit different. Yeah, he runs hos, okay? But Lester takes outstanding care of all the girls that have ever worked for him. He never hit a bitch as far as I know, but he will fuck up any nigga that gives him the wrong vibe when he's mad. Lester was crazy, and we all knew it, but he was always looking out for the kids and girls in the hood.

5

He didn't like going to Gucci's, and we didn't either because of Tony Guccione. He was the asshole that opened up shop here back when *Sweets* was running shit. He worked with Miles, the same nigga that sold crack to Maya's mom. Tony thought he was a pimp, opened this place, aiming to run hos out of the back. But Tony was snatching up pretty little girls when they got to look a certain age, he offered them work as a waitress, but they wound up getting raped, turned out, or dancing in the back.

Pretty Tony is a piece of shit, but his club is the only place around that doesn't ask questions when you got paper. If you go in back, people know you're there for the Strip Club/Brothel. But the dance club was where you go if you just want to party like a rock star and spend your money. I see a lot of rich kids there that know they can do whatever at Gucci's. It's the closest thing to Magic City out here in the country, open every night. Nobody fucks with Tony because it's on his private property, outside the city limits, and he pays enough people to cover shit he and homies do up.

Lester has been beefing with Pretty Tony for years over fucking up the young girls before they are old enough to make up their minds, hitting and raping women, and fucking with Cyrus. Yeah, Lester is white, but he's an ally. Kaliah told me that white people are messed up like us. Looking at peoples' skin without knowing their heads is the same as looking at us as a threat. I agree with that... All I know is Lester is not about fucking up the community with the bullshit that Pretty Tony Guccione has been on for years. Lester shows up looking for his ass to test him cause Tony is scared of him.

"What the fuck do you want?!" As we pulled into Gucci's parking lot, Lester screamed out the heavily tinted driver's window to a group of people eyeing his new ride. When Les pulled up on the block in that bitch I had to ride! I had never seen a car worthy of so much MONEY! That pretty 2019 white and gold custom Bentley Continental was the real deal! The chrome on those wheels was shining at night with barely any light! He had a burnt caramel and black interior with "Les is Extra" stitched into the headrests that were so sick I got nauseous."You niggas acting like you never seen a white man drive his brother around in a Bentley before, shit! Lionel, you wanna really fuck 'em up? Here, nigga, you push my shit!"

"For real, Les?!" I demanded, stunned as shit. Lester just bought this bitch, and it is clean! I had never seen a real Bentley before, and this nigga went and bought one just to flex! Niggas in THE VIEW don't drive Bentleys. Everybody and they Mama have those cheaper look-alikes. I know my big brother Lester dropped some paper cause he loves to aggravate fake niggas, to see who wants to fight, and Lester talks way more shit than me. I didn't have my license, and Hakim and Cyrus never let me drive. "You really gonna let me roll this shit?!"

"It's just a fuckin car, Nigga! Here swap out," Les snickered, putting that bitch in park.

He hopped out in the middle of the club entrance, blocking motherfuckers way. Les had a blunt in his mouth, a gun in his jacket, and dusted the ashes off his Versace shirt. His green eyes were red ass hell in the headlights, grinning at me. He reminded me of Kaliah with the same short red curly hair and green eyes. Les's tall, swoll frame was also similar to Kaliah's.

You know I'm gonna drive this bitch, right? I walked past Les, getting in the driver's seat. I put that bitch in drive, we cruised the parking lot, and niggas were watching like they saw Lil Wayne when they looked at me. I got chills everywhere…Ewww…!

It was ugly the way niggas recognized me, then their jaws would drop. I love that shit. Yeah, Nigga, I'm that nigga to give you those waves. You hate your life right now, don't you? I can see it all over your ratchet faces.

Kill yo self! This is the shit I live for! Oooh!

"Nobody is gonna believe me when I tell them this shit at school tomorrow, Bro," I chuckled, struggling to contain my excitement.

My knee was twitching; I was so damn happy. Les glanced over at me, passing the blunt. His eyes glossed over as he let a giant cloud in my face. His eyebrows drew together, smiling. Lester was the man in the hood that we all knew got the bag and the hos. He had every pretty girl around the way chasing after his cars when he drove by. But Lester is a player. He's always on the move across Texas, so he can't be tied down. I got brothers that are all about the grind and taking care of family. Lester is the breadwinner, and he is happy being the man taking care of his little brother now that his parents are as old as G.D. and Granny Sophie. I think that's why Lester kicks it strong with me. He treats me like Jamire. But Les pops up to hang out because he's rarely in town. That's why it's hard to turn down Les when he pulls up. My nigga is making actual moves. I try to hang and absorb as much as I can. I've learned how to treat these niggas and not trust these hos fucking around in the streets with Les. Hakim doesn't teach a class like Lester Woods.

"Lionel, you still in school? I thought you dropped out or graduated… How old are you, Nigga?" Les laughed as I took the blunt.

"Bro! You know Hakim would kick my ass if I quit school. That's Jamire that dropped out! I'm just 15. I got plans, and I need my degree to get my paper. I'm pretty sure I'm going to college. I don't know what the fuck for, though," I snickered, blowing the blunt while I parked.

"15? Nigga, I could have sworn you were at least 17! You look 20 with all that hair on your chin! I can't even grow a fucking beard, and here your bony-ass is looking like a damn billy goat! But bitches love smooth niggas. So, I'll shave all my body hair off, even my balls! I grow hair everywhere but my damn face! What…the…fuck, Lionel?

'I feel Hakim's struggle. But he pulls way more bitches than my broke ass!" Lester chuckled red as hell in the face. He was high as hell and running off at the mouth. His eyes kept scanning the parking lot, looking for any reason to pop off. I know, Lester; he never lets his guard down. That nigga sat forward, eyeing a bunch of dudes in a black car that slowed down staring at us. Lester opened his door and leaned over, staring them down with his gun, smirking. Those niggas got the fuck gone! Les dove back in his seat, laughing. "You still single, Nigga? I know you not checking for anything since May-May up and got taken. These hos ain't loyal, and the women don't know the real, so you better off fucking and moving around until they know you are serious. Fuck, you mean?"

"I don't care about no bitches, Les," I groaned, nodding. "Hos started begging too much since Hakim raised my spending cap. I'm not spending my paper on these hos. I get the pussy and goes about my way!"

"Man, Lionel, I love all bitches. I wish all of them could be my wife, really. I'd give them all the shit they want too. I don't mind providing for a woman that gives me what the fuck I need! I don't care I'll take white bitches, black bitches are beautiful, shit I've fucked a bitch from Greenland that lived in Iceland," Les thought toward me, watching the parking lot a moment more. "That was some cold-ass pussy! Her pussy was so cold when it got wet, my balls stuck to her ass. It was like that kid's tongue in *A Christmas Story*. I told that bitch next time we fuck, we gonna be in a hot tub or something! I can't lose my shit fucking the *White Witch* from *Narnia*!"

I loved fucking with Lester when he was high. He would go on and on about his business. Hakim never told me shit about what he was doing. Lester Woods didn't have any shame, and he loved talking shit like me. So I was gassing him up to keep sharing. He loved it…I know it boosted his ego. When he got a good vibe, Les would talk, laugh, wanna party, and start making it rain! I loved that shit, so I was down to boost my homie's ego. He did that shit for me all the time, and he was down to show me the best time anytime I rode with him. Yea, sometimes I had to fight, but fuck it…Better than sitting at home alone, worried about what my brother was out doing.

"You not fucking that much, Bro…But it's cool. I know how you operate," I chuckled, teasing him. "I've always seen you pull some fine dimes. But the sisters don't peep for you like that, though, do they?"

"Hell yes! The SISTERS be playing hard to get and shit. But I'm not mad at them. I understand, baby. You're infuriated at all the fucked up shit in your life that you can't control. I can put some milk in yo coffee, take a drank, and cover you in this cream. Then I'll get you whatever makes you smile until the next time I hear you crying in my ear. I don't chase the ones that don't want me, Bro.

'The ones that know what I got come to me, and they learn that I'm a cool dude. I let them know I'm not looking for a real thang, and I like to play around. If they down to play, I'll pay, and if they want more money, I tell them how they can come up. Some are down, and some ain't…but in the end, it's her choice," Les told me seriously but joking.

Then he scowled, watching the club thinking again. "The shit that Tony is doing has been going on too long. Every time I leave to work and come back…It's worse for the girls around East Texas. It's not the big cities…these little tiny towns…He's preying on girls nobody's gonna miss. Pretty Tony is asking for it, man!

'I don't get these fake niggas, Bro.

'Riddle me this, Lionel? Why the fuck all these niggas out here aiming to pull a bitch they know Tony and his boys probably ran through? They know what goes on here, talk all that shit, but won't bust one cap in his ass? These bitches don't have not one REAL NIGGA protecting them from that trash. Pumping up the rural area with Miles's poison, raping teenage girls, doping niggas up, set 'em up to get cleaned out by them scared hos he made, and the motherfucker got the nerve to talk shit about me behind my back. But act buddy-buddy in a nigga's face? I get one bad vibe tonight, Lionel…Bro…I may catch another charge, but you just get my ride home. I trust you, Lionel."

"You know Tony shits his pants when he sees either you or Hakim. He ain't gonna pull shit, Les," I laughed, pumping him up. He needed to come up a bit more. He was gonna pop that nigga if Tony said a word to him. Whatever Les heard had him pissed off enough to come to get me, so I know he meant that shit. Jamire was probably waiting for the call. He knew what was up. Lester and Jamire were tight and told each other everything. I wish Hakim and I had that kind of relationship. "Why you didn't bring, *'Jamie'*?"

"Jamire in his feelings over that bitch being pregnant and don't want to do shit. He keeps saying that bitch is a liar, now…I don't know…It sounds like a classic setup to me. But you know *'Jamie,'* he's smarter than he plays, kind of like you, Lionel. But Jamire swears that bitch is up to something. I SAY, just hit the bitch with a DNA test, but *'Jamie'* worried about what Mama will say. You know he hates making Mama mad. She's pregnant and wants *'Jamie'* to do the right shit, and I agree with Mama IF that's your baby. FUCK that ho if it ain't, shit, bounce!" Les laughed, shaking his head.

"Right!" I agreed with Les. "She can lie all damn day with that mouth, but DNA gonna snitch on that bitch!"

"I don't blame the bitch for attempting to get a payday. That kind of shit comes with the fucking territory when you got something bitches want. She doesn't want to get it for herself, so she expects a nigga to just hand it to her for a kid. She could have been a ho selling it safely, making bread, and no kids to raise if she was a down bitch. But naw…She's just a lazy ho. Big difference there, Lionel.

'You'll live longer and be gravy if you learn the difference between bitches and hos. Any woman can be a bitch. A bitch is gonna be in her feelings and not know why or how to get out of them. I just see all women as bitches cause that's how they gonna act when you do shit they don't like. But these hos are getting dumber as technology takes over. They think that a motherfuckers gonna blow their whole wad on their asses for a cute body and some makeup?!

'Then the ho doesn't want to take care of themselves, start popping out kids and turning them against niggas because they're bitter and can't accept they needed LOVE and lied saying it was just a FUCK. That lie is what is fucking everybody up. Say what the fuck you really want once you know…if you don't…then you shouldn't be fucking anyway. I know what the fuck I want! I want the pussy, and I want to help you if I like you, but I want you to leave me the fuck alone unless I call you. Simple, but bitches lie, become hos, and then bitter because I don't change.

'You got me all the way fucked up, bitch. I've seen many fine bitches all over the world. Only one ever made me want to spend it all, and you don't come close to the bitch. I like all my pieces on the side, like my pistols, so I can dump them if I have to run, and LOVE ain't an option fuckin wit nigga like me.

'You can't have it all, Bro. You have to pick and choose your priorities. It ain't fair to lie to a bitch when you know you can't be the man she needs, but who am I to turn down a bitch with a made-up mind about what she wants, Bro? That's all I'm saying. That's real motherfucking talk!

'I see shit totally different than most motherfuckers because I know I'm crazy, Lionel. I don't give too many fucks, nor do I expect one back but from a few. You, Jamire, Mama, Hakim, Cyrus, and all the kids that grew up on my block are the only people I trust. That's why I roll deep with you, Bro. We all struggling to get the fuck out of here for good, but it seems that bullshit keeps pulling me back," Les laughed, hitting the blunt. He glanced at me, then the club, frowning deeply. "You want to know something I learned from fucking with Hakim?"

"I never saw you kicking it with my brother, Les. He says that you're a bad influence on me. Since when did you roll with Hakim?" I died laughing as Lester shook his head. "He acts like he hates all white people. I can't see you talking to Hakim like you talk to me. You know he hates that nigga-shit you do."

"Hakim is a fucking savage, Lionel. But, he's smart as hell and taught me some shit," Les arrogantly said with a serious look on his face. He offered me the blunt and placed his gun inside the holster under his jacket. "Hakim doesn't like me, and I've always known it since you moved here. But we respect one another for the hustle and each other's twisted ways of seeing shit. We have words from time to time, it makes me admire him more, and he knows that shit.

'Your brother is the only nigga that could pull all the bitches away from me when he comes around. They want him because he makes them respect HIM and THEMSELVES enough to get out of here.

'I can fuck the shit out of a bitch, Lionel. But the bitches that won't love themselves that fuck Hakim...they never want to be away from him. They will throw everything away for a shot to be his girl! They want to be loved by Hakim so much that they will say fuck any other nigga. They all say that the shit that Hakim tells them when he fucks them makes them so happy they don't want another nigga! I don't get it, but it must be straight facts if all the bitches I used to run quit!

'Back when *Sweets* was on the streets, he used to tell me to watch your brother because Hakim was just 11, and he had all the women on the block watching him like he was made out of gold. It didn't matter how old a bitch was either…Hakim was hypnotizing 'em all with words and swag from the ages 10 to 50, and they were listening."

"Hakim got a hell of a past he doesn't like to talk about, Les. But it's not good," I groaned, not saying anything else.

"Shit, you think I don't know? I've fought that NIGGA, and Cyrus saved me from his ass, Bro! We all squashed things when Hakim explained shit once Cyrus was gone. It fucked me up, but I saw that shit and knew…He's worse than anything that I think about.

'That NIGGA scared the fuck out of me, and I couldn't clap that motherfucker...He didn't give me a second to think about hitting him. You know I always got my shit on me? Hakim knows that shit too. We had words cuz I called him Nigga. I call everyone that shit, Bro. Hakim and Cyrus know that shit too, but I guess Hakim wasn't hearing me that night.

Cyrus tried to calm him down, and Hakim turned on him. He talked pure shit to his best friend. Cyrus took that shit and still tried to stop him from getting at me. That's when I knew Hakim was for real. I blinked, thinking about if I wanted to fight him, and he knocked my ass smooth out."

"Damn, Les! I didn't know you and Hakim were beefing!" I groaned, shaking my head.

Lester Woods rolled his eyes and looked at me, saying, "I'm not beefing with your brother, Lionel. Shit, Hakim is my fucking hero! I wanna be like him when I grow up, and I'm 32! Shiiiiit... He's making bank, smart as shit, got the finest bitch on the planet now, a cool homie that's got his back, and you for a brother. Hakim is gravy, Lionel. You don't have shit to worry about as long your brother is looking out.

'He's gonna take care of his family. That's all he gives a fuck about. We get along on that shit all the time, but we bump heads on my ignorant shit. He's a little brother to me, but we've always had a black-love/white-hate relationship. I get it.

'I'm an enemy to him because of my skin, but that doesn't make me a monster. We compromise until we disagree, but we respect one another's tastes. I fuck with you because you respect me more than Hakim, and he's the one with all the keys you need. But he doesn't like to get down like us...that's why we vibe, Lionel.

'We alike, and I dig your waves, Man. I always want to chill when you kick it, but so be it if we do some ratchet.

'Let me call this bitch back real quick, then we gonna meet up with Carla inside. She brought her model friends tonight."

"Ask if she got a fine friend for me, Les?" I laughed watching niggas gawking from the sidelines.

"Nigga, I'm calling to check on my kids!" Les laughed, pushing my arm.

"You got kids, Les? Where they at?" I demanded curiously.

"They're with their Mama, Nigga!" Les snorted, slumping down in the seat, clutching his phone. "My wife...Why the fuck do you think I don't love these hos? I married my baby mama back when I was 21, Lionel. I've been making all this bank for my kids since I had my son at 17, Nigga!"

"Les, you're fucking married, too? What the fuck?!! You always in the streets and gone!" I thought, confused as shit.

"We got an arrangement, see, I give her what she wants with her gold-digging ass, and she raises the kids. She doesn't run shit, but her mouth. I put up with her crazy ass because she's always been a down-ass bitch to me since I was a kid. She knew I didn't want her or anyone, but we were going hard. When Tariq popped up, shit, I had to do what a nigga gotta do.

'My Mama was trying to throw me out, so I hit the streets getting paper for my son. I married the bitch because Mama told me that I owed her that much for getting her pregnant so young. She was just 14, so yeah…it was terrible. I did what I had to do. She never complained as long as I bought home the bread and took care of the kids. But she tries to come out of her neck talking crazy when I don't call her back.

'I told her crazy ass to leave. I wasn't stupid. She didn't have shit, and my folks weren't giving up the paper to her. I made her sign shit before I said I do or I wasn't gonna give her shit. I was gonna take my son and raise his ass with my Mama if she didn't. I knew her people were a fucked up mess. But she was a good girl, and I made her go wrong, so I took that loss. She knows I don't love her, and I'm just looking out. I love my three kids with her. She's the only bitch I've ever fucked raw. I don't love her, but I guess I trust her.

'It's more women out there than there are men on this planet, so I say play on playas if you ain't in love. I love all women, and I loves me a big bitch, Lionel! Fat bitches be so soft and sweet as hell. After you bust a nut, they want to feed you. I fuck better when I smell food cooking in the kitchen! My wife doesn't do shit, and she is skinny as hell, now! She used to be so fucking fine, but all her rich girlfriends got in her head.

'She's trying to be like bitches on *Love and Hip-Hop*, looking like bony-ass NEW YORK from *Flavor of Love*. All that fake shit, surgery, and she ain't happy with how she looks. It doesn't make no damn sense to me. I tell the bitch she was sexier fat! I was all over her chocolate ass when she wasn't worried about what the fuck people thought about her.

'Now, whatever her friends on, she tries to ride the wave. Botox and shit got her looking crazy and going off on me cuz I don't want to hear how unhappy she is for how she fucked herself up! Trust me! All bitches are crazy, no matter what you do to make them happy.

'She strutting around in Prada looking like a well-dressed ruler with no ass-at-all. Begging me to cuddle, and I'm scared to touch your ignorant ass because you don't want to fuck up your hair, fingernails, and wearing makeup in bed, taking selfies. Trying to fake it for likes on the internet because you don't think you're beautiful. I told her she was fine and needed to stop the bullshit. She goes and does more shit changing the outside.

'I thought she was trying to go through one of those phases like Hakim or Cyrus. Black Power and shit…? Yo…I would be glad if she taught the kids some of that shit! Naw…She cut off all her damn hair to a fade, then started wearing colored wigs. The internet has these hos lost, and niggas gassing them up believing the hype. All these bitches posting for likes looking for love…they need to love themselves. We gonna like what we see cuz we men, but who wants that for an old lady when she doesn't shut up about how ugly she feels?

'She ain't gonna answer! Bitch! It's cool. Let me call Carla to see what it looks like inside. I'll see if she got a friend that wants to fuck, Lionel. Just watch the man work!"

"Les! Nigga, you a fool," I died laughing as he sat up, ready to roll.

"Sup, you filthy nasty, Bitch?" Les asked, answering his phone. "You know you love that shit, Carla. Yeah, I'm coming, Baby. Me and Lionel on the way in now. You got a fine friend for him?

'...Naw! I don't mean that monkey-mouthed heffa, Shelia! She looks like she's been shooting dice with her teeth. If that bitch smiles at a cookout, niggas gonna call *Big Six*! Then she got the nerve to have a funky little attitude when you tell her to back the fuck off? I can't stand that Domino Dentist having-ass bitch!

'Oh, yeah…?

'Fredericka can get it…Tell her to text me a picture so I can show it to him. Alight, Baby, I'll see your slippery mouth in a minute, girl. I hope that you're thirsty? The Alcohol Hero is here to deliver, and I want satisfaction like the Rolling Stones. You let me know if that bastard Tony and the boys pop up tonight? I don't see his flashy shit anywhere. What he out kidnapping bitches, again...oh…Mia…?

'Alight, well we gonna kick until he bring that ass back or I gotta roll out. Take your panties off! I ain't got time to undress you, Bitch!"

"What's up, Les? Carla got a homegirl I can hit?" I asked, watching him hang up his phone.

"Oh yeah, Fredericka, she is fine! She's mixed with black and Chinese or something, has crazy eyes, and a big ole butt, too! Ricka is cute for her tiny frame, long hair, big ole titties, lean, and she's sweet too, Bro! Here, I'm gonna give you some bread to buy some drinks and get nice. Then you can tear it up," Les laughed, handing me three blue-faced bills.

"You the shit, Bro!" I thanked him, smiling.

"I got you, Lionel. Just lay low and watch my back. I'm gonna get a lap dance and smell some pussy. If Carla ain't acting right, I'll find the finest bitch in the spot and fuck her in the lounge. Fuck Pretty Tony!" Les died laughing but was still looking for him in the flashing lights to show up.

"Why don't you open your own spot? You got paper, Les," I wondered.

"I got too many jobs as is, Lionel. I can't keep up with all the bitches I have now. If I got a spot and sat still, I'd catch a case. My temper ain't made to be friendly to strangers. I tolerate ignorant motherfuckers cuz I look at most of them as kids out here. But if you want to grow up quick, come fuck around in Les's neck of the woods. I got extra bullets and enough guns to light up Chiraq if you want to test me.

'But they won't pop a punk-ass piece of shit that's fucking up the vibe around here, so I know they ain't shit, Lionel. You won't protect your women, then you ain't shit! I don't give a fuck what they do with their bodies to make bank. You don't fuck with a woman's capability to make a goddamn choice about what she wants. She can make up her own damn mind when she's ready.

'You don't force a girl to be a bitch! Little girls are innocent until we make them bitches, and I take full responsibility for every bitch that tells me her troubles. If she trusts me enough to tell me some shit…I'm going in to fix it! It's the least I can do for some pussy. What do I look like fucking for free? I better help if I touch it! That's why I'm fucking offended by a nigga that rapes a bitch!

'You got some nerve moving here fucking up the girls and making crazy bitches that hate themselves! All the good work I did after *Sweets* got locked up was undone in a year, thanks to Tony gaining momentum. I should have popped his ass back when he snatched up Angela. If I had caught him back then, James wouldn't have fucked up going after Miles. But I understand that shit why he did that shit, Bro! The what-ifs fuck with me a lot in these streets.

'Let's go see what the scene looks like? Ain't none of these bitches REAL NIGGAS, and if they touch my shit, they know I'll light it up out here and make them scatter like roaches," Lester mumbled, stepping out of the car.

I was never worried about shit when I rode with Les. He was not going to let shit happen to me. He was prepared to pop niggas lastly. Nobody wanted to fight Lester Woods because he was known for knocking niggas unconscious when he snapped. Lester had a short fuse, and he yelled at niggas that got in his way. He didn't like to be disrespected by anyone, but he didn't mistreat people unless they came for him or one of us. He was always strictly business unless he was on the prowl to fuck shit up. That's why I loved hanging out with Les. He was cool, calm, and ready when he made a move. He always had a plan, and he was looking out for anyone close to him. Sometimes I wished Hakim was more like Les, but Hakim would knock me out if I ever said that shit.

Anytime I bring up Lester Woods around Hakim, he gets pissed off and starts hating. Hakim doesn't fuck with Jamire too hard either because of Les. I don't know what *'Jamie'* did to Hakim, but Jamire always talks about my brother like he's Donnie Yen. He even calls my brother 'Hakim Donnie Dunn.'

But that's why I can't see eye to eye with my brother. He doesn't realize when he's won a motherfucker's respect because he can't turn the hate off. He thinks he's better than anyone not doing shit his way. Les and Jamire are the coolest brothers I've met in the view. At least, Les says that he and Hakim are cool. I didn't know that shit. I usually get pissed when I learn more shit Hakim is hiding, but this time…I got happy.

Les and Hakim not beefing meant Hakim wasn't a complete bitch under all that mean shit he wearing. I was ready to have fun when I learned that Hakim connected with niggas I actually liked.

"Yo, listen, Lionel, I gotta warn you to stay away from here alone from now on. Pretty Tony will try to fuck you off if he catches you slipping in his place. Tony is eyeing Cyrus for fucking Ms. Mia! He better be careful too. As long as he's running with Hakim, he's safe. Tony's scared of Hakim since your brother nearly gutted his ass with a blade in the parking lot two years ago. That shit was epic!

'Hakim was like Jett Lee! He took out four niggas and cut the fuck out of Tony with a short ninja blade. I laughed so hard I almost pissed myself! He's terrified of Hakim, so he'll put up with Cyrus fucking his old lady back in the gap, but he ain't forgot that shit, Bro. He's mad! Mia was trying to leave his ass, but Cyrus kept running off on her.

'I heard from a girl we both know that works here that Cyrus had Ms. Mia about to file for divorce, but she got scared because of his age and ran back to Tony. He was too young to be fucking with her fine-ass anyway. So, Cyrus cut her off, and Tony is still mad! When Cyrus comes to town, Ms. Mia doesn't want to work, and Tony knows she's in love with Cyrus's black ass. If she sees him and Tony is around, just get the fuck gone. Or you better hope me or Hakim is with you.

'These FAKE NIGGAS will watch these beasts fuck y'all off rather than stop Tony's bitch ass. I hate it here! That's why I move the fuck around!" Les told me over the top of his sparkling white freshly waxed top. The frown on Les's face reminded me of Hakim when he was ready to fight.

I didn't know that Cyrus and Hakim were doing it like that back when they were my age! What the hell? Lester was there and saw it all, too? Damn, shit just keeps getting deeper and deeper the more I learn about all the people I consider family.

"Niggas, stop hating and get some paper! You got a problem with my brother driving my shit? Let me know right now!" Les shouted, gazing at a few of my fans eyeing us as we started for the door. Les slowed down his stroll and glanced around, and those niggas all made themselves busy. Niggas knew Les wasn't bluffing. They called him 'Les the Pest' or 'Hot-Mess Les,' and he would pull the trigger just to see who wanted to fight. The niggas that don't run are who he wants. "Holla at me if you need a job, but if you gonna just hate and wait...try me! Tell Tony that I'm here to holla at him real quick when he brings his bitch-ass home! I know he lives on the hill!"

"Les, you a nut, Nigga!" I taunted Les, being messy as those niggas faded like jeans in bleach!

"Li-Li!" Billy-B., the watchdog at the door, yelled as we came up. Billy was in charge of making sure shit was cool out front, and only people with bank got in the door. He always let us in with no issues. "Hot-Mess! Nigga, don't clap nobody! We don't need the police here, Man!"

"Fuck the police!" Les laughed, shaking his head looking around critically. "You know I'm no old head, Billy-B. I'm a youngblood. If you don't give a damn, I don't give a fuck!"

Gucci's was packed wall to wall with people inside. The flashing lights, smoke, loud music vibrating the walls and floors, and people dancing everywhere were the vibes that set the mood. The dancefloor was out in the open when you got downstairs. But all up above, Tony had VIP booths and sections for his 'BIG SPENDERS.' Those spots were usually packed on the weekends. It was Thursday…actually Friday morning, and niggas were partying like it was a Saturday!

Les went straight to the bar behind the dancefloor to get in the zone. Once Les started drinking, he'd either relax, or he would be paranoid and trip all night long.

"Les, get me a bottle, Nigga?!" I hollered from the end of the bar, viewing the floor for a moment.

"Bitch, Lionel needs a bottle! Take him some Belvidere and put it on my shit. Naw, he doesn't sip dark like me. I ordered the Crown Royal! Only old heads like me appreciate the sophistication of dark liquor, such as yourself, Baby! You need some of this white chocolate in your life to eat your pussy, right?" Les laughed, firing up another blunt, eyeing a cute brown bartender. The girls that worked at Gucci's wore sexy shit to show off their bodies. It was always beautiful to see the girls up in front; they loved their jobs and danced like girls in the back! Les held up a hundred-dollar bill waving it to the bartender. She wiggled over and put her black bikini top close, reaching for the bills. I smiled as Les pointed at me.

"Anything he wants you can put on my shit, hear me, Bitch?"

"Whatever you say, Hot-Mess...Don't start no shit tonight? I'm making good folding paper tonight, Lester Woods," She replied, with an attitude, snatching his bills. "If you're looking for Mia, she ain't here...so Tony is out looking for her."

"Mhm, and yet here I sit in yo face not giving a fuck. Get our drinks, Bitch! I didn't ask for Mia's location, Cocoa. Best mind yo fucking business and keep it moving, or I'll burn this bitch to the ground, and you'll be back on the corner tomorrow," Les sarcastically laughed, shooing her away.

"I'll tell her you said hello, Les...Be right back," Cocoa informed him, rolling her eyes and moving to get his order.

"See what the fuck I mean about girls turning to bitches, Lionel? Cocoa's trying to protect the motherfucker that ran a damn train on her ass and is mad at me cuz this is where she chooses to work? Bitches don't know what the fuck they want," Les grumbled, spinning his eyes.

"You remind me of Hakim saying that shit," I sniggered over the music, squinting, catching sight of Carla. She had a gang of fine girls with her dancing on the floor looking like America's Next Top Fantasy…Lionel Edition! Les bumped my arm, showing me his phone. My eyes nearly burst out of my head seeing the female on the screen! "That's Carla's friend? Damn!"

I was floored by how beautiful she actually was. Usually, when Les said a girl was *fine*, she was just cute. Les would fuck any woman that gave him a shot. But when he said *sexy*, that meant she was gorgeous. Ricka was too sexy for words! This girl had long hair down to her ass, long silky straight, mocha skin like chocolate kisses, chinky brown eyes, a sweet face like a black barbie! Oooh, she had a body like she was raised to dance with the roundest ass and tight legs. I could see all her body in that black leather suit she wore. She had to be a model by how she looked so natural posing like a pro with that ass out. There was no way this girl was really here to talk to me. I was getting catfished!

"Les doesn't lie! She's sexy, young, sweet, and has been modeling with Carla on the side since she started school in

Houston a few months ago. They send me all kinds of neat pictures. Ricka likes girls too," Les chuckled, shaking his head at my response. He pointed to Carla and her girls again. That was when I saw her! At first, I didn't see Fredericka because she was so short and cute that the others surrounded her. She might be 5'2, but so fine to be petite and well put together. "Ricka has been trying to reel a nigga in with her sweet bait, but I think she's too cute for me. She looks like my daughter, Kayla. I can't see a woman when I look at her."

I poured myself a drink looking at that fine-ass girl! She had that cute face and high cheek with those eyes...looking like a short, brown Jhene Aiko! I was struck!

Maya had that vibe like Ashanti that I loved. With her sweet smile and high voice, I would give anything for her. But it was innocent, and nothing ever happened. One look at Ricka was like my dream girl walked right up on me with Carla, and I couldn't look away. Fredericka was a woman that had a body! It was so fucking crazy the way her eyesight seemed to spot me when I discovered her. She gazed over at me, and I witnessed the prettiest look in her sexy bedroom eyes. Oh, yeah, girl...? I see you, and I am on it. It was on!

They strolled up to Les at the bar. I watched from a few seats away as they approached, enjoying my drink and the view. I lit a cigarette and waited to see what was doing down.

"What's up, Les, Baby?" Carla's fine ass giggled as she winked at me down the bar. She waved her purple fingernails at me, and I raised my eyebrows and glinted back. Carla was a fine red-bone with long curly red hair and looked like she danced for Beyoncé in her black and purple bodycon dress. She looked fly! She rubbed her nails across Les's belly through his shirt. "What you doing, Li-Li? You're looking out for your big brother, again?"

"You know me, Carla-Cakes! I'm always looking out for the fam," I chuckled as Les nodded, grinning up at her trying to climb into his lap.

"Damn, Girl, careful, you know I pack that hot fire!" Les flirted with Carla smiling as she showed him her panties. "I got my gun, too…Don't make me pull both out tonight, Bitch! I'm so tempted!"

I died laughing as Carla shook her cute ass against his gun. Les shook his head and moved it out of the way, pulling her into his lap.

"Ladies, you look delicious! What's the business?" I requested, smiling at Carla's friends, but you know my eyes went right where my mind drifted. I locked eyes with Ricka and leered. "Have a seat so I can holla? You want to grab a table, or we can chill here at the bar?"

Oh, God is good! Fredericka moved closer to me, staring up curiously. Her sweet smile was so adorable I couldn't help but smile at her as she studied my braids. Her hair was as long as mine, and I love a woman that loves my hair. Carla's friends were suddenly interested when Ricka handled it.

"Can I buy you ladies a round of drinks?" I asked, taking out my credit card Hakim ordered me after school started.

"Oh, shit!" Les giggled, trying to fight Carla off of him. "Kill 'em, Li-Li!"

Les was getting tipsy, so he was relaxing. I turned to Cocoa and said, "Get the ladies at the bar what they want…Especially the beauty queen in the black dress that looks like my future baby mama!"

"Got you, Li-Li," Cocoa giggled at me, walking away with my card.

She went down the bar, taking orders while I watched Ricka enjoy herself. Les bumped into my elbow and pulled me to the side a second. I started watching around for Tony when I saw the heartless look on his face. He beamed over at Ricka as he glanced around the club, saying, "It's nothing to freak about, Nigga! Stop exploring, Dora! I'll move when I'm ready to jump. Oh yeah, I forgot to tell you something else about Ricka, Lionel."

"What? Les, you got me trippin' with your faces, Bro. Chill," I whispered, raising my eyebrows staring over at Ricka now. "It ain't nothing crazy like she's really a dude or some Springer shit, is it?"

Les choked and rubbed his face cutting his head, "Fuck, naw, Lionel! Ricka's got big bank! Her family got their own shit. She pays her nigga's way!"

"Say what?!" I asked, my voice going up way too high. Cocoa came over to us, talking at the edge of the bar handing me a fancy bottle of vodka. It had glitter, diamonds, and stones inside the glass and pretty colors in the diamond dust in a tube through the center. I held it up...Diva Vodka? What...the...fuck? (It's REAL...look it up!)

"That's the cheaper version. I don't know a bar in Texas that carries the real deal. It costs 3000 dollars for the less expensive I keep with me in the car. The real deal is worth over a million... home in Singapore. Keep the bottle. It's worth something," Fredericka told me as she touched my hair, pushing Les out of the way. "You want to know Ricka Han, you talk to Ricka...Lion...Your hair is sexy, and your face is adorable...Lionel. Les talks about you. He says you're the real thing. I'm looking..."

I took her tiny hand in mine, admired her pink fingernails with diamond tips, and kissed them.

"Lionel Dunn, beautiful, Han," I flirted, picking up all kinds of vibes from that woman. She was so superb and kept smiling up at me like she wanted to marry a nigga!

"Ah, you have jokes, I like, I like," She giggled with her eyes sparkling in the club lights.

"You're a long way from Singapore, Beautiful. What are you doing in the Dirty-Dirty besides making my night so special?" I asked, trying to get in her head. Fredericka Han was exactly my type, perfect in every way, so I had to try. The music got really loud as she was about to answer. Les handed me the keys to his car on the cool while she was distracted by the noise. "You want to go somewhere a little quieter to talk?"

"Okay!" She yelled over the bass.

I grabbed the bottle, a glass, and her hand. We went and sat out in the Bentley and smoked, talking. The longer I stared at her, the harder it was to look away. She was so beautiful and sweet. We were smoking, vibing, laughing, and yo…Ricka was dope as fuck.

"So, why are you in THE VIEW?" I questioned her, grinning as she took a sip, seeming tipsy like me.

"I'm a Business major at Rice University in Houston with Carla. She's from here, you know her, Lionel. Carla talks about you and your brother Hakim. She comes here to see Les. I have no classes until Monday, so I came for fun. Why not?" Ricka replied, passing me the blunt.

She was sitting next to me in the backseat, and I tripped on her hair and joked about it. She was giggling, pushing my hand. Ricka was soft and smelled like she was worth a bag. I had been with plenty of older women, but none had goals or swag like Ricka. She was 19, had a modeling contract, her family had paper, she went to school, and had fun with her friends between working and studying.

"No cap, Ricka, you're sweet, soft, fly, and fine as hell! I bet niggas at Rice going crazy over your cute ass," I laughed, pouring some of her bomb ass vodka in my glass and taking a sip. "This shit is smooth and goes down like water. It's nice!"

"I got a dude back home. It's an arranged marriage thing by my family. But it is good. He does his things. I can do mine before we marry. There is no love…we have not dated. It is all about Dinero," Ricka told me honestly.

"Damn, my brother got a girl in the same situation!" I thought, moping, as Mandisa exploded into my head.

"Yes? So, she is dipping with your brother, Hakim, until she gets married?" Ricka asked me with a tipsy smile and lowered eyes.

"No, my brother is in love with her! He is going to try to talk her father out of her marriage," I told Ricka smiling.

"Damn, lucky girl…most men hear about women like us and get a score and move on," Ricka confessed sadly with a shocked look. "I have been dating outside since I was 16. My mother's idea was to meet other men before having kids and settling down for the trust fund. She's a legacy too.

'My older sister... ran off because she's a lesbian ... and wouldn't marry a man. I'm the only child left to pass the family business.

'He's divorced, starting over, and adds value to the business reputation. Love is a fairy tale for women like us that have traditions to uphold."

"I didn't believe that shit still went down in the world," I frowned, hearing how calm she was with things. Or maybe she was just lying to herself?

"So, you have a girl here? I know you could not. A woman would never let a man as fine as you out of her sights for long," Ricka flirted with me with cute cheeks blushing. She pulled my braids and made me feel embarrassed. That shit was the wrong move.

"Naw, no girl, but I can't say I've been looking. You think I'm fine? I think you're gorgeous, so why don't we get together and make a fine-ass mess?" I laughed as she smiled at me and wedged out her tongue, taunting me. Cute ass! Ooh, Ricka was giving me wifey vibes now. I smiled and tilted my head, looking at her thighs.

"How old are you, Lionel? I don't like to see men too old. My future husband is much older, so I want to meet someone close to my age to be with when I fool around," Ricka told me.

"I guess that puts me out of the game, damn!" I sighed as Ricka kept yanking my hair. I was fucked up, and that shit felt so good. I know I was rock hard and didn't care.

"You're not that old, Lionel. I can see that," She giggled, twisting my hair around her pink fingernail pulling me closer.

"I'm 16, Fredericka," I confessed, grinning, drunk as fuck.

"No way!" She giggled, taking another sip, letting me go. "You're not 16, Lionel!"

"Alright, you got me! I'm 15, but my birthday is next month," I told her, looking for a cigarette. There was no need to lie to her about something that clearly didn't matter. She wouldn't be here with me alone if she didn't have a made-up mind about what she wanted.

Ricka leaned back in the seat laughing, then she paused, looking up at me, saying, "You're serious?"

"Scorpio, October 26th," I replied, taking a long drink, nervously a moment. She was a bit too astonished. I leaned back in the seat and glanced down at my shit growing against my thigh. Ricka's face went from a smile to confusion eyeing it. Her hand grabbed my shit through my pants, and she was trying to get a good feel. "Damn, Girl…You want me to help you see it?"

Ricka started giggling and sat back in the seat, "You're so sweet, sexy, and funny...it's so cute! Then you have something nice for me? I don't see why we can't have fun if you can keep a secret?"

"Hell, yeah, girl! My lips are sealed tight unless you need them for something," I answered, sticking out my tongue. She smiled at me and ran her nails up my knee, touching the head.

"So. Lionel, will you give me your number?" Ricka asked, blushing sweetly, making it hard to sit still.

"I can do that all day, every day, no problem, but I'm right here now. So what's up?" I asked her, watching her hand nibbling my bottom lip, grinning at her. "Careful, Ricka, that's the sleeping monster. He's gonna fuck shit up if you wake him all the way up."

"You ever fuck a rich girl in the backseat of a Bentley, Lionel?" Ricka questioned me as she pulled off her dress and climbed into my lap.

I reached forward and hit the locks on the door, and smiled laughing, "Naw, but I'm about to make it happen right now!"

I kissed her while I unbuttoned my shirt and grabbed her close. She giggled, taking off my A-Shirt but stopped staring at all my tattoos.

"Lionel, you are a bad boy, yes?" She asked, gaping at my chest and guns. Damn! Ricka seemed to go crazy the minute she realized I wasn't some punk!

"I'ma bad motherfucker, Ricka! You about to see how bad!" I laughed as she pushed me down and started unbuckling my belt. She unzipped my jeans, but I was trying to see her body up close in the darkness. I grabbed her close and tried to kiss her stomach. Ricka was trying to run from me as I buried my face between her soft breasts and kissed them. "You give it to me, and you gonna fall in love with this dick!"

"Mmmmhmmm…" She moaned and giggled, running her fingers through my braids as I sucked and licked my new favorite chocolate friends. Ricka's titties were so big and soft I wanted to die. I sucked them until she shivered and got mean. She slammed my head down to the seat and got my jeans open, and pulled them down my legs. "Niggas that talk the most shit can't back it up…It's not- Oh, God! It's bigger than…"

"I can back it up…Can you?" I asked, watching her staring at my shit as it lept up and slapped her in the face. "You know what they say about us loud-mouthed skinny niggas?"

"It's so big, Lionel," Ricks sighed as she grabbed it and slammed it in her mouth! Yeah, Nigga!

"Oh, shit!" I screamed as she sucked the hell out of my dick. "You a freak!"

"Mhm! I love it!" She moaned, putting it back and swallowing it down.

Ugh…I got chills all over, and my eyes rolled back. I needed to calm down, or I was gonna bust one right then! I had never had a woman that just dove on it like that. She was trying to swallow all of it, and it felt so damn good; if I didn't have my Jordans on, my toes would have curled up! No cap!

"Oh my God!" I groaned, seeing stars. "You, Nasty Bitch! Ooh, Shit!"

That shit made Ricka go harder. She tried her best to make me cum, but I have never lost it from a girl giving me head. It wasn't the same as pussy. My shit knew the difference because it was a much more intense feeling for me to fuck. I used more energy and felt much more relaxed afterward. But I was on fire from the crown of my head to the back of my hips. Ooh, Ricka knew how to work her mouth! She was so sloppy, licking and slurping that shit up. I lost my fucking mind, yo!

I grabbed her hair and pushed my hips up, and tried to ram that throat. She enjoyed that shit. My fingers ran along her thigh up to her skirt and found the Motherland! No panties! I rubbed her clit with my thumb and slid a finger into that pussy, and she started humming on my shit!

Oh, Jesus, marry me, girl?! She appreciated that shit so much she was soaking wet. My kind of woman, Ricka, give me that shit right now! I reached down and grabbed a condom out of my wallet and tossed her ass on her knees. I put that shit on so fast it made her head spin. Really, she looked back at me like she broke her neck.

"You like it Doggy-style, yes?" She giggled, eyeing me.

"Naw, what I got in mind for you is a little different," I chuckled as I yanked her sexy ass back into my lap, facing the back window. I pulled her legs around my waist and pushed my hips toward the edge of the seat, grabbing her shoulders. I went deep!

"Oh, my, God!" Fredericka screamed as I dug her out. I started pounding the hell out of Ricka's walls, and she loved that shit. Even wearing a condom, I could feel the grip on my shit. I love that feeling. It sets me on fire and revs up my motor more than a fight! I was rocking Les's Continental like a 64 Chevy with switches at a lowrider convention. "Fuck me, Yes! Oh God, Fuck me, Lionel!"

Oh, no, Girl, Lionel doesn't play with it when you give it to him. I like to stake my claim on a girl that lets me have it, so she knows it's here when she's ready for another go! I got plenty of dick and energy to give to the needy. She gonna catch this hook and spray a nigga with thanks. Ricka had already come twice, and I was not mad at all. She screamed and threw her head back. I grabbed her hips and pushed her down as I slammed my hips up. She gasped for air, fell forward, and started kissing my neck!

"Fuck no! Not yet!" I screamed as I came and fell back. My neck is my weak spot. I can go for a long time unless a girl does that shit. All that liquor had my head swimming, and it felt like I lost all my fluids when I came. My heart was beating my chest up, I broke into a cold sweat, and it was freezing. Ricka tried to kiss me. "Naw…don't touch me! I'm fucked up…wait…hold …oooh...stop!"

She was giggling as I shivered, trying to stop her. She ran her lips across my face and kissed my chin. I closed my legs, and she climbed down and started getting dressed. I started putting on my A-shirt and rolled down the window, tossing out the condom. She smiled at me, holding her phone, asking, "Now can I have your number?"

"Yeah," I replied, smiling. I put my phone number in. Ricka grabbed me, hugged my neck, and threw her hair to the side as she took a picture of us together. "What happened to zipped lips and keeping secrets?"

"No, we are going to do this again and soon, Lionel. You're mine, now!" Ricka giggled as I zipped my jeans and put my shirt back on. She climbed back into the front seat and made herself another drink.

"What you going to do with that picture?" I asked worriedly. I didn't have anything to worry about, but I didn't want her to get the wrong idea.

"It's for my memory only. I'm getting married next June in Hong Kong. So I need something that I can keep, for when I go home and say I do…I'll always remember you, Lionel," She told me with a horribly upset smile. "You're sincere, sweet, handsome, and an excellent lover."

"Yeah?" I chuckled, lighting a cigarette thinking. Ricka would be a cool girlfriend, but she has a situation that I couldn't think of getting in the middle of. I liked her. I thought she was so cute, and I was considering seeing what she really thought of me. But I don't have the kind of bank Hakim has. I can't compete with some dude that was about to get a lot of cash marrying her. "Your old man is gonna get a hell of a wife."

"Yeah?" She giggled playfully, then sulked, putting her heels on. "Why don't you have a girlfriend?"

I exhaled deeply suddenly in my feelings, thinking about Maya, "Cuz, I don't want one…I mean, I used to have a girlfriend when I was younger. We grew up together. But she moved away when I was 12, and I can't find her. You kind of remind me of her, Ricka. She was cute, had long hair, brown skin, and was always happy…like you…through all the bullshit…I still love her."

"What's was her name?" Ricka asked me sweetly. I rolled my eyes, looking away. "Come on now, you can tell me. Who am I going to spill it to?"

"Her name is Shamaya," I replied, glaring at the floor. My eyes felt heavy as I exhaled. "We were just kids but did everything together…I never told her how I felt."

"You'll find her, Lionel, and when you do…You hold on to her and never let go. If you do what you did to me, to her…she'll love you, too…. Women don't fall out of love easily. Those that say they can are lying. Maybe they don't know what love feels like, but some don't trip over feelings because it's not an option. But I'm glad I came to Longview tonight. I'm happy I met you, Lionel.

'Next year, when the madness begins, and I have to put on my 'good wife hat,' I'll have the memory of a sad little boy that showed me love and rocked my messed up tiny world. That's something I believe is worth remembering. Now, give us another picture and smile this time!? It's not so bad! Okay?" Ricka said, pressing my shoulder. She took another picture with me, and I smiled.

"Can you send me those? I want to remember this night, too," I asked her as I gave Ricka a kiss on the cheek.

"I will, so are you going to call me soon?" Fredericka inquired.

"You really want to see me again?" I worried, offering her a smile.

"Yes, I really do…I'll come every weekend if it's to see you and get that! I don't have much else to look forward to but a degree, a meaningless relationship with a rich old man almost three times my age, and my trust fund. It's enormous!

'But cash can't make you completely happy. You just have to find value in the memories or be a rich and miserable person, Lionel," She told me as she played with my goatee.

"If you don't love him, then why are you marrying him, Ricka?" I asked, eyeing her, confused by her happiness.

"It's just business, Lionel, and I love my family. They have me so spoiled that I hate to admit I don't even buy my own clothes. I don't know how to live without financial security, Lionel. Like my sister, if I say no, they cut me off and lose more cash than you can imagine. No college, car, credit accounts, and I wouldn't know what to do. The family could go under because of a selfish choice that could be a mistake. America is awesome! Freedom is priceless…Love is…a dream. I love my family enough to let go of a dream," Ricka explained, rubbing my hand. "So, when you feel lonely, you call me, Lionel. I will come…we will have fun and forget all the pain together, yes?"

I watched her get out of the car, and I felt so bad for her. That could be Mandisa if Hakim failed her. But Ricka wasn't going to give up that financial security for anything, I could tell. She loved being wealthy, and nothing was going to stop her from getting married. For a moment, I wanted to say something to stop her, but I just told her goodnight, "Alright, Fredericka, you be safe, Baby girl."

She came back around to my side of the car, and I rolled the window all the way down.

"I really care about you, Lionel, you know? The moment I saw you, I knew you were special. Be safe and take Les's old ass home to his wife!" Ricka teased me. I nodded, and she leaned in and kissed my lips. She was so sweet and sad, but she made her choice, so I wasn't trying to be that dude to fuck up a woman with goals from what she wanted. The scenario was similar, but Ricka wasn't like Mandisa. She reminded me of Shamaya, and if she wanted to fool around, I was going to see. But she wasn't girlfriend material unless you were prepared to get your heart broken. I know better than that shit. "Call me soon, Lionel!"

"Alright, Sweet thing," I replied, leaning back in the seat.

Ricka was so perfect that it scared me, but I knew I didn't stand a chance. I could never give her the life she wanted. It was best to squash any feelings or attachments. It could be just about sex. I felt my phone vibrate, and it was two texts. Ricka sent me the pictures she took. I smiled and saved them and her number.

"Thanks for the sweet memories, Ricka," I replied, smiling to myself.

I got fucked up sitting out in Les's car, finishing the last of Fredericka's expensive vodka. I held on to the bottle staring at the gems and crystal running through the center. People would do anything for a bag. Some would sell their own freedom too.

#

I was wrecked when Les dropped me off at home. It was nearly 4 am as I stared at my phone, unlocking the door giggling with the key.

"Yo, Lionel, call me tomorrow night, Nigga!" Les shouted, skidding off down the road, leaving burning rubber, smoke, and tire tracks on the street.

I couldn't answer, so I waved, but I was so slow I missed him. I held on to the last bit of Diva Vodka and closed the front door. I glanced back as I heard the loud slam.

"Oops, oh shit...shhhh...Nigga, you gonna wake...oh...That nigga ain't here," I grumbled to the door, frowning. I looked up at the ceiling as the lights came on in the den. "Oh, fuck!"

"Mhm, you been out all night with Hot-Mess Les. When Hakim called saying Ninon had the baby, we returned when he said that you here until morning. But we got home at 12:45, and no Lionel. It's 4:15 on a school night," I heard G.D. say from somewhere. The den started spinning the second the light came on. My stomach turned as I spotted my grandpa standing near the kitchen door. "God, Lionel, you're just like Sonny!"

"Hey, Gary, what's good, Old Nigga?" I chuckled, looking at his evil, angry face. He looked like Hakim with a fade and gray hair. No beard wrinkled up, but darker like Cyrus, and his one-legged ass was always yelling and chasing us with his cane or fake leg! "I mean...G.D. My bad, Pawpaw..."

"Nigga, have you been drinking? Never mind...I can smell it coming out of your pores. Have you lost your mind?" My grandfather yelled from the kitchen. I turned my eyes at him and tried to stand up straight. "You're not grown, Lionel! You're still a kid, and you need to act your age!"

"Why are you always yelling and shit? You so mean, G.D!" I groaned, holding my forehead.

"You're grounded, Lionel! Now, get your drunk ass to bed!" G.D. yelled, limping closer on his cane.

"You don't understand me. Nobody gets me! You, Hakim, Cyrus, shit, the only person close to getting me is Mandisa, and she ain't family, fuck! At least Les lets me be me! Why does everyone hate me so damn much?" I shouted, losing my temper but starting for the stairs slowly. I grabbed the railing as G.D. swung his cane, and I barely missed falling back on the floor. "G.D., chill, you could have fucked me off!"

"Don't nobody hate you, Lionel! You hate yourself! You're always talking about niggas hating on you, and you don't love yourself! Out all night, skipping classes, fooling around with nasty girls, and you're so blind you can't see the forest for the trees!" G.D. screamed down at me and smashed his cane across the top of my head.

I felt the pain and dropped everything as I hit the floor. It hurt so much I started to see flashes of light, and I bit my damn tongue from the impact. But I was too dizzy to stand up. I frowned as I saw the broken bottle on the ground shattered.

"Why you do that, G.D.?" I cried, trying to pick up the pieces of glass from the floor. He hit me again across my shoulder, and I held my arm as tears ran down my face. I took a deep breath and sat there, ready for another.

"Gary Dunn, you better not!" Grandma Sophie screamed, coming down the stairs. She stopped seeing the broken glass. She was barely awake as she looked at me and G.D., frowning. "Lionel, go to bed. I'll clean this up."

"Boy, you're going to end up sad and lonely. You are fucking up your life, and you just started living! Look at Hakim? He may be crazy, but at least he is getting his shit together. He makes good grades now, he has good friends that care about him and keep him out of trouble, and he has a sweet girlfriend that loves him," My grandfather announced to the world as I nervously stood up with tears streaming off my face.

"See, there you go again talking about Hakim! You've been comparing us since we were little. He's out on a damn school night too, but you ain't beating his ass!

'No, Lionel's the bad guy because he comes home every night. You don't know what the hell he's up to when he's out like this, and you don't ask. He's your favorite, and you chose him because of the money. Hakim this, Hakim that, and Lionel's the problem child? I get it. You hate me! Everyone hates Lionel, and you know what? I don't give a fuck no more!" I suddenly laughed as I stood up. I was pissed off, and my damn shoulder was throbbing. Granddaddy hit me in the head with the cane again. I hit the fucking floor.

"Since you lost your mama, you've been an evil little asshole, Lionel!" G.D. shrieked at me. I held my head and stared at him holding my breath. Tears were already falling from him, messing up my feelings, but you just have to mess me up when I can't fight back...That shit is petty; G.D. Grandma Sophia didn't say a word either. She just frowned and folded her arms when he whacked my ass like an Italian mob boss. "Hakim ain't my favorite! You are, boy! You act just like Luther! When he was 16, he started playing just like you're performing because he was stupid. He fucked up a good thing, and she didn't want to give him the time of day anymore. He was misbehaving for attention too. But being a dumbass doesn't change shit, Nigga. Get up and wipe your ass if you wanna change or lay in the shit. But you can't live here talking to me like that, NIGGA!

'Your dad thought he was hot shit until he got his ass whipped one good time out there and nearly got killed! Weed, women, and these fake friends don't make you real! You don't even know who the real Lionel is because you've been faking for so long, do you?"

I jumped up and ran upstairs, stumbling. I was so pissed I didn't know if it was because I realized I really fucked up. I just lost my fucking car! I was hurting from the beating as I slammed the door and hit the bed. I was dizzy as hell, and the ceiling fan would be fucking with my vision, making the room spin and the lights flicker.

"Now, don't leave this house unless it's to go to school or with your brother! You better be home before night, or I'll break this cane off up your ass, Lionel! Then, I'll put this fake leg so far up your ass you'll have a kickstand for when you stand on the highway begging for change. You better hope I don't change my mind by morning!" G.D. screamed through the bedroom door.

"Yes, Sir!" I replied as I shut my eyes, trying to stop the speed of the fan blades.

"Lionel?" Grandma Sophia called me through the door. "I'm coming in, okay?"

I opened my eyes and tried to sit up. I was starting to feel nauseous and held my stomach as I glanced at my grandmother. She was frowning and folded her arms. Granny Sophia had light brown eyes and looked like Mama with fair skin and brown hair. Hakim had the same eyes, and they seemed to look right through you. I loved my granny, but right now, I wasn't feeling well. I stayed quiet and listened because she would hit me if I talked back too!

"Lionel, what are you doing, Baby? You need to slow down and act your age. You knew when you got in that car with Les you were in trouble. Every time you leave with that boy, you get in trouble! It's a school night, and look at you! You look like you're going to pass out. You're so drunk! I would have beat your ass if I caught you too!

'G.D. gets emotional and angry about you boys because you both act like your father. Luther got heartbroken and thought he could sleep it all away with fast girls and drugs. But when you make a mistake, you have to face the consequences. That's how you learn and can get over things. If you don't meet your problems and accept your flaws like men, you'll run from them like boys.

'I don't compare you to Hakim because that boy has some serious issues. He's been running since we lost Vivianne. Only God and faith can purify a lost soul and scattered mind, Lionel. G.D. and I are terrified that we will lose you both to what money makes possible in this evil world.

'Nothing would hurt us more than outliving you all, Lionel...look at me...?

'If you and Hakim die before we die...How do you think we will feel? We'd lost both our children and our grandchildren. We moved you here to stop this from happening back in Georgia. Both of you were already going at it and scaring people. You wouldn't have survived in Atlanta. You and Hakim are still mad. You can't blame yourselves or one another for things you couldn't control, Baby.

'It was God's plan, and you have to find his plan for you. Life, death, and grief are natural. Unless you want to upset me and join your mother and father, you have to move on.

'Look at you, Lionel…? Handsome, talented, funny, and sweet...you're all those things, and you hate your own existence. Survivors Guilt is what I think you and Hakim are suffering from primarily.

'You have to find something to live for and start living! It's time to stop trying to die for some honor code you made up in your head. I love you, Baby. You're the last, and you have to grow up before you have us dressed in black at your funeral. That would kill me...

'I can't lose you or Hakim! I can't! Viv and Luther were too much for me! Without you boys and Gary, I might not have made it... God has a plan... Let him use you, Lionel. I know you still believe.

'That's all I am going to say. You try to sleep that sickness out of your system," Grandma Sophie explained, rubbing the tears from my face. She kissed my forehead. I just frowned as she shut the bedroom door. I laid back on the bed, tears trickled down into my ears, I nervously gasped for air, and I passed out!

# Chapter Two: Fear/Real

## Hakim Jahlil Dunn

Lionel! When I left the house last night, he was in the shower. I thought everything was fantastic. But G. D. called me at 7:05 in the morning, ready to throw my brother out of the house.

"Hakim, you need to come home, now!" My grandfather yelled at me through the phone, waking me up completely. I sat on the edge of the bed, looking back at Mandisa fast asleep, and Cyrus was out cold. My nerves were already bad, but now I knew I was about to lose it. I tried to stall.

"Grandaddy, not now. I have got something vital to deal with today. What happened?" I asked, scratching my head and running my fingers over my lock-wrap.

"Your brother has lost his goddamn mind! He's been out all night with Lester, drinking, smoking, and came in here talking crazy! The more I think about it, the more I want to choke his narrow ass! He's hungover, sick ass hell, locked in that room, and not answering the damn door! Get your ass here now! I'm too old for this shit!" G.D. shouted at me.

I sighed and shook my head. I needed to settle things with Mandisa's father before the effects of the new baby wore off. He was going to take Mandisa away this evening if he had his way. Shit!

Why today? Fuck! All I asked my brother to do was sit his bony behind down and chill until I came to get him. If G.D. put Lionel out for real...No...He wouldn't...would he? Fuck!

"Alright, G.D., I'm on my way. But Lionel's shit is minor compared to what's going on here," I replied, frowning as I grew more frustrated by the second.

"Whatever, Nigga!" G.D. yelled, hanging up in my face.

Hmph…?

I wiped my eyes and sighed, shaking my head.

"Cyrus! Wake up, Bro!" I shouted, hitting him. His eyes rolled around his skull a moment, and he glanced up at me. I motioned him to get up and be quiet. He exhaled, slid from under Mandisa, followed me into the den, and then shut the door.

"What's up, Hakim?" Cyrus asked, wiping his mouth. He wasn't a morning person, hated getting up early, and was slow processing until fully awake. I had to snap my fingers a few times to get his eyes open. "My bad…I'm up. What, Bro?"

"Look, I know we have a mission to take care of today, but Lionel has fucked up. I have to go home for a while. Then I have some business to handle before I meet Dr. King. You and Kaliah know the plan. You're the only ones I trusted with the information. If this shit doesn't work, then the new mission is to allow me to keep Dr. King distracted while you get Mandisa to Jamaica.

'Kaliah will have everything ready. I spoke to him last night, and he knows if I don't call him by 7 pm, that 'Exodus' is a go. I appreciate you helping with everything. I'm confident I can get in his head, but get her to safety if you see things heading south. Don't tell anyone! You know where everything is, right?" I explained, trying to stay chill. Talking about the plan always made me edgy, which is why I kept things quiet until now. The pressure was piling up by the second, and I wouldn't mess up the execution. I can't fuck up the moves I make, or it could be the end of my happiness. I don't want to think about losing Mandisa!

"Yeah, it's already in the truck. I'll take care of everything. What did Lionel do?" Cyrus sighed deeply, frowning.

"Lester Woods, need I say more?" I replied, staring at him, shaking my head. Cyrus crossed his arms and shook his head, rolling his eyes. "I'm heading home to pave things over. When I call, come to the hospital with your A-Game. Be calm for her, alright?"

"I got you, Bro. But I'm more concerned about Lionel! What are you gonna do? I know you're pissed off, but you can't go home fucking him up! He needs a friend, not a mad big brother putting foot to ass! Les is an asshole, but he's the only person Lionel looks up to for dumb reasons. Les may do ignorant shit, but he's always looking out for your brother. Lester just instigates shit because he treats Lionel like a grown-ass man," Cyrus educated me on the subject.

Cyrus knew I didn't like Lionel around Lester Woods. I didn't trust his crazy white ass, and he never failed to keep my brother in some shit that grown niggas wouldn't do unless they had a death wish! I've kicked his ass many times through the years for his fly ass mouth and coming at Cyrus or me about his bitches! He's a former pimp that just runs from place to place popping niggas and is a much better hitman than a pimp.

He thinks that because his stepmother and half-brother are black that he's black. Yeah, he is married to a pretty sister, but Les really thinks he's a nigga. He only realizes he's white when I slap the shit out of him about calling me nigga. I know he doesn't mean shit, but I hate he thinks I'm the motherfucker to test his luck. Les used to have all the women we wanted, but when Pretty Tony popped up, shit changed fast. He couldn't control his bitches. I remember that much watching him around the hood as a kid. You could say…I was always watching Lester's mistakes. He made a lot of them, so it was a hell of a learning experience.

Cyrus was right there, but he was always worried about the women than the shit Lester was up to making money. I wanted to know what the fuck all the girls saw in him. Obviously, it was Les's spontaneous not-giving a fuck attitude because when he ignored them, they chased him down. That shit was the first thing I saw when we moved here, and I noticed how Angela was on it. Everyone is my teacher. I'm no hater, but he doesn't need to keep putting Lionel in the middle of his illegal activities and dropping him off, tore up, and pissed off.

Cyrus seemed to be thinking as he sighed, "Hakim, in a way, I think Lionel follows Lester around because niggas are scared of him. The same way niggas are scared of you. Think about it, Hakim? The only time Lionel goes around Les is when you're gone!"

Whoa! Was Cyrus making a valid point? Yes, Les had a bag, cars, girls, respect, and people feared him because he wasn't afraid of anything, but he was nothing like... Damn it all! Cyrus was right.

"Lionel started hanging around Les when I started doing my shit and leaving all the time," I realized, holding my jaw.

"Yep, he just wants a friend like you, Bro," Cyrus added, turning on the TV and sitting on the sofa, smiling.

I stood thinking for a moment. I never thought about things that way. I saw Lionel doing dumb things all the time and never tried to see things his way.

"I'm going to head home. I'll call you later, Bro," I said, going to get dressed.

"Alright, Hakim, don't lose your temper, okay?" Cyrus stated, watching me, grinning.

"Yeah...I hear you, man," I replied.

#

"It's about time, Hakim! He's been locked in there all morning! Sophie is gone to work, and he won't talk to me. I don't play that shit, Hakim! He doesn't pay any bills in this house. So either he starts flying right, or he's got to get out tonight! He wants to act grown, then he needs to be on his own! We didn't raise you to disrespect us. He's messing with the wrong one! I'll kick his bony-ass, trust me! Boy, uh...get him or I will," G.D. fussed at me as I came through the front door.

"Alright, alright, G.D., I'll handle him," I replied, looking toward the stairs and back at my grandfather's frustrated face. When he started rhyming like Muhammed Ali, I knew he was serious.

"Don't put no holes in the walls or break the windows like the last time you two fought," G.D. warned me. I shook my head at the sudden memories of Lionel and me disagreeing all the time. It always turned violent, every time!

"I'm not going to hit him, Granddaddy, I promise," I sighed as I started upstairs.

I sighed deeply, hesitating by the bedroom door. My palms began to sweat, and I frowned, remembering shit I forgot years ago.

*I hung up the phone and walked into the den sitting on the couch. Our neighbor's daughter, LaKeisha, sat watching TV, chewing gum, and smiling.*

*"What's wrong, Hakim?" She asked, looking me over.*

*"I want my Mama!"* I cried, breaking down and hitting the arm of the sofa.

*"Hakim, they've only been gone three hours. They'll be home soon. It was just dinner and a movie. They go out every Saturday night. It's never bothered you before, so chill, okay?" LaKeisha tried to calm me down, but I wasn't hearing her. I know what I just heard on the phone, and she was wrong!*

*Lionel was seven, coming from the kitchen, and sat next to me asking. "Hakim! Hakim, what's wrong? Why you crying?"*

*He smiled, pushing my shoulder as I gazed at the clock. He didn't know what I had just heard. But I couldn't tell him yet. Maybe I had dreamed it all?*

*"What mama say? Why you hang up so quick? I was just peeing. I wanted to talk to them too. I'm gonna call back. Dad said he was going to the barbershop tomorrow and I want a haircut too. I hate having an afro like you," Lionel ran off at the mouth.*

*"Shut the fuck up, Lionel! Leave me alone!" I yelled, pushing him away from me. He stared at me and frowned up. "You talk too damn much, and I'm trying to fucking think!!!"*

*"Fuck you, Hakim! You're mean!" Lionel started crying and swung at me, I grabbed his arm, and we started wrestling in the den. I put him in a headlock, he pushed off the couch, and we fell back into the coffee table. It shattered into pieces on the floor. Glass and pictures flew all over the carpet, but I would not let that nigga go. He was still hitting me in the side as I locked my legs around him and put more pressure on his throat, trying to make him tap out! "Fu-ck...Yo- ...Bitch!"*

*"What the hell are you doing?" LaKeisha screamed, trying to break us up, grabbing my arm. She wasn't strong enough to break my hold on Lionel's neck. The doorbell rang. She let go of me and went to answer. "I hope this is them now! You're both going to get a spanking!"*

*I quickly let go of Lionel when I saw the policeman at the door, and both of us got up. G.D. came over from across the street where they lived.*

*"This is the Dunn residence, isn't it? Is Mr. Gary Dunn around?" The officer asked LaKeisha. He looked past her and spotted Lionel and me, and suddenly he looked familiar as he took off his hat. I knew him. He worked with Dad at the office.*

"Yes, but no one's here but me and the kids. He lives across the street. I'm sorry if they got a little loud. They were just playing," LaKeisha tried to explain, glancing at our grandfather limping into the doorway.

"What the hell's going on over here? Who called the police? Have you been playing on the phone again, Lionel?!" Granddaddy yelled past everyone at us, holding his cane threateningly.

"No, Sir, no one called us," The officer stated as he glanced back at G.D. "Mr. Dunn, I'm sorry to visit under such terrible circumstances, but I wanted to be the one to find you and the boys."

G.D. stared at the officer recognizing him, and glared, asking, "Arthur, what's wrong?"

"Gary, there's been a terrible accident. We arrived on the scene, and Luther was involved in a head-on collision on the freeway not far from here. We have the driver in custody fine. He didn't feel a thing; he was so drunk. But Luther and Vivianne died on impact. I need you to come with me, Mr. Dunn. I see the boys are in capable hands for now," I remember Officer Arthur Kennedy told G.D. He was trying to keep a straight face, but he nearly lost it, glancing at

*Lionel and me. He put his hat back on and looked toward our grandfather.*

*I ran upstairs, slammed the door shut, and locked it! I knew it! I couldn't breathe, staring at the door. My heart was racing! The room seemed to be getting smaller as I struggled for a breath through my tears.*

*I heard it all…*

*It was all my fault!*

*Why did I call them? I was so spoiled! Mama…I should be dead, too…why didn't I…*

*"Hakim, open the door!" Lionel yelled at me. I opened the door staring at him, annoyed and bored as hell. He was crying with a pitiful look on his face. "Why you lock me out?"*

*"I don't know…It's open now," I said, going back to my bed and picking up my book and trying to read.*

*"Hakim! Mama and Dad are dead!" Lionel screamed at me.*

*"Yeah…I heard…What do you want me to do?" I replied, trying to concentrate on the words over his crying. "I'm going to bed. Fuck this."*

*"What are we gonna do?" Lionel cried, touching my foot after I just laid still.*

*I looked up at him, pissed off. I didn't have any answers to his questions. I'm a fucking kid just like you, Nigga! What am I supposed to tell you? I'm fucking scared too!?*

*"What do you want me to do, Lionel? I can't fix it, I can't do shit, and neither can you. Crying won't bring them back, and nobody is going to care what happens to us tomorrow.*

*'You see Officer Kennedy's face? He feels sorry for us, but he didn't even know where we live. Some friend! How many times have we been with Daddy at the office? I hate fake people! I don't care about him, and I don't care about anything anymore!" I shouted, frowning. I laid down and covered my head with my pillow.*

*"You don't care about me either, Hakim? You're my brother..." Lionel cried.*

*I sat up, stared at him, and sighed, realizing I had scared him.*

*"I don't know what to do! I don't know what to say, Lionel. What we gonna do without them?" I cried, unable to hold it in. Lionel fell across my knees, crying. "I don't want to stay with G.D. I know he's going to get us in the end!"*

*"He's mean, Hakim! He's going to beat us all the time,"* Lionel cried, his voice shaken and high.

*"Maybe Ms. Louisa will take us, and we can grow up with Kaliah?"* I said, trying to comfort him with a lie. I touched the soft curls on his head, hating myself. Kaliah's mother was struggling. That's why he stayed with us for a few years. He was in High School and back in Los Angelos. No one could take care of us, and I knew that our grandfather hated boys. Grandma Sophie could only keep him off us when she was around. *"I'm gonna make a plan to get us somewhere we can be good. I don't know how long it will take, though."*

*"You gonna take me with you, Hakim?"* Lionel asked worriedly. *"You not gonna leave me alone, are you?"*

*"I wouldn't leave you alone, Lionel. You're all I got now,"* I frowned, hugging my terrified brother.

*"Uh, uh, Hakim...You got to promise me you not gonna leave me alone?"* Lionel begged me, pushing my arm away, frowning.

*"I promise that I'm never going to leave you alone, Lionel. You're my baby brother..."* I swore, so angry that I wanted to cry, but I couldn't do it anymore. I was done lying to my brother so he wouldn't be frightened like me. I didn't

"Lionel, open the door!" I yelled, knocking, trying to talk over the music coming from the room suddenly. Of course, he heard G.D. screaming at me from downstairs.

"Go away, Hakim! I don't need you fucking with me right now! Leave me alone!" He yelled through the door, and that nigga turned the music up louder.

He must not believe that G.D. would kick his narrow-ass to the curb this time? Whatever he said to grandpa last night has him so deep in his feelings he's still pissed off. I know Lionel, he shuts up when he's in trouble, so G.D. is pushing this one. Lionel has fucked up.

"Lionel, OPEN this damn door, or I'll KICK this bitch in," I cried seriously over the music. A second after my threat, the music went off, and Lionel unlocked the door. I opened the door and stood watching him. He flopped on the bed and covered his face with a pillow. He looked like shit in a dirty A-shirt covered in makeup, bruises, scratches, and the room smelled like puke. "I see you follow instructions well. How you feeling?"

"Like I ate a raw pork chop that sat out for three days," He moaned through his pillow. I went over to my mini-fridge and got him a sports drink. I opened it and sat on the bed next to Lionel. I snatched away the pillow, and he opened his eyes, leaning toward me. "Here, drink this...you're probably dehydrated."

"Why you being so nice? You spit in that shit? I'm good," Lionel said, taking the pillow back and covering his face again.

"Ain't nobody spit in it! Drink the damn energy drink, Nigga!" I yelled, grabbing the pillow back. He sat up too quickly and moaned, leaning over the edge of his bed.

"Ooh, shit!" Lionel groaned, looking at the floor. I grabbed him and pulled him up. I held it to his lips, and he took a sip.

"Let me guess. You didn't eat anything all night?" I laughed, watching him take the bottle and drink more.

"It was late, so I didn't worry about food. I was having fun," Lionel sighed, holding his head.

I went into the bathroom, wet a washcloth, and grabbed a few pain pills from my lockbox for my knee injury. I sighed and shook my head as I handed him two and put the cold towel on his neck.

"I can't believe you did that shit, Bro. I thought you were smarter than that? You let Lester Woods talk you into getting in trouble every time. But you keep rolling with him," I chuckled, shaking my head. I was considering the stuff Cyrus told me, and it was funny.

"He's my friend! We had a good time! Shit, it's better than sitting here at home bored as hell," Lionel said, rolling his eyes looking pissed off.

"You haven't been home alone in months, Bro! I left you here for one night, and you hit the club and acted a fool on a school night? I guess I was stupid for thinking I could trust you to be smart enough to just chill, do your homework, and go to bed," I groaned, frowning. I was more disappointed than upset. "You're cool when you're with us, but as soon as I let you out of my sights, you get on the dumb-dumb again."

"I don't need no damn babysitter!" Lionel protested, rolling his eyes around and holding his head, frowning.

"You could have fooled the shit out of me! You are always flying off the handle when I'm not around. Why?

You miss me that much?" I seriously questioned his actions, raising my eyebrows.

"Don't nobody miss your mean ass, Hakim," Lionel said, frowning as he stared at the floor, holding his drink.

"Is that right?" I inquired seriously. If Lionel would be an asshole after fucking up, maybe he needed to learn a lesson about the shit he was pulling...From ME! "Okay, then...I'm going to move out. You've wanted your own room for years. When I tried to move to another room, you started with the shit, and Cyrus got it. But Cyrus has his own spot now. If I move out of your space, then you can do you and not have to worry about what the fuck your mean-ass brother is doing anymore. You'll have all the privacy you'll need!"

Lionel looked up at me and got pissed off, "Why? Why you gonna move, Hakim?"

"Because it seems like my being here is a problem for you. I'm in the way. I'm the reason you can't do shit, right? It's me that makes you fight niggas and talk shit. I'm the motherfucker that made you talk shit to G.D., and now he wants you out. But it's my fault, so if I get out of here, you can finally accept who keeps fucking up Lionel's life. You're only doing this shit because you're scared to grow up, and it has nothing to do with me," I told him, exhaling deeply. I took my wallet, car keys, and phone out of my pockets.

"Naw, naw! You can't move out and leave me alone, Hakim! That's not fair! You told me you wouldn't do me like that! So, now the cash got you ready to bail on me for good?" Lionel asked, looking angry.

"The MONEY?! Are you serious! It's never been about the money! We're family, and I've been putting up with your evil ways for years. I'm eighteen, and you're about to be sixteen. You don't give a damn about anything! G.D., Sophie, and even Cyrus have tried to get to your heart. There ain't shit to get to in there. I thought you knew how much I care. I'm always flying to save your ass, but I'm tired. I want my own life! You've been fighting everything I try to tell you. I don't talk to hear my own voice, and I don't think I'm better than you!

'I do all that talking because I love you, Man! But if you don't give a fuck about yourself, why am I going to keep wasting my breath, my time, and my goddamn cash trying to help you commit suicide?

'You want to go to jail or die. It's too easy to do, Lionel. Believe me, I know, and I've been through more shit than you can imagine. Some Cyrus does not know. I feel like sometimes…I can't trust anyone! So I keep shit deep down. Who can I tell? You?

'Hell no, you'd use it against me. I don't mean shit to you! I'm your scapegoat!" I explained as calmly as possible, but I was losing.

"That's not true, Hakim! You're my brother…It's just…I don't know. The shit between us ain't never been smooth unless we fought. If we aren't scrapping together, then it doesn't feel right unless we fight each other.

'When mama was here, it was a fun kind of fighting. We just teased each other all the time. But that night they died, we both just got actually furious. It felt like the only way to get shit out of you when I know you are scared or mad. You overthink, Nigga.

'But when we on a mission to kick ass, it's like we're best friends. We can read each other's minds and body language like we're the same person. It's crazy and always feels good to fight niggas with you, Hakim," Lionel said, thinking back to our adventures in violence and street brawls.

"Yeah, that's true, but why can't we just vibe like that all the time? I was nice to you when I came inside, but you thought I was trying to fuck you off! You believe I hate you that much I would spit in your shit," I asked, a bit hurt over that. I nearly lost it when he turned it down.

"I know…I know…I got a fucked up way of thinking! I'm sorry, Hakim. You're my brother, and I don't want you to move. I'll do anything if you stay," Lionel sighed, putting the towel from his neck to his knee.

I'll be damned…Cyrus was right…Usually, when I tried to correct my brother, he would wait until he thought I was done and come for me! We'd wind up destroying something in the process of my trying to NOT kill the nigga because neither of us played when we threw punches. We always go all in like a Texas Hold 'em tournament, and it would end with Lionel getting fucked up along with the house, but it didn't discourage my brother. Lionel had more heart than any nigga I ever met on the streets. He would hound a motherfucker until they made him shut the fuck up, but there were not many out there that could best Lionel anymore.

Fighting me for years had turned my little brother into a boxing wonder. He knew he would always have to catch me slipping because he couldn't touch me in a fair fight. No one stands a chance if they attack me head-on armed or unarmed. I made sure that I learned disarming and incapacitating people growing up in Georgia. I physically trained my body to be a brick wall, so niggas hurt themselves trying to harm me. It backfired, though, because my muscle is so solid when I am angry I don't feel anything for hours until the adrenaline wears off.

Lionel loves to see the violent side of me, so he's not afraid of getting hurt by anyone out there. I finally get it now.

"I got an idea of how you can help me out today to prove your words. But I need you to slow down! Help G.D. and Sophie more around here, try harder at school, and watch your mouth. You only have two more years. How are you going to make it into a college if you can't survive high school?

"You want to party? Fine! You'll party with us, so I can keep an eye out for you. Hanging with Lester Woods is too dangerous. I can assure you when shit hits the fan, Les's white ass ain't going anywhere, but your black ass is gone!

"Now, give me my credit card, Sir!" I demanded with a straight face. Lionel frowned but took out his wallet and handed it to me. "I want a promise from you that you're going to fly straight. I kept my word. You messed up the privilege, so now you owe me a new deal. I want you to chill, do the right thing, and use your head more, Lionel?"

Lionel stared at me sadly and nodded, saying, "Whatever you want, Hakim, just don't leave me, Bro? You all I got. I'll help out, do the work, and stay out of trouble, alright?"

"I hope I can trust you this time, Bro. I have to make some serious decisions soon. If I can't trust you…I got to leave you behind to find your own path. I can't have you dragging me down. I need as much positivity around me as I can get right now. All the negative vibes are blocking my inner peace. I can barely center myself," I confessed, rubbing my eyes nervously. A headache was coming on, and I was trying to stay calm. But I was scared shitless of meeting Mandisa's father in a while. I'll admit it here and nowhere else. "I'm going to meet Dr. King this evening. I need you there for moral support. But this Lionel, not the crazy nigga I've been fighting for years. Don't break your word, Bro. A man is worthless if you can't trust him, and when he loses everything, his word is all he has. An untrustworthy man is unworthy of knowing if you want peace."

"Whatever you need, Hakim, I've got your back," Lionel assured me, nodding with a very calm expression that I had never seen before. Lionel looked sincere and serious because his face was completely relaxed.

I stood up and stretched, trying to think about anything but what was to come. But there wasn't much time to get everything done. I took a deep breath as the headache began dwindling.

"So, besides getting the following day reminder of how dumb it is to drink on an empty stomach, what did you do? You're not fucked up, so you haven't been fighting?" I asked, staring back at him from my closet as I opened the door.

"Les, let me drive his new Bentley! It was so sweet! I felt like the richest nigga on Earth, Hakim," Lionel replied with a huge grin.

"Wow! A Bentley? 2019? Coupe or Sedan?" I inquired, somewhat impressed.

"It's a four-door, and it's clean! It's all white and gold with a chocolate and caramel interior. That leather is so soft I want a recliner made out of that shit!

"I met this fine ass girl from Singapore, and I fucked her in the backseat," Lionel chuckled with an evil grin. His eyes looked like the Grinch that Stole Christmas.

"What?!" I laughed, shaking my head. "You're lying!"

"Uh-huh," Lionel insisted, showing me his phone. Oh! She was not lovely! She was gorgeous! I was very impressed. "She's nineteen, goes to Rice in Houston, and she's rich! The only thing is she's about to get married, so ain't nothing going to grow in that soil. But it's like

Mandisa's situation. Her people set it up. She ain't got no love for this dude. It's all for the trust fund."

"So, you fucked a Singapore heiress in the backseat of a two-hundred thousand dollar car?" I asked sarcastically, drawing a vivid picture for Lionel to view. "That sounds like some bucket list shit that some dudes could never get to happen, Bro!"

Lionel's grin grew even uglier, and he stuck out his tongue, saying, "Yeah! You're right...Shit like that doesn't happen to normal niggas. She said I was the best she ever had and wants to see me again!"

"You gonna do it?" I asked thoughtfully, staring at him.

"Fuck, yeah...Ricka is fine, and she's a super headhunter! She loves this dick, so I'ma feed her what she loves until she can't take more," Lionel laughed, suddenly feeling much better, I noticed.

"Even though you know there's no possible future with this woman?" I reminded him, raising my eyebrow. He poked out his lips for a moment. "All I'm saying is she's beautiful, rich, and she's a good lay too? You're going to catch feelings, and then what? Or what if it's the other way around?"

"Naw, it's not like that, Hakim. I know how to keep the 'L-word' out of a situation. I see a line, and I don't cross that shit. I know how to take things as they are because I don't want a girlfriend.

"Pussy is just pussy. Ricka's not going to be a problem, and if it does get weird, then I'll cut it short. I got this shit," Lionel explained, seeming like he knew what he was talking about.

"Well, I believe you when you say it like that. But there's nothing wrong with falling in love with a woman if she feels the same way about you," I told him, grabbing a suit bag from the closet and my dress shoes.

"You mean like Mandisa?" Lionel asked with an arrogant tone that I didn't like.

"Yeah," I replied, sincerely glancing back at him. "Why did you say her name like that?"

"I see you and Cyrus. Both of y'all niggas are sprung over her. I know she's a good girl, but I don't see any future for you with her either. Both of you are spending your paper and sniffing after her like you can both really have her?! Seriously?

"Ain't no way she's gonna go through with that shit! One of you is gonna lose...honestly... I think it's gonna be you,

Bro," Lionel said, sounding a bit concerned for me. He had no idea what he was talking about. How could he know?

"Oh, really?" I interrogated Lionel, raising my eyebrow and tilting my head. I folded my arms, analyzing his point. "Why would you assume she would pick Cyrus over me?"

Lionel looked at me seriously and stood up, "No offense, Hakim, but Cyrus has more swag, sex appeal, game, and he's funny. Girls love niggas that can make them laugh. Cyrus has more talent, his own spot, much more expensive taste than you, and he can sing and dance! He has spent some serious bread lacing her, Hakim."

"Mandisa doesn't care about the money and all the gifts, Lionel," I insisted, glancing through my sock drawer.

"Keep telling yourself that. When Mandisa fucks Cyrus first, and he pops that cherry, don't tell me shit, Bro! Just take it and let that shit go," Lionel said, raising his eyebrows and poking out his lips, teasing me.

"So, you really believe that Mandisa doesn't love us both? You think she's playing me for a fool?" I asked, frustrated as I stood up straight, watching him. I folded my arms, thinking as my headache began to make the top of my head throb. I hoped that he was making a valid point because I didn't want to hear the bullshit right now.

"I didn't say that…Hakim. Mandisa cares about you! But you both know she ain't woman enough for two real niggas! She's a virgin, shy, and scared of the dick! Mandisa ain't going to go all the way with that three-way shit!" Lionel chuckled, shaking his head. "Now you need to grow up and face reality, Hakim, you or Cyrus? Game over, Bro…Kill yo self!"

"Is THAT right? I questioned my brother, rubbing my eyes beneath my glasses.

"Yeah, Nigga, stop living in La-La Land! You lose, Bro!" Lionel said, throwing his pillow at me, knocking my glasses off. They fell on the floor, and the arm broke off. I frowned as I poked out my lips, knelt down, and picked them up. I glanced at Lionel and flared my nostrils. "My bad, Hakim, I didn't mean to do that."

I walked over toward him. Lionel nearly jumped off the bed as I reached down into my nightstand drawer and grabbed my spare pair of glasses. I gave Lionel a hug and then put on my glasses and smiled as I shook my head.

"You don't know what you're talking about, Lionel. Mandisa is MORE woman than YOU can handle. But Cyrus and I have her covered VERY nicely. So don't worry about me, Bro," I informed him maliciously like he did a moment ago. Now I was the Grinch.

"Aw hell no, Hakim! What the fuck?! You AND Cyrus FUCKED her?" Lionel hollered so loud that I grabbed him and covered his mouth, and pushed him against the bedroom wall.

"See? You've got a big mouth! That's why I don't tell you shit!" I whisper-yelled at him, wrinkling my forehead in anger. "Now, shut the fuck up and talk like a normal person. Quit yelling out my personal shit! She's not a ho. Mandisa's my future wife. If you want to know anything else, you better calm the fuck down."

Lionel gazed at me and nodded through my grip over his mouth. I made him sit on my bed and slowly let him go. I shut the bedroom door, and Lionel smiled at me viciously.

"You and Cyrus fucked Mandisa? Both of y'all, as in together?" Lionel whispered, wiping off his mouth with his sneer growing.

"Yeah..." I answered as I grabbed the safe out of the closet and set it on his bed.

"When? She seems the same to me? She ain't piped up like she's been fucking," Lionel asked, staring me down.

"No, man, last night while you were out with Les. She came on to me! I didn't expect that shit at all, but...DAMN!"

I whispered, getting excited thinking back. Those chills started hitting me all over again, and I shivered involuntarily.

"What was it like? I mean, it was her first time, so I know she was scared. It couldn't be that good," Lionel asked curiously.

"Bro, she was nervous, but no, it wasn't what I thought it was gonna be. I've been with a lot of women, and I have never felt pussy that good. Everything was so good! We did it more than once, and it gets better and better…ugh!" I groaned, still shivering, as goosebumps broke out all down my neck and arms.

"Word?! Both of y'all at the same time?" Lionel asked, sticking out his tongue.

"Yeah, both of us, and Cyrus ain't no punk! He's a beast!" I laughed, taking off my shirt.

"She let you put it in her butt?" Lionel asked, grinning.

"Nigga! Shut the fuck up! You don't turn a girl out like that the first time!" I bellowed and covered my own mouth as I realized I had raised my voice.

"I did the first time," Lionel laughed, sticking out his tongue at me.

"A woman has to be ready to do that freaky shit. You don't surprise her with anal! You can really fuck things up if you don't know what you're doing, Bro," I groaned, seriously offended.

"She asked me for it! Older women ask me for it all the time, and they love it!" Lionel chuckled, getting excited.

"Older women have experimented a little…well…some of them…a couple of them, okay, not many like that! They'll fuck you up if you try it without warning.

"The first time I went there, she was really drunk. So she didn't care what I did to her, but she remembered. She liked it, but after that, I did it when a woman asked," I laughed nervously. "Mandisa…That may take some time, no rush, because that pussy is superb!"

"She squirts?" Lionel asked me, squirming on my bed. "I bet it was wet and sticky? The finest women got the stickiest cum."

"You must have only fucked one kind of woman? Pussy is pussy! Fine or not, it gets wet! If you hit it right, they all will talk, squeeze you, and wet you up. Well…all women don't squirt, but you can make it cum hard enough to wet you up," I chuckled, getting dressed. "Ooh, when she moans…Bliss! It makes you want to let it go right there. I got goosebumps all over me right now just thinking about that shit, Bro…Mercy…Shit!"

"Eww, Mandisa is a freak…I knew it!" Lionel groaned, acting like he was shooting a jump shot. He raised his eyebrows, eyeing me. "Why are you getting so fly? You need to wear a suit and tie to meet her dad?"

"Yeah, this isn't a typical meeting. I've got to prove to Dr. King that I am good enough for his daughter, Lionel. If I go in there unprepared, he'll take one look at me, then reject my words. It won't matter how I meet him intellectually; if he has a made-up mind, I ain't worth hearing looking at my attire. I have to meet Dr. King where he can be reached. I did learn something by observing the white man for three years.

"Whites are notorious for being overly judgmental about brothers based solely on appearances. White man ain't gonna let just any nigger have his daughter. I'm no Uncle Tom, and I'm not going to smile in his face and bash my people. I don't care how nice of a person he is deep down. He's not going to let her go without a fight.

"This is warfare because he's already judged me, and he doesn't know me yet. But I got something for that ass…I'm about to tan his hide," I told Lionel as I straightened my tie and put on my jacket. "I'm going to show Dr. King just how wrong he is…not just about me, but all of us."

# Chapter Three: Dna/Control (Diss Record)

## Darius Cyrus Jefferson

Mandisa and I were watching TV in the den and talking. It was in the afternoon, and still no word from Hakim. So, I played it cool and kept her relaxed. But I was nervous, which meant I was doing anything for laughs, so I didn't overthink.

"I cannot believe you have me watching cartoons, Darius, of all things?" Mandisa giggled, putting her head on my shoulder. I played with her copper curls against her cheek. "SpongeBob Squarepants?"

"What?!" I asked, grinning at her. "Spongebob is the silliest virgin on the planet!"

Mandisa's eyes sparkled as she blushed, laughing, "It's a cartoon! How can you tell he is a virgin, Darius?"

"Okay, he lives alone with his pet snail that he talks to daily. Spongebob works in the fast-food industry even though he has other talents that would make much more money. He goes to a driver's school, but he's too nervous about driving the boat to pass the test. He thinks everyone is his friend, even Squidward, who hates his guts. His best friend, Patrick, is a moron that plays games, blows bubbles, and chases jellyfish, which would be butterflies up here.

'But besides his terrible taste in clothes, the worst clue is that he's been the employee of the month more than eighty-four times which means he's been working at the Krusty Krab for at least seven years. If he started there when he was sixteen, that would make him twenty-three years old, Queen. Ain't no way Sandy is giving him a nut," I chuckled, doing the math. "Either SpongeBob's a virgin, or he's completely gay! He loves playing house with Patrick…I smoke too much, I know!"

"You are silly!" Mandisa laughed, pushing her face into my arm. She was giggling so much it tickled me. "How do you not know that he might be just a freak behind closed doors?"

"I don't know about all of that, but I think he's gay on the cool. He likes to cross-dress too much and wears make-up. A lot is going on in Bikini Bottom, and I think it's a dude's bottoms he lives inside," I laughed, throwing my head back. "A lot of kids' shows have a hidden agenda… Bugs Bunny was bi-sexual or transgender. You never knew what he identified as when you were a kid. He was always dressing up like a female and kissing dudes in the mouth…straight…gay? We knew the Warners were white and not REAL BROTHERS."

Mandisa lowered her eyes and took the remote, and changed the channel.

"Oh, the Price is Right! I used to be the Master at this shit! My mama and I used to play at home watching the show," I chuckled, stopping her. Mandisa stared up at me like she was lost.

"How do you do that?" She asked, smiling.

"Oh, that's easy! You know, when they call people down to contestants row...you get piped up! Darius Osiris Jefferson Jr, come on down!" I yelled as I jumped up, looking shocked, and started running around the room. I was jumping over the sofa and table, making Mandisa laugh so hard she looked like a tomato. "Oh, but when I get down to the bidding, I do the fool! 'What's the item up for bids, Rod?' 'It's a new car!' 'How much do you think that car is worth, Cyrus?' One hundred dollars, Bob!"

Mandisa fell over forward, laughing, "One hundred dollars for a car, Darius? REALLY?"

"What? Too high? 'Alright, One dollar, Bob!' Yeah, Nigga!" I said, acting seriously excited. Mandisa fell off the couch and hit the floor crying. "The actual retail price is...15,769 dollars! If everyone else overbids, I win!"

"Darius, oh god! No! You are too silly…I…cann…ot…breathe…." Mandisa giggled gasped, rolling on the carpet, making me grin and shake my head. She sat up with her face pink, eyes red from the reefer, and looked so sexy in my tight-fitting black tee-shirt. Her hips were poking out as she struggled to climb back on the sofa in tears. I would help, but it was lovely watching her behind in her red panties, trying to stay underneath my shirt. "Why do you do that to me all the time? Lionel falls on purpose, but you make me fall out!"

"What?" I asked, looking innocent blinking rapidly. "What do you mean? What do I do, Queen?"

"You always make with the jokes and witty observations…then you pretend to be other people, and it is so funny…the faces you make…like…now! Why?!" Mandisa giggled, wiping her cheeks, finally sitting on the sofa.

I sat, telling her, "When I was younger, I used to get picked on all the time about everything from my skin tone, hair, and for being overweight. I'd get emotional and fight. Then I'd get a spanking when I got home. My dad thought it was normal for boys to fight. But my mama used to say that I needed to learn how to use my words to outsmart people rather than be violent.

'Whenever I saw something funny, I memorized it, and I practiced making my mama laugh. I watched so many shows and stand-up comics. It all just started coming together in my own material. My dad thought I was going to be a comedian. But it's just a way to make friends, break the monotony, and keep people off my back. I got so good at the dozens and roasting that nobody talked about me to my face. When I got mad, I'd really hurt people's feelings, and then they'd want to fight," I laughed, thinking back. "When I moved here, everyone tried me, and I shut them all down. The only person that never came for me was Hakim. He hated snapping, but he'd laugh if it was funny.

"Hakim never used to laugh, play, or act like a kid before I came around. G.D. told me he thought Hakim was never going to relax before we met. Hakim's actually chilly, but if you met him when I did, you'd know Hakim was suicidal. All Hakim did was read, go to school, run, and fight. Back then, he and Lionel fought almost every day.

"Lionel's always been, Lionel. He hasn't changed much at all. On the inside, Lionel's still a big-ass kid. Outside he's different, but he's still that mad tiny shrimp he was when he was eight. Lionel is slowly getting better, but I don't know what keeps setting him off. Maybe losing his little girlfriend…?"

"What?" Mandisa asked, glancing up at me, smiling in thought. "Lionel always says, 'I don't want a girlfriend…I don't need no one all over me!'"

"Lionel used to have this little shadow that followed him around, Little May-May! She was so cute. They were always together. She moved away, and he can't find her. He was in love with her. It fucked him up because he treated her like a friend. He was little, so he wasn't thinking about love. Now, he wants her so bad he can't get over it," I explained as I ran my fingers through Mandisa's curls.

"Darius, that is so sad…No wonder Lionel is so upset. He cannot move on," Mandisa sighed, frowning.

"Yeah, Hakim has been trying everything he can to find her, but nothing. Lionel's been looking for her for three years," I added, looking down at her.

"Poor Lionel," She mumbled, pouting her plump pink lips. I kissed her sweetly and held her hand, thinking. Mandisa rubbed my fingers. "Seeing us together must upset him so?"

"Maybe, I'm not really sure. But Lionel can't fuck away the pain. I've tried. It doesn't work. The only way to drown the rain is with real sunshine. Pain comes back like weeds when you keep trying to bury it," I groaned, trying to not think about it too long. "Can I ask you something, Mandisa?"

"Of course, Darius, anything," Mandisa answered, leaning closer again and smiling.

"If I asked you to marry me, would you say yes?" I worried as I watched her playing with my hair. She twirled the locks between her pink fingertips and smiled.

"I would marry you, Darius. You make me happy and keep me smiling. I know that it wouldn't be like it would be in a forced situation. We'd have fun, you would want me to live a happy life, and I would never worry if my kids would have a loving father," Mandisa replied, looking at me through her fingers, blushing. I smiled down at her touching her chin with my thumb. She didn't have to think about it for a second. All I needed to know…now I just need a beautiful ring.

"When we get married, I'm going to spoil you to death, you know that, right?" I chuckled as she wrapped my hair around her finger.

"Darius, you spoil me enough. I have told you that the gifts are nice. It is you that I love, not the money or what you buy," She reminded me for the fiftieth time.

"I hear what you're saying, Queen, but that just makes me want to give you everything. Just like I said last night, you might think that was in a fit of passion, but I meant every word, Mandisa. I love you!

"My life would be so different right now if you never told me how you felt that night. I was so terrified of what I would do if I said anything to you, and you didn't feel the same. I've always fallen in love, and then the girl just didn't want me. They liked me, but that was because of the game I kicked or the money I wasted. But then I became suddenly too immature or slow. I didn't think you could really cared about me because every woman I've ever loved used me to get to Hakim," I explained sadly.

"Darius, I would never ever use you or hurt you that way," Mandisa told me, putting my hand on her cheek. "You never have to buy me another gift or spend another penny. I just want you, Darius. I love you.

"Oui, I love Hakim. I fell for him first, but I am not interested in hurting either of you. I only wish to give you both the love you give me."

"I know you wouldn't use me, Queen," I assured her, kissing her hand. "But you can't stop me from buying you things. It's an obsession, I'm a pleaser, and I need help! Can't you tell how sick I am?! I love feet. I like when my woman needs me, but I need her more, and I can't be satisfied unless I know I made her smile at least three times a day. I'm hopeless!"

"No, you are perfect, Darius. That is not hopeless. It is Cyrus, and I love him. Who cares what people think?" She giggled, kissing the back of my hand, flirting. I smiled and tried to fight the insane vibes Mandisa gave me. She was so lovingly affectionate, understanding of my personal hangups, and beautiful through and through. I never felt sad telling her anything because I knew Mandisa accepted people just as they are and didn't try to change them. But being herself around us was making my family more like her. Mandisa was healing us all slowly with her gentle nature and kind, wounded heart. I fell in love with her the moment I laid eyes on her, and the things that I was ashamed I did were what Mandisa loved the most about me!

Her physical appearance was all I obsessed over for years, searching for a woman to love. You have to understand that I have it so bad for Mandisa because of her natural beauty. Yes, she's a light-skinned sister with dazzling eyes that seem to change color, and her hair is long and so lovely and light. The things that Mandisa hates about herself are the things that I love! Her hips, thighs, figure scream sexy black goddess! Some hate the idea that brothers dip with other races. It's fucked up because, at the end of the day, none of us had a part in being put here, so you should make the best out of your fucked up existence and find someone that is really down for you.

Mandisa and her mother have been used and abused by her father. Being in the room with the man, I saw that he was terrifying the hell out of his family. Mami is afraid he's going to snatch Mandisa and run to Paris so he can marry her off for money. She sees the cycle about to repeat with Amani if he gets away with it. But you can see that Ninon and Mandisa are beautiful black women, deserving of the same love as any woman. It doesn't matter their race in this situation to me because Dr. King is wrong! These are his kids! Mandisa is frightened of him to the point she won't say a word or make a move in the room with that man.

He's got her trained to be seen and not heard, and I don't want to imagine what he did to make her that way. Mami seems to know that Dr. King was verbally abusive, and he hit them both, but Mandisa doesn't remember her father beating her for some reason. She doesn't talk about how he fucked her up. Mandisa just knows that she doesn't like him and what he's done to her mother. Queen's taking so much medication for her heart deformity, depression, anxiety, and Mandisa has pills for epilepsy, psychosis, and Mami insists that she needs them all to be ordinary. She snapped when she turned fourteen, and Mami said that Mandisa had to be hospitalized for weeks afterward. That was when Mami said enough and started running.

Mandisa can't remember much after that age until now. She's tried to kill herself with sleeping pills, and had a major meltdown, and ran away from home when she was sixteen. Dr. King found Mandisa and brought her home. Mami told him they were leaving because she was pregnant, and Dr. King attacked Mami. Mandisa assaulted her father, and it scared them both so much that they locked her away. Dr. King thought Mandisa would be fine in the hospital for a few weeks, and he could marry her off anyway. Mami checked Mandisa out of the mental hospital and ran, coming here with the help of a friend.

She couldn't depend on her own mother because Mrs. Brown was always taking money from Thomas King, so her loyalty was to the dough. She never wanted a child anyway, so selling Ninon to Dr. King's father wasn't a big thing. Sylvia Brown didn't care if she didn't have to worry about her bills and debt. Ninon caught on the last time she ran, and Thomas showed up the next day. That's why Ninon came here...there was no way he could find her. She had no ties to Longview, Texas. But I think that she called him and that's why he's here now.

"Ayo! They made a sequel to Coming to America?! It's got the original cast?!" I screamed, looking at the screen, trying to read.

Mandisa burst into laughter, watching my reaction to the ad. I was trying to read the story plot, and she popped me on the head. My locks absorbed the shock as I looked back at her. Mandisa handed me my glasses, saying, "You cannot read if you cannot see, Darius. Wear them. They make you look cute when you read."

I groaned, staring at my reading glasses in her palm. I hated wearing glasses, and after moving here and meeting Hakim, I didn't want to look anything like him. Everyone was saying that I was trying to be like him, but Hakim wasn't listening. I heard it all, and it sunk in deep. It's hard for me not to think about what other people are thinking. I grew up around Hakim and Lionel, and people were always talking about the shit they did.

By association, that was a shot at me because they were my family. I took a lot of shit personally, especially what the women said about me. So I let Hakim do the book thing, and I kept the funny coming so he could operate. I could read, but I hated doing it because it meant I had to wear glasses. If I read aloud, it comes out slow because my brain flips the letters around, so I have to read each word carefully, or I'll start making things up that look right.

"I think I'll be good, Queen," I chuckled, shaking my head.

"Darius, did you ever think the reason that your struggle with reading is because you are afraid to be smart, so you think the funny will go away?" Mandisa asked me, putting my glasses on her eyes. "Wow…It's like I can see the future they magnify so much…I think I can see our son! His name…is…AYO!"

I died laughing at that shit! This is why I fell so hard for Mandisa! When we are alone, she makes me feel like there isn't shit in the world that can bring me down. I would pay every dime I have to keep her sunshine near me. Hakim found the perfect woman, and somehow, she's brave enough to try some shit most wouldn't and love us both so we can be friends. I didn't think it was possible at all, but Hakim has been so calm about this it shocks the shit out of me. Then last night!

When Mandisa got excited playing peek-a-boo with me, she went after Hakim being curious…I was just trying to see what she was after, but she wanted us both. A virgin let us both have her, and it was so damn good that I fell even deeper into my feelings. I didn't think Mandisa would ever do that shit! She did everything we asked, and I know Mandisa loved what we did to her fine ass. The way that girl moans and screams gives a Brotha goosebumps just thinking about it. The faces she makes are so innocent and sexy, but that pussy is so good that I see stars, and it feels like Jody is having a seizure fighting those walls. I'm getting tremors right now thinking about it, and it's right there.

Understand that I've been around Hakim when he's doing him, but that was not the same brother that I'm used to handling at all. That was Hakim! He was nervous, and he was worried about what was going to happen to Mandisa afterward. Elyeuh doesn't give a fuck, and he would never let me touch a woman that he was fucking! He would literally fuck the shit out of a woman if she looked at another man near him. Then when he was done with her, she never wanted you again. But he doesn't want her, and she's all heartbroken, still feenin' like Jodeci!

You see, HE talks lots of shit to get the girls interested in a fuck, but when he gets her naked…and collared…He says the most player shit to boost her ego until she can't take it! He fucks her so good that she can't take another nigga touching her unless he can make her feel like that. That's why Nicole was the only one that ran after she took the money and gave the collar back. Nicole figured out that

Hakim and Elyeuh were two different brothers. She only wanted his money to get the fuck out of here, she had a man boosting her up, but he didn't have the money to save her. Nicole didn't fuck him until after giving him the collar back but danced for Hakim and did anything Elyeuh asked until the nigga proved Hakim was going to give her the money. Once she knew HE was honest, she gave him his shit, fucked him, took the hundred thousand dollars, bounced without warning. Nicole ran off with her man and left Hakim looking dumb. His ego got bruised, but HE respected her for knowing what she wanted and following through.

All the other girls that sold their shit or still have it want Hakim or Elyeuh and will do anything to be in Mandisa's shoes. But Mandisa hasn't met that nigga, and I'm trying to keep things calm so HE doesn't return. So far, so good. Mandisa seems to have a healing effect on my brothers and me. We're blessed to have her. That's why we can't lose her to this fucked up situation. Hell, no…I'm going to marry her! I'm going to get a ring once all the shit dies down…I just have to pick the perfect time to propose.

I'm never gonna get a vibe like this from another woman. I've been with countless through the years! Many of them were with Hakim, too. But none of those women ever got to know the real me, showed me the kind of admiration

Mandisa gives and would do anything to make me happy. One woman can love two different men effortlessly if she's really learning who they are. Mandisa's submissive nature makes us succumb to her healing energy naturally because she's so humble, beautiful and aching too. It's a fucking small world, after all.

I heard my phone ringing as I lifted Mandisa from my lap. I carefully got up, ran to the table grabbing it, and froze as my heart stopped. I glanced at Mandisa as she stared at me, worried.

"Bro, I'm on my way to the hospital. Get there in about thirty minutes.

"Here's the idea, try to look as black as you want…be yourself. I want an honest reaction from Dr. King after meeting you last night. Let him see you, NOW! His prejudices will come out fast if he's hiding them," Hakim calmly explained. He didn't sound pissed off, nervous, or worried.

"Alright, Bro, No problem," I replied, nodding to Mandisa.

"Make sure she's in her school uniform, Cyrus. I want Mandisa to look as young and innocent as possible as I can pull raw fear from Dr. King. He won't see a little girl if she comes in dressed like a model," Hakim warned me. "Tell her to put her hair in pigtails. That will really get his head fucked up. No makeup. We want sweet, innocent, and hide her curves under the jacket."

"Yeah… I see what you're going for, Hakim," I chuckled as my brother's plan started unfolding before my eyes. He was an evil genius! "Thirty minutes, and we will be there!"

"Try not to worry Mandisa with too many details. Just tell her to trust in us," Hakim said. "I got this shit, Bro!"

I glared at Mandisa as Hakim hung up the phone and said, "Queen, hit the shower. You need to wear your uniform. Your motivation is little schoolgirl, innocent, sweet, and no makeup. We don't want your dad to think of you as being eighteen. We need to remind him you're his baby like Amani."

"I understand, but what is Hakim doing, Darius?" Mandisa asked me with a terrifying stare.

"Don't worry," I assured her, grinning. "The only thing I can say for sure is Hakim can hold his own in a fair or unfair match-up. Whatever he's got planned with Mami, it's organized. So let's hit it. We can't keep him waiting."

Mandisa and I took a shower and quickly got dressed. I made sure I didn't look like a schoolboy. I dressed like I was about to fall into a club. A-shirt, jeans, a flashy belt buckle,

Brooklyn chain, diamond watch, clean boots, a fly designer shirt, black, and gold everywhere, so the diamonds shine, and I let my hair hang free.

I smiled at Mandisa as I walked into the den from downstairs. She looked so sweet, like when we went to the mall in Dallas the first time. She had her hair back in two pigtails with blue ribbons on the ends with adorable sunflower clips up top matching her vest and the gold in her skirt. The oversized school sweater hid her body from sight, but her eyes still made her look so sexy. I couldn't help but see the sweet angelic face before me and love Mandisa more than anything. I had to shake my feelings and the growing fear to get in the truck.

"Darius, I'm afraid," Mandisa sighed, looking out the window. She peered at me sadly with the darkest eyes I had ever seen. They were green like moss on the side of a tree. Her fingers trembled as she tried to rub her hands together. I took her hand and held it in mine as I drove.

"I know my brother, Queen. When Hakim tells me he's got this shit, then he's not going to fail. The only thing you've never seen is his ability to manipulate people's emotions. He can make you love him or hate him. His mouth is more deadly than any punch or kick he can throw. I trust him. Hakim knows exactly what he's doing," I explained, setting her mind at ease the best I could.

#

It was 4:44 in the evening when I knocked on the door. I didn't realize the day had gotten away from us. Time flies when you're having fun.

"Come in," I heard Mami say. I let Mandisa go inside first, and I followed her quietly. There were a few extra chairs for visitors near Mami's bed. I wondered who had been by so early? "Hi, Baby!"

Mami smiled, giving Mandisa a hug as she glanced up at me sweetly. Dr. King stared at Mandisa. He stood up and hugged her, playing with her pigtails.

"Don't you look cute in your school uniform," Dr. King asked, smiling at her. He suddenly glanced in my direction as I hugged Mrs. King. His eyebrows wrinkled as his blue eyes seemed to get darker! "Nice bling! Don't you look…flashy?"

"Yeah," I replied seriously as I stood up straight and popped the collar on my Versace shirt. "Yesterday, we were in such a hurry to get Mrs. King here that I didn't get home to change. So, I looked kind of…generic…I know, I'm funky fresh, though, right?"

111

"I see…" Dr. King mumbled, giving me the once over, frowning up. "Where is your quiet friend from last night?"

"Oh, Lionel? That's my little brother. He should be here in a few minutes," I confirmed as Dr. King nodded, staring at my watch, suddenly hypnotized. He didn't like my style at all, but suddenly…he noticed my shit was real! "I have the New York fashion that people around here don't possess. I love Rolexes, and expensive timepieces are something I collect for fun."

"I have a few myself. Not quite as flashy as yours. What was your name again?" Dr. King asked curiously, suddenly relaxing his face.

"Cyrus Jefferson Junior, Dr. Thomas King, nice to meet you…again," I chuckled as he shook my hand and admired my icy blue watch face. "I've got a guy in New York that does superb custom work that makes all my family's dreams real. He's pretty reasonable once he knows you're going to do more business with him."

Mami winked at me as I smiled at her from the corner of my eye. I caught sight of my girlfriend in her bassinette and was ready to go for the kill. I smiled, seeing her tiny peach foot kicking under her blanket. Did Amani hear me talking? Mami giggled when she saw the baby start to stir from her nap. Dr. King glanced over as Mandisa and Mami started laughing. Amani wiggled in her covers and threw her arms around, and let out the sweetest whimper toward me.

"Aww, Darius! She wants you to hold her," Mami sighed.

"Oh, good, then she's got that power nap out of the way," I laughed, reaching for Amani and picking her up carefully, and holding her close. "Girl, I am about to roll to the club tonight, so you need to wake up so we can drive my truck. I already got your outfit out in the trunk. I found some baby Prada for my supermodel girlfriend."

Dr. King laughed and rolled his eyes. Mami pushed his arm, laughing as I playfully nibbled on Amani's tiny toes. Everyone enjoyed having a ball with Amani, and she was so precious I couldn't help but be happy holding her. Her blue eyes followed me all around the room as I acted a fool to get her giggling. It was the sweetest thing I had ever heard in my entire life. A newborn baby smiled at me and actually giggled. I suddenly realized why Hakim sent me in first when I saw the way Dr. King softened up with me once he saw I was harmless. I actually wasn't worried about the man once I focused on Amani.

But my heart stopped when I heard a knock on the door! I took a deep breath and raised my head as Mami said, "Come in!"

The door opened slowly, and all I saw were tons of roses and balloons. Mami's face lit up when she saw a giant teddy bear walking into the door. I stood up and grabbed the bear from Lionel, sitting it in a chair, and started to shut the door. A hand touched mine on the handle. I saw a pair of black Stacy Adams, a grey trench coat, and I pulled the door open!

Hakim looked me in the eyes and smiled as he stepped inside Mami's room.

WTF?!

My brother's dreadlocks were gone! Where his crown once hung was short, neat, and covered with waves! He wore a fly-ass grey suit and black tie, looking like a brother from Wall Street. He had a briefcase in one hand and a leather binder in the other. His designer frames caught the light as he smiled up at me and offered me his hand.

"Cyrus!" He called me smiling, giving me his briefcase. He gave me a hug and fixed his glasses.

"H-Hakim?" I mumbled, trying to accept what the fuck I was seeing!

I had never seen Hakim with short hair, nor have I seen him smile like this and so happy! WTF!? He was someone completely different now!

Oh, the nigga looked like Trey Songz before, but that was his fucking twin with no hair anywhere now. I was gonna roast the fuck out of him later!

"Yeah, it's me, Bro! You look fresh to death," He said, knowing I was blown away. I reached over and touched his Dark Caesar and suddenly felt happy too. I couldn't believe his hair was gone, but he looked happier without it! Hakim told me he was never gonna cut his hair, and I couldn't believe that shit.

"Hakim?!" Mami screamed, looking Hakim over as he came inside the room. Mandisa played with Amani in Mami's arms, and tears ran down her cheeks when she laid eyes on Hakim's hair. She didn't say a word but covered her mouth, sadly looking away a moment. Dr. King stood up and stared right at Hakim the moment Mami said his name! "Where have you been hiding? I missed you, Sweetie. Tomny, this is-"

Hakim didn't acknowledge Mami because his eyes locked on Dr. King the second he stood up. Hakim stared him dead in the eye and held out his hand, saying, "Hakim Jahlil Dunn, Dr. Thomas King…good being here to meet face to face."

"Please, everyone, have a seat," Mami insisted, trying to ease the tension between Dr. King as he stared at Hakim critically and didn't shake his hand. Hakim kept his eyes on Mandisa's father a moment longer. He studied him, blinked, and smirked, suddenly glancing at Mami shaking his head. "What, Cheri?"

"Not yet…" Hakim said, grinning, but his eyes turned back to Dr. King. "Your husband and I haven't met yet, Mami. In the south, it's tradition to shake a man's hand if he offers you his."

Hakim glared at Dr. King, and his grin grew suddenly deadly, still offering his hand. Dr. King finally rolled his eyes, took Hakim's hand, and turned red as he shook it. Hakim suddenly locked his grip and jerked the man's arm with force as Hakim shook his hand. Hakim made that man feel him and let Dr. King know he knew that he hated him. Hakim rudely tossed Dr. King's hand free, peering over at Mami, and beamed.

His smile had turned back to the same sweet guy that walked in the door!

I'm used to spotting changes in Hakim's behavior because I've observed the levels of his insanity for years. Strangers would probably see this and go, oh, Hakim's just really trying to put on a good show right now. He's trying to show he's an alpha male to Mandisa's father and all that bullshit. No… That's not what I see going on at all. All I can

116

do is tell you what happened and was said… Maybe you can figure this shit out. I'm stumped… Who the fuck is that?! I'm just going to call *him* Hakim because I will mess up trying to explain this shit any other way.

Hakim slid the binder in the chair nearby and took the dozen pink and white roses from Lionel.

"These are for the sweetest mother and her new princess," Hakim told Mami as he touched the pink ribbon, offering them to Mandisa's mother. Mami blushed, nodding as she placed Amani in her bed. Her face lit up looking at that gorgeous bouquet. Lionel brought the fluffy bear for Amani to see. He offered Hakim the huge red garland. "These are for the most beautiful girl in the world."

Mandisa's hands trembled as Hakim moved in front of her father and offered her the flowers. She had tears in her eyes, staring up at him as he smiled at her. Mandisa took the roses, weeping, "Hakim…these…are so beautiful."

"Nowhere as lovely as you are to me, Queen," Hakim sighed, smiling down at her. Suddenly, Hakim turned his attention to Dr. King. "Pardon my rudeness, Dr. King, but you have a gorgeous family, and I get tense until I speak to them. They're the most beautiful women I've ever met."

Hakim's eyes drifted over toward Amani as her little hands reached up at the sound of his voice. He looked over at Mami, and she nodded to Hakim. He walked around the bed and over to the bassinet and touched Amani's tiny hand, smiling. Hakim carefully moved her blanket and threw it over his arm as he lifted her gently. He laid Amani on his arm and cuddled her.

"Look at you, Mini-Disa. Wow! I've been waiting a long time to see you, Amani. Longer than everyone here, but I'm here now, Sis," Hakim whispered to her and kissed her forehead. Her tiny fingers grabbed Hakim's lip and held it as she opened her eyes and yawned. "Oh, you like kisses?"

Hakim kissed her hand and put her foot in his mouth. Amani started trying to kick Hakim in the lips. Hakim chuckled, "Oh, you want to learn martial arts? Amani already got kicks and sneaking me!"

Mandisa and Mami were blushing and giggling as Hakim loved on that baby. I had never seen my brother act like that before, and it made me feel happy. Lionel was smiling, and he looked like he was trying to get Amani from watching Hakim.

"You would melt the heart of any brother in close range with a smile, like your sister, Mandisa. You're both gorgeous and sweet in every way," Hakim exhaled, gazing at Mandisa but cuddling Amani. He bit his bottom lip and gently laid Amani back in her bed. Hakim grabbed a chair, moved it directly in front of Dr. King, and sat looking at him eye to eye. Hakim smiled as Dr. King stared him over bizarrely but wouldn't say a word to Hakim. Hakim stroked his smooth chin and raised his eyebrows, laughing. "You don't like me, do you, Dr. King?"

"I don't know you…I've heard of you, Ha-Keem, and I can't say I like what you're doing. Mandisa is NOT supposed to be dating ANYONE. Period! She is here to attend school…and make a friend or two…but that is it!" Dr. King replied with a relentless stare that made me dip back.

Okay…wait…one fucking second….I know I said that I was just going to tell you what happened. Yeah…but no! Dr. King's eyes went from blue to the darkest shade of brown that looked black! His whole attitude went from slacked and watching to solid and tempered talking to Hakim. When Mandisa said her dad was a crazy white man, she meant that shit literally! Dr. King has a crazy motherfucker inside of him, just like Hakim! And they were having a severe staring contest scaring the fuck out of all of us!

"Well, Mandisa has been here a few months, and she's made quite a few friends. Some are here in this room. My brother, Lionel with the braids, and my best friend, Cyrus, who you keep eyeing suspiciously… Though he hasn't made a move since he got here to alarm anyone," Hakim chuckled as he sat back in his seat and smirked charismatically. "So, I suppose she was doing well when you ran off the only other friend she had? If not for your wife, she wouldn't have anyone but you to lean on to tell her who she's becoming, right?

"I can read your mind.

"I know you don't like me because I'm not a doctor, the profession that seems to command your utmost respect thanks to your father's brainwashing. I'm not white or fair-skinned, so I'm not good enough for your beautiful daughter, in your expert opinion. But your wife would strongly disagree with that if she felt comfortable enough to say so herself."

"I didn't say that," Dr. King laughed, relaxing as he leaned back with an amused grin. "My wife's judgment may be a bit biased because she feels Mandisa disapproves of her planned future."

"You didn't have to say it, Dr. King. It's written all over your face. No one in this room is worthy of your daughter, and it has nothing to do with our professions. But I digress; tell me about Spencer Patesh? Why's he a better man than me?" Hakim went in, staring at Dr. King without blinking.

Dr. King glanced over at Mami, then back at Hakim chuckling, "He's wealthy, comes from a long line of legacy doctors, he likes my daughter, has from the moment he saw her, followed her growth and rearing over the years, and plans to secure a wonderful life for MY daughter. There's nothing else that matters more to a father than seeing his daughter married into success."

"Is *that* right?" Hakim inquired with a cold stare right into Dr. King's eyes. When Hakim says those words, it always means… "You don't know shit, and I'm going to tell you why!"

Dr. King laughed at Hakim's question and adjusted his glasses, "Yes, this is something someone like you could not possibly understand, Ha-Keem, no offense.

"I respect Dr. Patesh because he's a man of honor, has a respectful background, and he knows that it takes real money to be a good husband. Spencer decided when he was twenty-nine and never married, waiting on *my* daughter to grow up. He made sure that there was no doubt in MY mind about what he wanted. Others seemed interested in using her, but Dr. Patesh actually cares. He understands that you don't stand a chance in the world without status, honor, and success. These qualities you…boys lack. So, I'm sorry if you have feelings for Mandisa, but I don't really give a damn about your feelings! You'll get over it!"

Hakim glanced over at Mami and bit his bottom lip, nodding. He looked back at Dr. King and raised his left eyebrow over his frames. That meant, "It's on!" I saw that look too many times. Usually, it suggested he was about to punch someone in the throat or face. But not this time. Hakim loosened his tie a bit, exhaled, and aimed just for the…heart.

"Traditions? Legacy? Status? No offense to you, but those words don't have much meaning to poor people. I didn't grow up with a silver spoon in my mouth like you. Many black people could care less about some of those words because we aren't blessed with many opportunities. But honor and pride?

"We were born with honor until someone takes it away from us. It takes lots of honor to grow up in poverty and to overcome adversity to find success. My father was a police officer. My mother was an elementary school teacher that specialized in educating gifted children. Both of those professions are necessary and honorable, but we have no status because neither of those jobs receives the proper monetary compensation they deserve, Dr. King," Hakim chuckled arrogantly, but his face was gravely serious. "But, yet status is given to doctors, lawyers, engineers, and business executives based on a capitalist pay scale. To you,

you get your honor with the money you make, but to us, it comes from the hardships we face.

"Both of my parents went to college. My father served this country in the Marine Corps. My grandfather was in the Navy for over twenty years. They all loved us and raised us well, and taught us values. But my parents both died too soon to see my brother and me growing up. They were killed in a car accident when I was nine years old, and my brother was seven. The guy driving the truck was too drunk to react when he got a flat tire, stuck the median, hit them head-on, and knocked them from a freeway overpass. They never had a chance to react either.

"I'll never forget the night the policeman my father worked alongside for years came to the house to tell us they were dead. He looked at us like we were a lost cause. My mother was six months pregnant with a baby girl. Her name was going to be Janelle, which means God is gracious. But I haven't thought about going to a church since they died."

Dr. King's face was red as he stared at Hakim but dropped his head. Mami and Mandisa were so upset they were in tears hearing this shit. I know I was crying. I didn't know how it happened. Lionel had dropped his head in his seat, weeping. I never asked because Hakim would get so upset talking about his parents he would snap sometimes.

"My grandfather tried to raise us in Chicago alone, but he was old and disabled. My mother's mother tried to take us to Georgia. It was too hard for her to work with us. She sold her house, and Dad's father moved in with her here to take care of us. They eventually got married. It was ironic because they dated before our parents met but cut it off. They got back together once Mom and Dad died.

"I read so many books looking for answers to every question I could think of, seriously. History, religion, philosophy, psychology, law, chemistry, biology, you name it, I read it, and I probably read it two or three times. I wasn't even twelve yet. I have an IQ of 145, Dr. King. I only know of one other person that's higher, my best friend, Kaliah. He's a genius! Me, I'm an educator with gifted tendencies."

Dr. King sat forward and scratched his head, saying, "That's impressive, Hakim. My IQ isn't close to yours, and Mandisa's was tested at 140 when she was ten. I respect intelligence. I'm proud of my daughter, love her, and only want the best for them. That is why I am so protective of her."

"Do you love her enough to see her happy or just yourself satisfied?" Hakim asked, suddenly angrier than before. Dr. King glanced at Mandisa and then Amani smiling back at Hakim.

"Dr. Patesh *is* going to secure her education, financial security, and he's going to make her a happy woman," Dr. King insisted, giving Hakim the same evil stare. "Her husband is going to make her happy, Hakim. She's going to have to make a few sacrifices as her mother once did. But it's all necessary for her to complete his family.

"Your friend and brother are good kids. You are an alright kid, but you're still kids. Your love for my daughter could never provide for her. She needs a man that is capable of supplying her needs. Both of my daughters are going to be happy with their husbands.

"They'll learn to love the choices I make for them as their mother has done. She hasn't given me a son to carry on my name, but it will go on regardless. Mandisa and Amani are *my* flesh and blood, and I *will* have the last say in their decisions to wed. END OF DISCUSSION!"

"What?!" Mami cried, staring at her husband, screaming. "Tomny, you can't do this to them! They are just babies and deserve their own lives and make their own choices. You're treating our girls like they're property, not people!"

"Amani is going to marry a wealthy doctor as well, Ninon! My girls are not going to make dumb mistakes and be some gangster's baby mamas!" Dr. King shouted, standing up staring at Hakim gravely.

He was turning redder by the second. I stood up. Lionel jumped out of his chair, seeing what I saw in that motherfucker's eyes. I was about to floor his ass, but Hakim held up his hand. He motioned all of us to sit but kept his eyes on Mandisa's father standing over him. There was no way I could relax with him standing over Hakim looking ready to swing any second. Lionel didn't hear that shit either, squaring up Dr. King.

Hakim hadn't stood up, but Dr. King lost his temper and suddenly realized what he looked like to all of us. Quickly three against one didn't seem like good odds as he did the math in his head and slowly took his seat. Hakim waited until Dr. King sat down and smiled.

"You're absolutely right, Dr. King, your daughters are going to have a happy, secure, and have a prosperous future. They're going to have honor, status, traditions, and success. Mandisa will have a wealthy, strong, and honorable man that loves her no matter what. No gangster could ever love her and financially support her or her precious baby sister," Hakim said with dark eyes on Dr. King.

"Then you understand where I'm coming from? I'm sorry, but I could never let this puppy love thing go on in confidence," Dr. King said to Hakim as he stood again, offering Hakim his hand. "It has been nice meeting you all.

Mandisa will be going with me when I leave in a few days. You understand I can't leave her here knowing that you feel so strongly, Hakim?"

Mandisa looked at Mami and burst into tears, and Mami glanced back at Hakim. Hakim took a breath and stared back at Dr. King's hand. Lionel and I were both still on our feet, ready to knock him out and just take Mandisa and get to a plane.

"I'm not finished yet, Dr. King," Hakim groaned, staring at Dr. King's hand with disgust on his face. Hakim reached back toward me, and I remembered the hefty case he brought inside and handed it to him carefully. "Mandisa is going to be HAPPY."

Hakim set the briefcase on the floor and opened it. Inside were stacks of bundles of cash. Lionel's eyes lit up like Christmas lights seeing all that money. I smiled as I remembered Hakim asking me to stop playing and get serious…

*"Bro, we can't let this go down!" Hakim informed me, frowning once we got home from the mall that first night.*

*"I'll do whatever it takes to save her, Hakim. Life would never be the same if her father took her away from us!" I replied, smoking at the bar. Hakim nodded as he took a sip from his cup.*

*"Time to man-the-fuck-up! Give me five million dollars!" Hakim demanded seriously. "I'm going to buy my woman's freedom from her slave master, and you're going to help me if you love her too."*

*I watched him as he began to put things together and agreed, "Let me make a few calls. I'll get it for you in two days tops! She's worth more than that... I'll give you all I got if we can stop worrying about her dad taking her away!"*

*"I feel the same. The important thing is to show this family we are serious and put our money where our mouths are. Her dad is so determined to sell Mandisa to strangers for money. Let's see if he really loves her or if he's just an asshole?" Hakim growled, folding his arms glowering.*

*"If he doesn't take money from us, then that will prove he is just a racist asshole, and Mami is going to play the trump card, isn't she?" I questioned Hakim, putting shit together smiling.*

*"Yep, it's going to suck to part with the money, but the only thing that works against white power is black unity. I'm going to save Mandisa by any means necessary, Cyrus!" Hakim told me, holding out his fist. I gave him a pound, agreeing.*

"I'm done playing around here. I'm no gangster. Neither are my friends and family. But if you keep stepping on my feelings like I don't matter, I'm going to get gangster in here! Your daughter IS going to be happy with ME, Dr. King!"

"I'm a businessman, and this just became an auction! You're trying to sell my black wife to another man for money. I don't care if you like me or not, I'm not sure if I like you at all, but I respect you for WHO you are. So, you're going to respect me as well."

"To me, you're a slave master. A white man married and slept with black women, breeding and diluting our bloodline with your sick games and hidden agendas for control to feel superior. This isn't family or about love to you....this is a business deal! Since you're so prominent to sell your daughters' freedom to the highest bidder, Dr. King, I'm putting my bid in for both of them! RIGHT HERE and RIGHT NOW!"

"Dr. Patesh is 45 years old, and he's trying to marry your precious little angel. He's been INTERESTED in her since she was just a BABY...like Amani is now....Hmmm....Kind of like me with all this money....sitting here....looking at that beautiful little girl....But I see Amani as an innocent little baby. Spencer took one look at Mandisa...just like that....and wanted to fuck her!"

"He's not buying a wife to love...he's going to treat her just like you treat Ninon. But she's gonna do the right thing and stay when he mistreats her....then...she's gonna kill herself just like she tried to do the last time you let that motherfucker touch her....Right....Isn't that what happened? When you hit Mami? Did Mandisa scare the shit out of you....or....it wasn't Mandisa...was it? So that's why you have her hidden away? You're trying to marry her off to money because you've made her crazy....?"

'Spencer Patesh is a therapist that specializes in a CERTAIN field, and you're chasing him hoping he can fix what you fucked up! Stop me when I get something wrong. I know money talks, but I just had to share what I discovered doing a little research about you, Dr. King."

Dr. King was distraught at Hakim as he assassinated his character, unable to say a word. But, there was one thing that made that motherfucker shut up and listen...That money on the floor had Dr. King ready to lose his mind.

"It would seem that you're broke, Dr. King. You have been a naughty boy, and your many mistresses are coming forward. Too bad they're all girls, huh? Not one boy in all that fooling around, and Dr. Patesh suddenly up and vanished on you after the Belgian geezer bailed. Hmmm…You need that money, don't you, Dr. King. If you go broke, Ninon isn't going to stay, is she? Not after you hit her, and you saw how you've fucked up Mandisa."

"You want to count it, Dr. King?"

"Mandisa's not some toy to purchase. She's my one and only. I have ten million dollars in cash right here to prove my words. So go ahead, count it. I'll wait!"

"As long as it takes, but I'm not going anywhere without you signing her freedom to Mami. I bet no one made you an offer like that," Hakim insisted as he kicked the open case over to Dr. King. Hakim grabbed the binder from the chair and snatched a pen from the breast pocket from his coat. Hakim flipped through a few pages. "I love Mandisa, I'm going to take care of her, and that money is just the start. I can give it to you because I've got plenty more in the making. You sign this contract, and you're not selling me your daughter's body."

"You're allowing me to buy her freedom from you. I'm not going to force her to do anything. I'm setting her free to make up her own mind about what she wants for the future, Dr. King."

"Mandisa's not going to be pressured into anything she doesn't want, and she's not obligated to me. If she chooses me or not, this money is yours to keep. All I care about is seeing her happy and free," Hakim told Mandisa's father as he handed him the contracts and pen. Dr. King stared at Hakim, absolutely shocked and stunned a moment. Suddenly he gazed at Mami and Mandisa as a tear ran down his cheek, and he flushed. "It's all there, black and white, and no gray…read it? I can wait! I wrote it up myself and had my lawyer look over everything. I love that woman, and I want her to be free. If you loved her as much as I love her, you'd wish the same thing.

"I'm going to finish law school in a few years. When I pass the Bar, Mandisa's gangster-looking boyfriend will become a lawyer. After that, I'll be on my way to a promising career and starting my own practice. I hope to become the youngest black man to serve this country on the U.S. Supreme Court and be a foreign diplomat. Who knows? I could run for the Presidency?"

"Once I graduate high school, I won't have much running to do since money isn't an issue for us now. I made my status possible by manifesting the money, but I've never lost my honor. That's why I can talk to you as a man and not seek a negative resolution to something that can be easily negotiated between two men."

"You'd make a hell of a lawyer, Hakim! I can see it when I look at you and hear it in your voice. There is a nervous passion that is fighting to get out….I am starting to think that you and I are alike in many ways…oui…I can sense…something…I'll sign it. You keep the money. I was wrong about you. I was wrong about a lot of things, I see," Dr. King agreed and signed the contract with a damn smile on his face?

"I'm truly relieved you had a change of heart. It made me see you really do love your girls. But I'm sorry I lied to you," Hakim said, looking over Dr. King's signature and pulling the contract away.

"What?" Dr. King asked as Hakim handed him another paper. He looked over at Mami and frowned.

"That's not 10 million, it's 15, and the other 5 was for Amani. I want them both, sigh here? The other five are hers's no matter what. I'm giving it to her as a trust fund. I've always wanted a little sister and lost mine. But meeting your wife and daughters has changed me, Dr. King. I'm going to take care of all of them. They're my family now, and if you want to be near them…you're going to respect all of their wishes," Hakim told Dr. King, showing him where to sign. "I'm not here to play games. The money belongs to Mami, and she's in control of it all, but Mandisa is free from now on."

Dr. King sighed both contracts Hakim gave him. Hakim took them to Mami and gave her the pen. Mami was in tears, and she was so emotional now. Mandisa's face was buried in her mother's lap, crying. Mami stared up at Hakim, wiping her eyes. She signed both the contracts and gave them to Hakim.

"Merci, Hakim....I love you," Mami cried, gazing at Amani and rubbing Mandisa's back. Hakim smiled brightly and caressed Mami's chin. Dr. King grabbed the other papers Hakim was holding, but Hakim grabbed them quickly, shaking his head offering them to Mami.

"What is that?" Dr. King asked Hakim curiously.

"Oh, these?" Hakim smiled, teasing him viciously, holding the papers. "Well, Mami was so concerned that you might really be an asshole, thinking you weren't going to give up, had me talk to another lawyer I know. You can tear it up IF you won't be needing the divorce since you signed these. But if you try to take the girls anywhere, it gets filed.

'You won't ever get custody because you have a bad reputation now, you can't raise a little girl alone, and you let pedophiles around your daughters. Courts don't like that shit, Dr. King, no matter where you're from. You still have your career, your lovely wife, and your girls. But you have something you didn't have before....You got a rich-ass nigger for a son-in-law. Now, that's a new legacy to build on! I'm replacing the traditions of your ancestors and their dirty money with a new family for us all. You signed everything, you get to have it all, and enjoy the ride too.

'Excuse me, Family, I'm going to turn these into Artie. He's expecting me with the papers before 7 pm. He'll be glad he's not going to divorce court. He's a beast. Artie can destroy a prominent career and leave you bankrupt if he doesn't like you.....

'Lionel, let's go! You have homework.

'Mami, I'll come and visit soon, and I love you.

'Cyrus, take Queen home so she can finally relax."

"Queen, you know I love you, right? I only wanted the best for you," Dr. King told Mandisa, catching her hand and looking in her eyes.

Hakim and Lionel hugged Mami and left. I watched all that money walk out the door with them. I couldn't believe Hakim had just got his way and didn't have to give a dime to that man. Mandisa watched Hakim leave and smiled at me. She looked at her father.

"I know you love me, but I know what is best for me. You never listen. I love Hakim and his family. He's a good man, and if you had given him a chance, you would have seen that without all of this, Daddy.

'They're wonderful people, they love us, and we all love them! They've been here for us more than you ever were," Mandisa stated with tears in her eyes as she came near me. I took her hand, smiling. "I love you, Mami. I will be by to help get you home tomorrow, and I will call in a little while…Dad."

I let Mandisa go on ahead and said my goodbyes, "Mami, love you.

'Dr. King, it's been a pleasure. We'll talk more once things die down. We're going to all be family, so we have to learn to get along. Hakim's going to be a good man for her. I'll make sure of it."

# Chapter Four: Black Friday/Loyalty

## Mandisa Isoka King

I rounded another corner heading for the elevator, and ran right into Hakim! He was pacing the far hallway with the most upset look on his face. He panicked as I grabbed him, examining his face and hair in disbelief.

"H-hey," Hakim's voice apprehensively trembled.

"Hey…," I gasped, struggling not to cry, stroking his soft short waves. "Look at you! Your hair is gone! Hakim, why?"

"Because…" Hakim sadly exhaled. His brown eyes were glowing red with tears as his jaw quivered. "I said I'd do anything for you. I'd pay any price to set you free…It's only hair besides I can grow it back, Mandisa. I could never replace you.

'Yeah…I cut my crown, but I got my Queen. That's all I care about now."

I was so emotional touching his hair. Hakim looked so different now. He was still very handsome and clever, but he didn't seem like my Hakim anymore. He squeezed me close in tears and caressed my cheek. Darius came up behind, grabbing me and kissing my hair.

"I told you! Hakim knows what he's doing! Didn't I say to trust him? When he says, he's got you, just roll with him. I've learned!" Darius exclaimed, so excited that he scared me. He put his chin on top of my head. Lionel grinned, hugging Hakim.

"When Hakim is on a mission, he's on it!" Lionel laughed, touching my shoulder and giving me a hug. I squeezed him back and pulled his braids. "I love you, Sissy!"

"I love you too, Lionel," I told Lionel but noticed Hakim's half-smile on his face. He appeared anxious.

"Damn, Bro! I told you that you looked like Trey Songz before! I didn't say turn into the nigga!" Darius laughed, fingering Hakim's waves. Hakim blushed and dropped his head.

"You got jokes, Cyrus, I see you," Hakim chuckled, popping his collar up and posing. "Don't hate me because I look good no matter what I do to the outside!"

"Bro, before you were like I Gotta Make It, Trey, but now you're 'Passion, Pain, and Pleasure'! All you need is a mustache and beard! Bottoms up, Nigga!" Darius teased Hakim. I giggled as he pushed Hakim's arm, but Darius was not lying. Hakim's baby face and tiny lips reminded me of

Trey. He had those same eyebrows, and now with short hair…

"Man, shut the fuck up!" Hakim yelled, laughing. "Do you know how long I have heard that shit?!"

"Oh, Shit!" Lionel died laughing at Hakim's face. "Yo! Cyrus is right, Hakim!"

"And I wish I never did it! And I wish I didn't love it! I cut my hair, and now it ain't no way I can't be Trey!" Darius sang, beating on Hakim's chest crying.

"Whateva, Lance, cut your hair, and we'll see who's the look-alike," Hakim laughed, slapping Darius's hair away from him, frowning.

"Oh, no! Cyrus will never cut his hair! My pride is all tied up in here," Darius said, rolling his finger around his head. He squeezed Hakim's cheeks, grinning. "You so sexy now, Baby!"

Hakim pushed Darius back, laughing. Lionel was laughing with tears in his eyes, struggling to breathe, "Y'all niggas are crazy!

'When I saw Hakim's shit, I couldn't believe it was him. I thought we were getting jacked. G.D. got all emotional, and Sophie was crying, talking about 'Baby Dunn' growing up.

'I'm never gonna cut my hair, but Hakim, that shit is tight on you!"

"Yeah...well, fuck you anyway! As long as Queen likes it short, I may never grow it again. It was heavy, hot, and I started feeling different as soon as it hit the floor. I didn't want to do it initially, but I wanted to be taken seriously by Dr. King.

'I knew my hair would get in the way of that.

'If you could have seen the way he was eyeing you, Cyrus, you would have busted him in the jaw. But once I got him past that fear, he saw something else. Of course, it's gonna take time before he understands who we are and all of THIS...us...But you're free, Queen, so who cares what he has to say from now own?"

I clutched Hakim beaming and threw my arms around his neck, kissing his sexy lips. Hakim glowered and pulled away, shaking his head. He grinned uneasily and demanded, "Can you take those pigtails down? You look like a little girl for real. I want my wife back. My name is not Spencer!"

I giggled, stroking the side of his cheek playing with the diamond studs in his earlobe, "Maybe I like pigtails now!"

"Then you need to take that sweater off, put on some sexy heels, and pull your skirt up a little. I'm confused because I know you're 18, but you look 12...My dick can't be a pedophile, Queen," Hakim chuckled, struggling to pull away from me seriously. "I feel like a sex offender touching you...stop...no...don't...Mandisa!"

Darius and Lionel were laughing at Hakim's silly behavior. Darius caught his breath laughing, "Damn, now you're full of jokes, Bro? That's my damn department!"

"I'm serious. The haircut did something to me! I haven't felt this free in my life!" Hakim said, glancing at the suitcase. "I need to take all this stuff to the office so Artie can file it, put this back in the safe until I can get it to the bank, and take Lionel home. You're grounded, and Granddaddy ain't beating my ass tonight!"

"Whatever, Hakim," Lionel laughed, rubbing the top of his head suddenly. Lionel seemed different. Usually, he'd be ready to start a fight with Hakim. But now, Lionel was calm and full of smiles. Both he and Hakim were like two totally different brothers. Lionel took the case and binder. Hakim gave him his car keys as we all started for the elevator.

"Bro, pull Shun around for me. I'll be down in a minute," Hakim told Lionel smiling. Lionel went ahead alone.

"What the hell is going on here?" Darius asked Hakim raising his eyebrows acting silly.

"Lionel and I reached a compromise today. I think things are gonna be alright. He's still hard-headed Lionel, but he's listening to me. He's serious about slowing down. So, I'm giving him a chance to back up his word. Of course, he's going to fuck up, but that's my brother. I love him. I know he loves me, too," Hakim said, staring at Darius thoughtfully.

"What a difference a day makes," Darius replied jovially. "I'm going to make sure he doesn't get jumped in the parking lot. That's a lot of fucking money!"

Darius ran to catch up with Lionel. Hakim stared at me a moment quietly. I was overwhelmed and so grateful I didn't know where to begin to show my appreciation! I was still aiming to wrap my head around everything he had done for all of us.

"I cannot believe you stood up to my father. You were so confident, brave, and determined to be heard. You were willing to give that money away? How did you think of doing any of that?" I questioned as he scanned me, suddenly growing emotive.

"Honestly, bravery had everything to do with it, Queen. I was terrified. I've been afraid from the moment you told us that he was going to take you away. I was ready to run. But why should you have to run?

'You have the right to be happy without being trapped with me for the rest of your life. I can't just force you to stay with me while you miss your family. I decided that if money was the only thing that mattered to him, I would give him more than he could ever expect. Cyrus and Kaliah made it possible too. I owe them both for helping me set you free.

'I know I don't deserve you, Mandisa. I'm not perfect by a long shot, but I knew if I could get that monkey off your back, then you could finally be happy. I didn't expect what happened last night to go down, ever! I would instead appreciate you single and happy than hear of you somewhere married and miserable.

"But when it did, it motivated me more to see you free. If you decide you want to move on or just want to be with Cyrus….I won't be mad. I'll miss you every day of my life, but at least I saved you from doing something horrible to yourself."

"Mami told me about the pills, and I know if Spencer got you, you wouldn't last long before you hurt yourself. If you die…then a part of me dies with you, Queen…."

"You're all I want and need. I wish you would marry me? I'd spend my life worshipping you and every penny I have to make our family happy. But we're young, and you've just started living. I've been doing so much shit….I feel like I'm on my second life."

"I'm ready to settle down, but you've been living in fear of marriage your entire life! I can't ask you to do that if you're not ready, Mandisa. You can't be sure I'm what you need if you've never flown before. You have your wings now, so you can go. I'll always love you, okay?" Hakim explained to me. He seemed so unhappy. It was as if Hakim had shattered his own spirit and had convinced himself I didn't want him anymore. He breathed and ran his fingers across my lips, and tiny tears rushed down his cheeks.

"Hakim," I moaned as I stole his hand. "A moment ago, you were so pleased and full of enthusiasm. So why are you pushing me away now? You believe I don't want to be with you?"

"That was just an act for Cyrus, so he wouldn't see how upset I am. I know your father would never accept Cyrus right off the bat. So, I did what I did to leave the window open for him. Dr. King will never look at us the same anymore. He saw his mistakes.

'I want you! I love you! But….I understand that I've done…my shit….and I'm ready to ..face the music. I've got some terrible things to reap. This haircut made me see that much….Everything is going to come back to me. The weight of all that guilt has been killing me.

'I can't make you stay for all that! If I do, I'm no better than your father-," Hakim confessed sadly.

"I'll never let you go, Hakim. I gave myself to you. You're my King. You're my sweet running fantasy, and I don't care about all that other shit. So don't think of me as a blind little bird in a cage. I know what I'm doing, and you're not a mistake. You're my savior. You set me free, and I'll never be able to repay you for what you just did out of love.

'I owe you my heart, my life, so don't try to make me leave you alone. You saved Amani and me from a fate worse than death. I will never forget you. I belong to you, okay?! I said it! Now, if you want me to go, then just tell me to leave!" I cried, staring up at him, losing my composure. "You wish to have other women and leave me?"

"Hell no! Fuck no!" Hakim cried, grabbing me. He held me close and exhaled in my ear. "I love YOU, woman! I'll never tell you to leave…I just thought…."

"Shut up and kiss me! You talk too damn much!" I giggled, stroking the back of his head, missing his ponytail so much.

"Ooh, attitude!" Hakim chuckled, putting his lips on mine sweetly. He glanced away, blushing. "For real, Queen, take those damn things down! I hate pigtails…You're not Shamaya Lockhart!"

I froze!

"What?!" I asked, pushing him away from me seriously.

"Lionel's little girlfriend…that's been missing in action, Shamaya…Lockhart," Hakim said, staring at me confused.

It couldn't be the same girl! Shamaya lived in Philadelphia! I needed to find out where she was and talk to 'Giggles' now!

"Darius said her name was 'May-May'?" I informed Hakim, confused. Maybe he heard me say her name before…no, I can't recall saying it.

"May-May was one of her nicknames. Her brother called her that. All of us called her May-May or Maya. Why are you tripping? She was LIONEL's little friend… She was like a LITTLE SISTER to Cyrus and me," Hakim said, attempting to comfort the wrong idea.

"Hakim! I know, Maya! She's my friend from Phili!" I yelled, covering my mouth.

"What?! You're shitting me, right?!" Hakim yelled back at me.

"No! Maya is short, pretty brown skin. She smiles and laughs all the time, has long pigtails that hang down her back, and has a big brother named James that is in jail. She was always talking to him on the phone or writing him letters," I screamed, pushing Hakim again.

"Queen, you really know her! Oh, shit! What's her number? Where is she now?" Hakim asked, excitedly grabbing me.

"I…I don't…know! But I'm going to call every barbershop and nail salon in Philadelphia until I find her. She's got to know Lionel misses her! She always told me she had a boyfriend, but her grandmother wouldn't let her talk to him. So she's been wanting to see him again," I told Hakim, hugging him.

"Damn, Queen, how do you do that? How do you keep fixing people without undertaking the job? If this happens, do you know how my brother is going to react? His melon head might explode!" Hakim laughed, squeezing me tighter. "He needs that answer. It could be the only thing that fixes that tear in his heart. We have to find her! Don't say a word to anyone until you do. I want to talk to her!"

I nodded understanding as we went out the hospital doors. Hakim stared at me strangely now, and it made me worry.

"So, what do we do now?" I asked nervously as he held my hand.

"Now, we're going to live and be happy, all of us. But for now, I'm going to change, take my brother home, and then we're going to celebrate! You're free, and we're all going to live it up! Take those pigtails down! Put on something sexy and spread those wings!" Hakim laughed as he ran and jumped in the car with Lionel. Lionel burned rubber as they sped off. "I LOVE YOU!"

"I LOVE YOU, TOO!" I yelled back, laughing as I got inside the truck with Darius.

"Everything alright, Queen?" Darius asked, touching my hand smiling.

"Everything is perfect!" I screamed, losing my mind.

"Ooh, look at you! I've never seen you smile so beautifully before," Darius laughed, squeezing my hand.

"I've never felt this good in my life! Meeting you all had made me so happy. Hakim has done the impossible...I feel as if I just got out of jail! I want to enjoy all this...everything! I want to do it all!" I giggled, rolling down the window and leaning my head out as the cool fall breeze kissed my face.

"I hear you, Queen," Darius laughed as he drove the truck. I sat back in my seat and smiled to myself. I was free! I pulled the ribbons from my hair as we hit a hill and let them go watching the wind take them away.

I was about to make critical changes in my life starting from that day forth. I would live my life my way and let my fears and doubts fly away like those ribbons. I was always holding back due to fear. Losing my virginity was just the beginning. I was going to tame all my fears one at a time and finally live and love limitlessly.

#

As the days went by, we were together, Lionel, Darius, Hakim, and I. School was okay because we did the work, hung out, and had fun. But everything changed! On weekdays we were responsible kids hanging out at the mall, playing with Amani, doing homework, and being best friends.

But when Friday came, Mami gave me the nod, and we were off to Dallas! We hit every club we could get into. Darius could buy his way into any door he approached, and Hakim could back up the money with action when things got too hot.

We drank what we wanted, smoked great weed, yes, me too, and we danced the night away. We made love into the early hours of the morning, and then I modeled for Antoine Sundays.

All the while, Hakim took me on the best dates, shopping, amusement parks, sometimes we checked into expensive hotels and 'Did it Big,' as Hakim called it. Hakim was so affectionate, sweet, and giving. He wanted to spend all his free time that he wasn't running or playing ball with me. He kept telling me he never wanted me to think he even thought about another woman. I thought it was adorable. His new look was getting him so much positive attention, along with his very recent shift in energy. Hakim had become an intriguing conversationalist and very popular at school.

On the other hand, Darius will not stop buying me things no matter how much I keep telling him no more! My closets at Hakim's house, my room, and Darius's condo are full of clothes, shoes, bags, and gifts he keeps buying. Once one closet was complete, Darius would just clean out another room and keep buying more! I appreciate every single thought he has of me, but his spending is getting out of control. It was not so bad at first, but it seems that once I was free….Darius wanted to buy me anything he thought I wanted, especially if Hakim got me a gift.

Darius and Hakim are constantly challenging one another to gift-giving contests for no reason, and sometimes I have to tell them I don't want anything and run, or they will argue until I choose who gave the better gift! It…sucks! Women think they want these kinds of problems….or do they? I don't know….Sometimes, it feels like I am being pulled in two different directions struggling to keep Hakim from losing his temper and Darius feeling secure with me.

I'm very proud of Lionel. My baby brother has calmed down so much for two terms gotten straight A's. No one is prouder than Hakim. Those two, wow! They are so close now….They have these moments where one would talk, and the other would finish the thought! It was funny. I called Philadelphia hoping to find Maya, but so far, no luck. I was not going to give up. But I never told Lionel what Hakim and I were up to, so Lionel had his weekends when he stayed home and did his own thing.

I thought he had a serious girlfriend, but when I asked, he said, "Naw, she is just something to do, Sis....It's just sex."

But this girl was spending a lot of money on him! Lionel would come home sometimes, and he'd have new watches, diamond earrings, chains, and clothes all the time. He must have been doing something right. But after Mami's birthday on November the 5th, something happened. Lionel stopped seeing her, I guess, because Lionel's always with us now. When I asked what happened to the 'Million Dollar Diva,' he told me, "She fell in love too deep and wants to be serious. I can't commit to her!"

He even tried to return all of her gifts, but she wouldn't take any of them back. So Lionel packed it all away and never touched it. He even put the bling away when he cut her off! Darius was amazed, so was Hakim.

I had never celebrated Christmas before, but the boys' family did, so I spent it with them just to see what all the fuss was about. But I did NOT want any gifts! That was my condition for coming. It was Christmas Eve, and Darius and

Lionel were helping Grandma Sophie cook dinner for tomorrow. I was looking up anything and everyone I could remember that could help find Maya. Hakim was studying law books lying across his bed. We left the door open because Granddaddy always talked dirty to me when he thought we were fooling around. Grandma Sophie would beat him up. The boys thought it was funny.

It was getting late, and I was frustrated. I took a break and turned from Hakim's computer screen. He glanced up from his book over his glasses and smiled. He flexed his shoulders and spun around, sitting on the edge of the bed. He playfully began to tug at the strings to his gray sweatpants and rolled his hips.

"Can I help you with something…" Hakim sang as he winked seductively.

"Yes, find my friend, Magic Mike!" I joked, putting on his glasses after snatching them from his face. "What is your vision? I am going blind just looking through these!"

Hakim burst into laughter, taking back his glasses, "I used to have 20/20 vision, but I strained my eyes badly, reading as a kid in the dark by flashlight under the covers. I really fucked up my eyesight because I squinted my right eye and strained the left. Now it's like 30/110. It's bad. I can see much from across the room without glasses or contacts, but up close…I'm as blind as a bat."

"Wow!" I giggled, staring around the room, holding up my hands. "I just saw our grandkids in my left eye!"

"Oh, you got jokes?" Hakim chuckled, spinning me in the chair.

"Yeah," I laughed, putting my feet down stopping him, dizzy. "Bad news, Hakim…they're all white!"

"Oh, HELL, no!" He died laughing, ticking me. I laughed, taking off his glasses and setting them back on the desk. He sat on the foot of the bed and stared up at me. "So, are you excited about tomorrow like Cyrus and Lionel? I hate Christmas. I haven't celebrated since Mom and Dad died. Grandma and G. D. love the holidays, but they all know I hate this time of year. We lost them two days before Christmas. Cyrus doesn't like Christmas but loves any holiday you can eat and give gifts."

I giggled, pondering, "Sounds like Darius. Anything dispensing food, he will be there….I can't say I am excited…It is different."

"I like the gift-giving part, but the tree, star, and Santa shit is so fake. I like to see the lights sometimes, and when we lived in Chicago with G.D. before we moved to Georgia, it snowed. It doesn't snow much in Texas, maybe twice since we've lived here. I love cold weather. You can get close near the fire, get under a blanket, snuggle up, read, talk, or….well…you know," Hakim suggested wiggling his eyebrows playfully. I giggled and shook my head.

I had to keep changing the subject with Hakim. He was always in a flirty mood when he wasn't distracted. It was cute how he tried to get me to let him have his fun, but I was terrified to be alone with Hakim when he was like this! Hakim would catch me alone and have me screaming for hours, and then he would want to fuck me! It was terrific, but I did not want people hearing the sounds that we made, and Hakim was not a quiet lover…at all! He talks too much doing that too! Oh, my God! The things he says once he gets going…It's scary but so hot! I needed Darius around to keep Hakim from losing his mind. So, I had avoided sex alone with Hakim, and he knew I was scared of him. It made him even more aggressive.

"A day to get gifts is kind of unnecessary for me. You all give me too much! If I get one more gift, I am going to scream," I groaned, spinning myself in the chair, throwing my hair around.

"Is THAT right?" Hakim flirted with me upside down as I spun in the chair.

"Stop doing that, Hakim! I know what that means! Darius told me," I warned him, stopping the chair.

"Oh, DID he now? So y'all are decoding my vocab now?" Hakim growled, lying back on the bed. "I can give you a dynamite present if you close the door?"

"Hakim, no!" I giggled, quickly turning back to the computer.

What was Maya's family's name...? She had cousins close to her age. Her Aunt Key-Key, but I couldn't think of her real name. What did Maya say Key-Key's daughter's name was?

"Nigga, you dumb!" Lionel laughed, coming inside the room and diving on his bed, followed by Darius. Darius stood in the door as Lionel watched me sign out of Facebook. "Sis, how long are you going to leave your relationship status, 'It's complicated?'"

"Forever!' I laughed, rolling my eyes. "Until Facebook adds married Polyandrist Wife as relationship status, then it's complicated is good enough. It's no one's business whom I am seeing. I don't know the 4 thousand friends I have. Most of them are customers from Zola. The rest are people that like my pictures."

"You need to see my page. I've got about 3 thousand friends, and they blow my shit up! I have close to ten thousand followers on Twitter, and I'm viral on Youtube because of all the fight videos and movies I put up there! I'm an internet sensation. Everyone loves Li-L Dunn!" Lionel chuckled as Darius concurred.

"About 2 times that many for me," Darius chuckled. "Dance performances and just me acting a fool and balling...."

"I don't fuck with social media because the government is constantly monitoring for terrorism. I don't like all the ads they frequently put in your faces to distract you so they can watch what you want and influence your purchases. It's a marketing scam, and since I consider myself a threat to national security....I'm good.

'Conscious brothers are considered terrorists. That's why I use private websites by people I know and interact with other people on the same intellectual frequency. I hate arguing with ignorance," Hakim laughed as Lionel stared at him suspiciously. I just giggled at them both.

"You need to see Les's Facebook!" Lionel laughed, getting up signing in over my shoulder. "Check this out!"

Lionel showed us his friend's list and found Lester, 'The Molester' Woods. There were many pictures of a white guy with red hair and green eyes, and he was surrounded by women, holding guns, flashing money, all over the place, and Lionel was in many of Lester with him posing or partying. There were pictures with musicians, celebrities, and lots of this friend worldwide traveling, but he wasn't smiling in one shot.

"Lionel, your friend, is having fun, but he's not a happy person," I mumbled, looking at the pictures. Lionel was grinning and seemed very happy, but not Lester. "He's miserable."

"Cause Les is rich, but he doesn't give a shit about anything but partying, his kids, and getting pussy," Lionel said, raising his eyebrows.

"Whoa! Les has kids? Oh, Jah, no!" Darius yelled, falling on the floor.

"Hell, yeah, that nigga's married and has four kids," Lionel told us, laughing.

"His wife lets him fuck around like that?" Hakim questioned Lionel shaking his head.

"Yep, He said he loves her, but she's a gold-digging ho," Lionel said, scratching his scalp, and I messed with his curls.

"Damn!" Darius sighed, crawling up on Lionel's bed. "I gots to be more careful…they almost took me out of here…."

"They who?" Lionel asked Darius frowning.

"Deez nuts!" Darius chuckled, pushing Lionel on the floor and taking over his bed, stretching out. Hakim shook his head as Lionel crawled up and sat next to him. "I can't believe you still fall for that shit, baby bro!"

"Who's this on your page with all the tattoos?" I asked, glancing at a profile picture of Jamaican flags and flowers.

"Oh, that's Kaliah's page," Hakim said over my shoulder, clicking it. There were no pictures of his face, just motorcycles, friends, sunsets, beautiful beach scenes, and ocean views. All his posts were quotes, poems, and lovely but sad images. I read the last post and sighed. It was sad. His relationship status was, 'It's complicated. I frowned as Hakim scrolled down. I read another and had to look away.

"Love is fresh like a rose on a misty morning, only if you keep it pure and don't leave it to die for too long. If you forget about it, love dies, withers, and is not as beautiful. When love dies, you have nothing left to admire and follow. Love is like a rose…It can wither and live in a heartbeat if you let it.  Kaliah- 'But I never knew looking back on the laughs would make me cry."

"That's horrible," I sighed, looking at the date on the last post. It was 15 minutes ago!

"Kaliah is deep!" Darius stated, smiling. I gazed at him and nodded approvingly. Hakim picked up the phone and dialed a number. He put the phone on speaker.

"Dunn-Dunnie! Sup, Bro?" A silly high pitched voice answered, nearly making me laugh.

"Ka-Li-Aaaah, Merry Chrima!" Darius yelled playfully.

"Aye-aye, Cyrus! Same wishes to yuh, Bro! Where be Lionel?" Kaliah answered with a lower, handsome chuckle. I caught his island accent and sneered at how he initially sounded like Lionel talking to Hakim.

"What's uppers, Kaliah? I'm here chilling with the fam," Lionel said, leaning closer to Hakim. Lionel's eyes lit up, and his smile was enormous. "What's up with it?"

"Li-Li!" Kaliah shouted, making me giggle again. "How yuh be, baby boi?"

"Shit, it's all gravy here...I'm staying cool. Hakim and Cyrus keeping me on point," Lionel told Kaliah, smiling.

Hakim frowned and asked, "How are YOU? Your Facebook page is depressing as shit, Bro?"

"Bah! Everything is everything...jus git in dem moods and mi put shit bothering me dere, right? No worries, no worries, Bro!" Kaliah replied, straining a bit. He chuckled anxiously and cleared his throat. "Yuh having fun?"

"Oh, as much as we can around here. So, you ready for all of us yet?" Darius asked, smiling at me.

"Got everything handled, Cyrus...When yuh come wi party-party have big fun! Mi take the whole week off just tah chill wit yuh, Family.

"Mi canna wait, Brothas! Wi gonna do it big, Jamaica Style! Yuh gonna love it 'ere," Kaliah screamed joyfully.

"Spring Break!?" Hakim shouted, jumping up and dancing in a circle happily.

"Aye-aye! March canna come fast enough for mi!" Kaliah chuckled.

"Wait, what?!" I asked them entirely in the dark. No one told me anything about going to Jamaica. I knew that Hakim and the boys had a brother FROM Jamaica, but he lived in LA. So now he was IN Jamaica, and we were going there?

"We be going to Jamaica, Mon!" Darius laughed, slapping Hakim's hand and joining the dance seriously.

"Yep, yep," Hakim confirmed, winking at me flirtatiously.

"Are you serious? Jamaica? Oh, Jah!" I screamed, losing my mind! I had seen so many beautiful images of the scenery and nature around the islands and secretly wanted to visit them all one day. But I never dreamed that Hakim would set me free and make it possible for all my dreams to come true. Hakim was doing everything to make me feel like a real queen. I loved him so much more as I realized he wouldn't do this if not for me! "Hakim, Mon Cheri, Je'taime!"

I grabbed that sexy brown boy and tried to smother him with kisses! Hakim screamed, losing it, "That is what I am talking about! Show everyone your King's got the sauce!?"

"Who DAT be?" Kaliah asked after listening to Hakim and I wrestle.

"Oh, that's right....you two have never met or spoke. This is Queen, Kaliah," Hakim replied, smiling.

"Oh, EH, aye?" Kaliah said, confusing me. "How yuh be, KWEEN?"

"Lovely, Kaliah, good to finally speak to you. Hakim, Darius, and Lionel talk about you all the time. Good to have a voice with the name," I answered, sitting on Hakim's lap and pushing Darius off of me for messing with my earrings. "Stop, Darius! Put your hands in your pockets!"

"Okay, Queen....I'll be good! You're so cute! I'm sorry I can't help myself...let me rub your feet?" Darius groaned, falling on the floor and staring at my slippers. "Please, Queen? Let me rub your feet, and I'll be good?"

"Fine, but if you don't calm down, I'm going to go home! You all are too hyper," I giggled as Hakim rubbed his face in my neck. "I need a vacation.....But I can't leave Mami and Amani here alone for an entire week."

"It's already arranged, Queen. Mami wants you to go and gave me permission months ago," Hakim told me holding the phone smiling up at me.

"I'm going to Jamaica? We're going to Jamaica!!!" I cried about to attack Hakim again.

"Aye-aye! Dere yuh go! Mi love dat shit! Yuh git hyped up, then when yuh git ere Kaliah show yuh the time of yuh lives. Neva waan go home!" Kaliah playfully teased me with a mellow tone. "Need more family ere tah play wit, Queen. Yuh bring mi brothers, so mi got nothing but love fi yuh. They never wanted to come around me much until you showed up. So, I'm in your debt as well."

Kaliah's sudden change in tone and accent seemed to make him seem much more mature. His playful demeanor vanished the moment his accent faded, and it frightened me a bit. Hakim smiled and shook his head, asking, "You haven't been sleeping much, Bro?"

"Spending lots of time with Mom, Hakim. She loves having me home. I'm not worried about shit, but you know how I get when I can't sleep. Taking sleeping pills, anything to get relaxed…Shit's too crazy upstairs…." Kaliah chuckled calmly. It wasn't that he was hyper…Kaliah was trying to keep himself awake. The more exhausted he was, the clearer his voice became. He had to make himself laugh so he wouldn't fall asleep. Why was he keeping himself awake for days at a time? "Mom fucking forgets that I'm a grown-ass man, Bro! I've had to tell her about herself just to get her to take her fucking medication…You know me…Mom is my heart…She's just insane…I'm no better."

"Kaliah, why don't I have your number?" I worried suddenly, concerned about what he was saying. Kaliah was going through a lot! It sounded like he wanted to talk about things, but he was staying away. Lionel frowned as he sat on the bed and started searching for something on the floor. Lionel…

He was the one that told me that Hakim and Cyrus kept Kaliah away because of his wife! Now, I understood…no wonder Kaliah was so sad talking to them. He missed them and wanted them around but knew they feared his wife. But he was with his mother, and she was sick? Poor Kaliah…

"Na, KWEEN, Hakim nah let yah anywhere near Kaliah. Hakim scared Kaliah steal yuh away?" Kaliah flirted with the heaviest accent I had heard from the man. I leaned back, and Hakim frowned and shook his head. "It's true…I know my brothers better than they know themselves. Hakim has always been a hater, but Kaliah is a lover, KWEEN…Aye?"

"Ugh! Don't call me that! You can't call me Queen. Your accent sounds horrible saying it," I groaned, ignoring his flirting.

"Aww, KWEEN, why yuh hate mi? Mi a gud guy wit BIG surprises, AYE?" Kaliah teased me. "Yuh CUM to

Jamaica...and...FEEL ALRIGHT...! Kaliah got da medicine, KWEEN!"

"Eww!" I groaned, rolling my eyes, seriously offended. He didn't have an off-switch, like Lionel! It was getting annoying how Kaliah kept flirting, knowing that I was with Hakim. "Bye, Kaliah!"

"Yuh nah be mad, Love! Mi jus play-play! Tell Hakim to give you my number. I'll send you pretty poems, nice songs, and pictures of Jamaica. Then, all you have to do is tell Kaliah ...WHAT.... will make you HAPPY...?" Kaliah begged me as I glanced at Hakim. Hakim shrugged his shoulders, laughing.

"Yeah, we'll see..... later! Ugh....Nasty-ass niggas always start out sweet then turn into fuckboys. That shit is annoying as fuck," I mumbled under my breath, moping.

"Wat-wat!?" Kaliah giggled like a girl. "Sounds like mi ex-wife fi a moment! Da fuck yuh say, woman?"

"BYE, KALIAH!" I hollered as I strolled out of the room. I heard all of them dying of laughter as I left, but I was not in the mood to play. Kaliah was funny, but he rubbed me the wrong way. I understood now why they were all so tight. They were all alike in one way or the other.

"Mandisa, you and Kaliah fight like y'all married! That shit was funny, and I ain't never heard you talk like that before! You got ghetto on his ass!" Lionel cried, chasing me downstairs.

"Ugh, why are you following me, Lionel?"I wondered, glancing back at him up on the steps. I was blushing and didn't want anyone to see that Kaliah had upset me. Lionel was still laughing, and I folded my arms, frowning. "If you don't stop! I'm not feeling this shit right now, Bro!"

"I wanted to talk to you about something. You know, girlfriend-girlfriend time?" Lionel laughed down at me. I nodded as I went into the kitchen and poured a glass of juice. I sat at the dining room table and smiled, noticing the lights on the Christmas tree.

"What's up?" I questioned Lionel watching the twinkling lights. I just so happened to notice the clock on the living room wall reading 11:11 pm.

"I've been looking for Shamaya a lot lately, and I found her brother, James. I wrote him a letter and got one back! But he's in lockdown in Southern Texas. He gave me the number of her cousin, Nina, but nobody answered when I called. No one returns the texts I send. I'm trying, but I'm lost, Sis," Lionel told me with a seriously frustrated glance.

"Who's Shamaya?" I asked, taking a sip from my glass.

"Come on, Disa? Every time you use our computer I check the history. You're looking for her because Hakim told you, right?" Lionel questioned me, smiling.

"No!" I replied honestly.

"Disa???" Lionel sighed, leaning his head closer, frowning.

"I am not doing this for Hakim. It is for me, she's my friend from Philadelphia, Lionel. I didn't know you knew her until the day at the hospital. Hakim called me her name because of my pigtails," I confessed.

"You mean...you've seen her? You know, Maya?" Lionel interrogated me.

"Oui, I used to have her number, but it is disconnected," I sighed, offering my phone and showing him the number I had saved. I dialed it to show him it didn't work....And...it rang to my surprise! I've been searching for her too," I said, frowning again.

"Wait! It's ringing!" I gasped, confused, looking at the screen. There was no way! I had tried since we left Philidelphia...Someone else had to have her...

"Yes?" A sweet high female voice answered. "Who is this?"

"Giggles???" I cried nervously.

"Beyonce!?" She screamed in my ear so loud I pulled the phone away. "Oh GOD! Thank you, Jesus! It's really you?!"

"Maya! Oh, my goodness…I have been trying to reach you for months! Sadly, this number was off!" I yelled, unable to believe it.

"Yes, Oh god…I'm so sorry! I got this number turned off to catch up on the bill. Aunt Key-Key and Nina ran up the family bill and didn't help pay. I paid off their contracts and got my number back last month. I called your other number, but I knew that it was over when your Dad took you away," She explained, so excited that I was crying. "I had this other cheap government phone that runs on minutes just for clients and work."

"I got this phone the moment we left Paris and tried to reach you. You need a Facebook page! I've been trying to find you-," I remembered.

"I do have one. It's under a nickname. Come on, Beyonce…didn't you look for 'Hair by Giggles Rene?" Maya laughed. I never thought she used my nickname for her business! It was too funny.

I glanced over at Lionel, and his countenance was so grim it looked frightening. His eyes were wide and his eyebrows so high I thought someone was behind me!

"Maya….I have a friend that stays near me that would like to talk to you," I insisted without spoiling it.

"You have more friends, Beyonce? Who is it?" Maya giggled adorably.

"Just say hello," I told her, handing my phone to Lionel. He nervously took it in his hand and gazed around, sticking it to his ear.

"Hey…Maya…how you been, Girl?" Lionel asked with a trembling voice.

"Who is this?" I heard Maya ask with a nervous giggle.

"Oh, so you move from Texas to the East Coast and just forgot your old friends? How you gonna play me like that, Maya? I thought we were tight like a size four on a fat size nine foot?" Lionel groaned, teasing her.

"Wait….I know…Who is this…really?" Maya giggled nervously.

"How does this jog your memory? You used to always ride my bike because James's long-ass kept taking yours to the store. I started getting my hair braided because I called him my braided up brother?" Lionel hinted with a smile.

"Lionel..." Maya gasped and got quiet.

"Yeah, how you been, Maya?" Lionel asked, his voice lowering as he tried to smile.

"Lionel Dunn?" She questioned, whispering.

"Yeah...It's me, Lionel...how have you been, Shamaya?" He asked again, getting emotional.

"Lionel!" Maya screamed suddenly. "Oh, my God! No...no! Somebody is playing a joke on me!"

"Uh-uh...it's me, Maya. I missed you, Girl. I've been looking for you everywhere. Why you not in VA? How did you end up in PA?" Lionel chuckled, finally smiling again.

"This isn't Lionel. Your voice is too deep," She said.

How was Lionel's voice deep? I didn't hear any bass when he talked. Then again...Shamaya's voice was squeaky...Maybe Lionel's voice was deep for their chipmunk tribe...Kaliah could be the chief with that squeal of his.

"Um, I'm 16, Ma. I'm not a little kid anymore," Lionel chuckled. I called her on facetime and waited for her to answer.

"Hold on! I have to turn on a light…I was in bed!" Maya yelled.

The light came on, and there she was, beaming as she sat back on her bed. She was still my beautiful supermodel friend with her long braids, brown skin, and gorgeous smile. She looked exhausted with puffy eyes as she wiped her face with her long blue fingernails, and blushed trying not to look at the camera. I waved to her, and she stared forward and nearly burst into tears.

"Beyonce!? Look at you!!! You look so sexy!!" She screamed, shimmying to the edge of the bed.

"You look adorable as always, Giggles! Still got it, girl!" I teased her.

"Uh-uh…you look like you doing some thangs…." Maya giggled at me.

Lionel turned the phone toward him and waved, smiling, "Hey, Girl, you look so beautiful."

"Lionel….look at you! You're so grown up, so different, but the same. You're so tall! I can see the door behind you that goes to the garage. We used to hide from Hakim and James when we got in trouble in the park back there," She giggled, embarrassed with her eyes twinkling. She looked like a chocolate Barbie doll in her oversized Cardi-B teeshirt and pink shorts.

"You remember me....I'm glad...I thought you forgot about me," Lionel sighed, staring at the screen.

"No way, that was the best time of my life! We had so much fun. I can't believe how much you've grown up! Your eyes, smile, and...you're so handsome! I don't know why I thought you'd still be short with that same high voice like when you were 12. I guess I still look at this and get confused," She said, holding up a picture of Lionel with a shocked look on his face standing in front of a school bus. It was cute! Lionel laughed when he saw it. He pulled out a picture from his wallet and showed her.

Hakim came downstairs and grabbed me, saying, "I missed you. Why did you leave me with that pervert, Cyrus? He keeps trying to cut my toenails. I told him that's your thing, now he's mad!"

I started laughing, and he kissed my cheek. I pointed to my phone and covered my lips, winking to him.

"What's up?" Hakim asked, looking over Lionel's shoulder. Lionel turned the phone.

"Beyonce…who is THAT?.... Oh…Shit, that's Hakim! Hakim!!? Oh, my GOD…Look at you…." Maya groaned, covering her mouth.

"May-May? Wow! Look at you! You look beautiful! Shame….exactly the same…Your hair's longer, same smile, and you're a big girl now! Cute thing," Hakim told her, smiling.

"You're smiling, Hakim? Wait? Where is your hair? You had locks…like," Maya thought, staring at the screen. Darius came over messing with Hakim. He was pretending to cry, pushing his shoulder.

"Fuck you, Hakim! I don't need to fix your feet! I'ma find a new man that loves me for me!" Darius whined. Hakim fell over crying.

"Cyrus!?" Shamaya screamed. "Holy Shit! Sweet Morris Chestnut!"

Darius looked at the phone, confused a moment…Then his eyes exploded as he gasped, "Oh, shit! May-May?! Where in the hell have YOU been, Bitch!? We have been trying to find your sweet chocolate ass since your brother turned himself in. You better leave a goddamn number so we can reach you, or I'm coming to get your cute ass!... Right now! Sitting there looking like a Chrima present! I'll kick your ass if you ever vanish on us again!"

"Uh-uh, Nigga! I gots that hot fire for you, Bro! They know around here not to step with that Woop-Woop! Damn, Cyrus! You're tall as hell now! Your hair's so damn long! Both Lionel and your hair is longer than mine…Damn, son!" Maya taunted Darius with her cute attitude, making us all giggle. "The whole crew is all grown up and still together…I wish I could be there too. You look so happy…wow!"

"Hakim, Bro, We've got to get her here for….," Darius started, and Hakim nodded and glanced at me. Hakim stole my phone from Lionel and ran upstairs.

"How Hakim just snatch the phone from a nigga like that, Sis?" Lionel growled, stunned with his mouth open.

"I see you got your answer, Lionel. Do you feel better now?" Darius asked him, smiling and yanking his hair playfully.

"Yeah…I do feel better just seeing Shamaya again. But I still need to see something else. I'm going to get my answer before Christmas is over," Lionel thought aloud, smiling. "Damn, she's so fine now!"

Lionel suddenly grew impatient and began to pace between the stove and the sink. He threw his head back and groaned, pulling his hair.

"Fuck!" Lionel yelled, smiling to himself. "Did you see her, Cyrus? Oh, my god! She's got a body with her fine ass! She was always cute, but Maya looks like a short-ass model with all that damn hair…oooh…my shit is waking up! She's so beautiful…."

I smiled as I headed upstairs. Hakim had been on the computer doing something as I touched his shoulder. He turned in the chair and smiled, handing me my phone. I texted Lionel Maya's number. Hakim saved her number inside his phone, and his smile grew.

"It will be a nice Christmas present for them both," Hakim began as he offered me a slip of paper. He had written 11:45 am Dec. 26th, and March 21st, 10 am?

"What's this?" I asked.

"I booked Maya a flight here for New Year's and brought her a ticket to go to Jamaica with us," Hakim said, grinning. "He's not going to believe it. So I told her to keep her lips sealed about it until tomorrow night."

"Hakim, you're amazing! He's never going to forget this! Neither is she! They both have been waiting for years to see one another again," I giggled, running my fingernails across his waves. Hakim stared up at me and nodded. He took off his glasses and glanced over at the door as Darius came inside the bedroom, grinning from ear to ear. "My brother is going to be as blessed as I am, Queen."

"That nigga is happy as hell right now! Queen, you are amazing! How did you find her?" Darius asked me as he stood nearby, shaking his head, amused.

"It was an accident. I dialed Giggles' old number…it was disconnected. But she answered! It was like-…I don't know…I was thinking about her and wanted to talk to her…." I remembered.

"One of those weird coincidences…? It happens to me all the time… after I talk to Kaliah….I'd cuss him out…Then someone I miss will call me or pop into my mind, and I'll call them. That shit is crazy," Darius thought, staring at my phone.

"Wow!" Hakim chuckled, gawking at me, chewing his bottom lip. "Lionel got a hell of a Christmas present thanks to you, Queen. So….can I unwrap my Christmas gift now? All we have to do….is close…the door?"

Darius raised his eyebrows, tilting his head back, thinking, "Come on, Queen. I've been a good boy all year. Gimme a Chrima nut? It's been almost two weeks?"

"Hakim, we are at your house! Your grandparents are at the end of the hall," I giggled, rolling my eyes.

"So, G.D. and Sophie be getting it in, too. Then they're out for the night. They love you, Queen! They don't really care as long as we're out of sight. G.D. sees all that ass, and he'll have a heart attack!" Hakim teased me, falling back into his Channing Tatum mode. He started rolling his hips toward me.

Darius died laughing, "Nah, Bro…G.D.'s got that one leg, so you've got to lean with that shit!  'I'm trying to get this nut! Shut up and stop playing with yourselves! My damn Viagra ain't kicked in yet! I'm trying to focus…oooh, Sophie! Watch my stump, girl!"

"Darius!" I died laughing as Darius started hopping on one leg, chasing me.

"Come on, Queen….close the door?" Hakim whispered, tilting his head flirtatiously. He relaxed his face and made the saddest face poking out his lips. Hakim made his adorable lips quiver and held out his arms. "Ain't I cute? Don't you want to give me a kiss? It's Christmas, and everyone gets a gift from you but me and Cyrus? Pwwweeasse?"

"Hakim…" I giggled, struggling to run from him as he slowly caught me by the door. His hand stretched out, clutching my jeans, attempting to unzip them."Stop…no…not here…Hakim!?"

Darius suddenly lept over Lionel's bed and held up a little bunch of leaves over Hakim's head. Hakim glanced up and grinned viciously. Darius burst into laughter, "I got you, Bro! Come on, Queen, mistletoe is a Christmas tradition. You have to kiss him under the mistletoe!"

"That is correct," Hakim agreed, poking out his lips again and placing his glasses on the tip of his nose. "Ain't I sexy, Man-DISA? Hakim just wanna kiss?!"

"Okay, just one kiss!" I laughed, spinning my eyes.

"Yeah!" Hakim yelled, dragging me nearer. "Gimme them lips!"

Hakim took the mistletoe and held it over his head. I leaned closer and rubbed my nose against his, and gently kissed his chops. My tongue played with his lips, and I sucked them playfully.

"Mmm, dammit! I'ma start a new Christmas tradition…Cyrus, close that damn door," Hakim demanded, plucking me up from the floor and tossing me across his bed. He twirled the mistletoe over my lap as he began to unzip my jeans again. "I'm gonna kiss you under the mistletoe my way!"

Darius snatched it away from Hakim suddenly and fixed it over his private parts, laughing, "Um…Queen, I want my kisses right here, though! You're so nice all the time, be naughty to me. Come on….it's Christmas?! Let's tease the season?"

# Chapter Five:  Momma/God

## Lionel

"So, you've been in Philadelphia all this time?" I asked Maya with a smile over video chat.

"Yeah, for nearly three years now," She answered with a sweet smile that made me feel shy.

"You didn't look for me?" I teased her, pretending to be angry.

"Yeah, I did, a lot of times. I thought I found you, but I didn't recognize any pictures. There are a few Lionel Dunns out there, you know. But I work braiding hair, painting nails, and things I haven't had much time for social media unless it's to get clients. I'm the only one paying the bills here. Aunt Key-Key has never worked or taken care of the girls. So when Granny died, this was the only place I could go," Maya answered me with her cute dimples showing as she smiled.

"I'm 'Da Realest Li-Li Dunn,'" I laughed, staring at her.

"I can't believe you're talking to me right now. This feels like one of those dreams where you wake up, and it's the same. You know what I mean?" She asked me as she sat back with her pillow propping up her phone so I could see.

"This is the best Christmas present I've ever received. I owe Disa bigtime!" I laughed as I leaned back on the couch. She giggled sweetly, covered her face, and blushed. Maya was so damn cute now. She acted the same as when we were little, but Shamaya had some swag! Philidelphia had her attitude right with some flavor that turned me on. Her face was still gorgeous with those dimples like New-New from ATL! Oooh, I loved when Maya smiled. Now her face seemed to just explode into a beautiful heart attack for me. Maya was slim, but she had some thick hips and tight thighs...looking at her skin in those shorts...ooh, they looked so smooth I just wanted to touch her. I didn't care if she hit me in the nuts if I could rub that ass for a few seconds.

"So, where's your man, Maya? I know you got niggas in Philly trying to snatch you up and put those handcuffs on your fine ass? You're too beautiful to be single. So, come on and break my heart...tell me the facts," I asked, keeping it real.

"Lionel...I've never had a boyfriend. The guys around here are so nasty and weird. They try, but I don't feel safe with everyone alone. I work all the time, so I don't waste it," Shamaya told me.

"Nobody?!" I questioned curiously.

"Nope, no one," She giggled sweetly, blushing. "I do have this imaginary boyfriend in my picture."

"So, you really missed me?" I worried.

"I thought about you all the time. Everyday....We used to have so much fun doing the silliest stuff. Even being bored was fun for me. I used to tell James I was going to run away and move back to Texas with y'all. G.D. would let me, and Sophie loves me!" Maya giggled.

"Yeah, they both were crazy about your wild ass. G.D. used to call you 'Chocolate Piya, Maya'," I chuckled, remembering. "I think he likes you more than I do. You know he got it bad for Mandisa, too?"

Maya laughed, falling over, and I looked up at those shorts and saw those sexy thighs and nearly lost it! Damn it, Lionel! Stop being nasty!

"I'm not gonna sit here and lie to you, Maya. I've been waiting too damn long to see you again. I missed you a lot. I've never had a friend as sweet as you, Girl. We used to do it all together. I still think about you all the time, too. If we could have stayed together, I know we'd be linked up. But I hope it's not too late, now? I want a chance to be your man. I don't want to be just your friend," I managed to say as my stomach knotted up tightly. My nerves were so bad that I could barely hold my phone steady. I was scared she was gonna laugh at me.

"Okay," She answered, smiling over her pillow. "If you're really serious, Lionel. You're the only boy I've wanted, and I love you."

I paused and sat up straight, saying, "I love you, too, Maya. I always have….I was just too stupid to say it."

"You're not stupid, Lemonhead! We were kids…Neither of us knew what to do or say. But I can't keep pretending that I have a boyfriend now that I have you back. I want the real thing," Maya sighed nervously.

"I know…now…If I knew then what I know now, I would have been cool and waited for you. But I've never had a girlfriend. I fooled around a lot. I couldn't commit to anybody cause you stole my heart when you left me," I confessed as I stepped out on the front porch. Maya smiled, watching me as I lit a cigarette and blew the smoke out the door.

"What?" I asked, staring at the phone holding my cigarette.

"You still smoke, really? Kools?" She asked me with glowing eyes.

"Killers Out of Longview, Fa Sho!" I laughed, remembering the joke. Maya held up the green box and giggled.

"Old habits die hard, huh?" She asked as she opened her box and lit one with me! Maya was my best friend, yo. We did everything together…really. All of this was too much for me. She was doing precisely the same shit as me, but Maya couldn't replace me with anyone. It made me feel like shit because it meant she had way more faith than me. "I guess we do still do everything together…huh, Lemonhead?"

"You're my old habit, Maya. That's why I can't quit," I admitted frowning. "Whenever I'm sad, I smoke and think about you. I wish you were here now. I'm all twisted up. I need a hug! I want a redo on that last kiss, too!"

"Don't be like that, okay? It will happen. Just be patient. We've waited this long, right?" She begged brightly to me.

"Yeah…" I agreed, nearly losing it. I was so emotional I wanted to cry.

"You want me, you got me, and I'm not going anywhere. So, smile? We're going to see each other again. It's going to be fun, and we won't take the time we have together for granted again, will we?" Maya asked me as she blew out smoke.

"Never, Maya, you're all I ever wanted. I even wrote James trying to find you, Girl," I told her, thumping ashes out the door.

"He never said a word to me, and I talk to him about you all the time. All he says is, "If you love him and he really loves you, it will happen. Just keep looking, May-May.'"Maya said, acting tall like her brother, making me laugh.

"Just like Hakim," I laughed suddenly. "Every time I start flipping out, he would bring up your name and make me shut up. He was always preaching, 'She's out there, and I bet she's thinking about you, too....' But you know Hakim.... 'Yadda, yadda...blah...blah...stop being dumb, Lionel!"

She giggled as tears ran down her cheeks. She sighed deeply but didn't stop crying! I had never seen Maya cry before....it broke me up.

"Yo! Don't...do that...okay? You never...cry," I gasped, frowning at my phone.

"Everyone cries, Lionel. I always cry when I'm alone...." Shamaya sobbed, hiding her face from me.

"You're not alone...kay? I'm here anytime! Just call, and I'll answer. I promise, hear me? You're my nigga! Don't punk out on me now! You gonna make me cry," I told her, smiling, trying to cheer her up. "You get some rest. I will call you in the morning, okay? I love you, Maya."

"Alright….I love you, too, Nigga! You better dream about me!" Maya teased me, wiping her face.

"I always do," I sighed honestly. I hung up the phone and put it in my coat pocket.

Yeah, I got my nigga back!

I glided out on the porch and blew out smoke as the cool air hit me in the face! I shut the screen door behind me as I felt how cold it was, but it felt alright. I glanced around, and all the memories started coming back.

We used to sit right on these steps, and she braided my hair the first time. After that, Maya and I rode our bikes up and down this street for hours until we got tired. She always used to race me and do crazy-ass stunts.

We shared ice cream in the summer because we sometimes didn't have enough money for two. She laughed at me when I tried to sing songs and forgot the words. I used to get mad, and we'd play fight. Maya gave me a black eye when we were wrestling in the front yard, but then she held ice on my face for over an hour because she felt terrible.

Then when she left, she gave me my first kiss and took my heart away. Now that I had got it back…I wasn't giving it to anyone else.

I sighed as all the old questions I had answered suddenly got replaced with new ones. I was going to hang in there until I got all the answers I needed. I wanted to keep talking to Maya, but when she started crying….it got me. I didn't want to cry in front of her anymore. When we were kids, I was always crying. Maya was always smiling no matter what. It was my turn to keep a smile on her face so she could be braver. My phone vibrated and scared me. I grabbed it out of my pocket.

"Lionel, I miss you already," Maya texted me.

My phone rang, and I answered it quickly with a smile. I was so happy that I nearly screamed, "I miss you too, girl, you couldn't sleep?"

"I'm coming to Longview. I want to see you, Lionel!" A familiar accent said.

My mood immediately dropped as I frowned. It was Fredericka, and I didn't want to talk to this crazy bitch! I ground my teeth and pulled my hair.

"I told you we are done, Ricka! It's been two months, so why are you still tripping? I'm done…This Dunn doesn't want none!" I told her, scratching my head getting pissed.

"You can't stay mad at me forever, Lionel. I said I was sorry. I didn't mean to hurt you like that. It just happened…Come on?....please?" She begged to try to tempt me.

"Naw, I'm good, Ricka! You burned me! I'm so good. The one and only time I trust a girl, go raw, and you burned me! You don't know how much medicine I had to take! If my Grandma didn't work at the health clinic, I would have had to tell my brother!" I yelled through my teeth. "You up there in Houston hoing away all that pain because you can't keep me! I ain't the one! I was so close to loving you, then you fucked me all the way up with that shit!"

"You got me! I'll take that shit, but it ain't happening again. I'm out! You come here looking for me, and I'ma get ghost on your ass, peace!"

"Lionel, come on, don't be like that! I miss you don't you want me?" She begged me. "We can use the condoms, but I promise I'm clean!"

I hung up the phone, went inside the house, and shut the door. I needed a fucking drink! I knew where Hakim hid the

Crown Royal, so I poured a glass and downed that shit. My phone rang again. This time...I checked that shit before I answered. It was Maya.

"Hey, Girl....what's up? You can't sleep?" I asked, failing to hold my shit together.

"No, I couldn't sleep," She sighed quietly. "You sound upset. What's wrong, Lionel?"

"Uh...naw, I'm good now. I'm talking to you," I lied, pulling my hair, trying to breathe and relax. Awkwardly, Maya knew me too well, and I couldn't hide how Ricka had me fucked up in the head.

"You want to tell me what happened with her?" Maya asked, breaking me. How did she seem to read my mind? All my nerve was gone, my swag vanished, and I couldn't stand up straight. "You gonna get quiet on me now?"

"What? W-who?" I asked, collapsing back against the kitchen counter.

"Come on, you said that you had girls before? She's got you upset, and I can hear it in your voice, Lemonhead. I know the difference between your angry voices. If it were a guy, you'd be hyper and high. But now it's deep and slow, so it's a girl. What did she say?" Maya asked as I slid down to the floor, frowning.

"I love you, Shamaya…." I gasped, my voice cracking as I lost it again.

"Don't cry…Hey, remember what you said a minute ago? You're not alone…just call. Something told me to call you back," Maya said seriously. "Let me see you?"

"No!" I groaned, covering my face. I was hiding my tears like she could already see me.

"Lionel, I want you to see my face so you know I'm for real," Maya told me as my Facetime rang. I answered it and looked at her. She was smiling and waving as I sat up. I waved back sadly. "You need another cigarette? Come on, Baby, let's smoke one together…? Tell me what happened?"

I got up and turned on the back porch light and sat in the rocking chair, then lit a cigarette. Maya hit her's and smiled at me. Then, she folded her pretty legs and sat forward.

"Come on, you can tell me….you know that, right?" Maya asked, holding her cigarette.

She was pointing her middle finger at me as she used to when we were kids. It was cute, and I smiled. Then, I took a deep breath and told her everything. I told Maya about Les,

Fredericka, how I tried to stop seeing her after she tricked me, and how Ricka wouldn't let me return her gifts.

Then I had to tell Shamaya about how Grandma Sophie had to treat me for both Gonorrhea and Chlamydia. She had to give me shots, and I had to take all kinds of pills for weeks to get rid of that shit. Now Ricka was calling, trying to get me back. I didn't want to think about Fredericka Han's lying ass.

"They were not lying when they said it only takes once in school. I learned my fucking lesson. I never fuck a girl without a condom, and the one time I did, she got me. But never again," I sighed, wiping my eyes.

It felt good to get all that off my chest. I hadn't told anyone what happened between Ricka and me. Grandma Sophie knew that bitch burned me, but I didn't talk about her with anyone. I was ashamed that it would get back to Hakim and Cyrus. I didn't want to hear the I told you so's.

"You did the right thing by telling your grandma. You took medicine, and now you're clean, right?" Maya asked, looking worried.

"Yep, I've been checked every week since it happened. Nothing, but it scared the shit out of me," I said, frowning.

"Good, so stay away from those nasty women!" Maya giggled. "Everybody makes mistakes. Just learn and move on."

"You're right," I sighed, scratching my forehead, relieved. "Why are you so cool? Any other girl would be like, 'Stay away from me, you nasty!'"

"I told you, I love you, Lemonhead, and I meant that shit! Fuck them, hos! You got me now....That's the past, okay?" She reassured me with a smile so beautiful it made me happy. "Feel better, now?"

"Yeah, much better now. Thank you for everything," I told Maya smiling again.

"Any time, Nigga! Hey, it's over. Try not to beat yourself up. If you have to change your number to ditch her, just call and let me know. I can't lose you again!" Maya told me. "Besides, Beyonce, you're my best friend. Losing both of you really hurt, I was in a bad place for a while, but I got you both back! I'm blessed. Fuck fake friends, get some good positive people around you, and be happy. Drama is so stressful. I had to learn to let shit go, or I'd kill myself worrying about ignorant people."

"You keep talking like Hakim, and I'm gonna scream," I laughed, taking a drag.

Maya laughed and asked, "It's Christmas, Lionel. New Year's is next week. Are you going to make a resolution like we used to do when we were little?"

"Yeah…I haven't done that in years. But I'm gonna start over this time for real," I confessed as I thought about it.

"Good, so what do you want for Christmas?" Maya asked, looking at me suspiciously. She started giggling. "A Cadillac on 23-inch rims with four bad bitches holding pizza? So you can eat and roll on dubs?"

I fell out of my chair laughing as I remembered telling her that shit when I was eleven! I couldn't believe she remembered that stupid shit!

"Naw, I got my Christmas present. All I need is one good girl. Fuck those bad bitches! Somebody else…fuck those bad bitches…I am good!" I laughed and smiled as I found a blunt under the picnic table. "Fucking Cyrus!"

Maya started laughing when she saw me hold it up, "Some things never change…Lionel?"

"Yeah, Baby?" I asked as I took a puff, watching her smiling.

"I want you to be my first...?" Maya whispered, smiling nervously. I choked and dropped the weed! I looked all over the porch until I found it on the step.

"You said what, now?" I asked, thinking I heard wrong.

Maya blushed and hid her face laughing, "You heard me!"

"After all that shit I just told you, you still want to do it with me?.... Wait...you're a virgin?! I heard something else," I wondered, scratching my goatee confused as hell.

"Do you believe what you heard or me?" Maya asked me, frowning.

"I believe you....but the shit I heard was foul as hell, Maya," I started as I thought back. Niggas do lie.

"Whatever you heard about my mother and me is not realistic. She was fucked up really bad, but James protected me. That's why he's in prison. He saved me, but he caught an assault charge for trying to kill Miles.

'If James wasn't in jail at the time, I never would have left The View. They lied and said he was trying to sell dope. But he got involved with those guys to get close to Miles trying o get Mama to come home. He had weed all the time, but James wasn't a drug dealer. He was getting paid to fight grown niggas for Pretty Tony. But when he tried to touch me, James fucked them all up!

'The police got called, and those niggas tried to say my brother had a gun. He did have one, but he never used it. James always boxed niggas. But he took the lesser charge and got four years. So he's only got a few months left. I don't know what he's going to do once he gets out. If he can't find a job, Lionel might do something dumb and end up right back. You know he has anger issues," Maya explained, looking worried for her brother.

"I'ma talk to Hakim, Cyrus, and Kaliah. We'll handle James. He's gonna be good when he gets home, so don't even think twice about it," I assured Maya smiling. She stared at me, and I nodded. Maya nodded to me and just listened and trusted me like that. She didn't doubt my word for a second.

"I'm going to lie down, but I'll call back if I can't fall asleep," Maya giggled, lying down.

"You can leave the phone on so I can watch you sleep," I teased her. But secretly, I hoped Maya would do it.

"Silly," She giggled, blushing. "Night, night, Lemonhead."

"Maya?" I called her feeling happy as hell.

"Hmm?" She answered, looking up exhausted.

"I'm gonna take care of you, for real. I love you," I told Shamaya honestly.

"Love you, Lemonhead," She giggled, hanging up. I was still staring at the black screen, hoping she would come back as my phone locked.

"Why are you sitting out here in the cold alone?" Hakim asked me as he came through the screen door.

"Why y'all lock the bedroom door?" I retorted, being messy as I passed him the blunt. Hakim sat at the picnic table and dropped his head.

"What you talking about, Willis?" Hakim laughed, sticking out his tongue and licking his lips. But then, Hakim hit the blunt, and I had second thoughts about hitting it again.

"Ew, Nigga, you nasty," I laughed, lighting a cigarette rolling my eyes.

"That girl is a beast!" Cyrus groaned as he came out behind Hakim and sat on the picnic table near me. Hakim passed him the weed, and Cyrus shook his head and slapped me with his hair.

"What y'all do to her?" I asked, laughing as I pushed Cyrus's hair away from my face.

"Shiiiiit, it's the other way around. It was funny as hell! We were just acting silly, and once we got her going, she tore my ass up! Mandisa's so sweet and shy at first, then she tears your ass apart!" Cyrus mumbled, smoking staring straight ahead. He glanced back at Hakim and shook his head. "Bro, we created a monster!"

"I'm good, Osiris! I can handle her, but you get her in the zone with all that begging," Hakim laughed, shutting his eyes. "Please, Baby-cakes, come on, Queen, ooh baby, yes…you know she likes all that shit!"

"Uh-uh! You started that shit… talking about 'let me unwrap my present…I'ma kiss you under the mistletoe…MY WAY! Fuck! Don't put that Evil on me, Ricky Bobby!" Cyrus laughed, hitting the top of Hakim's wave cap.

"But I wanna go fast!" Hakim said, raising his hand as I puffed the blunt. "If you ain't first, you're last! You know I'm all about speed, Bro! You're gonna have to learn to Shake it and Bake it, or lay there and take it! Mandisa is destroying her Black-ass Stallion!"

"Y'all niggas straight stupid!" I choked as Cyrus wiped a tear from his face. He looked really fucked up. Hakim was dying of laughter. Hakim slapped my arm and couldn't even get the shit out because he was laughing so hard.

"Fuck you, Hakim! Shut the fuck…up!" Cyrus groaned suddenly and stole the blunt, and walked away.

Hakim put his head on the table, crying, "Cyrus… can't hang! Mandisa….oh shit! OOOhhh! He talks all that shit!…. But, Bro, he was out of there! I can't….he wasn't 10 minutes…I can't…."

I had tears in my eyes laughing at Hakim laughing at Cyrus, who was so pissed off that he didn't even want to look us in the eye. I wanted to die! But I couldn't stop laughing to get that shit out. Hakim slapped my arm and held his stomach, saying, "Lionel…Every time he begs like Keith Sweat and cums faster than the police in white neighborhoods! Bam!…. OOOh, Queen!"

"Fuck you, Hakim!" Cyrus shouted from near the BBQ pit. I died laughing. "Nobody complains about the thunder that I put down under. I'm not trying to fuck Mandisa crazy like you. On the contrary, I make love to her, so she isn't scared away by your piston-pumping action and kung-fu grip, G.I. Ho!"

"So, what happened with May-May?" Hakim chuckled, ignoring Cyrus's temper tantrum.

"What do you think happened?" I asked, smiling as I bit my bottom lip.

"So, what are you gonna do about Fredericka Han?" Hakim questioned me seriously. "You don't want her popping up like Trisha starting shit with the fam? Or are you more like Kaliah than I thought?"

"Look who the fuck is talking!" Cyrus chuckled, making Hakim roll his eyes.

"Oh, and Sami Reed and Ms. Mia aren't still trying to get some Chocolate?" Hakim sarcastically shot back at Cyrus.

"Right…right…low..blow….Truss…? I'm done…." Cyrus groaned, sitting down.

"Fuck that bitch! It's been over with her, Hakim. I'm changing my number," I told him, smoking my cigarette again.

"Oh, now it's fuck that bitch?! You didn't say that shit when she was spending all that bread, you man-meat!" Hakim laughed, rubbing his hands together. Cyrus fell over laughing. "For real…what really happened?"

"The nasty bitch burned me!" I groaned, rolling my eyes.

"What?!" Cyrus asked, staring over at me critically. "What did I tell you about dressing the soldier for war, Nigga?"

"I do! I always have, but the one time I didn't, she got me," I told them, shaking my head.

"You take care of that shit?" Hakim asked worriedly.

"Yeah….weeks ago. That's why I stopped fucking with Ricka's nasty ass," I replied, twirling my chain around my finger.

"That's a relief," Hakim sighed, rubbing his wave cap. "The last thing you need is to see Maya and burn her up. She'd never talk to you again."

"Yeah, but….WHAT?!" I asked as Hakim covered his mouth suddenly.

"So, that's what you were up there doing?" Cyrus laughed, pushing Hakim. "You invited May-May to come here for New Year's! Look at who can't keep a secret?"

"Hakim, stop! Don't play with me like that…." I groaned, taking the blunt from Cyrus.

"Damn it! I knew I should have just stayed in bed with Queen, Fuck!" Hakim shouted, rubbing his eyes.

I sprung at my brother, knocking him off the bench. I hugged him so tightly he suffocated. We rolled around on the porch play-fighting for a minute, and he bounced up chuckling.

"Hakim, why? Why are you so nice to me?" I questioned as he leaned against the screen door.

"Lionel, Maya is not some ho! She's home for you. You haven't been the same since that girl left Longview. If all I have to do is book a flight to make my brother whole again, then I'll spend whatever.

'You've changed, Lionel. You're not the same as you were six months ago. Watching you start to grow up made me remember how cool it is to have a little brother. We're not so different. I did fucked up shit because I never wanted a girlfriend, but you fucked shit up because you lost one," Hakim told me seriously. Cyrus smiled and nodded, agreeing.

"Yo, I need to show you this letter from James," I remembered taking the envelope out of my pocket. Cyrus stared at it and shook his head, and handed it to Hakim.

"You know I hate to read aloud, Bro. So why're you trying to play me?" Cyrus replied, frowning at me.

"Bro, you could read if you stop playing and take your time! You don't wear your glasses, and you know you need them for school," Hakim began preaching to Cyrus. "I haven't seen you wear them since you started seeing Sami. She fucked you up, Bro., but it's the past. So why are you still worried about what she said?

'I bet your vision is worse than mine now? You're not dumb! You could read if you tried. Here!.... I'm not doing this for you!"

Hakim handed the letter back to Cyrus, took off his glasses, and put them on Cyrus's eyes.

"James has Dyslexia, too, Cyrus. Why do you think he was always two-piecing niggas for calling him slow? Y'all used to be tight. Don't you want to know how he's doing? He's been in prison for almost 5 years," I asked, watching Cyrus fold the letter. Cyrus's eyes suddenly looked sad, and he fixed Hakim's glasses on his face.

"Alright-alright! I'll read it…but I hear one giggle, and I'm done!" Cyrus grunted. "Li-on-el, go-od to hear from you, Bro. Shit's deep in here, but I'm us-ed to it now. Ev-ery-one in here is mad for shit they re-gr-et, but I don't re-gr-et shit I did. I sh-ou-ld have kil-led that nigga, Miles when I had a ch-an-ce. But, now, my mama is dead…."

Cyrus got upset and frowned. Then, he shuddered his head and grumbled, "I can't do this...I can't...."

"You're doing great, Bro," Hakim encouraged our brother with a smile. I nodded and motioned him to keep going.

Cyrus looked back at the letter and sighed, "Do-n't give up on May-May, Bro. You two are me-an-t to be to-get-her...together. Keep loo-king! Au-nt Key-Key's num-ber is 610-576-4492.

'I do not talk to her any-more be-ca-u-se of shit that went down when we were kids. F-ou-l shit, Bro. I won't bore you with it. I st-ay to my-se-lf, so I don't lo-se my te-mp-er. I try to read, but it is hard. May-May he-lps me with money.

I love my si-st-er. May-May loves me, and she loves you, Li-on-el. You are my br-other. Tell Cy-rus....to.... smoke one for me. Let Hakim know that his preaching helped me deal with some things...I couldn't handle it at first. He is one of those awakened brothers that I hear about here.

'But, who wants to be free of mind in a place like this? I'd sooner do my time and start over on the outside. Fuck prison, bro, you don't want to live like this...niggas is apeshit in the jungle.

'So, we will vibe once I get out, Bro. I miss you all…Be easy…. I hope to hear from you soon.     Your Big Brother, James Tyrone Lockhart Jr."

By the time Cyrus finished the letter both Hakim, and I was grinning. It was like the moment Cyrus connected back with James…he wanted to read that letter! I was happy as hell watching Hakim's eyes light up, noticing it too. Cyrus was in tears as he folded it.

"Hakim, J-Rock was our boy! How did we lose him?" Cyrus groaned, shaking his head.

"When his mama got hooked on that shit, he started hitting the streets all the time. But, you know he was older than us, so he tried to be the breadwinner," Hakim said, frowning.

"James never asked for handouts, he was too proud, and he did the best he could to keep his family safe," I told Cyrus. "But he got caught up trying to protect Maya from that nigga Pretty Tony, and Miles was keeping his mom fucked up to dance. So James fucked up Miles for trying to fuck with Maya over dope, and Pretty Tony blew the whistle on him. Y'all know James only smoked weed, and he hated dope pushers because his dad and mama both smoked crack!"

"We've got to help him, Bro. James is family. He saved Lionel's ass more times than I can remember, and he's always been a positive person. But James couldn't stop the negative shit from happening around him and did the only thing James thought would keep that nigga off his family. When Maya moved away, she was eleven, so James was 15, now he's almost 21! He's the same fucking age as Kaliah! This shit is crazy…."

"Yeah…What the fuck is going on? Since Mandisa came around, I'm starting to feel that more of us are beginning to come together for something. It's a weird sensation when I see these coincidences, and things seem to magically work out perfectly now," Cyrus breathed nervously to Hakim. "I don't know how to explain what it feels like, but it's a buzzing in my brain like quiet-static. It's creepy shit when you start to spot shit as it happens. I've never wanted to read. But I haven't thought about James, May-May, or anyone else…until I met Mandisa!

'I don't know why but when I saw James still thought about me…It fucked me up. I let my brother down….Pretty Tony and Miles got Sweets and Les off the streets and took over right in our faces. Then…they started snatching up our family…really…there aren't many of us left here because of his shit!"

"Fucking Pretty Tony," Hakim exhaled deep-rooted in thought. "That motherfucker…The club is cool, but all the drugs and shit got worse when he started that bullshit brothel in the back."

"He's foul as fuck, Hakim. Why you cut him a few years ago?" I asked, wanting to know what Les didn't.

"He threatened my brother! I hate his PUNK-ass! I don't say those words often, but he's got one more strike, and he's out of the game. Cyrus might have fucked his wife, but that ho chased him down.

'If he'd stop raping little girls and took care of Mia's pussy he wouldn't be on my shit list! So you chill at Gucci's if you want to, but Tony knows I'll fuck him off if he messes with my family.

'You notice how Miles came up missing, right? I don't play that shit!" Hakim told me with the angriest face I had ever seen. His eyes were so dark that it scared the shit out of me as he stared at Cyrus. It didn't sound like Hakim talking. His voice was too damn deep! Cyrus's face was absolutely blank, gazing down at Hakim. "One more strike and it's permanent retirement for Tony Guccione…and his PUSSY-posse. We'll start a Go Fund Me Account or send Mia something via Cashapp for the funeral. I know that bastard is broke!"

"Why you talking like Les, Hakim?" I questioned my brother.

Cyrus's eyes shot over to me, and he shook his head quickly. Hakim suddenly looked over at me and said, "Sup, Little Bro? You still kicking it with that piece of white trash because you're afraid to roll with the big dog? Fuck Lester Woods in the ass! That motherfucker got all his game from me! All I learned from him is how to build a better mousetrap. I don't fuck with him, and best believe he knows not to fuck with me. So you stay the fuck away from that crazy cracker. I'll pop him if he keeps pulling you into MY shit and telling MY fucking business!.... Good help is so hard to find....But easy to hire. I'm going to bed....I'm exhausted and irate...."

Hakim stood up and stared at Cyrus a moment, considering him like he had a problem. Cyrus waited until Hakim was long gone before even he moved.

He blinked and gasped, "Lionel...Don't bring that motherfucker Pretty Tony up around Hakim! We might be fucked. That's not Hakim anymore....and I don't think I can calm him down. He seems really pissed off at me for something….I'm gonna go and check on Mandisa. Hopefully, he'll be cool if he goes to sleep.

'But if HE leaves…We're going to have to run interference. ELYEUH cannot fuck another woman! If he cheats on Mandisa, then it's going to fuck Hakim up. He'll kill himself if Mandisa breaks up with him over this shit! So you're gonna have to keep an eye on him from here on. Fuck! We're gonna revive THE PACT between me and you, Lionel. I'm gonna call Kaliah…we might have to get him here sooner! We have to make sure ELYEUH is a good boy when he gets out, so Hakim stays fine."

"Cyrus…that nigga is talking about killing motherfuckers for real?" I asked, terrified by what the hell I heard.

"Yeah….He means every word he says….ELYEUH doesn't waste his words. You notice he didn't say shit to me?" Cyrus mumbled, frowning. "He only talks to who he wants and dares anyone else to say shit. For some reason….He got out to talk to you! Hopefully, the JACK goes back in the box after his nap, or this could turn into an episode of Snapped, Cheaters, and The First 48 from one Nigga!

"Fuck that!" I yelled suddenly, thinking I was going to have to really fight that nigga! "Hakim kicks my ass! There's no way I can stop a nigga probably 10 times as solid running on pure rage trying to fuck a bitch or kill a nigga! You better call Kaliah right now! I'll go watch Hakim."

"Good idea...ELYEUH doesn't like being around you...maybe he'll go to sleep if you stay close. I'm gonna call Kaliah right now. He's gonna flip out...damn!" Cyrus groaned, putting James's letter in his pocket. "I'll give this back once I get his info."

"Alight, Cyrus...let me know what Kaliah says, Bro. This shit is getting deep," I worried as I went inside, leaving him to make the dreaded call.

# ACT TWO

BLACK PANTHER/GODDAMN!!!

# Chapter Six: Lust/Bloody Waters

## Hakim?

"Hakim, wake up!" Lionel screamed, jumping right into my chest, waking me up abruptly.

"Nigga, get off me!" I shouted, pushing his bony knees off me, looking like Tigger from Winnie the Pooh, leaning over my face.

I wiped my eyes as he moved. It was bright in the bedroom and seriously cold outside the covers as I sat up. I glanced over at the clock, and it was after 10 am. I reached over and grabbed my glasses. Mandisa was laughing as Lionel pulled her legs from under my red and black comforter. Cyrus's long-ass was lying off the foot of my bed, still sleeping. Lionel dove over Mandisa and landed on his back!

"I don't wanna go to school, Mama!" Cyrus yelled as Lionel bounced up and down on his back. Then, the foot of the bed suddenly slammed down into the floor!

"Oh, shit!" Lionel yelled, staring right at me. He lept over his bed and shot out of the door.

Cyrus rolled off the bed and hit the floor. He sat up, waking slowly, wiping his mouth yelling, "What the fuck?!"

I laughed as I stood up looked at my destroyed bed. I had replaced everything inside the house but the damn bed in ten years. I was never home once I turned 14. When I was home, it was hard to sleep, so I read all night. Lionel stood in the doorway, observing me nervously.

"My bad, Hakim, I was just excited. You mad?" Lionel worried, eyeing my face strangely.

"No, it's cool…I need a new bed anyway. But, after last night…It's time to put her to pasture. It was too small anyway. She's seen too much action, Captain, and canna take any more!" I chuckled, grabbing Mandisa's foot and humping it.

"You've got to see this!" Lionel laughed, opening the bedroom window.

The cold wind blew into the room, and I saw what looked like…snow?! I ran over and looked outside. Holy shit… It WAS snowing! I suddenly started to think about the shit Cyrus mentioned a while back about…thinking about things…then it happens. I know I said some shit about snow last night!

"What?!" Cyrus laughed, peering over my shoulder. "It's snowing in Longview, Texas?"

"What?" Mandisa asked, stepping behind looking at the blanket of white covering the yard. Tiny flakes rained from the skies above like powdered sugar out of puffy gray clouds. I gazed at them and sneered as I ran to get dressed.

#

We all ran outside into the cold morning air like kids. It reminded me of when we used to stay across from G.D. in Chicago. Dad would be shoveling the driveway for him while Mama sprinkled salt ahead of Dad. Lionel would be tackling the snowmen down the block to make the other kids mad. I would stand or sit on the porch and watch everything. It was my favorite pass time as a kid in Chicago.

It was always so quiet when it snowed like this. It felt like the world was hushed, or my ears would go deaf for a moment. I would sit and enjoy the sound of the silence. Sometimes when cars drove by, the calm was still too loud. The cars barely made a sound, trying to break the hush. I used to question…is that what it feels like to be at peace? To be somewhere and be unbothered or disturbed by any noise but what you choose to hear? I loved the peace that silence brought me.

Lionel broke my train of thought as he dove headfirst into a pile of snow in the yard nearby as I stepped off the porch.

"Nigga, you still silly," I chuckled, imagining Lionel doing that shit when he was 5.

I walked out to the street, still not hearing much but my own footsteps in the snow. The sounds of everyone else seemed drowned out by any noise I made. There were a few kids throwing snowballs and trying to make a snowman down the road. But, they were going to have to move fast before all the snow melted at noon.

That's Texas weather for you….you don't like it…stick around…It'll change. Texas is the  Bipolar weather state. That's why all the other stars went to other flags. No one can deal with the environment unless you're prepared to lose your mind…the weather has a crazy effect on people mentally.

I'm trying to come up off of my high horse. Mandisa made me realize that I mouth off more than I educate, and I may be too militant. I really don't care what I look like to random niggas, but my queen made a valid point. I waste too much energy warning niggas about shit that they should already realize about me. Why am I wasting so much time trying to prove that I'm worthy of anyone's respect aside from myself? The more questions I ask myself, the less I react, and the more I stop worrying about others' motives. But that only gets you so far in the face of true evil and that ratchet shit!

*I can pretend to be enlightened like Kaliah and become passive....But I would never be happy kissing everyone's ass or feeling equal to a motherfucker that I know only means harm. Peace is nice...But war makes shit happen, and motherfuckers love to make peace happen once the bullets start flying. So I've been a peaceful brother by minding my own business....which, as many of my brothers have learned through history...that's the wrong fucking move unless you want shit to get worse.*

*That's precisely what happened when I listened to motherfuckers talking about stay in your lane, that's grown folks business, kids can't stop niggas like that or my favorite....REAL NIGGAS gonna take care of them. Funny.....apparently....I'm the only REAL NIGGA that's been around THE VIEW in 10 years...It must be why I'm so fucking popular? Right...?*

*Niggas have nothing better to talk about when you live in towns that people spit on. So they make their own drama just to break the monotony. That's why the American Dream for Hakim…Is to get his family the fuck out of here. I'm about to give my brothers all the help they need. But first…It's time to test the loyalty of the family.*

*I'm getting tired of dragging dead weight that loves to talk shit! Either this bitch will stop playing with me, or he's going to have to let my wife go. I'm okay with Hakim needing his HOMIE to be happy again. But that nigga is a lazy distraction that will fuck up everything with his childish games. I'm trying to build a fucking nation, and he's fucking with the church's money!*

*I walked over to Cyrus's truck, grabbed a handful of white, and balled it up in my gloves. I slowly began to put everything together in my head…I raised my eyebrow, spotting Lionel making a snowball to start a snowman. Cyrus was, of course, playing with Mandisa and watching me more than usual. I smiled playfully as I tossed the snowball, and it splattered upside Lionel's head.*

"Oh, shit!" Cyrus laughed, grabbing a handful of snow from the ground, balling it up. "You can't be blind-siding, baby bro!"

*I ducked left as Cyrus's snowball whizzed past my head. Lionel tossed one back, and I caught it as it exploded in my hand. I grabbed more snow, made another ball, and flung it back at Cyrus. He rapidly ducked and stuck out his tongue at me. I immediately ducked back just in time to watch the next one pass my nose, but I froze as the cold busted me right in the right side of my face! Lionel and Cyrus fell out, amused.*

*I gazed over, and Mandisa was cackling so hard she had turned red. She gave me a wave of hello, trying to catch her breath. I forgot all about her messing with Lionel and Cyrus! She got me! Oh, it's on…Three against one!?*

"That's my sister!" Lionel shouted. I glanced over, and G.D. was on the porch laughing his ass off at me.

"She got you, Hakim! You didn't even see her coming! You got your eye dotted!" G.D. laughed, holding his stomach crying. *Mandisa got the whole fam on her side…I see yah…Queen! Good form…* A snowball buzzed from behind Cyrus and hit Granddaddy in the hip.

"What the fuck!?" G.D. screamed at Cyrus. Cyrus moved over as Grandma Sophie poked her head from behind the bushes. She was crying, pointing at both G.D. and me! *Not you too, Granny…Mandisa…No! This shit is crazy! They don't play with us anymore!*

"Grandma Sophie got an arm on her! She hit G.D. from the road!" Lionel laughed, watching granddaddy trying to get the snow off his pants.

"I used to play softball for 15 years as a pitcher," Grandma Sophie laughed, giving Mandisa a high five. "My Diva! You got him!"

"That was a huge snowball, Granny Sophia," Cyrus laughed, pointing at G.D.

"The backyard is completely covered. There aren't any trees to catch it like up here. Piles up to my hips back there if you want big snowballs," Granny laughed as she kissed my grandfather. I was wiping the snow out of my ears. I was lucky it wasn't close range...It might have knocked my contacts out. *I got you, Queen.* Cyrus was having a field day guffawing, and Mandisa was so crimson it was cute.

"Hakim, that shit was priceless! You should have seen your face! It was like....oooh shit!" Cyrus laughed, closing his eyes in slow motion, then grabbing his stomach, then staring at me wide-eyed. I nodded, picking up a rock and tossed it straight above, arching it toward him.

"Nigga, that was way off!" Lionel laughed, gazing at the rock flying overhead.

"Is THAT right?" I requested as I heard the rock strike directly above the tree branch. I smiled at them as a pile of snow fell out of the tree, covering Lionel and Cyrus. I started rolling as Cyrus tried to get the snow out of his locks. "I bet you wish you cut them snakes off now!"

Mandisa was giggling, seeking to help Cyrus get all the snow out of his hair. Sophie and G.D. were snickering from the porch. Granny shook her head, laughing, "That was precise, Hakim! You killed two birds with one stone!"

The branch suddenly rattled again, and another pile of snow fell, and Mandisa was covered. All the snow she got out of Cyrus's hair was back!

"Now, THAT is precision!" I laughed, falling to the ground. "Revenge is so very…very…sweet…when served COLD…!"

"Oh, my Goodness!" Mandisa screamed, trying to shake off the white. The tree loudly shifted again, and they all took off running. *That's how it works….when I strike…I cover ALL targets.*

My grandparents had the fun of their lives watching them run away from the falling avalanches caused by one damn rock. Come on! I know this house's structure like my dick! All the trees touch in certain places. How simple is it to cause a chain reaction from making a few waves in the silence? I'm not a completely bad guy. I do love my family, and I love to play games. But...I make the rules and decide who gets to participate if I pay to play. That's why it's time for Cyrus to shit or get off the pot.

I got up and chased after them to the backyard. However, I slowed up when I saw Mami walking around her backyard holding Amani. She must have been enjoying the snow.

"Mami!" Mandisa giggled as she stopped near the fence. "Isn't it too cold for her out here?"

"We only came out for a few minutes, and I bundled her uptight. I wanted to look at the snow. I haven't seen any since we lived in London," Mami told Mandisa, bouncing a pink bundle with brown curls, blue eyes, and a purple pacifier. Mami was slimming down, and she looked so happy and youthful in the morning sun with her hair up outside in her sweats and robe."The snows...so...Queen! You're soaking wet! What happened to you?!"

"It was my fault, Mami," I confessed, laughing. "We had a snowball fight, and things got out of control."

Mami glanced at everyone and giggled, " There is no need to ask who won, eh, Hakim? You are the dryest!"

"Hakim cheated!" Lionel hollered, knocking snow out of his hood.

"It wasn't cheating…I implemented a strategy," I replied, smiling arrogantly as Mami ran her fingers over my waves.

"Mami, I found Shamaya!" Mandisa announced, wringing out her now damp hair.

"That's wonderful, Queen! She's such a sweet young one and cute, too. I believe she is about your age, Lionel," Mandisa's mother hinted, looking toward my brother. "You two would be so cute together, Lionel…she's so short…you're so tall…all that hair…both of you…I never thought of it until I looked at you now."

"Already a done deal, Mami," Lionel said with a wink. "She's my best friend that used to live HERE. Now that I got her back, I'm not messing that up. I better go call her and wish her family Merry Christmas!"

Lionel gave Mami a hug and messed with Amani before racing back to the house. Cyrus shook his head, laughing as he rang out his locks.

"Not you too, Darius?" Mami hooted at him.

"It's alright, Mami! Hakim best sleep with one eye open, or I'll put his hand in warm water and make him piss the bed!" Cyrus rolled, taking the melted snow out of Mandisa's collar.

"Oh, You!" Mami laughed, checking on Amani. I held my hands out for her, and Mami let me hold her.

"Getting big, girl," I said to those blue eyes inside the blankets. Her hand grabbed my finger, and she smiled at me with those creamy chubby cheeks. Mandisa grabbed her binkie as Cyrus started playing with her dark pink lips, and Amani wrinkled her nose and started kicking. "Cyrus! Stop aggravating her! You're putting her in fight mode!"

"You should teach her some Kung-fu, Hakim, for real," Cyrus chuckled. "Amani will dominate the bullies in daycare! Amani Kang, she's the baddest baby on the monkey bars!"

Mandisa pushed him, giggling. Mami made a suspicious face at Cyrus and reached for Amani, saying, "I better get her inside before she catches a cold. But, Queen, you better get dry before you suffer the same fate!"

Mami took my sister, and I waved as they headed inside.

"I'll be back shortly," Mandisa told us with red cheeks from the cold. She followed her mother as I stood watching her from the fence….thinking quietly. Mandisa looked back before closing the door. I mouthed to her that I loved her silently. "I love you, Hakim."

I glanced around, and Cyrus was gone! *Damn, he was fast… I wonder what scared him off?*

I smiled, brushing away snow as I climbed up and sat carefully on the fence. Mandisa didn't notice me there yet. I took my phone out of my pocket and called her as I caught sight of her undressing in her bedroom window.

"Hakim…I just left…you miss me so soon?" She giggled with a smile candidly in front of the window.

"I miss you every second you're out of my sight, Queen. When I can't see you, I have to think about you or talk to you so I can breathe. But…yeah…I miss you, Baby. So what are you doing?" I replied with a smile, watching her take off her coat.

"Aww, Hakim…you are so sweet, My Love… You know I must change my clothes. Or did you forget that you snow bombed us with a tree? I'm soaking wet," Mandisa giggled, throwing her damp hair to the side. I smiled, biting my lip…she began to take off her shirt…I straightened up my back.

"Soaking…wet, you say? Mmm…" I began to tease her. I heard her giggle, and I inhaled deeply. "I think you know what I think about when I hear those two words together, Goddess…? I'm so glad that my playing around got you so wet that you had to rush home and strip. Did I make you shiver, Baby? I usually don't like to use ice to do the work. But, my tongue is right here…I can heat up any place you're shivering, Queen."

"Very funny, Hakim, you know what I meant. You are so nasty lately…and as horny as a devil…." Mandisa giggled in my ear. I blushed…*Oh, if you only knew…I've been wearing a halo over my devil horns for so long now…I may just fuck me an angel…May as well since I'm looking at one. She is divine! I must applaud Hakim for his immaculate tastes! Mandisa…You creamy, curvy, innocent honey pot. Mmmmm Mmmmm Mmmmm?*

(rrrrrrrRRRRRRRRRrrrrrr)

Was that the sound of a car leaving the house?

"What was that sound?" I asked, pretending to be dumb growing excited.

"Mami is going to find a supermarket open to get cereal for Amani. She is cranky because she isn't getting full nursing anymore. I offered to go, but I think Darius is driving her," Mandisa replied while I watched her lips sync with the phone. I suddenly leaped to my feet and stood upon the fence, staring right into her room.

"Is...THAT...right?" I taunted her knowing she still hadn't noticed me watching. But, instead, I smiled as it suddenly grew scorching outside.

"Hakim...stop that!" She giggled, taking off her shirt.

"Stop...right there!" I sighed, staring through her window. Mandisa paused and laughed, spotting me. "Open the window, Queen...let me cum over...you have to let me cum inside. I only want to say hello...?"

Mandisa came over to the window opening it staring at me in her bra. Then, she burst into laughter, "Have you been standing out here watching all this time?"

"I couldn't resist...I'm sorry...." I apologized, smiling at her. I jumped down and walked over to her house. I grabbed the window sill below her, pulled myself up, and sat in her window. I must have moved too quickly because she backed up. She smiled at me with nervousness glowing her eyes as I hung up my phone. "Where's Amani? Is she with Mami?"

I licked my lips, noticing her wet bra as the cold air made her nipples hard. They tried to poke out and say hello, and I wanted to help. So I stood up and moved closer.

"Amani's in the nursery!" Mandisa gasped nervously, stopping me as she held up her hands. Mandisa blushed innocently and covered her damp chest. *She's still afraid of me....I love this shit!*

"Oh, okay...I'll go check on her while you take your shower," I assured her.

I walked past Mandisa and went down the hall into the nursery to check on Amani. She was lying under her blanket in her crib, sucking her pacifier with her eyes shut tightly. I turned on the mobile and watched her drift off to sleep. I glanced around, spotting the baby monitor I bought her. I set the receiver near her feet, and took the speaker with me and set it on Mandisa's dresser, and turned it up as loud as it could go.

I cracked her bathroom door. Mandisa was nearly undressed, standing in front of the shower turning on the water. She took off her bra, and I sighed as her supple skin came into view. I didn't open the door. I just watched her undressing quietly. Her curves were so soft and sexy, with her skin creamy like butter. I took off my jacket and tossed it on the chair near the window. I snatched off my shirt and opened the door, still watching unobtrusively.

"Need some help?" I asked when she noticed me. Mandisa nervously shook her head, ogling my chest. Her sunset curls danced around her face and shoulders, and I smiled sitting on the stool near her vanity. "Alright, I'll just sit and watch?"

"Hakim, really?" She snorted with red cheeks.

"What? Don't let me stop you," I informed her, grinning seriously.

She stepped into the steam and closed the door. I glanced over and noticed the shampoo on the vanity and grabbed it. I was about to hand it to her....

I took off all my clothes, closed and locked the bathroom door, and got in the shower with her. Mandisa paused when she felt me start to wash her hair. I ran my fingers through her curls and massaged and scratched her scalp. She shivered and smiled as I rinsed the bubbles from her hair.

"What are you doing?" Mandisa asked, looking back at me.

"Nothing...I'm just helping," I replied, smiling as I took the conditioner and ran my fingers through Mandisa's hair again. "It's so beautiful…It just keeps….growing…and getting…longer, fuller, and thicker…."

*I used the sponge to wash her back and covered her skin with silky, slippery suds—the sweet smell and water trailed down those dimples on her hips. I never cared about the cellulite, stretch marks, or minor imperfections…There was the only thing I wanted desperately…but if I got it….*

Mandisa popped my hand! I bit my bottom lip as I realized I was squeezing her behind. *I wasn't trying to fuck her! I was mischievous….I really think she's adorable…*

*Hakim is the one that is always eating the Pussy! So I get to wear them out once he's had his fill. He was so afraid I would GET HER. I loved teasing everyone now that they knew about me. Mandisa seemed to be the only one that could never tell I wasn't Hakim! I thought that was so damn sweet, so I started sneaking out more and more to play with her when we were alone. I know she's scared because Cyrus runs his mouth about his past, which links us. She's so accepting of Hakim, and that makes her the perfect woman for ME to wife. So, yes, ELYEUH wants Mandisa too, and Cyrus won't stop me from getting it. But he's expecting me to treat her like my other toys.*

*No...I think with a bitch like Mandisa as my number one, the games can be much more fun! She's already bringing May-May back for Lionel. Did you hear her response to seeing me? I think little May-May may want a taste of Big Brother Ha-KIM! I can make that happen...all day, every day.... No problem! I love all flavors of chocolate, and I'm starving for a taste. You fucked up and opened the buffet too early. Should have let the nigga put a ring on it first....smh....*

*Oh well, Queen Bee...I'm gonna do something that is going to fuck Cyrus up. If he doesn't get his shit together after this...there's no hope for him. I'm gonna have to cut him loose.*

"What?!" I asked as she broke my concentration. I glanced down and moved back so my shit wouldn't shove against her hip. "Oh...My bad...I was deliberating ...too...hard."

Mandisa laughed at me, then she turned, taking the sponge after that washed my chest. I raised my eyebrow, chuckling, "Oh, you're bathing me now?"

"You bathe me, so I will clean you in return...." She whispered, scrubbing my arms and shoulders. Mandisa's fingernails scratched my weak spot on my neck, making me shiver. When I looked down into her eyes, they were so blue it was like staring into the ocean! I couldn't look away. "Hakim?"

"I told you not to call me like that, Baby…you think that I can't hear what you're asking for? That pussy is so lonely without me, and I want to make you sing my name…just like that…Let me make you happy, Queen?" I whispered as I knelt down and reached for her knees. "You don't have to be afraid of me…I'll let Hakim fuck you…But I'm going to eat your pussy! We're going to switch games…just for you….and you're the only bitch I'll ever do this for."

Mandisa stared up at me with those crazy blue eyes and sulked at me suddenly.

Her pink lips slowly parted, and her eyes turned bright green! I frowned as I suddenly felt a different vibe from her accent as she said, "What the fuck do you think you're doing, Nigga? You are always talking shit! We gonna fuck or what? All Cyrus talks about is how scary your ass is, and all I hear is big talk. You can leave if that's why you're here. At least Cyrus lays the pipe like a man and makes me feel like a woman. You always fucking like a bitch wants to lose her legs or some shit. How many bitches sued your ass for abuse?"

I backed up suddenly…and realized what the hell I was doing! Mandisa stared at me strangely with those eerie green eyes a moment. Something was wrong! What was I seeing?

#

"This ain't no bachelor party, cuz you ain't getting married! You just turned 17!" I laughed, looking at Kaliah's high-yella ass. He shook his head, blowing out a heavy cloud of smoke with red eyes and face. His hazel eyes scanned the hotel room a moment, and he nodded.

"Aye-aye, Bro, mi gonna marry har! Trisha asked mi, so mi say yeah!" Kaliah laughed as his eyes turned blue while still in thought.

"Trisha?" Cyrus asked, frowning as he shook his head. "You're a damn fool, Kaliah. No way you can handle that woman! No man can hold her."

"Mi got har covered! Stanley says she's as sweet as pie since mi started fucking har. She gives mi anything mi want. All I have to do is knock the walls of dat pussy down. I make her cry, and she loves dis dick! No cap," Kaliah chuckled, passing Cyrus the weed.

"You cool with her fucking like she fucks?" I worried, raising my eyebrow curiously. "You don't need a ring to

232

fuck the pussy. I wouldn't with her jumping from bed to bed. I don't see how you can share one woman with another man. A woman that needs that much dick has issues. She didn't have a problem fucking around on Stanley to pull you. Who's next…?"

"Har always be like dat since she left Jeffery. He twisted her up in the head, Bro. I got tha cure. Her heart all fucked up because that man did her dirty. Trisha thought he loved her, but he hit her, cheated, got her pregnant, and ran the streets. Now she's always dancing…so fine…She's sweet to mi! Mi in love wit har. So, mi say wat tha fuck?" Kaliah sighed with his eyes glowing as he smiled.

"It's your life, Bro, Yolo! But don't be a fool," I groaned, rolling my eyes. "I'll be back. I think we need to talk about this shit some more… It seems like a bad move."

I got up and went to the bathroom. I couldn't believe Kaliah was seriously calling this get-together his bachelor's party. Kaliah was my brother, but he had no idea where his life was heading. I could see that shit as clear as day. He knew that Cyrus and I had both fucked her, and he still didn't care. She was wild, crazy, and when she got drunk or high, she was a loud-mouthed evil woman.

Yeah, Trisha was rich, she was fine as hell for her age, but she had too many issues. She loved to take niggas on a trip to places they had never been before. I hated women that acted like her. She talked shit about everyone, and she loved to test people's limits. Kaliah was blinded by the sweet side she wore when she was around her kids, I guess. I never saw it, though. She was always fucked up around us.

I knew my older brother was about to make a huge mistake. He wouldn't listen to us, so what could I do? I closed my eyes, trying to think.

"Ha...Keeem? Let me help you with that?" I heard a voice whisper into my neck. I tensed up as I opened my eyes, feeling someone grab my shit out of my hand! The bitch was in the damn bathroom with me, and she was drunk as fuck! Her hazel eyes were bloodshot red, her black dress was clinging to her crooked frame as she smiled, trying to catch herself from me pushing her off. She didn't have any underwear, and her skirt wouldn't cover anything because it had been torn by someone else.

"Fuck you doing, Trisha?! I'm trying to piss!" I yelled, moving away from her.

"It's not like I've never seen it before, Hakim...What's wrong, can't you relax? I'll help you out...come on?" She said as she stood up straight and smoothed her dark straight hair in the mirror and fixed her dress, but still couldn't cover her exposed lips. She blushed as she realized her dress was torn. "Easy access…right?"

"I'm good…Trisha!.... Kaliah is right out there with Cyrus…oh, Wait! " I yelled as she fell on her knees trying to suck my dick! "Get the fuck off of me! Tha fuck is wrong with you…Are you high again!?!

I pushed her ass off of me and ran close to the door. Trisha crawled after me faster than I could move! It scared the shit out of me as she grabbed me, and I fell back and hit the floor. Trisha climbed up on top of me and stared down into my eyes. Her eyes were glowing green, and her frown shook me to the core. I could smell all the liquor as she exhaled vodka and everything on my face. She was sticky with fluids and sweat her skin was so clammy.

"Don't act shy now! Is it because of Kaliah? You love me, too? Just tell me it's okay…." Trisha growled like an animal pulling at my shirt with her fingernails. "We can do it again…you'll love it this time, Hakim. You were just scared the first time…I can fuck you right…Let me make it better?"

"Kaliahs's my brother! That shit that happed last time was a mistake! You caught me drunk! I don't want you, Crazy Bitch!" I yelled at her honestly. Trisha heard me and blinked…her eyes seemed to get darker, turning nearly black as she suddenly glared at me.

"You're the bitch! I can look at you and tell you that you want this pussy! Cyrus loved it! Baby brother needs it! I'll fuck whoever I want to fuck! You'll give it to me because you're all scared, little bitches! The more of you little bitches that I fuck, the stronger I get. There's power in this pussy, Bitch!" Trisha laughed with those freaky dark eyes as I fought from under her and grabbed my shit.

"I'm not scared of you! I don't want to hurt Kaliah! He loves you! You crazy bitch!" I screamed, pushing her face getting up. Trisha stood up, staring at me, glowering, and looked furious and injured. She suddenly caught me by the neck and thrust me against the wall!

My head slammed against the door so hard my locks bounced. I felt her struggling to take off my pants again as she held me with one arm! She was so strong! Why was she formidable than me?! Her hand forced my face into the door, and I panicked.

Trisha put her face closer to mine and looked up into my eyes…Wtf!?

Her eyes were all red!

Her face did not look the same at all. That looked like a man staring back at me! When Trisha opened her mouth, the bass in her voice made me start pissing, saying, "You love me, don't you, Hakim? SAY IT! IT'S OKAY!"

"No, I don't love you, BITCH! I HATE you!" I laughed suddenly. "But you're gonna love me, you crazy BITCH!"

I grabbed her hands and threw her off of me, snatching a handful of hair as I held her to the floor. I slammed my shit deep inside of her ass! I hoped that I had torn her apart. Instead, she screamed and suddenly started laughing? That pissed me off so, I fucked the shit out of her!

I tore her ass up. It wasn't good, I hated her, and I was sick of her bullying us with her rotten games. She had broken Kaliah, then got Cyrus, and I was 13 when she came after me the first time! Now the bitch was talking about going after Lionel, and he was 13! I wasn't having that shit! The only reason that I knew her was because of Kaliah. I tolerated her because he blindly loved her. But she really was a crazy ho. I wanted to fuck her nasty ass to death.

When Trisha came around, she pulled her crazy stunts once she was fucked up. She bought all the drinks, took us to strip clubs, and then let us get fucked up so she could have her way with all of us. I couldn't let her do Lionel the way she fucked us up. I snapped!

"You think you scare me, Bitch! If you touch my baby brother, I'll break your neck and make it look like an fucking accident! I'll be NICE for Kaliah, but you stay the FUCK away from Cyrus and Lionel! I'll have you come up missing, BITCH!" I hollered as I snatched her hair back, ramming the point home.

"You think I give a damn about you or your fake-ass family? Go ahead…Kill me now…You're such a bad motherfucker…Black Dynamite!" Trisha laughed back at me. She could be drunk, high, or whatever, but she didn't give a fuck about anyone! Those evil green eyes were laughing at me. I was near squeezing her windpipe, but I couldn't hut Kaliah. "Just like I thought! You ain't shit…just like Kaliah ain't shit, Hakim! Fuck you!"

I slammed her head into the floor. I know I knocked that bitch unconscious when she shut the fuck up talking shit as I stood up. I pissed on her back as she laid there, probably blacked out…Hmph…I suddenly didn't care if the bitch was okay as I left her on the floor and when to tell Kaliah.

After that night, I hated pussy, women got on my nerves, so I gave them what they wanted. But I was gone before they could spin around. I was dressed and out of the door once I was done. Whenever I got near a woman, I could tell what she wanted once I smelled her. It was like another sense to me, and any woman drove me crazy. I couldn't stand any of them. I loved my grandmother, but I started staying away from the house because being near her made me feel physically ill. That was how I discovered the underground, where people don't ask questions when money is power, and green is the only thing that makes the rules.

The Parade!

It was an underground club scene privately owned by business owners around the world. They had a Texas chapter that met in different houses, office spaces, or private gatherings and specialized in true B.D.S.M. These people are not playing. They lived this lifestyle at home or on Parade. The man that I observed was known as 'Lord Chaos.' He was a Master that saw how women gravitated to me. He taught me the rules of Dominance and Submission, but I was never allowed to participate because of my age. The lifestyle taught me the discipline I lacked when I was fucking everyone when I was Vanilla, free fucking…no rules. I did my own research visited meetings for months. I needed the boundaries and regulations to control the parts of me that couldn't feel anything. Once I found what worked for me and I was in.

I decided to make the game temporary to keep myself incognito because I didn't want to keep anyone permanently. The contracts were my way of keeping things very civil and also evidence of consent. I'm not stupid, bitches will lie and try to get it all! It was supposed to be my way to scare some stupid girls out of the strip clubs and run off some annoying bitches that just wanted to fuck. But they fell in love with the shit Hakim says when he's in his feelings.

All these bitches were little girls ages 18-55 fighting for my love, I didn't want any of them, and I couldn't give away something I never felt. There was no love. They were begging me to fuck them all, but I saw how crazy they went once I got them. So Hakim just ate them and broke their hearts. He made them all cry…Georgie Porgy…Kiss the girls and make them cry…poor pudding…sad pie…no cap. They knew the deal. WE don't love you, Bitches!

When they got too disobedient, I took my collars and set those bitches free. Then it started; the lustful urges took over, starting it over again. I had been with so many women I couldn't remember names, faces, and my mind kept slipping. I started to lose track of time. Cyrus was the only person I trusted to talk to. He helped me find help. I learned that all the trauma, sexual frustrations, and years of anger and rage had taken a severe toll on my mind.

So, Hakim secretly started taking meds. He meditated and ran to keep my head straight after we nearly killed a good girl. Hakim was done! If ELYEUH came out for sex, then Hakim just wouldn't have sex anymore….I locked him away…and drowned him in celibacy. It worked for over a year….?

#

The loud whimper stirred me.

"Are you alright, Hakim? You look like you are not well," She worried with sad gray eyes moving toward me. I ran and slipped, tumbling to the slick floor out of the shower. Mandisa giggled, viewing my naked ass struggling to get up off the bathroom floor. I grabbed a towel and covered myself as I heard weeping from somewhere! Mandisa looked around. "That's Amani!"

I got up, quickly dried myself, and put my clothes back on, and went to check on the baby. Amani was fussing, kicking her little legs, and crying. I checked her. She was dry, so I wrapped her and held her in my arms. Amani calmed down as I hummed, walking around the room. Amani looked up at me from her blankets with her beautiful blue eyes. She smiled as she pinched my lips.

I wanted this….not to steal…Amani. I wanted a baby!

Mandisa came into the nursery, and she viewed me with her sister for a moment and smooched my lips. Honestly, I was tripping because everything in the last few hours seemed like a dream. I could have imagined what I thought I saw in the shower. But the voice that I heard…reminded me of Kaliah's fucking wife! It scared me enough to stop everything…

Whatever I was trying to do?

Mandisa was nothing like Ms. Trisha! I just need to take a nap. Oh yeah…my bed…I would have to do a lot when I got home.

"You're really good with her," Mandisa giggled, blushing at me.

"I always wanted a little sister, and I got Lionel's crazy ass," I laughed as Amani grabbed my finger. "I don't know why little girls like me so much. Boys hate me…not the gay ones…them I wish couldn't see me."

"You seem to get along well with all the women that come around, Hakim. They all think you are the sexiest man alive, like me?" Mandisa added with redder cheeks touching Amani's toes.

"Oh, really? What about Cyrus?" I teased, calling her bluff. "You know you have two brothers trying to lock you down for good. I thought he was your favorite?"

"Darius is beautiful, but I find his personality more appealing than his physical appearance. His sense of humor is contagious. I love how he can make you smile or laugh with just a look or by touching you. It's natural and never forced. But I'm more physically attracted to you.

'Your smile, eyes, and that brain of yours are intriguing….not to mention you have the body that I bet Trey Songz wishes he still had," Mandisa giggled nervously. "Both you and Darius are different, but you have enormous similarities too."

"Ha! Ha! Ha! Like what?" I play laughed sarcastically. Amani thought that was funny because she put her feet over my lips, shutting me up.

"You dress alike, somewhat. But, you're both very loving and caring men to me, you like babies, you're very generous, talented, strong, proud, beautiful black men, and both seem tormented by mistakes you've made in the past," Mandisa enlighted me putting Amani's pacifier in her sister's mouth.

As I watched the baby, I couldn't find anything Mandisa said wrong. Mandisa went into her room, and I heard her drying her hair. Amani looked around for Mandisa and got fussy again. I think Amani gets her mother and Mandisa confused sometimes. But they look alike. I nearly thought Mami was Mandisa coming into the nursery. Mami watched me trying to calm Amani down.

"You look so happy holding her, Hakim," Mami stated, coming to save me from the tiny feet attacking my chin. "Oh, she's hungry. I'm going to get ready to nurse her. I'll be right back."

"Yes, Mam," I replied, rubbing Amani's cheek as she held my index finger suckling her binky. Nobody knew how much Mandisa had transformed me. Before her, I never thought about getting married or having kids. I only cared about getting the hell out of THE VIEW. Lately, those two things were all I could think about. But how could this work out with Cyrus?

Everything was golden, but I knew he had a side he had never shown Mandisa. Yeah, Cyrus was funny, charming, and romantic…but he was very insecure. I wasn't jealous of Cyrus…he tried to keep me away from Mandisa to keep her to himself more and more. But Cyrus was still playing around, thinking that Hakim would keep playing about what we wanted.

If Cyrus were to walk in my shoes from day one, he'd never let my ass anywhere near Mandisa! I knew that because of Samantha Reed! When I first told Cyrus about that girl, he thought that I really wanted her. I was trying to help him out. So, I set her ass up! After he heard my proof, he got pissed off at me, then just left. So, I know if he doesn't get his way with Mandisa, he'll do the same shit and blame it all on me. But this time, he won't come back.

I'd lose my best friend and my girl. Mandisa would never stay with me if Cyrus hated me or the other way around. She's too devoted to following her own heart. It will kill her to come between us. So, I believe she'd leave both our asses if we fought over her. That's why Cyrus needs to stop playing his little game with me. I'm serious about Mandisa, and he seems to only be interested in showing me up. But it hurts his feelings when Cyrus comes up short, dropping the ball. He needs to start looking at the big picture. I've been focused on the view. My glasses just need cleaning from time to time. I'm straight…for now…I'm good!

# Chapter Seven: Big Shot/Blood Diamond

## Cyrus

I was standing on the back porch for a few minutes, smoking and thinking. I knew Mandisa had gone home to change. Lionel was talking to May-May on the phone. Granddaddy and Sophie were exchanging gifts, but where was Hakim? I was waiting for Mandisa to come back, but no one had seen Hakim for a while. His car was parked in front of mine in the driveway, so I knew he couldn't have gone far. I looked down at my phone to see if he had called me back after calling three times, but there was no answer.

That was when I happened to glance up and notice Mandisa's bedroom window wide open! I know I saw Mami leave a minute ago while I was helping clean the driveway. So, I guess that meant that he was over there? I didn't mind...Queen was always with me...She could be alone with him for a few minutes and be fine...But why was I feeling like I was being ignored? I called Mandisa a few times too. Same thing, no answer, but she could have left her phone somewhere...?

I sat in the rocking chair staring at her house when Hakim suddenly flipped out of her bedroom window. I shook my head and burnt my blunt. Hakim cleared the fence and ran across the snow beaming. What was he so damn delighted about? I wonder…?

"Sup, Bro?" I questioned, gawking at Mandisa's window. "You didn't get my calls?"

"What calls?" Hakim queried, halting short of the chair. He checked his pants pocket, and I bobbed, peering at the trails of prints in the snow. "Oh, damn, Bro! My bad…it's been on vibrate. I didn't even feel it, I guess."

"You were probably too busy with your pants down," I snickered to myself. Obviously, He was doing HIM…didn't waste any time, either…I see you… "Where's Queen?"

Hakim sulked at me and glanced back at her house, saying, "She's helping Mami with Amani. She's nursing, and I didn't need to stick around for all that! It's too tempting to watch."

"Big-ass titties!" I laughed nervously, spotting Mandisa coming out of the back door carrying a black and pink bag. She switched through the gate and smiled at us. She looked sexy as fuck! Red knee-high boots, tight leather pants, a hot red button-up Christmas sweater, and her hair up in a festive ponytail. "You sexy motherfucker…."

"Sexual Chocolate!" Mandisa exclaimed, smiling at me as she came closer. Hakim fell over laughing every time she called me that shit.

"Randy Watson!" Hakim laughed at me, and I bit my bottom lip as I handed the blunt to Mandisa. She grabbed it in her fingers and blew it with her ruby red lips, and I nearly screamed! When Mandisa smoked, she looked like an A1-certified Baddie!

"Damn, girl, those lips look hazardous on that blunt," I groaned, scratching my neck. She passed it to Hakim, glancing at me with those gorgeous eyes like a cat! She rubbed my lips with her thumb and kissed them as I took her bag. I smiled as she climbed the steps. I wiped her lipstick from my lips, smiling at that round ass in those tight black leather pants... "Ouch! What's all this? You got us Christmas gifts?!"

"Yes...Is that a problem?" Mandisa asked me, blushing as Hakim opened the door for her. "Coming?"

"Hell, yes...I will cum...all you had to do was ask!" I replied, following that ass. "But you said you didn't want anything....But you know I never listen when you say that, so, oh well!"

"Darius! I'm going to kick your butt!" Mandisa threatened me as she pushed my arm away from her curly ponytail. Ooh, I loved it when she got spunky with me!

"What?! You thought I was going to just leave you out on Christmas?" I teased her as I touched my pants pocket, searching for her gift. That bracelet was worth enough to make ELYEUH sit the fuck down. He didn't spend big bucks on his collars. I knew if I got Mandisa something costly as far as bling went…He would stop the picking he was doing lately.

Hakim was really a chill dude until we went to Gucci's that one time with Mandisa. I just wanted to show her the places we used to party growing up. Pretty Tony and his boys took one look at Mandisa, saw she was with me, and tried to start shit. Hakim and Lionel tore the place up while I got Mandisa home safely. But he was so pissed off that when anyone said anything about Gucci's or Pretty Tony…That NIGGA started trying to get out more and more. Then last night…when I read James's letter….Lionel just had to bring up that old shit! That was ELYEUH…he seems to be sleeping…but he does not go away simply! He's faking, and I'm the only person besides Kaliah that can see this shit until he really gets serious.

I told you that he is fucking crazy…YOU didn't believe me….He has no idea how sick he is…I really don't know to be honest. I'm kind of going with the flow until Kaliah gets here tomorrow. I didn't tell HIM that I called Kaliah. But after last night…we can't trust Hakim to stay calm. I only want things to be golden. So far…He seems good! It's Christmas, so I'm just gonna roll with it and do me.

"You look very festive, Man-Di-sa!" G.D. flirted, eyeing at her tight pants, cheerful. "Looking like a Christmas cookie! I just need to take a bite!"

"You'd drool all over her without your teeth in, Gary…Sit down!" Sophie hissed, pushing G.D. back in his chair. She messed with Mandisa's ponytail. "I love your hair, Diva. You're so beautiful…Hakim…I'll whip you if you run her off."

"Granny! I'm not going to run Mandisa anywhere! I love her!" Hakim grumbled as he jumped over Lionel on the sofa and landed on his head.

"Hakim, get yo ass off of me! You better not fart either!" Lionel screamed, struggling to pull himself from beneath Hakim. Hakim moved over as Lionel sat up and died laughing. "That's why I keep saying you're gay, Hakim! How you gonna put yo nuts on my neck like that?!"

Mandisa laughed, sitting on the sofa, and I sat next to her as I offered her the black bag's ping handles. She set it on the floor and smiled, looking around at everyone. G.D. raised his gray eyebrows and offered Mandisa a box.

"You didn't have to get me anything, Granddaddy!" Mandisa gasped, embarrassed.

"It's your first Christmas with us, so you deserve to get something to help you feel like family, Baby Doll," G.D. replied, waiting with a smile on his crinkled-up face…looking like Lionel…even sounds like Lionel when he yells. "Go ahead and open it, Sweetie?"

Mandisa tore off the paper and covered her mouth. She smiled flushed, saying, "I love it!"

She took the framed picture of the Dunn family out, displaying it to everyone. G.D., Sophie, Lionel, their Dad, Luther, Ms. Vivianne, and Hakim there smiling sweetly. It looked like an old Christmas picture with them wearing red sweaters and matching smiles. Hakim even had a giant grin on his face. Hakim stared at it and nodded, smiling to himself.

"I remember this picture. I was seven, and we had it done at the mall when we went to see you in Georgia, Grandma Sophie!" Hakim laughed. "I never saw it after we took it."

Lionel stared at the picture and said, "I want one of these too!"

"I got you all one! I found the card and had them blown up for the family. Man-di-sa has been asking for a picture where you're all smiling," G.D. laughed. Granddaddy had one for all of us. But he handed me a blue box. "Open it, Cyrus?!"

I tore it open and laughed. It was a picture of Hakim, Lionel, and me when we were kids. We were doing poses like gangsters in the front yard. I must have been eleven.

Lionel chuckled, pointing to his braids, "That's when we first started kicking it strong, Cyrus! I was just eight, look at my hair! Hakim's mean-ass looks more gangster than all of us!"

"Shut up!" Hakim laughed, pushing Lionel's forehead. "Real gangsters don't smile for pictures!"

"Grandaddy! Oh, God!" Lionel screamed, opening his picture. He held it up. It was Lionel and May-May on their bikes in the yard. "This is perfect! G.D., where did you find this?!"

"You know Sophie, and I took pictures of you kids all the time. I had a bad-ass camera. That closet in the hall has over 15 albums of nothing but pictures we took over the years. We went through all of them and found some memories I had forgotten back when Sophie and I were the finest thangs on Earth!" G.D. laughed as he showed us a picture of him and Sophie at the wedding when Luther and Vivianne got married! "Sexy Woman!"

Hakim and Lionel were laughing at their Grandad as he smacked Sophie on the behind. She was covering her mouth, laughing with Mandisa. I had to agree! Grandma Sophie was a fine woman back in the gap! She was light like Mandisa with curves, too. Grandma Sophie looked like she could have been a model with her thickness. Oh, my! G.D....you dog! Grandma Sophie still looked good for a woman in her 70s.

"Mr. Dunn! You look just like Lionel! Oh, my God! So handsome and tall!" Mandisa laughed, coloring at the picture.

"Girl, I was too fine for words!" G.D. teased Mandisa. "I may not have my leg, but I can still work it out!"

"Mr. Dunn, No!" Mandisa screamed, falling on me.

"Gary, you gonna leave Mandisa alone!" Sophie giggled as G.D. caught her. Sophie looked over. "Hakim, aren't you going to open your picture?"

Hakim leered and unwrapped his picture. He sucked his lips and nodded and chuckled, "G.D., you the nigga of the year! Oh, man!"

He showed us the picture of his mother and father with the Black Panther Organization. They were at a rally, and Ms. Vivianne was speaking, and Mr. Luther was standing guard armed to the teeth. He looked just like Hakim when he was mad. Mrs. Dunn looked like she was nearly in tears speaking. Black berets, jackets, afros, and the picture just screamed 'Power to the People!'

"How old were they in this photo?" I asked G.D.

"Let's see…that picture was taken…about 1974 after Luther came from the war. He was 22, and Viv was 19, so yeah…They both went to the University of California to meet Mr. Huey Newton.

'Luther was against activism because of his military service. But Viv hated things back then here. She told him that she wasn't going to be with a slave to the system…Luther got his shit together for that girl," G.D. laughed, moving his glasses.

"Mama was a G. That's deep," Lionel said, smiling at Hakim's picture.

"Your Mama was a gifted child, just like you, Hakim. She disliked seeing people oppressed, and when she was 13, she just… 'woke up.' She said that she wasn't going to take it anymore. She was protesting, boycotting, and speaking out against anything unfair. People just came to her. She called anyone that refused to stand up for their rights a 'slave.'

'I didn't understand Viv until she grew up. I realized my daughter was just struggling with enlightenment. But as she aged…things fell into place…you need life experience to really start a revolution…mentally. What good would it do to uproot the system without a new device to replace what's broken?

'More will come and take over and make matters worse. The people going through the system can change, and that would force the corruption to be exposed. That's how you wreck oppression. That's why she began teaching children and helping them to find uses for their gifts."

"Everything I learned I got from her and the books I read. It didn't just happen overnight. Mama was always my hero, and I wanted to be a man just like Dad was with her. I love this, G.D. Thanks, I'm gonna keep it forever," Hakim sighed, touching his mother's youthful face.

"Very welcome. I think memories are better than anything you can buy in a store," G.D. said, nodding. He pushed Hakim's shoulder and laughed. "Now, I want a 96-inch plasma screen smart TV, so I can watch HULU and Netflix…You know I don't like computers, but those Smart TVs are the shit!"

"I told you it was time to upgrade," I laughed as G.D. nodded, agreeing with me.

"I've got you, Granddaddy! It'll be here before Friday," Hakim laughed, agreeing. Hakim got up and grabbed a big red bag from under the tree. We all stared at him.

"What?" He asked as we all looked confused as hell at what we were seeing.

"You bought Christmas gifts, Hakim?" Lionel asked, flabbergasted.

"Yeah…Everyone always gets me stuff, and I felt bad I wasn't getting anyone anything through the years. So, I thought this year I wouldn't be a Grinch. I hate Christmas because of all the hype, but I still love you all," Hakim stated, glancing around.

He handed all of us a different-sized box as he read the tags. He got Lionel an excellent professional camera. I opened mine, and it was a new pair of wireless headphones. They were the costly ones. He handed Grandma Sophie an envelope. She smiled, glancing up at him as she opened it.

"Oh, Sweet Jesus! Hakim!" She wept, revealing it to G.D. "Two tickets to Las Vegas! Hakim the Belaggio is a five-star hotel!"

"I felt bad that you spent your anniversary here instead of going somewhere nice. I know you both love to gamble, so," Hakim recounted, smiling.

"That's sweet, Hakim, thank you," G.D. exclaimed, clutching Sophie grinning.

"It's on hold, so you can pick a date to go anytime," Hakim added, nodding.

"Hakim, this camera is bad-ass! It makes movies and has all the software to edit things expertly. I'm taking this to Jamaica!" Lionel howled, filming us laughing.

"Thank you, Hakim, for this. It's really nice, Bro.," I thought, clutching my gift, eyeing him, smiling.

"Bro? You didn't open the box?!" Hakim snickered.

"What?" I asked, opening the box. Inside was another box. Inside of that box was a custom-made Rolex watch!

"Hakim!!! What the fuck, Bro?!" I shouted as I glanced at the golden face laced with diamonds with the black band with 'Osiris' engraved in gold!

"Damn, Nigga!" Lionel screamed as I put it on my wrist. "That shit is player-made! Where's mine, Hakim?"

Hakim unexpectedly handed Lionel a long box from inside his bag. Lionel opened it. That nigga jumped up and took off running! Lionel nearly ran out the back door. He turned around and returned, sporting a platinum chain around his neck with his initials in blue and silver stones… 'LED'! And that shit was sparkling like the lights.

"Yeah, Nigga!" Lionel wept, clasping Hakim in tears! "This is the best, Hakim! I ain't never gonna take this off! I wear every single chain, even when I'm in the house! Nigga, started from the bottom, now I'm HERE!"

"This is so dope, Bro! I need a hug!" I cried, stepping up and snatching him. Lionel dove on Hakim's back, screaming.

"Ugh, Look who's gay, now!?" Hakim grumbled. "Alright, I feel the love now…."

Mandisa was enjoying the madness of us loving our gifts and behaving ridiculously. I suddenly glanced at Hakim and frowned…I know he didn't overlook to get Mandisa a gift?

"Hakim? You really didn't get Queen a gift?" I asked worriedly.

Hakim gazed at me critically, shouting, "Bro, she said NOT to buy her ANYTHING for Christmas…So I didn't. I respect her wishes."

Hakim threw the empty bag in the trash and walked over, taking something out of his pocket, saying, "But I didn't get this for Christmas. I got it for your birthday, Mandisa, but I was too scared to give it to you when your dad showed up. I put it away. I was going to give it to you on Thanksgiving, but I chickened out then, too."

Suddenly the vibe in the den got really heavy for me. I took a step back as Mandisa watched Hakim open the package, taking out a velvet box. She abruptly stared up at his face as Grandma Sophie gasped.

"You're the queen of my heart, Mandisa. Everyone you touch, you bring them closer. You keep linking us together, making the bonds of this family…my family, more essential. I want to worship you until I cease to exist on this planet.

'The money I spent having this made is nothing. But, your love is priceless, and I'll spend it over and over if you'll always be mine? This diamond is my heart now, but I thought I didn't have one before we met. So, I'm giving it to you because I know you won't break it. Will you take care of my heart, Mandisa?" Hakim proposed to her, kneeling close by on the floor staring up at her.

Hakim didn't tell me that he bought the ring on her birthday. Mandisa's Birthday was back at the end of August before we started school. He never mentioned Thanksgiving either…he never talked about when…Hakim just always said he would propose.

I guess I assumed he was going to wait until she graduated high school, at least. Hakim moves faster than me! I was having Mandisa's ring made to give her on Valentine's Day! He was making a bit of scene proposing in front of his family, but it made me realize something significant.

We hadn't told anyone about *The Contract* yet. As long as that was a secret, then Hakim was the only one that could propose! I think he knew that Mandisa may never tell her parents about me! That might be why he was moving so fast. If we didn't tell Mami about us, then she was just going to be married to Hakim, and I'd be the family secret...or joke...? So, that's what HE thought of me? I'm the joke?

"Hakim, I'll always love you," She sighed as her face colored red like her sweater. Hakim playfully set the box on her knee and rested his head on her foot. She took the box and screamed so loud that I knew my fate was sealed. When I saw Mandisa's tears, I knew Hakim wasn't joking.

"Mandisa, will you please marry me?" Hakim begged, taking the ring out of the box. She covered her face falling back on the sofa in tears. Mandisa couldn't reply. She just nodded. Hakim wiped the tears from her face, and I glared at that massive diamond as he put it on her finger.

It was gorgeous! The way the platinum band had golden links looping around it, there was a tiny red ruby heart inside each loop, tiny sparkling diamonds like stars that spelled out 'Queen' under what must have been a 5 karat diamond! It was serious....I know my shit...Hakim spent close to 300 thousand making that ring! I had chains with less shine than that one beautiful diamond band! The lights hitting it were like a light show of color. It was unbelievable Hakim did that shit....I needed to step up MY game! If he spent that kind of paper, I had to top him.

But it wasn't the ring alone that got her so emotional. It was Hakim's sincere proposal, too. He was so genuine. In addition, that ring was a symbol of his devotion to her. He was the master! I bowed to HIM right there after seeing that shit!

But…When Hakim locked eyes with me while holding Mandisa, the look in his eyes gave me a vibe. I hadn't seen that look before, and I knew…THAT was not Hakim. That Nigga was challenging me to jump with his eyes. I could almost hear him saying, "What you gonna do now, BITCH!?"

I nodded, letting him know that I knew it was HIM. ELYEUH smiled and hugged Sophie and G.D. I eyed Lionel, who didn't seem to notice the change in Hakim's demeanor. No one saw the way he threatened me, and it was fucking with me. IF he's already fucked Mandisa, then there's nothing that I can do. I'd know as soon as she started treating me differently or talking crazy about me. IF Mandisa began ignoring me, then HE would get everything he wanted…so I would leave. So, that's it? If I don't ride HIS wave, follow HIS rules, and live by HIS code, then he's going to run me off. Hakim needs me, but THAT NIGGA will use Mandisa as bait to pull in more beautiful women to fuck. She'll be so in love with him she won't care. It's ALWAYS like THIS! Why do I keep falling for the women that he wants?

"Congratulations, Queen! Welcome to the family," Grandma Sophie cried, holding Mandisa. G.D. hung on to her smiling, and Lionel was so happy he was crying. This would be a beautiful moment for the family if THAT NIGGA wasn't giving me the ICE GRILL. I kept staring at THAT RING; it was taunting me just like his gaze. I was getting pissed off when I realized I couldn't say a motherfucking word.

"Look at this shit!" Lionel screamed, staring at Mandisa's ring. "You will never find anything like this on display in a store! Everyone is gonna know your husband loves you, Sis! When I get some serious money, Maya's getting a rock like this! Damn! You did the fool with this shit!"

"You don't buy a symbol of love off a shelf, Bro. When you have the money, you imagine it and make it happen," Hakim told Lionel, eyeing me with an arrogant sneer. He leaned closer and squeezed Mandisa and ran his fingers through her ponytail but never stopped watching me. "All those gifts on the shelves are for the slaves...Kings manifest their futures with vision…they don't feast where the pigs slop."

I stood up from my seat, and Hakim's eyes followed me a moment. I was so close to letting my fist fly. I didn't realize my fist was balled up until I noticed the watch on my wrist. I excused myself for a moment. Hakim was obviously in there, and HE got me the Rolex! But now, I was so damn confused. Was that ELYEUH or Hakim, or both? It seemed like he was Hakim, then suddenly that RING…Fuck! I took a sip of water in the kitchen, watching as Mandisa began to pass out her gifts.

Hakim stared at me sinisterly, asking, "Cyrus? What's wrong?            You            look            pissed? My phone vibrated in my pocket before I could respond. I reached in, checking it.

"Merry Christmas, Darius," Sami had texted me.

I wanted to throw my damn phone suddenly. My mood dipped suddenly, and I needed to relax. I scratched my head and glanced around as my stomach growled. I hadn't eaten today. I hadn't even given out my-

I had left the bag of everyone's gifts in the closet by the door at home! I remembered Mandisa's bracelet because it was in my truck! Okay, I could just swing by my crib and pick the gifts up.

"Cyrus? For real, you looked fucked up, Bro?" Hakim asked. This time he looked sad and worried with a nervous frown. Okay…I'm tripping…The ring must be playing tricks on my mind. Hakim is really responding to me. I must look crazy as fuck!?

"Yeah, I'm golden, Bro," I lied, attempting to smile.

Mandisa smiled at me as she came over and handed me my gift with a sweet smile. I put my phone on the counter and took the offering. I opened it and smiled at the irony. She got me a new phone, Mandisa loved Iphones, and I hadn't bought a new phone in years. Mandisa always gave from the heart when she thought of people. She was always thoughtful, and I realized all the shit I bought her…I was just buying because I could. The damn bracelet wasn't really from the heart. I was just trying to show out because I believed Hakim would drop the Christmas ball. He never celebrates Christmas….I didn't think Mandisa had changed him that much…Staring at that ring on her finger made me feel like shit. But I couldn't fuck up her vibe. She was happy, and Mandisa deserved to be satisfied with a ring like that.

"This is just what I needed, Queen," I thanked Mandisa smiling. "Really, I'm about to change my number."

Hakim's frown grew more severe as he stood and came closer to the kitchen. Mandisa grinned, saying, "I never know what to buy you. Darius, you have everything. I only wanted to get you something I knew you would use."

"No! What? I really needed a new phone, Queen. Thank you so much for thinking of me. I've got to start thinking about when I spend.

'Say, I just realized…I'm gonna run and grab everyone's gifts," I tried to assure Mandisa.

She didn't seem convinced that I liked her gift. That wasn't it at all. Sami's texting and EVERYTHING was messing with my head. I was starting to think I was seeing and hearing shit when I looked at Hakim. I reached to get my coat from the hanger. Hakim caught me as I stepped out on the porch.

"Mia or Sami, Bro? I know that face!" Hakim worried as he closed the screen door.

"Sami, this time," I answered, frowning. "I'm done, Bro! I can't take it anymore. It's been going on for months now. Someone's always calling and fucking up my head! If it's not Samatha Reed or some chick…it's Mia! I don't have anything to say to any of them.

'Sami has been calling and texting just to piss me off. She doesn't want shit but to get in my pockets again!"

"Do whatever you need to do, Cyrus. Don't worry about that girl. She knows how to get to you if you let her. You can't be afraid of her, though. You're going to have to confront her one day, so she gets the point and lets you go for good," Hakim told me, concerned. "I've seen her back around THE VIEW, but she doesn't recognize me without my crown now. But I don't talk to her. She's still crazy, Bro!"

Hakim glanced back, watching Mandisa pass out the rest of her gifts and give hugs. I stared down at her and suddenly wanted to know. I hit his arm, asking, "Hakim, why didn't you tell me about the ring?"

"You knew it was coming, Cyrus. You just didn't know when me either. I've had it for months. Every time I tried to propose, I got this feeling that she might say no. I know she loves me, but I guess I was afraid that she loves YOU more. Of course, that's probably Lionel's fault. He hyped me up to the thought.

'Today, I decided that if she did shoot me down, at least I'd know who she would say yes to. It wouldn't be the end of the world if I lost to you. So, when are you going to propose? The longer you wait, the more doubts you're going to have….You know how anxiety starts to build up with you? Well, that ring has driven me crazy for months!" Hakim confessed, shaking his head with a frown.

"It's the most beautiful thing I've ever seen Hakim…and that speech… I could never say something like that, Bro," I sighed as I folded my arms, thinking. Hakim really had me beat in all departments. I was hanging on by a thread, but Mandisa just kept smiling at me sweetly. "She deserves it all, and I just want to be the one to give it to her. I want to make her happy, Hakim. I think I get what you mean by picking and choosing my battles. You can't win them all. But, in the end, the smile on her face is worth more than all the money in the world."

"Cyrus, Man, stop trying to compete with me! I'm not the enemy, remember? We are brothers, and that woman loves us both. You're just going to have to learn to chill with the over-the-top shit and get serious about what SHE wants, not what you want to buy her, to complete your desire to flex," Hakim said sadly, shaking his head. "What are you going to do with your life? If Mandisa marries me, I will be the kind of man that she would be proud to say is her husband. If WE take this all the way…like we're doing….WE need to know that you will not just use US for the ride when you spend all your money, Cyrus….That's ALL…I'm trying to get you to see. A king has to provide income so that there is security for the queen, remember?"

I was pissed off, and I didn't want to hear that shit again! Hakim's favorite subject lately was trying to get me planning for shit! I didn't know what I was going to do! Shit, we're still young! He acts like he's got his shit all figured out, so we all have to be on his level. This is the shit that Lionel hates when he says Hakim thinks he's better than everyone else. He very arrogantly rubs his Master Plan in your face and keeps asking, "So what are YOU gonna do?"

I smiled at Hakim and nodded, "You're right, Man. I don't know why I'm always trippin. As long as Mandisa's pleased, then nothing else matters, right? I'm gonna run to the crib for the gifts…Don't eat all that food!"

I got in my truck and sat in it, warming it up a moment lost in thought. Mandisa came outside. She walked over and put her hand on the window. I let it down as I stared at that damn ring. I frowned…It was getting late…and that motherfucker was glowing in the darkness.

"Why are you so sad, Darius? I can see you are upset about something…Are you angry with me about something?" Mandisa worried with the saddest eyes touching my cheek. I smiled as her warmth affected me, but I couldn't look at her wearing that ring. I shook my head and peered back, faking a grin.

"I'm fine, Queen. I'm just making a run to the crib to get the gifts. But I have yours right here," I remembered as I hoped that maybe the bracelet would make her see. I really spent a lot to see her happy. I offered her the black velvet box. She took it in her red nails, and I smiled at her little snowmen on the tips. Those gold and black diamonds set me back nearly 25 thousand. But I knew it didn't come close to *Hakim's Heart*. "Darius! This is so beautiful! I'm going to treasure it. You ARE coming right back, oui? We will have dinner soon, and I KNOW you are HUNGRY."

Why did it sound like she was making fun of me? Mandisa would never…I just needed to get the fuck away and think for a minute. I was gonna come back. But I needed to clear my head.

"You are disappointed in my gift, Darius? I am so sorry…I only wanted to get you something-," Mandisa tried to apologize.

I shook my head and backed out of the driveway. I knew she was going to say that. Mandisa took everything so graciously with a beautiful smile and open heart. It could have been one of those plastic braided bracelets we used to make in school, and she'd love it. But she wouldn't love anything…like that ring.

I headed home. After grabbing the gifts and changing clothes, I dove back into Mercedez, but I still felt down. The longer I thought about that ring and going back around Hakim….the angrier I got. I tried to clear my head, so I turned on the radio. They were advertising a part for Christmas at Gucci's. The radio kept taunting me, making me laugh, "Cyrus…night….holy…night?... Maybe I was too high…? I had sat and smoked a blunt.

I smiled as I started the truck. Shit, I might as well go to see what was up since I had changed and didn't feel like sitting in Hakim's arrogant face. I could get a drink and have a little fun without him, and I needed to have some fun. Anything would cheer me up.

At least Kaliah was gonna be arriving tomorrow night. I just needed to avoid Hakim for a bit longer. He was rubbing me the wrong way on purpose….No…Hakim was trying to help…It's THAT NIGGA that was trying to fuck with my head. But he was scared of Kaliah. I didn't really like the idea of Kaliah coming to Texas. Of course, Trisha could pop up, but Hakim was scaring me, and I knew Kaliah would knock him back in his spot.

So, I made a right, hit I-20, and headed West just outside the city limits to get my head right.

#

"Cyrus?! Bro, what up? It's been a minute! I thought you were out of here again, Man?" Billy-B chuckled as I slid through the door, handing him a bill.

It was nicely decorated, music was dope, the Dj was playing that new *Cardi-B* single, and the ladies were tearing up the floor, so I headed to the bar watching the dancefloor. Niggas were everywhere, moving and vibing.

"What can I get you, Hot Chocolate?" I heard a cute voice ask from behind. I turned around and froze. I could have swung, but instead, I stared at her. Her big green eyes locked on my face and slowly scanned. She had light creamy skin, sandy blonde hair like caramel waves down her shoulders, and her sweet face made me want to break her nose. Samantha Reed smiled at me, and I pretended to be glad to see her.

273

I lit a blunt and exhaled, struggling to raise my spirits. Finally, I glanced at Sami, asking, "You work here, now?

"Yeah, for about four months now. Where have you been hiding?" She questioned me, leaning over the bar. Her long hair fell over her shoulders and covered her breasts barely covered in her Santa bikini.

"That's great! Give me a bottle of Remy Red! It's Chrima, and I need to get in the fuckin spirit," I demanded, flashing away back at the dancefloor.

There was no way I was going to sit here and be friendly to this fake bitch. I knew what was coming…If she mentioned it…I swear…I might snap. I was gonna have my drink, make some moves, and get the fuck away from Samantha Reed. I don't hate…many people…but she can't seem to get the point that I HATE her.

I glanced at my baller-ass new Rolex, and it was only 8:30. I wasn't going to stay much longer. I just needed a buzz to let some steam off dancing and then head back to the Dunn's crib. I had plenty of time. I kept looking at my gift from Hakim! That shit looked so fly in the club lights! The diamonds with the gold look like sparkling Christmas lights!

Sami sat my bottle nearby, and I took out my wallet and handed her a bill. She took it, and I noticed she was wearing the ring I bought her years ago. Samantha noticed me staring and smiled with her eyes sparkling at me.

"I never take it off, Darius. It means a lot to me," Sami explained, frowning. "If you want it back…you can have it."

She sighed, watching me, and started to take it off, and I stopped her as I filled my glass. I shook my head, saying, "No, I don't need it! You keep it…What am I going to do with it?"

"Darius, look, I know I hurt you back then. I was really messed up, but you were always so sweet to me. I took you for granted. I'm sorry, but if it's not too late-," She started as he tried to touch my hand, and I pulled my glass away with my hand smiling.

"I've got a girl, Samantha," I interrupted her thought. She sighed sadly, with her face suddenly devastated.

"I should have known by the way you wouldn't speak to me. She's a lucky girl…Look, I'll stop the calling, okay? I'm not trying to ruin anything for you. I thought that maybe if you were single and lonely….you missed me…a little? I hope we can be friends again one day? We used to have so much fun when we were kids. I miss the old days. How's Hakim and Lionel?" Samantha asked. That did it! I was pissed the fuck off even more now! Always with Hakim! Really?

I rolled my eyes at her taking a sip shaking my head. There was always going to be someone I cared about who thought that Hakim was better than me. Well, guess what, bitch? You're not good enough for him, and I'm going to hurt you, now.

"Hakim and Lionel are doing great, Sammie! Hakim just got engaged to a gorgeous girl. She's so beautiful that she's a damn model for a high-end place. He's thrilled!" I laughed, noticing the sudden dip in her spirits. "Oh, and Lionel is with May-May, now. He's good, too! We're all doing Gucci!"

Samantha stared at me, lost for a second, then faked a smile, "That's wonderful, Darius….I'm glad you're all so happy…wow! Hakim has a girlfriend? Really?"

"Fiance, he bought her this big-ass rock! It has to be worth a couple hundred thousand. He's dead serious about his Queen," I added, being messy as hell correcting her rudely and smiling like a demon. I sipped my Remy and raised my eyebrows. Whoa…It's hitting a little quicker…right…no food today…I'm cool…I just need to pace myself.

"Wow…Hakim? That's crazy…." Sami sighed, moving her caramel waves back, appearing disappointed.

"Oh, yeah…I've started thinking about proposing to my queen soon. I'm just trying to figure shit out for the future, but I know she's ready for me, and I'm in love," I chuckled, rolling my eyes playfully, taking another sip.

Okay, I'll admit it. I still loved Samantha Reed, but I hate her guts now. She sets me off because I know she fucked Hakim, and neither of them will admit that shit! It's written all over her sweet, sad face. Hakim knows how much I loved Samantha, and he'll never tell the facts. I know he's lying, and that's why I can't trust HIM completely. Both of them….are liars.

I might be a little tipsy right now. But I know enough about myself to admit my true feelings and intentions. I keep getting the feeling that ELYEUH is trying to use all of us. Hakim may be losing his hold, and THAT NIGGA may take over for good. Then what? That's the future that Hakim hasn't planned for, and he expects me to stick around to stop it from happening. But treating me like trash isn't keeping me close. I'm at my wit's end, and THAT NIGGA shouldn't be merely my responsibility. I'm not his fuckin father, and he's not going to keep talking to me like he's my dad! I don't speak to my DAMN DAD! He doesn't need me, and I don't need him!

Hakim needs me. I miss him when I leave, but I can get ghost, and no one will know where Cyrus went. But I can't leave without knowing where I officially stand with Mandisa. I love that woman, and I don't want to let her go, but if she chooses ELYEUH, then there's nothing I can do but let her go…just like this one.

I hate it here. I should move around, but I'm starting to feel really good. So I'm gonna have another drink, and then I'm gonna get down the floor, like a pimp…quoting David Banner.

"Sammie! Here!" I heard someone calling and glanced over….Miss Mia! Sami went to the boss lady.

I couldn't help but stare. Mia always looked like a million dollars tucked in a short black dress, with that beautiful long black Indian hair, creole skin, pretty brown eyes like a thick chinky-eyed Barbie. Those curves should come with warning signs. Fine like wine aged with time, a drink of sweet sexiness, shaped like Thicky Minaj with those big ole hips and titties! I blinked and tried to look away as she had Sami make some drinks and take them to the V.I.P. section above.

That skirt was tiny! Too short, so teeny if she bent over a nigga could see the pearly gates! I knew she never wore panties, either! Her thick thighs ran down to those stiff calves, and she wore those heels with the straps that wrap all around the women's legs up. Oh damn! A Chrima pedicure with matching nails! Fuck me!

I glanced away, finished my glass, poured another, and left my bottle on the bar. I knew no one would touch it. I went to the stage and just started getting active to clear my mind. I was in the zone, yah boy was feeling no pain, I was high and feeling good! Remy got me feeling terrific! I was feeling so damn right. I danced with every woman there! I didn't care…I was just dancing. Every thick girl in the club was my target!

"Come here, big girl! Let Cyrus show you how to make that thang work!" I screamed, twerking with a lovely thick sista. I was lit!

I ran back to the bar to get my drink and was right back out there on it! I was smoking, drinking, and working that motion in the ocean. Then, when a slow jam came on, someone tapped me on the shoulder. I was out of it as I turned around laughing.

"What's up, Big Man?" Miss Mia giggled as she yanked my hair. I smiled, staring at her plump, sexy, red lips. She had the mouth that made 'Jody' jump, and she knew how to kiss him.

"Oh, hey, Mia," I managed to say nervously. She smiled, coming closer. Her hips wiggled just taking a step, and her ass wobbled under that miniskirt, and I exhaled deeply, looking around scanning for Tony. Miss Mia had a body that would make a nigga toss a check…nothing on her was small…she was a juicy peach. I was avoiding her because I knew….I knew if she saw me…She wanted to FUCK!

"What are you doing here on Christmas alone? No Lionel and no Hakim…just all the chocolate I can swallow…I must have been a good girl to get this gift?" Mia flirted with me as she touched my stomach with her red tips.

"Um…I'm just here for a minute. I haven't seen the place in a while…It brings back memories," I told Mia, glancing around because she was getting too close for comfort. My head started swimming suddenly.

"You've danced with everyone but me, Cyrus…come on?" Mia sang, pulling me close. She twisted my hair around her red and white Christmas nails, and I took a drink right out of the bottle. She put her arms around my neck, and I grabbed her hips, slowly began to wind against Mia's softness, and stopped….Whoa! No! What am I doing? Nigga are you crazy!? "Why haven't you called me, Cyrus?"

Mia gaped up at me, entertained as she pulled my hands lower to her behind. My fingers slid down, and I squeezed that soft yet firm giant peach. Miss Mia got a big ole ass that's so soft and round. God, why did I do that shit!? I groaned as I shut my eyes feeling 'Jody' starting to wake up. I bit my lip and moved my hands back up as I pulled my body away from her. But Mia doesn't dance distantly…I knew that shit…That's how she got me the first time!

Mia has been fucking me constantly since the first time we danced when I was 15. One dance with me, she got Jody excited and wanted HIM, not Cyrus. She loves this dick but keeps running back to her evil, raping, lying, cheating, beating, and crazy half-Italian husband. At first, I felt terrible for Ms. Mia because I had feelings for her. I really thought that I could be the man she needed to be happy with. However, once the sex is over, She can't leave the man who made her what she is today. She loves the club life, and she'll fuck any dude that feels sorry for her enough to catch feelings. I realized the last time I left…when I broke up with Sami…Miss Mia will never leave Pretty Tony. I tried to get her on a plane to come to New York and visit, and she made up a big lie. Strangely enough, I only hear from her or see her when I come to Gucci's, so I stay away. But tonight, for some reason…why are my exes all here trying to get me back? I got Mandisa, and I don't need the drama these other women bring. I don't get it…I wasn't good enough back then…so why do they keep sweating me?

I stared around at all the pretty flashing lights trying not to focus on her at all. I kept telling myself, now is the time to leave! My head was so heavy, and I was dizzy. I made up a lie really quick, "I've been busy with work, school, and bullshit…you know? I…don't…get out…much anymore, Mia."

"Look at me, Darius?" Mia called, putting her nails on my chin and stroking my lips.

"Naw, that's not a good idea, Mia….I got a girl, you've got a crazy-ass man, plus he's probably watching your ass right now! You know he hates me!" I chuckled, looking around, ready to get gone. Instead, I took another drink from my bottle.

"Fuck that nigga, Darius! He can't make me feel like you," Mia giggled, stroking my chest through my shirt. I chuckled to myself nervously and took another drink. "We can go out back, and I can show you just how much I missed you?"

Mia's hand moved down my chest, and she grabbed my shit! Jody started growing as I jerked back nervously, hitting the barstool.

"I got a girl now, Mia! Don't play with me like that, alright? We're just dancing. You know you won't leave that nigga for anyone. You always…do…this shit…I'm …cool," I told her, smiling, but I was wrecked.

"Where's your girl, Darius? Is she here now?" Mia asked, putting her head on my chest and squeezing my ass.

"She's at home with the fam…." I told her.

Looking across the dancefloor, hoping the song ended. I wasn't sure what music was playing…I was that far gone! When I tried to take another sip of liquid courage…My bottle was empty! Good! I needed a reason to move around. I headed back to the bar and left Mia on the floor. I tossed the bottle and sat at the bar. Samantha came leaning closer…I noticed her frown and shook my head.

"Darius, you need to stay away from Miss Mia…I'm not playing! Pretty Tony is going to fuck you up! Everyone that works here knows he's crazy about his wife….Go home!"

Sami said seriously. I stared at her, and my head jerked back as my eyes bugged out.

"I know you're not talking to me! You don't give a flying…fuck…about Cyrus….Samantha! I ain't good enough, I'm too immature, so I'm just trying to like Hakim, right?" I laughed, trying to hold my balance and light my blunt. I suddenly fell over sideways, laughing. I needed to get my fucking swag back. Went to see Djay!

"What's up, Osiris!?" Djay laughed, setting up the music as I climbed up, trying to maintain. "You look like you're wasted, Bro! You need a bump to get right, man?"

"Fuck yesh! Set me up, Mr. Djay! You are my nigga!" I laughed.

I was leaning on the wall holding myself up while he cut me a few lines of coke. I tried to roll the bill, and he laughed at me and helped. I leaned down and snorted that first line…It hit my brain, and I coughed. I held my nose, and Djay fixed another. I took the second on the other side, and….my heart started racing…the lights grew so soft and pretty…the music felt great against my feet through the floor as I took a step down. I was high as fuck! I fell into a fucking mode.

I flew back to the bar, sat, fired out my blunt, and rolled my eyes as Sami came back with the bullshit, "Darius, go home!"

"Fuck that shit! I'm a grown-ass man! I'll go home when I'm ret to go home! Give me another bottle! Your job isn't a therapist. So get my damn drink, and don't worry about Cyrus! I can handle my shit!" I yelled, smoking my blunt. My heart was pounding wildly, and I was talking 100 miles a minute. Samantha stared at me then walked away. "Chop! Chop! No sippy, no tippy!"

I shook my head, laughing as I looked around as the lights started changing again. Shit...I needed to be in motion! I ran back to the dancefloor and started getting it in again. I was on every song, feeling like the world was mine, and I loved that shit!

"Cyrus got the floor tonight!" Djay shouted over the mic. I laughed my ass off and didn't give a fuck as I took over the club. I had the night of my life, and I was just getting fired up. I wasn't about to go home yet. I was still in the zone and was gonna ride it out until I sobered up. What the fuck! It's Chrima...and I'm partying.

I went back to the bar to get my bottle, and Sami stared at me as I paid the bill.

"What's wrong with you?" She asked me, frowning with her face all twisted up like a witch.

"What? I'm not the same lovesick puppy sniffing around after…you anymore, girl. I've changed, and I don't need you trying to be my mama! My mama is dead, and that position is not accepting applications alongside dad," I told her, frowning back at her with the same damn face. I took out about $600 and put it on the bar as I grabbed my shit. "Here, for you! That's all you want anyway…right?"

I got up and started to the back, where the real shit was going down. The club had girls on poles, topless dancers, waitresses, and less Samantha Reed for me to deal with back there.

I sat at a table and put my bottle down. I took a drink and sniffed. Shit…my high…lifted, and the room looked so cloudy and colorful. My phone vibrated, and I grabbed it out of my pocket. Lionel?

"What up, little baby bro?!" I laughed, talking fast.

"Yeah….what's… up, Cyrus?" Lionel asked, talking slowly as fuck! I laughed because Lionel's mouth was always a motor…I was just really high!

"Shit, I'm chilling, Bro! What's good in the hood? What's new in THE VIEW?" I chuckled, glancing around.

"Where you go? Hakim and Mandisa said you were coming right back? You got the music turned up…" Lionel started with a million questions being too nosey.

"Hey, Baby, you need anything?" A dancer wearing nothing but a G-String and a smile asked me.

"Come back in five minutes. I'm on the phone, Delicious One," I laughed, sticking out my tongue at her as she wiggled away.

"Nigga! You at Gucci's without ya boy?!" Lionel screamed in my ear. "That's fucked up, Cyrus! Come get me! We can tear that shit up. It's just 10 pm!"

"I'll be back in a few, Bro! Just chill until I get there, peace, Ase, and holla!" I cried, hanging up. I gazed around, grinning. I brushed my nose and shut my eyes, taking a drink.

"Merry Christmas, Cyrus…" I heard Mia say to me.

I opened my eyes, and lights had me dazed. My vision was fuzzy, and the music was buzzing in my ears. Mia stood in front of me, holding up a piece of mistletoe. I blinked as she sat in my lap and held it over my head. Mia leaned toward me, and her breasts nearly popped out of the top of her dress! I groaned, seeing her more and more as she rubbed her softness against me. Jody was wide awake now. I fell back in my seat, and she opened her legs, pulling my hand down…and making me touch her pussy lips.

"Damn, Mia, you're so wet…." I moaned as she smiled, grabbing my keys out of my pocket.

"Come on, Baby, let me taste some of his sweet chocolate?" She whispered, taking my hand and pulling out the back door.

#

The next thing I knew, we were parked in the back of the club. I was wrapped uptight, and Ms. Mia was riding Jody like a jockey at the Kentucky Derby! I must have blacked out a minute ago after we came outside! I don't know how I got in my truck! I couldn't remember what happened, and all I could do was cry as I realized what I was doing! If anyone finds out about this shit…It is a wrap! Everyone is going to hate my guts for how I fucked up shit! How could I be so fucking stupid when I knew in the back of my mind it was just me up in my fucking feelings because…I want to tell Mami how I feel about Mandisa, but I'm too afraid. People are going to look at me like a punk for trying to share my girl with Hakim.

I know what niggas will say…I've said that same shit about Kaliah. I didn't believe that the Contract would work, so I became jealous and made Hakim get serious. All of this…even that ring…it's all my fucking fault. Now I'm gonna lose Mandisa…this is my goddamn karma for not believing in her. I deserve these women because…I don't know how to accept real love. This is precisely what I should have known was coming from all those strange coincidences trying to warn me to really change and get serious about what I need. Get off of me, woman! I couldn't feel much of anything as I came to suddenly able to more and quickly pushed her off me.

"Stop…Mia…get off of me!" I yelled as I came to frowning. Mia stared at me as her eyes teared up. "What the fuck is going on….I'm really high right now! Stop! I got a girl, this is so fucked up…what the fuck…?"

"We're already here, so let's just finish what we started. Nobody will know," Mia sighed, trying to climb back on me. I grabbed her face and made her look at me. I was so angry I wanted to hit her, but I couldn't. I was the one that fucked up. I failed the fucking test! I couldn't be angry at anyone but myself, but Mia was not trying to let me be great! So I had to make her feel me this time. I was really done!

"Get the FUCK out of my car, MIA! I love her!" I screamed as the tears ran down my cheeks.

Mia lost it and started swinging on me! I opened the door and pushed her out. As she fell to the ground, I pulled myself together and fixed my clothes. Mia was so mad she was red in the face. I got out and offered her my hand because I wasn't trying to hurt her. I was angry and scared.

"Fuck you, Darius! You ain't shit!" She screamed, refusing my help.

I bit my lip and nodded. I hate those words. When a woman said that to me, it reminded me of Ms. Trisha, Kaliah's wife. I took the condom and tossed it in the grass, and left her sitting there. Mia got up and skated. I was about to jet, but I couldn't find my phone…

Fuck! I must have set it on the bar inside. I stretched to get my car keys, and as I reached into the ignition, I heard a loud click! I felt something cold touch the back of my head through my hair. I backed out of the truck.

My head turned slightly left to see the barrel of a 9mm pointed toward me, and I froze, spotting several of Tony's boys with guns drawn! How did they get here so fast? I didn't see any signs of the nigga or his homies the entire time. Or…maybe…they were here the whole time…and I didn't notice because I was fucked up?!

"Sup, Cyrus?!" I heard a familiar voice laugh from behind me. "Turn around, slowly, Man? Let me see them black-ass hands. I know you keep a piece in there somewhere, nigga."

I slowly took a step back and turned around, holding up my hands. Tony was staring at me…. face to face. His high-yella, bald-headed, half Italian, girl raping, drug pushing, pimping, pussy-ass nigga, all that, plus short stroking Vienna Sausage having-motherfucking-ass was laughing at me? In what fucking world is he living in…? I've never been afraid of Tony; that's why I fucked Mia the first time. But I do not fuck around because of this same shit here. He doesn't fight niggas. He jumps niggas, so he doesn't have to fight. Then he usually runs a nigga off, or they come up missing. I typically get ghost because he's never caught me slipping like this, but I keep pressing my luck. Been a while since I'd seen Tony.

He was getting fat…must be eating well these days. He was starting to look more and more like Tony Soprano, with more hair on his arms, than his head. How you gonna put on open designer shirts with white teeshirts and still look like a picnic table with those horrible khaki pants and white sneakers…? Then think you flexing with those rusty gold chains and tacky pinky rings. Kill yourself…niggas…no taste…unless it's for all kinds of spaghetti…I bet? You fuck with only the sisters but act like you're white and better than us! I never saw Tony fuck with white women or any other color but black! All the girls he fucked and raped were all black. That's the main reason I couldn't stand his FAKE mobster ass.

One of his niggas brought him my cell phone.

"Lose something?" Tony asked, holding up my phone. My eyes lingered but drifted when I saw Mia come up behind them. The bitch actually stood by her husband. "I told you if you fucked up and came around my shit alone, I was gonna make you feel me, Baby!"

I glared at Mia, starting to feel like this bitch set me up! What the fuck would she get out of telling Tony I was there? I bet she didn't tell him what she was doing to keep me here? My lips parted, saying, "Couldn't have it your way, so you ran back like a good bitch again, huh?"

Tony's eyes shifted toward Mia, and he chuckled at her, "There you ho again, Bitch! Just when I think I got you trained right, you go and bite my goddamn hand? That's three strikes, Bitch! You're out!"

Tony snatched her by the hair and hit the shit out of her. He didn't use his hand. Tony used the butt of the gun; Mia hit the ground and laid there, not moving! My senses went back to Tony as he rolled his eyes, telling me, "Bitches are a dime a dozen, Cyrus! In my world, a fine bitch is like a dollar. You save some, you donate some, except you can always make more!

'But for YOU and ME....THIS ain't about a HO, not MIAAAA....Nooooo!

'I've always known she's a ho! But Courtney, that's my BLOOD, Nigga! I don't give a FUCK about Mia anymore, but my DAUGHTER?! You can't walk away from this bid, Homeboy. You gots to do your time, Potna!"

Oh, Shit! This nigga was trippin! I never fucked Courtney…that was the girl that Hakim had to take to the fucking Emergency Room. He was getting us mixed up! I was in New York when that shit happened…but there was no way Tony Guccione could know that. I had stopped coming around once he found about Mia the second time!

"Tony, I swear to God, I didn't touch Courtney! We were just friends," I told him honestly, raising my hands higher as Cory, Tony's brother, pushed the back of my head with his gun! I really never fooled around with his daughter. She liked me, and we hung out. She wasn't my type. Courtney was light but too skinny for me. I didn't mess with slim girls...ever. "You know me, Tony. I only like thick redbones....I don't even holler at skinny girls. I've been coming here since I learned to drive."

Tony walked around thinking for a moment, and he glanced down at Mia on the ground. He leered at me and nodded.

All I could think about was how much I had fucked things up. I kept telling myself I should have gone back home. I was jealous about a ring and Hakim's proposal. I should have just sat down with them and had a talk about when we were going to tell Mami. I would have had answers instead of a headful of doubt. Mandisa was the only girl that truly loved ME, and I had fucked up everything! There was no way she would forgive me for this....I felt a tear run down my cheek as I exhaled into the cold night air. My heart broke as the wave of disappointment and shame that facing them meant flooded my thoughts.

Tony suddenly popped right in my face laughing again, "Why you crying, Bro? You scared?!"

"Yeah, I'm scared...." I answered seriously. "But ...I'm not scared of you, Tony. I fucked up....I may never see my girl again. If she finds out about this shit...she'll never....

'Go ahead and clap me! If I lose her over this....I don't want to live."

Tony suddenly grinned at me and dozed, asking, "Oh, you mean that fine piece of sunshine you bring to the party with the Dunn boys? She's out front right now! I think I'll let you watch while the boys and I have a little fun with her. Then she can watch us pop you! Cory...Dog him!"

"Don't you touch her, you piece of shit!" I shouted about to floor, Tony.

I heard the guns go off! I felt only a little after that, a blow to the chest, something made things go dark hitting my head again...I know I was on the ground...pain...from everywhere...but I couldn't move...it was so hard to breathe so cold...and dark...

# Chapter Eight: Element/I Am

## Mandisa?

I stared Hakim down while Lionel tried to find Darius. I started to get the feeling that something was up after Hakim proposed. Darius was okay one minute, and then he suddenly didn't want to be near me!

"Hakim,… what did you do?" I questioned him sadly. I couldn't help but feel that their little game had gone too far! Why did my intuition keep telling me something horrible was going to happen? The longer Darius was gone, I became so anxious I couldn't eat, and it was getting late. Hakim seemed unhappy about something, but he was not saying much. Hakim was very loving toward me. But he would tell me Darius would return and to stop worrying when asked. Hakim was too calm! Darius was distraught when he left, and he didn't say goodbye! I turned fearful for him as I grew more tired…then I got mad. "You noticed his face just like I did! What happened?!"

Hakim abruptly stared at me thoughtfully through his designer gold frames. He glanced toward Lionel in the kitchen and frowned, saying, "You know how Cyrus is, Queen. He's in his feelings. Just let him be Cyrus. If we chase him, he'll just make up a lie and run. He never wants to talk about what's annoying him. He'd rather leave. You can't baby him, Mandisa. Cyrus is a full-grown-ass man!"

"You didn't tell him about proposing…? But we agreed that once school was over, we would tell Mami then move in together, making things official?

'I didn't expect the ring today. I knew you were going to ask, but not so soon. I'm happy to know you're sure, but it's not fair for you to act like Darius doesn't have a say in things. We are supposed to be equally invested in this relationship. A family…REMEMBER…?

'No wonder he is so upset! He must think the worst of us!" I breathed sadly, trying to keep my voice down. Sophia and Granddaddy were upstairs, and I didn't want them to know what we were discussing. But I was losing self-control as I grew more distressed about Darius's behavior and imagined he must hate us! "God, Lionel, can you please help a bitch comprehend what the fuck is going on!?"

Lionel grimaced with the most dismayed face and replied, "Calm…down, Sis. He'll answer…

'He's probably got it on vibrate. I'm gonna keep ringing until I get an answer. Hakim…why you so calm? You know what's up? Cyrus's possibly gonna bail; you did him dirty!

'I realize I was fucking with you about THE CONTRACT and shit....but it was just my way of seeing if you were seriously going through with it. I didn't think it would work at first. But you niggas operate equally...I can admit I was wrong about shit.

'You really don't care about our brother? Oh, I see...it IS just like I believed....you abandoned KALIAH for the same reasons....YOU'RE A HATER!"

"Lionel, Bro...It's not like you're thinking ...Cyrus... He just needs to stop performing so much...He needed this wake-up call to make him get serious about the future. I get sick of fussing about if he was going to find a purpose...He's my brother, Lionel!" Hakim grunted furiously. He glanced over at me, and I wobbled my head. "Don't look at me like that, Mandisa....I didn't make him leave! I tried to get him to chat with me, but he decided to move around independently. I'm concerned, but Cyrus can't keep playing with my feelings either. I STARTED THIS SHIT!"

"Got 'em!" Lionel shouted. I heard that, but my eyes stayed locked and loaded on THAT NIGGA! Oh, he must have gotten me confused with some OTHER BITCH?

I was relieved the instant Lionel got Darius on the phone. But now...I was pissed off at the nigga sitting on the sofa next to me informing me that HE governed this QUEENDOM!

"You clearly have me confused with one of those bitches that you said you bought, Nigga! Since when did THIS SHIT begin with you?! The last time that I checked, I was free? Thanks, nigga!

'But you don't own me, Nipsey Hussle & Flo, and you don't get to play Father MC to Cyrus or me! I don't display a fuck around Thomas King, so what the hell makes you imagine I was substituting HIM with YOU, 50 Shades of Pussy, Hakim Jahlil Dunn?!" I barked at him.

Hakim's eyes swiftly grew sad, and he skimmed over at Lionel apprehensively. Lionel was clutching the phone, gawking at me. Hakim blushed, staring at me, and droned, "Queen, can you please…. lower your tone…Sophie and G.D.?"

"Mhm….just like a sorry-ass nigga to be all mortified of his own affairs. Why're you nervous about getting exposed now, Hakim?! You didn't think about that shit when you were sneaky-freaky? You love to play the 'Master of Manipulation' because you're a narcissistic piece of crap deep down, and you don't want to get better…do you?" I demanded, seriously.

Hakim's eyes swelled redder. Lionel didn't make a move as Hakim's features hardened. I didn't care anymore. I was sick of the bullshit going on in my face and behind my back. Both of these niggas had to be bamboozled if they thought I would keep playing like I couldn't see. I went along with shit because….Yeah…WE wanted Hakim and Cyrus…They are fine as fuck…and love US…but I don't like what the fuck THIS NIGGA assumed HE got when it comes to US.

Uh…nah…I've learned enough from Lionel to smell the bitch in a nigga….That ELYEUH motherfucker is scared of ME, and I want to talk to him…RIGHT NOW!

"Keep Cyrus talking, Lionel…find out where he is….," Hakim stated promptly but holding his gaze on me as he withdrew backward on the sofa. His forehead crumpled while flaring his nostrils and smiling savagely handsome. The brown of his irises intensified into darkness, and he began scanning me as I crossed my arms. "Wifey…why would you talk to Hakim like a bitch off the block and not think that I wouldn't tell you how you DUNN fucked up!? You wanna FUCK or ….what?"

"I'm sick of hearing about YOU and your fucked up contests, Nigga!

'YOU got my sexual chocolate all in his feeling over a fucking ring, and for what? What's the FUCKING plan? You can't RUN me NIGGA, or did you not figure that shit out after the first time we fucked! I'm just like you! What is it....ELLIOT? ET? Or whatever you're making, the weak-minded hos call you! You are a NONFUCKIN FACTOR when it comes to ME!  Bottom line...I HATE YOUR GUTS!

'You never struck fear into my heart...there ain't much of that shit left after Tomny fucked me up...I'm much crazier than YOU motherfucker..... I'm the bitch that got her ass beat until she went crazy by A FATHER just like YOU!

'I kicked HIS ass and scared the motherfucker in HIM too. That's why he wanted to marry MANDISA off!

'Mami is scared of ME because I talk the talk, and I will walk that walk, nigga. I ain't scared to DIE...but you are...cuz...you're afraid of PAIN! You pop out to run women and intimidate men, but you don't really do shit but talk and fuck! How many bodies you got under your belt? You ain't down for the fam! You just a mad ho! How you a REAL NIGGA and you can't make the connection between love and lust, BITCH?

'You just like hitting motherfuckers that can't hit back....I have been watching you...You won't fight...just talk all that shit! Hakim has more heart. At least he would stand up for Lionel and Cyrus. YOUR BITCH-ASS just ran to find a bitch cuz you want your MAMA! I've been getting MY ass kicked by the white man my entire life...So...MAN, THE FUCK UP, BITCH!

'I know you better go find my OTHER NIGGA, or I WILL cut your bitch ass off and ride 'Jody' into the motherfuckin sunset...! But, since you allegedly started this shit...I'll finish it now!

'...WE want HAKIM....NOBODY here likes YOU, ELYEUH!" I told him seriously without lowering my voice. I was in that nigga's face and about to swing on his bitch-ass. "You want US, then YOU better give me some ACKRITE, like The Chronic 2001. You talk too damn much, BITCH-NIGGA! Stop scheming and looking hard...you ain't gangsta, BITCH!"

"He hit you...Queen?" Hakim wheezed as tears ran down his cheeks. Lionel's face nearly exploded with his eyes as he covered his mouth and hit the floor, trying not to let Hakim see him laughing. I was not trying to play with baby bro. If this didn't stop tonight...I was gonna put him on blast and cut him off for good. But I don't leave a motherfucker with a good impression.

Mandisa was just gonna have to overstand how you can't love some niggas out of shit. I knew he was a lost cause…but Paula… wanted him for his sweet side. All sweet AIN'T sugar, Sis…this nigga is ANTIFREEZE. "You never told me…why?"

"AND…? YOU HIT YOUR BITCHES, DIDN'T YOU?" I shouted. "That's how you get off…right? You mess with little girls' heads and beat them up so you can feel like a big man when you throw away your money? You can't accept that most of those women only spoke to you because they needed the money! You ain't that fine! Those hos want the cash security, and you just so happen to PROVIDE false SECURITY with that big mouth. The only HOPE you give a HO is that you will provide them with the cash, shut up, and leave. There's always another nigga that can fuck her better out there. But he doesn't have YOUR money, BITCH! YOU PLAYED YOURSELF, KHALID!!!

'You clowned Cyrus for trickin on bitches n shit being nice... wow! I see YOU paying mo money to fuck a bitch into submission, but that doesn't mean shit to a BITCH that grew up getting her ass beat! I don't need your money or your FAKE LOVE, Sadist Drake!

"You're inferior to Cyrus, projecting a false illusion of different, so you won't expose how weak you are under all that muscle! Now, look at you...the BIGGEST BITCH of them all...trying to run off a REAL NIGGA...because of what?... He has slight spending addiction? So he doesn't know what he wants to do with his life yet? He's 18, Nigga! Let him be great finding himself, BITCH...Why are you, Russian, since you always Putin on the white man so damn much? That's all you have on Cyrus...HUH?"

"BITCHES that try to FAKE being WOKE to run shit with no real heart ain't worthy of my time. So, if WE can't have just Hakim....then I don't NEED YOU...You can have your ring...If Darius is not in MY face in the next 30 minutes...That entails...YOU getting Cyrus home or ME to him in those 30 minutes....That's the time you've acquired and all I'm offering you to complete this task, NIGGA! I'm about to yeet yo ass off this ship, IMPOSTER!"

Lionel hung his head, attempting not to laugh as he put his phone in his pocket and slapped Hakim's shoulder. I was dead serious as I hit the stopwatch app on my iPhone. Hakim wiped his face and peeped over at Lionel, announcing, "He's at Gucci's, isn't he?! I had a feeling that he was going to run there to get fucked up. We got to move now! Tony will fuck him up if he knows Cyrus is alone! Go warm up Shun. I'm going to get my gun out of the big safe in the garage. Mandisa…YOU can't GO! *(Did this nigga just tell me what to do??! I'm about to fuck him up!)* Stay here with G.D. and Sophie…."

I gazed at him like his brain must be absolutely corrupted. Then, finally, I slanted my shoulders and rose, saying, "The FUCK did you SAY? Oh, now I'm rolling with Kid N Play, fasho! You can't tell me what the fuck to do!

'Leave me if you want…I won't be here when you GET back, NIGGA. TRY ME…"

"Am I the light-skinned dude with the big hair or the player, Sis?" Lionel questioned me, overthinking too damn hard but messing with Hakim. I raised my right eyebrow abruptly at Baby Brother, and he moved closer to the garage door, observing us. "I get it…My hair..and I'm the Kid brother…and ELYEUH is Playing too much…You funny, Disa!"

"NO!!!…. *(DON'T YELL AT ME, NIGGA!!! I know you see me saying this with my eyes, BITCH!)*… I don't want you there, Queen…It's too dangerous…. *(Thought so, BITCH, I am not playing with YOU anymore!)* We'll go find Cyrus...and bring him back...I'm sorry...I was stupid...OKAY...I'm sorry! I'm going to get my brother, but I can't take you!" Hakim wept, motioning Lionel to get to the car. Hakim put on his coat, crying like a child. "If anything happens to you...."

"This is ALL your fault for playing games with US. You've been using US all the entire time, so you could get what you wanted in the end...right, NIGGA? YOU trying to start a little harem, BITCH?

'Uh-uh...NOT using US!

'If anything happens to Cyrus...YOU'RE DEAD!

'I'll make it my life's work to destroy you...I SWEAR! Not only do I not want you to touch me, but if you try to fuck Paula, I will get out and fuck you up, just so you can't stay out, BITCH. YOU won't beat ME...I'm THAT BITCH that will help Hakim end it and go with HIM wearing a smile on my FUCKIN FACE! By any means necessary, ELYEUH...or whoever you want to be. We can both die tonight if you don't get me to my SEXUAL CHOCOLATE, Nigga! Let's Jet, Lee!" I terrorized HIM.

#

Hakim vaulted into the driver's seat, flew out of the driveway, and we headed for the Interstate Highway. He was driving like a bat out of hell because he only had 22 minutes to get to Gucci's, and I was keeping the time from the backseat on the very gorgeous golden watch Darius got me for my birthday on August 12th.

I loved how it has a digital app for my iPhone! I have to recommend this shit for the Queen with a busy schedule. I keep up with my modeling schedule with Antoine, school projects, test dates, nail and hair appointments, spa days, AND…It's perfect as a GPS for when you need to roll up and kick a nigga's ass! The navigation app connects to anyone you send your location to and will stay on until you find the area or turn off notifications.

Darius was so afraid Daddy would snatch me away…he bought it thinking he could find me anywhere on the planet. I thought it was cute. Hakim thought it was a waste of money…So, now I'm using IT to calculate how long it takes him to find MY MAN…Oh, look…20 minutes so soon? I'm just getting angrier the longer it takes me to see that MY MAN is okay. I planed to make this BITCH fear me like SATAN! Since he wants Paula so severely, I can fuck his life up. Paula is my sister, and BITCH she doesn't like YOU either. I will drop Hakim, and WE will love all on Cyrus's black ass. HE fucked up!

"We could have been at Gucci's sooner if SOMEONE wasn't acting like a NARCISSIST with the people that love HIM…HO! Those niggas wouldn't run up on Cyrus if Lionel was in charge. Too bad PAULA fell for the WRONG Nigga…I know SHE loves Hakim's ass, but I only fuck REAL NIGGAS. You ain't SHIT, ELYEUH!

"You better act like this is a damn snowmobile and get us there right quick! MELISSA wants HER man, and you're running out of time, BITCH!" I warned him, polishing the screen of my iPhone. I flashed my Christmas manicure, gave him the finger in the rearview mirror, then I glanced at Lionel in the front passenger seat and grinned. "What's Brackin, Baby Bro? You ready for this shit…you know them niggas gonna be expecting y'all, right? I think I can distract them so you can find Cyrus. I play dumb, and you get to my nigga? We don't know how Flipptiy-Dippity up there is gonna act under pressure. He's a BITCH!

'I depend on you to hold shit down if he goes dumb-dumb. I don't think he gives a fuck about anything. But it's breezy ….I know HE has 15 MINUTES LEFT!"

"Sis, you fucked up in the head like Hakim? You don't talk to nobody like this…I'm confused as fuck! I'm trying to stay focused on the mission, but….This shit is turning me on! That's shit you said about Bitch Niggas…Chronic 2001?…Classic Funny!" Lionel moaned, spinning around in his seat. "Can I put my dick on yo shoulder so you can put it on yo mind later on?"

"Shut THE!!!…. *(YOU BETTER NOT TOUCH MY BROTHER, BITCH!!! I'm watching your every move now…These eyes stay wishing a NIGGA WOULD!)* fuck up….Lionel…" Hakim unexpectedly snickered as he smashed on the gas gazing back at the highway. "I'm … catching feelings… too!"

"FUCK YO FEELINGS….again…you ain't man enough for this Gansta Boo! I can pull a ho from Texas to Guatemala, teach you three ways to run you a ho, then show you four more, and you still won't know. So if you're not down to ride…KEEP YOUR Bitch-ass in the spectator's seat!

'This is the NBA draft, and your stats are being called. I don't know what you're thinking, but you will not have me out there sweating for a paystub. I'm no player! I'ma coach, and I'll teach you bitches how to lay up. You better play hard or go home…YOUR TIME…is nearly up," I warned that nigga seriously sick of his fucking BIG EGO. I checked my phone and kicked the back of his seat. "10 MINUTES, BITCH!"

#

I know that NIGGA got us in that parking lot with 6 minutes to spare!

Now I really didn't care as long I found Cyrus.

Elyeuh could jump off a cliff and do a swan dive! I knew he couldn't be trusted when he started trying to get me alone all the time. That's why this morning, I messed with his head so he would get off OUR dick for a minute. His games with Cyrus were pissing all of US off in here.

When I saw HIM picking on MY man…I started taking the wheel more and more. He goofed when he fucked US and let Melissa out. I only get out when Angel's mad, plays too much around CYRUS, or when ELYEUH tries to fuck PAULA. WE are triple mad at THIS NIGGA for fucking with all of OUR emotions. Surprise! Now you know!

It was ME that saw that CHOCOLATE GOD and pulled him in, and this little BITCH is not going to take MY KING from ME! I love my baby, and THAT NIGGA, fucked up giving him to US. So yeah, CYRUS is MINE! PAULA can keep Fake Songz! A REAL NIGGA makes a woman feels like a QUEEN in every way possible. Cyrus is always making US feel like gold, and THAT NIGGA just keeps playing so he can ho…He can GO! AND I MEAN THAT SHIT! He's going to straighten up this ACT of his, or WE will show him crazy! YOU don't know how many motherfuckers are in HERE. I ain't the WORSE…LMFAO!

I have to put on this fragile act so Tony will take the bait. I HATE playing the WEAK BITCH…that's ANGEL always crying and shit. Let's get this shit over…I need a foot rub, and these boots are making my feet hurt! Now we're here at this rathole, and if Hakim fucks over his family, he won't have to worry about the money he spent on the ring. I'll shove 5 karats up his ass when I give back!

Hakim gazed at Lionel over the top of his car as I got out, inspecting the parking lot for Cyrus's SUV. Lionel's eyes fastened on my face, worriedly, before he glanced at Hakim. Then, finally, Hakim shivered his head, sluggishly assessing, "We get inside, rush the club, find Cyrus, and get the fuck out of Dodge. You hold my piece, Bro! They never check you for weapons. They know I always have weaponry when I come, so I'll take the pat-down…. Queen can get in without any trouble.

'Queen? Oh...yeah...Melissa... Please...trust me on THIS? I know you are mad. But this is gonna get really intense quickly. Stay by the bar in front! Do not go anywhere near the back door without Lionel or me with you! If you see Cyrus, tell him to take you home, now, then call me. We can fall back when you're safe. But not before....okay?"

I nodded, agreeing because the nigga had a plan and seemed sure. If he came with the bullshit...I would run with Lionel and say fuck, Hakim. I knew Hakim could fight, but he held back all the time, afraid to throw down for real. This was not the time to nut up and be the BITCH that he is deep down inside. But I couldn't let him assume I was gonna do what he commanded, either. I wanted to see where the fuck Mercedez was. She wasn't anywhere in the front, and Cyrus doesn't play about his truck! He trusted me with a spare set of keys. I keep them in my bag because he is always getting lit and locking them in the trunk.

I walked around the club's side, ignoring Hakim scanning all the cars in the front parking lot near the club. Cyrus would never park where he couldn't get to Mercedez in a rush. So that meant he parked in the back of the club.

I've only been to this raggedy excuse of a kickback once, and we didn't stay long. Cyrus and Lionel got into a big brawl because that nigga Ugly Tony tried forcing me to dance with him. Hakim actually boxed the nigga off of Cyrus and got us out of here. But…here I am again…wondering what's so great about this shed?

I heard people sniggering and chattering round back, and as I skirted the building, I saw Mercedez parked under a tree. I ran over and unlocked the door, locating Darius's coat but no keys or phone in the pockets? He usually left his phone in the truck when he was in a club. That's why I was surprised Lionel got an answer at all. He hated talking over the music and didn't text unless it was an emergency.

The seat was pulled all the way up on the driver's side, and Darius's knees would hit the dashboard if he drove Mercedez like that. So I sat my bag down, inspecting the interior. I moved the driver seat back with the button and saw something sparkling on the floorboard. I reached down and picked up an oversized diamond hoop earring…I'd never seen it before…It didn't match any I owned…Okay…? But when I saw the golden condom wrapper on the passenger side floor, …near the door…

The wind picked up, it hit differently, suddenly colder, and I didn't have my coat with me. I must have left it home. I looked around in confusion…closing the door to the truck.

I put the earring in my back pocket as I started back to front. I was infuriated…. I wanted an explanation because I had put 2 and 2 together now CYRUS was in 4 it!

The nigga at the door, B-something, spotted me attempting to shoot his shot, "Hey, Sweet Love, Merry Christmas, Angel…! You look hot in red with those fly-ass boots…ooh…leather is so damn sexy. Save me a dance…please…Make my life complete? What's your name, Angel?"

"Sure," I pretended as he swung over, holding the door. I combed everywhere for Lionel or Hakim but didn't see them. "Melissa…Angel's my mother's name…I don't like being called that shit."

"Are you going inside, Babygirl, or do you intend to party out here with me?" That DUDE sweated me.

"I'm going in…I want to dance a little…I'm looking for my homie Cyrus? I know I saw his car outback, but I don't see him inside…You know him, right?" I tested, pretending to be some plain chick.

"Nope!" This lying-ass nigga replied seriously. "Never heard of nobody by that name, Beautiful Melissa. Your eyes are the greenest I've ever seen. But why you here looking for cars.….What car you talking about? Niggas cars all look alike all over here."

"Mhm…" I fake-agreed and went inside.

That nigga is a liar! The only time we came here together, he let us all in. He knew me, Cyrus, Lionel, and Hakim!

I glared around the dimly lit room with led Christmas lights. Smoke was dense in the stuffy space. There were decorations all over the walls, and folks were all over the dancefloor. The bar was active, and it was much more than it appeared from the outside. As I made my way across the floor exploring, I spotted Darius's friend, the Djay, and made my way over. Finally, I got close to the booth and waved my hand to him.

"Hey, Sugar-Cakes!" He laughed from above. This was the guy that Cyrus always talked about from Hot Wheels. He was Stevie's brother, so I knew he was straight! Mr. Djay was a fine piece of chocolate like Cyrus with a smile like money. But he was too old for me!  "Where's Hakim? I saw him at the bar a second ago."

I glanced back around, not seeing anyone, and frowned, asking, "I must have missed him. Have you seen Cyrus?"

"Yeah…he WAS swaying with the ladies and having a good time before he went in back. But 'ole girl, Sami, at the bar, must have pissed him off cuz he got out of there quick. But hey, you see Lionel, tell him I got a new song I want to hear him sing…."

The Djay stared down at me thoughtfully and gestured me to the backdoor with his big hazel eyes. I nodded as I shook his hand as I moved to the bar. I wasn't running back there alone. I believe Hakim when he said that shit gets real back there. That nigga Tony said some shit about making me his future wife if I danced as good as I looked! I heard that Gucci's was a strip club, but that's not what was going on in the back here the Djay was pointing.

As I got near the bar looking around for Lionel or Hakim, a cute young-looking girl wiggled toward me in her red faux fur bikini. I guess this is how hos tease the season around here? Texas gets some snow, and niggas don't know what to wear. Black rubber boots and fur bikinis…wow… it looks like these ho ho ho's are going hunting over the river and through the woods. She glared me down and faked a smile.

"What you need?" She questioned me with an attitude.

Okay, she was cute with her light green eyes, blond hair, tits, and ass all out, but she wasn't THAT damn cute. I would fuck the bitch up for acting sideways with me. But I was on a mission.

"I'm not thirsty…Do you know a tall black guy with long dreadlocks? His name is-," I started.

"Cyrus? Yeah, I know him. He's….an old friend that grew up across the street. He's here…somewhere. He's fucked up, and my Manager is-," She began seemly nicer to me, but stiffening up, and rushed off.

I glanced over my shoulder, and that nigga, Tony, was standing his half-light, bald-bull from Tyson's Punchout-looking ass behind me staring. I don't know who he thinks he is, but he seems like a fucking joke.

"You need something, Babydoll?" He asked me coming closer to me at the bar and sitting next to me. I pretended I couldn't hear because of the music and shook my head, smiling. He smiled at me with those gold teeth in his mouth and reached over to 'ole girl. That was when I spotted THAT motherfucker was rocking MY MAN's Christmas present on his wrist! I saw 'Osiris' in gold on the black band changing color in the lights. I held my snuffle. "Let me purchase you a cocktail, Sexy Lady? You don't come here often. I need to demonstrate that I'm a wonderful guy. God…you seem to get finer every time I look at you. What's your name, Sweet

Thing? I'm Tony Guccione, and if you play your sexy hand right...all this could be yours, Baby. I'm looking for a fine fresh fragrant fascination to fix my fucked up feelings."

"I'm sorry...Did you say drink? I do not drink much," I yelled playfully in a sweet, ignorant tone smiling. I had to wipe down my face like Lil Boosie from all the fucking F's he was spitting at me literally.

"How about a bump, then? Do you get down? I can get you anything to get you in the zone," Tony offered to try to flash MY Man's watch in my face holding up a bottle.

"A WHAT?" I asked, pretending to be dumb.

"You know...a line...coke...powder...that white girl? Shit...you're so cute. Where you from, France or some shit? That accent is sexy as fuck, Baby," Tony continued trying to pick me up politely. I pretended to be stupid to keep him from finding Hakim and Lionel. He couldn't be in two places at once...They could discover Darius and get him out of the club if I kept Tony interested long enough. He seemed too easy stuck on just everything he saw. So I played like I was interested in his little FIASCO, like Lupe.

"I do not experiment with the hard drugs. This is because I have a terrible heart condition that could be deadly if I get too stressed," I pouted sweetly with a sorry glance around like I was about to leave.

"Oh...No, Baby...don't look like that...I understand...My daughter, Courtney, ....she has a heart condition, and a nigga got her fucked up and nearly killed her. But, I would never mistreat a sweet angel like you...You're a flower...and I know your pussy has power!... Niggas would respect you because you're too delicate and lovely. They will adore the floor you walk on...Mmm...bad-ass boots, you got flavor.

'You're too superior for these ratchet hood niggas. I can put you somewhere where niggas with REAL money will compensate just to watch you change those sexy outfits. You'd never have to be met...but you need to leave that rotten Cyrus alone. He's too reckless and wild. He's a kid. I saw you model walk your fine ass in here and wiggling all over him the last time. You got some dangerous marmalade. What you think about that?"

"Tony, where's Ms. Mia?" The cute bitch from before interrupted Tony's ranting. I was happy as fuck because this nigga's game was anemic! He couldn't possibly be dragging all the bitches around here with this shit! I'm starting to think ELYEUH might be right about the hos he's been fucking. All these hos must be dumb as shit to fall for this thirst trap! I know 'Giggles' and me could tear this bitch up on a horrible day If we rolled like that. But we are bitches with class!....

These hos are like school in the summertime. You'll go to get to the next grade...but you don't want to pay for that shit....AND if you gotta pay...you only taking the shit...that you REALLY want.

"Mind your business, Sami...Mia quit," Tony told the server, amused. The bartender watched at me with the most frightening glimpse in her sad green eyes. She looked like she wanted to say something to me, but she strolled away in tears. He peeked back at me, and I pretended to be stupid, spotting the door Djay indicated.

#

Tony noticed where I was staring and grabbed my hand unexpectedly! My heart skipped several beats...I felt a stabbing pain beginning inside of my chest... I panicked! Suddenly...I realized who Sami was...and how she knew Darius...!

"There's no need to go in there, Angel. Some sick shit goes on back in THAT room," He chuckled.

"What?" I demanded, eyeing his hand as he suddenly stroked my shoulder.

My heart began to race more when he caressed me, and I didn't know what was happening! I kept glancing around for Hakim, Lionel, or Darius, but I didn't see anyone I knew. I nervously reached for my purse for my pills and suddenly realized. I must have put it back in the car after I took Darius's keys out. I stroked my temple as I suddenly felt overheated.

"You came here trying to find Cyrus? Oh, he's in the back…I wouldn't go back there, though…You're too fine to be here alone. Cyrus loves to visit the sex room and spend big paper on the girls in there. They love him in back," Tony hinted to me with a gleaming smile.

"Sex room?" I repeated curiously.

"Oh yeah, for the right amount of money, you can trick around with any of my pretty little girls here. All pussy has a price….after inspecting the size of that rock, Cyrus paid plenty for your cherry pie. Unfortunately for you, Angel, Cyrus can't keep his burnt dick in his britches, and he made me have to cancel one of my best bitches. But I suppose this is a good thing for me…looking at you makes a nigga's palms itchy…You know what that means?" Tony posed, staring into my eyes seriously with a frown and straightening up. "Snatch HER….She's mine!"

The moment he said that shit! Someone grabbed my mouth, and something was put over my head!

The cover was snatched off of my head after I was escorted through the door. It was brighter inside of this room than in the club. It looked like a storage room. There was only the bolted exit and shelves with boxes stacked like a warehouse. Tony stood in front of me and looked me in the eye. He had about six other men inside of the room. All wore the same dark shirts and light pants. As I nervously looked around, I struggled to remember what Hakim told me before we got here. I couldn't recollect much now. I spotted Darius and somebody else lying on the floor in a pool of blood and gasped, grasping my chest.

They were submerged in blood! Darius's clothes and hair were saturated! The floor all around him was dark red…I'd never seen so much before…

"DARIUS!!!" I sobbed, realizing the worse.

"Whoa, whoa, Babydoll, as you can see…Cyrus is a nasty nigga! The bitch next to him, my ex'd wife, Mia, she's a ho! When you place nasty niggas and hos together…well, shit happens. Don't it, Mia?!" Tony shouted as he yanked me away. I didn't fathom I had tried to run to him. But, I knew that something had happened all along.

Darius seemed like he was asleep with his mouth open but all the blood...! The woman lying suddenly stirred, sobbing on the floor next to Darius. She struggled to sit up and spotted all the blood and Darius's body, and started screaming.

She was crying. Her face was inflamed, bloodstained, and bruising, "Cyrus's just a kid, Tony! Let him go! I'm sorry, okay, but you're sick!.... I can't do this…all the raping and-,"

"Shut the FUCK UP, BITCH!" Tony barked at Mia. Tony struck her and pounded her out. I noticed one oversized diamond hoop in her right ear as she fell to the floor….

Tony glanced at me as I hid my mouth, pulling my arm back. He snatched my hand and groaned. "So, I got to take out the trash. But you…you're young and fresh….I could be persuaded to let Cyrus go…if you…do something for me. So what's it gonna be, Babygirl? You give the boys and me a sample of that French Cherry Pie, and I'll hand over your UNFAITHFUL piece of shit fiancé…huh?"

I moped, watching every man in that room eyeing me. They weren't going to take no for an answer, and Tony wasn't going to let Darius go! They had the vilest heckles on their faces. The only way out of the room was through Tony or his friends obstructing my retreat near Darius. That door was double deadbolted from inside, and I couldn't get it open fast enough if I escaped. I was petrified as I sensed my lungs panicking in nervous hilarity as Tony clasped my wrist tougher.

Tony smiled cruelly and yanked the sleeve of my sweater powerfully. I fought him and screeched, "I need my pills! What are you doing…Daddy? Stop…don't…please…?"

Tony ripped my sweater from my limbs, exposing my naked chest, and froze suddenly hearing. First, he peeked at me as I immediately shielded myself. Then, his smirk swiftly changed to bewilderment, demanding, "What did you say?"

"You're mad because my heart won't heal…I'm sorry I'm dying…Daddy…." I wept, covering my face. "I'll be good and marry him so you can have the money if you stop hitting Mami…just don't hurt my sister…please? You can kill me…don't hurt her…she's just a baby, Daddy…I don't care about the money…I didn't tell her that you let that man touch me….I am a good girl…oui?"

"What are you talking about? I'm not your Daddy, Girl?" Tony grunted, clasping my sweater, hesitating to touch me again.

"Queeeeeen....!" I heard a rattled shriek from the floor. Darius unexpectedly was struggling to move. He couldn't budge, but he was trying to get up!

"Darius!" I whimpered as I spotted his horrid face stained in blood, reaching with trembling arm for me. His braided locks were full of blood and dripping down to the pool below as his head shivered.

The walls of the room began vibrating close to Darius, getting louder and louder. Then, unexpectedly Hakim crashed through the back door!

His eyes were enlarged, and his countenance was grim as he sprinted through Tony and tackled him like a football player before anyone could make a move!

Hakim vaulted for the person closest to me and swung, knocking men out one after the other with overwhelmingly sharp strikes. He was shifting stances so fast, swinging his fists that I could feel the power from every strike he flung as I backed away toward the door. HE focused on protecting me and didn't stop moving until no one was left on their feet or conscious but Tony.

A coat was put over my shoulders. Lionel walked from behind me, holding the gun up with a smile on his face, and his eyes were wide as he stepped in front of me. Lionel made Tony stand up and pointed the gun at his head, gazing at Darius. He didn't even look at Hakim as he kicked the last man completely through a rafter, making the entire shelf collapse.

"So, you fucked up my brother because you can't control your bitches? I'm supposed to let your sick-ass rape my sister, too? Nigga, you are dumb…You know that we don't fuck with you, and then you fuck with us?" Lionel questioned Tony dragging the hammer back on the gun and laying it on Tony's head, tickled. "Did he touch you, Disa? If he did, I'ma blow his fucking mind!"

"I didn't touch her! She's fucking crazy as shit! I swear, Dunn!" Tony screamed, putting up his hands. Hakim abruptly squinted at Tony and dashed toward him about to swing until Lionel waved. His eyes grew darker than midnight. I gasped as he strode up on Tony. Tony gaped down at Hakim as he saw the horrible look in his eyes; he attempted to turn, and Lionel waved his head with the pistol. His gaze tried to burn a hole through Tony's face. "The fuck is wrong with all of you?!"

Hakim changed his mind heading to Darius, but as he walked, his steps were slower. Hakim picked Darius up from the floor carefully. Darius opened his eyes and saw Hakim and wobbled his head weakly in wrenches. He was hurt really bad, trembling, gripping his side, and when he tried to take a deep breath…he nearly lost his balance. Hakim had to keep him up.

"Qu…een," Darius sighed as he climbed to his feet. Hakim restrained him securely and tried to take off his shirt to see the wound. Darius struggled to fight Hakim away, watching me, but Hakim obstructed him.

"Did HE touch you?!" Hakim shouted, glowering at me swiftly. I shuddered, realizing…it was THAT NIGGA! I wiped my tears and shook my head. "Lionel, take Queen and get her out of here, now! Get her home! She needs rest and her meds….I'm taking Cyrus to the hospital…."

"Naw, Hakim…I say I deposit a couple bullets in this pussy-ass nigga! The second he thinks his ass is safe, he's gonna have a squad of niggas on us. He's grimy ass fuck, Hakim! You know that shit! Let me drop his bitch-ass!?" Lionel implored Hakim, forcing the handgun up Tony's nose. "Say yeah, Bro…I've fantasized of mutilating him over Maya's mama a red hot minute!"

"No! No! That was Miles…What!? I deal with coke and pills…HE was the ROCK man! Dunn, get your brother!? I won't retaliate. Just keep Cyrus out of my shit!

'….All of you get out and don't come back! …...I see you here again, and my boys are gonna fuck you up..." Tony exclaimed, striving to sound intimidating to Lionel but more frightened of Hakim. His eyes didn't avoid ELYEUH from the moment ELYEUH rocketed in his face.

#

Now, I know that Angel was thrown in the seat for a moment when that motherfucker scared US. But for some reason, when THAT NIGGA … got genuine near me! Angel's fear turned to anger toward Cyrus, and boom! Melissa's back BITCHES…!!

Oh…I do love my little brother, Lionel! He's so brutal. I'd let him pop this piece of shit if I were Hakim. But we know what will happen if he does. Not a good look for them Dunn Boys round here. It looks like it's up to Melissa to get us out of here without a hitch.

I strode over to Cyrus and peered at ELYEUH a moment as I zipped up Lionel's coat. I squinted down at Mia on the ground and flung her earring on the floor next to her. Darius stared at me and tried to square up straight. He groaned as Hakim let him go a moment.

"Seriously?!" I yelled at Darius. "Really, Darius, REALLY?!"

"Queen, I'm…. so…sorry…I fucked…up," Cyrus struggled to apologize. Lionel kept the gun on Tony as I nodded.

I glowered at ELYEUH when I cocked back. HE was to blame, but I was pissed off at My Man for fucking that bitch! I reached back and swung with all of my might and sought to knock Cyrus back to the floor. Hakim captured him, and Lionel's eyes exploded with Tony's. Nobody imagined I would do that. Hakim quickly collected Darius and got him out of that door once I cracked his lights out. I needed to be messing Hakim up, but someone needed to get MY Man to the hospital, and I ain't carrying his rogue ass.

"Fuck this nigga, Lionel! Let's bounce…He ain't shit!" I uttered as I took a step back, and he followed me outside, stepping over Hakim's victims. He didn't turn his back on those niggas until we were inside near Darius's truck. I handed Lionel the keys, and we caught up with Hakim in the front in Mercedez. Lionel stepped out, helping Hakim get Darius into Shun's backseat.

Darius woke up after I pressed him hard enough for his father to get a headache, but he fought when he saw ME get out of his truck. Hakim suddenly appeared before me, and he stared at me and snatched my shoulders.

"He's not going to stop this shit as long as you're around. Go home so I can get him to the hospital. He won't let me see how bad it is. I'm not going to leave him…go get some rest! Queen…you're trippin!" Hakim breathed in tears.

#

I gasped and climbed into the truck.

Lionel was struggling to get Darius in the car. Hakim decisively turned to help.

I was in tears, blubbering, trying to recollect how this could be happening to us.

Hakim sped out of the parking lot, then Lionel drove us home.

We could still see Shun's tail lights flying ahead of us as Hakim's hazard lights went on, and he suddenly was a blur of red lights vanishing over the hill down the highway ahead. I didn't say anything as I felt chills all over my body. Nothing felt like it would ever be the same again after this.

Suddenly I burst into tears, and I couldn't stop myself from shouting, "Follow them, Lionel!"

"No! Hakim said to take you home…I'm listening to my brother. You ain't dressed to sit in the E.R! You really are…trippin today…Sis…I'm not saying it's Danger Doom…But I think you DO need your medication, Gnarls Barkley. I'm with Hakim on this. Cyrus might just look bad. But Hakim is not going to fuck Cyrus off like you believe. We're brothers, Sis.

'We really don't plan to kill each other…we just do and say shit to one another to keep a nigga on his toes. Hakim didn't plan on Cyrus doing that shit!... You know that, right?" Lionel strove to defend.

"Oui, Lionel, I know Hakim loves Darius…it upsets me when they fight…over me…and now…." I sobbed, hunting for Shun's headlights ahead. Lionel put the safety lock on the gun and passed it to me. I held it nervously. As I put it in the glove box…inside Darius's secret spot, it was heavy.

I never liked guns. Daddy used to go on safari in Africa with his wealthy friends. They all got their sick kicks shooting animals for sport. That's why I don't eat meat. Daddy killed so many rabbits, squirrels, wild hogs, deer, and game that he kept as trophies in one house we stayed. When

I was little, I was terrified of all animals seeing all those dead creatures stuffed.

Once he tried to take me to the zoo, I screamed, thinking that Daddy would kill them all. But, the only animals I knew he couldn't kill were fast and strong enough to escape…the wild cats. A few might get caught, but it would take a lot of skill. They were too nimble. But…Tony…he shot my black panther, T'Challa, Darius…God…No!

# 

We pulled into the driveway behind Sophie's car, got out, and Lionel took both guns out of the truck. As I went inside the kitchen through the garage, I saw Lionel opening a hidden door behind a shelf. He put the pistols away. Afterward, he reached into the dryer and gave me one of Hakim's teeshirts. I quickly turned and dressed.

Lionel caressed my shoulder, moping, and whispered, "Come on, Sis, I'll make you something to eat. I know I'm starving. You must be hungry too."

"You cook?" I giggled skeptically.

"Oh yeah, I've been cooking since I was six years old. Both mama and grandma taught me how to throw down. I even know how to make that vegan shit Hakim likes. I took

Home Economics for three years in middle school. I got good at making different recipes and sewing," Lionel chuckled playfully, watching me sit at the kitchen island. "I can make anything I see in magazines and cookbooks. I have drawn some designs and patterns for little girls' dresses and uniforms for cheerleaders. A few of my ideas in the classes got picked up for Elementary Schools. It was for school, and I made it having fun."

"Lionel?" I called to him, holding in my laugh.

"Yeah, Sis?" He replied, offering me a cherry soda grinning.

"You know you're gay, right?" I shot at him, making him snicker.

"Oh, now you're coming for me? How you gonna call me on that, Sis? Sewing and cooking don't make me gay. I took Home Economics because I like fashion, and I wanted to make my own clothes.

'That way, no one would rock my shit but who I made it for. Dope, right?" Lionel groaned with the most relaxed tone I had ever heard from him. He took his wallet out of his pocket and showed me an adorable photo of him and Giggles. It made me smile a bit, but I was heartbroken and uneasy. I only wanted to hear his voice and know Darius was okay. Lionel seemed to be reading my mind and trying to cheer me up. He can be so gentle when he cares. "Oh and Maya…she always helped G.D. and  Sophie with cookouts. We had Home Ec. together that last year that she lived here. I keep the picture of us in my wallet. It was my way of keeping her with me everywhere I went. I'm never getting rid of this picture. I owe you for bringing us back together, Mandisa. You're my sister….I can't believe this shit happened…That bitch set him up…I can feel it…."

"How can you be so calm? I want to scream right now. I don't know what to think. I'm so angry, but I'm terrified that…I just want him to come home!" I suddenly wept, losing control. "How could he do that to me? I knew he had a past, but he told me he would never cheat on me! I understand that what WE have seems so strange, but it felt right. I thought he was happy with me. If he wanted someone else, he …could have…just told…me. He could have always had his freedom…I told them that I didn't…no one should feel forced to stay with me. I'm no one special…I'm crazy, and I know it."

"Look, Sis, niggas do stupid shit when they're in their feelings. Cyrus has been fucked over so much by falling in love he doesn't know how to chill. Every girl he's ever cared about did him dirty. But nobody changed him like Samantha

Reed. He was desperately after her from day one, but she wanted Hakim.

'So, Sami started dating Cyrus to make Hakim jealous, but Hakim didn't like her like that. He was happy that Cyrus got what he wanted, but Sami started acting crazy. When Hakim told Cyrus, he turned on him. Cyrus stopped coming around for a while and was still seeing that bitch. Hakim saw him all the time, but they weren't talking. We missed our brother….

'When Sami saw that Hakim and Cyrus weren't cool anymore, she tried to push up on Hakim. So WE tricked her mean ass. I got Cyrus to come by one night. I lied, telling him some stupid shit about Hakim being hurt. I knew it was mean, but Cyrus needed to hear the facts.

'Hakim put her on blast when she called the moment Cyrus wasn't around. Cyrus didn't talk to anyone for weeks. He was so mad that he went back to New York. Hakim started to blame that shit on himself and shut down the first time. I think he was 13.

'I think I get them both a bit more now. Hakim shuts down every time Cyrus leaves, and I think he's grown to where he'll do anything to keep him close permanently.

That's why he put y'all together. He'll share you with Cyrus if it makes you all happy, so Cyrus won't run away for good.

'Cyrus is different. His feelings are getting hurt all the time. That's why he's always cracking jokes and acting out. The funnier he gets, the sadder or happier he actually is on the inside. But if Cyrus gets quiet and overthinks, it means he's gonna leave. Hakim knows this too, so he's always trying to fix him and keep him talking, so he has nothing to run from.

'But Cyrus takes shit personally because he does feel inferior to my brother. I don't understand THAT PART. Shit Cyrus is probably the sanest out of all my brothers. But he seems to think everyone is better than him except for dancing and bringing the funny. I get that Hakim wants Cyrus to plan for the future if he's talking about getting married.

'What woman wants a husband that doesn't have a job but wants to pop out babies? Hakim's delivery still sucks...." Lionel explained to me, very intellectually sound. "They both changed so much since you came along, Sis. Before Cyrus was ever around when Hakim used to get sad or mad …guess who he'd turned on? I couldn't do anything without my brother wanting to fight."

"So, every time Hakim was hurt, your brother made you a target?" I sadly sighed.

"Yeah," Lionel replied, nodding. "After Cyrus bailed the first time, my brother just stayed away from home for two years. Now, WE know what he was doing back then.

'But when we were kids, Cyrus and Hakim were close. So G.D. started letting Cyrus stay with us all the time while his dad worked. Next thing you know, Sophie gave him the guestroom here, but that nigga slept in our room on the floor. I couldn't get my own room in this house, and Cyrus turned it down! Cyrus said that he wanted to be like us. If we had to sleep in the same room, then he was gonna kick it with us. So now it's just a room no one ever uses. I tripped when I saw him still doing that now.

'I thought that Hakim and Cyrus were gay back then. Sometimes I woke up in the middle of the night, and Cyrus'd be in bed with Hakim. But I saw it wasn't like that at all. That's how tight they actually are…they're closer than I am to Hakim. Hakim won't let me sleep on his bed. So, yeah, I was jealous. He had a best friend, and I was his real brother, and we ain't that tight.

'Cyrus saw it and started treating me the same. He was always…trying his best to make me act right and get Hakim to take it easy on me. Kaliah was the only person that did that for my brother and me before Cyrus. Kaliah helped me realize that I didn't hate my brother. I just want Hakim to be proud of me and hang around. Kaliah told me not too long ago, he thinks all of this shit is happening because Hakim thinks he had something to do with what happened to mom and dad."

"That's impossible! It was an accident. You were just children, Lionel. Why would he think like that?" I frowned, signing. Lionel offered me a sandwich and nodded.

"Hakim blames himself for everything bad that has ever happened to this family. After mom and dad died, I started getting into fights, and I got hurt a lot, so he thought he was supposed to save me at first. If G.D. fell down the stairs and got hurt, Hakim would take the blame for the fucking gravity. He wants to be the nigga that dies trying to save everyone. What's that shit called?" Lionel went on frowning.

"A martyr?" I answered, growing upset.

"Mhm," Lionel mumbled, chewing his cookie. "He used to make up all these plans about how he was going to get killed trying to save someone. First, running into a fire, or jumping in front of the bus, then revolutionary shit…

'Hakim started reading more, and his plans started evolving, but he was still trying to die! Some of that shit scared the fuck out of me. Hakim had plans where he was doing this shit when he was 11. I used to hate how he could trick Grandma Sophie into letting him drive her car when he was 13, but Hakim was stealing it when he was 11. No one said anything to him, and I don't know why.

'We were fighting all the time back then. Hakim could talk his way out of trouble. I only saw G.D. hit him three times. We broke windows, put holes in the walls, and got the police involved a few times. Grandma Sophie couldn't handle us. G.D. couldn't stop us because we were so violent as kids. Hakim gave me black eyes, he cut me with his blade once, and I broke my hand trying to swing on his ass twice.

'When I got older, I realized I was never going to stand a chance against Hakim head-on. So, I started waitin for him to go to sleep. I'd bumrush his ass the minute he'd pass out! Then, THAT NIGGA started sleeping in chairs for weeks at a time, and if I made any move, he'd fuck me up! So, I calmed down and started letting shit slide because he wouldn't let me get any sleep or go take a piss some nights!

'I told Kaliah about the shit I found out. Kaliah started sending Hakim books he read about ancestors, past lives, and spiritual meditation...Kaliah was already in college...He came to visit...things were good. Hakim never wanted to fight, I didn't talk shit, and Cyrus was silly as hell when Kaliah was around back then. But once he got engaged...it was a wrap. Nothing was the same once Ms. Trisha came around us. It's been hell on earth for the whole family because of that one woman. I know she fucked all of my brothers, and she made Hakim and Kaliah insane! Cyrus, he flips when Kaliah or his wife comes around and gets fucked up. I saw Kaliah nearly kill Ms. Trisha when she tried to get me when I was 13. Kaliah went to jail that night, the bitch bailed him out, laid this enormous guilt trip on him, and he felt so awful he hurt her; Kaliah married her anyway...and moved away. He knew that none of us liked her, so he settled for the misery. He avoided his own mother for years because Ms. Trisha hates Mama Louisa. She's the biggest bitch birthed anybody could meet, Mandisa....

'That bitch is like you and Hakim, and she has niggas in her head all talking at the same time getting out when she's fucked up. The nigga that tried to get me in the bathroom was not a woman! That monster was faster, stronger, and uglier than all of us put together. So when whatever it is touched Kaliah trying to get me...It was like what happens with you and Hakim but different!

'Sis....Kaliah turned into a nigga like the Incredible Hulk, and he put her ass through two hotel walls! Hakim ran off out of the blue long before that, and Cyrus and I had to stop Kaliah from destroying the whole suite! Cops came, Kaliah took the charges and paid for the damages…but went to jail for months. He copped an insanity plea and got off because of HIS violent past.

'Kaliah's been trying to find anything that will help for years…Now, I want to help too. I see this shit is real. I just don't know what I can do….I know I'm talking a lot, but if I don't keep talking, then I'm gonna get pissed off and go back and finish that nigga like Mortal Kombat, Sis. You know I talk too much..," Lionel groaned as I touched his hand, nodding.

"You're keeping me calm talking, Lionel. I'm learning a lot listening to you. Why didn't you tell me this before?" I worried, trying to keep him going.

"A lot of this shit…I didn't remember until we went to Los Angelos this summer. When I talked to Kaliah about Hakim trying to…you know…the trip to the mall? Kaliah was the one that reminded me about that night in the hotel. I didn't realize he knew all along Hakim was messed up when mom and dad died. That was why Kaliah kept calling and getting Hakim studying, so he would stop planning to pass away and make money to provide for a family he'd make of his own. Hakim took that shit literally. It started when he met you and your mother, and we believe that he wants us all close, but ELYEUH doesn't need anyone but YOU.

"You scared the shit out of both of us earlier, and I believe you made that NIGGA fall in love DEEPER…I've never seen Hakim fight like that…he was moving so fast I couldn't keep my eyes on him. We were trying to figure out the best way to get to you when we heard you screaming. Hakim ran full blast and kicked that bitch in.

"I came through the club, following them niggas once Hakim got the door. He trusted me and knew that I wasn't gonna let shit happen to you. But once he saw how bad they messed up Cyrus…Yo…I think that was ELYEUH the whole damn time. So that means you got THAT NIGGA all in his feelings just as sincere as Hakim about Cyrus now.

"What you gonna do, Sis? That's sort of like 3 niggas on your shit. You about to become a pornstar? I mean…I know you not a ho or nothing….but…Why do you love my brother so much? How can you be with him and Cyrus at the same time? It's not normal. What are you doing? If I didn't know you like I do….I'd swear you were just using both of them."

I finished my sandwich and wiped my mouth, contemplating everything Lionel said about me. I couldn't be angry at Lionel for his honesty. Lionel was consistently honest, no matter how he felt. I respected that quality above his many other abilities that he often hid from others, but my little brother confided in me. I felt safe giving him reciprocity. I realized he wanted to keep me talking so I wouldn't overthink as well.

"You want to take a walk with me to get some fresh air?" I suggested glancing upstairs. Lionel nodded and grabbed my coat, and we walked out into the front yard. I found myself staring down at the slush in the streetlight as Lionel smoked his cigarette quietly. "Lionel, when I moved here, I was a scared little girl. It didn't matter my age; I didn't do anything that felt like living all alone. Maya was my first REAL friend. She thought that I was so beautiful, and I thought she was so adorable. Giggles made me happy to be a girl no matter my circumstances telling me about her family and how she was raised. Maya loved my mother, and I wanted her with me because she made me happy to be alive when I wanted to die.

'She was a tomboy, but Maya has so much style and attitude. Her courage inspired me and made me want more than my father decided for my life. First, she braided my

343

hair, and we talked about everything from boys to things we hated about life. Then, I watched her go to work and transform people's images and self-esteem with just a haircut, dreadlocks, braids, or even weaving…Maya is so terrific! She made great money, but she paid all the bills at her aunt's and sent the rest to James, Lionel. I admired her for being so strong at such a young age. After that, I knew I had to find my Giggle Pie.

'But I had no idea when I met her two years ago that I would be standing here today engaged to HER boyfriend's brother! I am so amazed at how small the world seems to become the more I meet people. But I was so afraid to speak to boys at all. My father verbally abused me for years to obey him or anyone he told me to. When I grew older, he hit me when I questioned him about all the men he wanted me to be around. He used to lock me in my room and scream through the door daring me to leave. If he caught me trying to talk to my mother alone, he would take me away to hit me. He was sleeping with many of my private tutors, au pairs, and he was afraid I would tell my mother what I saw, and he got worse.

'It made my heart condition worse, and they said I needed a transplant before I turned 13, so he wanted to marry me to one of those men. I suppose he thought that someone rich could maybe fix what he broke, but he wasn't giving me a say in my own existence and treating me like I didn't matter. I wanted to die until Maya and Amani. I tried…many times…but nothing worked…I'd wake up confused and afraid again and again.

'Then I started painting, but when I turned 14. Daddy introduced me to….this man…A German therapist…I don't know what he did to me…but Daddy left us alone to talk. I didn't like how he looked at me and the things he said.…were…strange.

'I woke up in the hospital, and I don't remember anything that happened. Nothing has been the same for me since I met that man…I know he didn't rape me. But it was obvious he wanted a young woman for sex. I didn't think my father loved me after that…whatever happened…he let it happen to me and tried to cover it up.

'Mami and I started running when he hit her. She caught him sleeping with my dance instructor. We couldn't go back to Philadelphia because granny would call Daddy, so Mami ran to a friend that she knows here. He told her he would let us stay as long as we wanted. I haven't talked to him, but I know he lives in Dallas, and he's a doctor.

'You asked a complicated question, Lionel. I…never thought that I was ever going to fall in love with anyone.…

'I WAS going to kill myself if Mami went back to my father. But I just wanted to live to see if Amani was healthy. I don't think my father would have been so evil with me if he could have fixed my heart when I was little.

'Mami said when the surgery didn't take...Daddy cried for days...then he just snapped. I was four, and he didn't want me to do anything anymore. Sometimes...I feel like I'm still that scared little girl...Then other times...I'm angry and want to fight, but I hate violence...Maya told me that I needed to stop being scared of motherfuckers and start to wreck shit when they treat me like I don't matter.

'I couldn't fight, and I haven't hit anyone, but Darius...tonight...I remember doing that and why....but honestly...when my feelings go too extreme...It's NOT me...and I'm NOT ME right now...I don't know who I am...or why I do anything. I've been living off of instincts like a caged animal for so long...I feel like a lion in the zoo, and the more people that see me..., the more I change, trying to understand what they all see...." I found myself explaining thoroughly.

"I was afraid to talk to people after my father started coming for us. So I sat in my room with my window open and painted a world like Maya and I imagined, where I could have whatever I wanted. We talked about going somewhere to shop, dance, party, and sit and talk on the beach any time we wanted. It was our fantasy world. I wanted to live there.

'I watched Hakim run by the house every day. I saw that hair, those lips, and his sad eyes. I thought he was so beautiful and I wanted to know why he looked so sad. There was so much physical attraction there for me I couldn't hide it. It was like seeing the perfect man run by my yard, and I was terrified. Finally, Mami gave me the courage to speak. She saw how sad I was from my paintings, and when she saw the one I painted of Hakim before we met…She told me I should at least say hello. But I thought he would laugh at me," I confessed sadly, thinking.

"Why would any man laugh at you? You're so beautiful, Sis?" Lionel chuckled, staring out at the streetlight in the cold.

"I've always been alone. All the women on TV are so thin and pretty, so I thought I was too fat. I had no idea what thick was until I met Maya. She started calling me Beyonce because she said that my curves made me a savage. After that, both Hakim and Darius kept telling me I was crazy…I was fine and thick. But Darius has a problem…HE loves us bigger than life!" I giggled and unexpectedly frowned, thinking of everything. "I didn't expect to love…anyone…

Especially…not two best friends. I blame Hakim's games, but …maybe this wouldn't have happened to Darius if I didn't…love him?"

"Naw, Sis! This ain't your fault! I know for sure that when you came around, my brother wasn't mad like he used to be anymore. The only time I have seen Hakim mad now has been when something happened to you or Cyrus. Oh, and when I fucked with him too heavy….We didn't have a big family, Sis. So when we met you, it just felt like you were that missing piece that put us all together. G.D., Sophie, Cyrus, Kaliah, Mami, Amani, and you….Shit! That's it! That's the circle, Mandisa!

'Hakim doesn't let too many others kick it close. I know he cares about J-Rock and Maya because they were always looking out for us. Hakim isn't a nice guy, but you changed him a lot. I'm glad I got my brother back. He's my hero, Sis. But you can't tell him I said that shit?! That's our secret!"

"Oui," I giggled at Lionel's embarrassment. I hugged him tightly. "I feel better after talking to you, Girlfriend-girlfriend!"

"I got you, Sis," Lionel told me, smiling as he rubbed my back, squeezing me close. He held my hand, staring at me curiously a moment thinking. "So what you gonna do now? I know you're pissed off about Cyrus, but you could still do something stupid if you don't think about things. If you throw Cyrus away, he's going to run, and that might kill Hakim.

'Cyrus is a man, and he had a moment of weakness. Of course, we all do, but do you STILL love him is the question?"

Yes, I loved BOTH Hakim and Darius, and I wanted things to work out. But, some things needed to change…we needed to add more rules to this shit if it was going to last…

#

"Yeah, I still love his black ass, but shit's gotta change if he's gonna keep this BITCH for his Queen. I love Cyrus…I know THAT NIGGA is the one trying to push MY MAN away, Babybro. I'm gonna find a way to make THAT NIGGA get with the program or get GONE, Lionel…." I told my brother seriously. I shivered and shook my head. "Let's get back inside…It's colder than an Iceman's dick out here!"

# Chapter Nine: Pride/Pray For Me

## Lionel

I stood in the back door, lit a cigarette, and called Hakim. Mandisa, Melissa, or whatever CHICK calls herself, was sitting on the sofa trying to watch a movie. She needed something that would make her laugh, and I knew just what would keep her calm. That CHICK is loud when she yells at a nigga! Yo! That's my SISTER…but when she gets like this….she is sooo fine to me!

Mandisa's face will look so sweet and innocent, then suddenly her eyes will turn green! After that, her eyebrows would arch up like everything was a damn surprise. Then, she would pop her hands in your face, roll up on you if you don't pay attention, and snatch a nigga quick! Then when she started talking shit…it was funny as fuck to me! She could say some shit that made me laugh at myself! I have to play like I am a girl, so I don't flirt with her. It's not the first time I've met her…I started calling her DISA.

The first time I met that CHICK was the night that Hakim got Mandisa and Amani's freedom. We went out to celebrate at this tight spot! Mandisa had on this tight red dress, and that ass was so right. Her titties were all out, and you know me? I asked to dance with her, and…I tried that old shit trying to get a face rub, and she waited until we got outside in the parking lot and snapped on me. Hakim and Cyrus thought I was walking her to the ladies' room, and so did I until she jerked my ass out the backdoor and told me off!

#

"What is your fucking problem, Nigga?!" Mandisa asked me as she slammed me against the wall once we were outside. She was so strong that she made the brick crack as I hit the wall. I didn't know what the hell to think as she smiled at me with those beautiful green eyes. I couldn't stop smiling, and it pissed her off even more. "I got shit on my face? I've been trying to not fuck you up, Bro! But your hands are getting too fucking friendly. I got enough niggas trying to throw their rods in this pond than to worry about what you want to do with your hooked worm."

"How you know my dick got a hook in it, Mandisa?" I chuckled but was nervous as shit.

"Shut the fuck up! You need to overstand that WE don't want you, so you need to stop with the nasty shit…or I'm going to pop your head like a big ass boil. Then I'll fix the hook in your rod with my boots…okay?" She threatened me

351

with a smile, but her eyes were so bright green that they scared the shit out of me.

It gave me the eeriest feeling and made me tremble like a bitch. She meant every word she said and didn't let me go or down until I agreed to stop that shit. If I said anything else, she would have stumped the shit out of right there...I was not going to test my pipe density...Fuck that.

I learned to keep my hormones under control around Mandisa, and I watched my mouth so I didn't piss her off. But, each time I met HER...She gets angrier...now she's talking more and more like ELYEUH.

But...I know that Elyeuh's got it BAD for HER, too, now...It's getting bizarre around here. I'm worried about Cyrus, but this shit keeps taking the front seat! I hope...Hakim, my brother, answers the phone, and not...HIM.

The phone rang a few times, and I was sick of leaving voicemails telling him to call one of us and let us know what was up. I was about to hang up when Hakim finally answered.

"Lionel, how is Mandisa?" Hakim asked, his voice the lowest I had ever heard. He was so emotional that it almost had me crying. But, I could tell...it was worse...

352

"She's waiting to hear from one of you. I'm keeping her calm, but...how is Cyrus doing?" I whispered, stepping outside. I didn't need her hearing something and losing it on me!

"He...they shot him twice and broke...three ribs...then...they had to wire his jaw shut," Hakim gasped, breaking down.

"Fuck, Hakim! He's that bad?" I groaned, pulling my hair struggling not to cry. I could hear Hakim straining to breathe. "Hakim!"

Hakim coughed, clearing his throat sighing, "He took a shot to the shoulder...they got that bullet out. But the second shot was to the back of his head. They cut off all his hair...trying...Mandisa can't see him like this! You can't let her near Cyrus until he's good. I called Kaliah and told him...and Cyrus had already called....for me! He'll be here...tonight! What...the ...fuck...? I think I'm seriously going crazier, Bro! He can't die on me! I can't lose my brother!!!"

That was Hakim, and I lost it hearing the frustration and hopelessness in his sobs. When Hakim cried...it always messed me up, and I sobbed too. I couldn't stop it no matter how much I tried. I hated it...but I knew...I cried because…He was my brother. I loved Hakim, and it tore me apart when he hurt because I felt that shit too. Now, with Cyrus…it was like taking two bullets to heart! I fell to my knees on the porch, and I cried. Nothing was gonna be right with Cyrus gone! Hakim may do something crazy!

Mandisa might be worse. If I lost all of them…what would all the money and shit be for without them?

I couldn't believe that Cyrus went off alone, knowing Tony had been checking for him like that. I cried, thinking…how many times I went in there thinking I was bulletproof. Yeah, I was always with Les, but those niggas never fight fair, and I knew it. I wasn't thinking…just like Cyrus. Now…he might not make it, and I would lose more family because of that fake motherfucker!

"The only reason he didn't die instantly is his hair cushioned the impact. It didn't go in all the way, arched, and grazed the rest. They shaved it down to see how bad it was, Bro. He's been stabilized with surgery…His jaw is broken, and he can't talk. I don't want you to tell Mandisa! She'll flip out!" Hakim warned me suddenly.

"Hakim, SHE's going to freak out if SHE can't see him. So why do you want me to keep her away?" I worried, wiping my face. I'm not dumb. That CHICK doesn't like for nobody to tell her what to do. So if I tell her, Hakim said to stay away…SHE is going to kick my ass. "Naw, Bro…you can't just dump her off on me. SHE is mad and scared…like all of us…you can't keep playing with her emotions. Or did you forget she said she would cut your ass off?"

"Lionel, SHE broke his jaw….Cyrus could talk before Mandisa hit him in the mouth! She was so mad she didn't know how hard she could swing. It was too late when I realized what she was doing. Cyrus was alert the majority of the ride, Bro. He knows that she did it…but he went into shock…and they had to rush him into surgery. Cyrus's stable, and they're going to move him to a hospital in Dallas. …I know it will destroy her if she realizes she did that shit to him…I know Mandisa didn't mean to hurt him…she was just pissed off…it is all my fault!

'I….I called Maya, and she's upset, but ….I couldn't talk her out of coming. So you use Cyrus's truck like it's yours. Keep the girls busy, and don't come until Kaliah or I tell you he's in the clear, please? You know…me…I don't…want…him to die…I should be the one…Uh…I'm going to come to grab some things and change. I'll follow him after I get all the details. But if I'm not home by 10:30, go to the airport and get your girl.

'You've been waiting for years for this, Bro. In my safe, the one in the closet, get your credit card. The combination is your birthday, two-digit month, date, and year. It has a hundred thousand dollar limit now. So get it, spoil Shamaya, have fun, and send her back to Philadephia with a smile until…hopefully…Jamaica. I'm not changing any plans, and I'm not abandoning Cyrus. I'm all he has, Bro!" Hakim said with his voice straining.

"Hakim, I can't abandon him either! He's my brother too!" I cried, frowning.

"You're not, Lionel. You're helping us all. If I know Queen is with and Maya, I won't worry about her so much. I can be here when Cyrus comes to. He needs to pull his head back togcther before he faces her again.

'Cyrus was gone before he passed out!

'He couldn't even talk…and kept crying her name…Just give us a few days, alright? I never ask you for anything, Lionel, please?" Hakim wept, frustrated.

"Alright, Hakim, anything you need. We won't come until you give us the word," I replied, rubbing my forehead.

"I'll talk to G.D. and Sophie when I get there, but …I'm so fucking scared, my Nigga! You know that if I hadn't have gotten Cyrus to emancipate himself and add our family legally as his people that they wouldn't have let me know shit and would have tried to call his father? Mr. Jefferson won't answer the fucking phone when Sophie tries to talk to him about Cyrus, Lionel. I don't know what the fuck went wrong…Oh…shit…they're going to move him now! I…I gotta go! I love you, man!" Hakim told me.

"I love you too, Hakim…tell Cyrus I love him, too, alright!?" I hurriedly said.

"I will, Bro, hold my wife for the both of us. I hope I make it there before you leave to get Maya," Hakim sadly said, hanging up.

#

As I walked back into the kitchen, I tossed my phone across the countertop. Mandisa stood up from the sofa, watching me with the prettiest puffy gray eyes. She seemed so serious, and when she came toward me…Her walk…made me stare at her hips as she rounded the island!

"It's bad, isn't it, Lionel? Hakim didn't want to talk to me because it's bad…right?" Mandisa sweetly asked, putting her hand on my shoulder. She was so gentle when she touched me it made me flinch. After that, she only stared at me with that beautiful, sad face and those starry eyes, and then she

357

kissed me on the cheek! "It will be fine...Hakim is just distressing and afraid. He is always terrified, and it makes him unhappy.

'Darius will be okay...he just needs to learn his lesson about playing with the laws of attraction. We all have lessons to learn, Lionel...We are a family, so we will get through this together...by any means necessary. Mandisa cannot help anyone...she hasn't been awake in years.

'What you do not know is...You have never met the real Mandisa. I am who you all met...Antoine calls me PAULA, and I like it...Angel is the sad, suffering child. Melissa is the angry bitch. I'm what's left of her self-confidence...I'm her pride...there are weaker ones in here that can't get out yet. But Mclissa is taking over more and more because of ELYEUH. He wants me...but he's scared of HER. She wants Cyrus, and Cyrus knows SHE's not me.

'Their little games were much worse than Hakim going after Cyrus with the ring. Hakim was trying to run Cyrus away because Melissa didn't want Hakim, and he knew it. So, our relationship status is beyond complicated...Facebook will never have a name for this shit...

'I've been painting, dancing, and writing…anything…to get someone to realize how many are in here. But once Melissa or Angel takes over…There's nothing I can do inside of here but run around in the darkness trying to find another way back to the light so I can drive…or hope that someone on the outside boosts OUR self-esteem enough to trigger me to get out longer. As long as we're in our feelings…WHO you get is gonna be WHO you get…only the pills can suppress these fits. I took them…

'I get out because of the pills until someone else gets me emotional enough to trigger THEM from the dark place. Mandisa…she won't wake up.…None of US know just how many are here, nor much of what happens once we're driving unless we meet up inside of here. It's pitch black inside of the mind, and you can hear the voices calling, but it's not safe running around in the dark. Some don't want to get out…they only wait for US trying to wake Mandisa up…to try to get out…Then we have to run for the light…They can kill US. We've lost a little sister to THEM. Angel is the oldest…she's like our mother…splitting off of her got US here…It's very…deep…Lionel…."

"Wait…what? Angel? ….The paintings…? Oh, shit! The nigga in the dark…HIM…?" I remembered suddenly. Model

Mandisa nodded sadly. "So, you're the pretty girl in the mirror?"

"Now you're starting to overstand, Baby brother…I couldn't tell my mother how bad it really is because of Daddy. Of course, she saw some, but she doesn't know…

'Daddy hypnotized Mandisa when she was in control…now she can't wake up…

'Angel took the wheel for so long…she needed help…I was born…but Melissa came when Daddy messed up. She really isn't nice at all. Melissa's more like ELYEUH than she will admit and kill if she gets powerful and too angry. Melissa tried to kill Daddy, and Mami had to drug US to get her off of Daddy!

'I'm the closest thing you're going to get to the real Mandisa for now…Someone better may just pop up. The more you all keep upsetting Angel, the more she splits trying to make you all happy. We really don't need any more feelings trying to drive, Lionel. I'll take the pills, but we have to find a way to balance our emotions or stop the triggering! There's no cure for this…

'That's what Dr. Patesh was studying…he wanted to help me. He was a good guy that listened to Angel about Daddy.

He knew something was wrong, and he started looking to find a way to stop what was happening.

'Daddy didn't want Dr. Patesh at first because of his skin…but…When Mandisa was 14, and Daddy cheated on Mami, and she saw it. He hit Mandisa, Melissa got out, and she attacked him the first time. Daddy got US another therapist, and… he sexually molested Angel, then…. THE DEMON got out and went after Daddy!

'THE DEMON's one of THOSE that hides in the darkness. It never hurts Angel…but he will kill anyone if HE gets out long enough or any of us in here. I couldn't tell you any of this until I saw Hakim lose the cheese off his cracker.

'I actually felt relieved that I'm not the only person in the world going through this…I know…Angel wanted to die…with Mandisa not waking up…if not for US being born here…She would have found a way to end it all by now, Lionel. Hakim, Darius…all of you being accepting…is healing us in a way…it's not going to be easy to fix what's broken within all of us.

'But I NEED you to overstand that I do not want ELYEUH to touch me. Angel is afraid of him, too. Melissa hates him…I love Hakim…but HE would destroy the last of OUR self-esteem with Mandisa sleeping and me driving. It would kill me if he hurt me, and Angel would have to chauffeur OR Melissa. Melissa will kill US all if you make her angry enough…Daddy broke all of US. We have memories connecting some of us together…

'Angel…Melissa…Me, Mandisa(The Body), and Francois…we are a family.

'Francois only gets out to talk to Mami; he speaks only French and is blind. So when Mami cries too much…Francois tries to cheer her up.

'He and Angel were made together when Daddy started mistreating Mandisa. They were her friends when she was kept in hospitals and clinics. Then when Daddy started hitting Mandisa…Angel began splitting…Me…Melissa…Then more and more…. So many are weak because they're afraid of the light…only those of us that will go into the light can get out to live outside for Mandisa. But they don't want us outside either. Francois stays protecting Mandisa while she sleeps, so we can keep moving. But with more of us popping up because of ELYEUH…it's getting crowded and more terrifying to try to get back to the light. I started praying to get triggered, so I don't have to go out THERE with THEM.

'Without Angel's halo, Francois's lantern, or the locket…we couldn't see anything…only those that heal Mandisa have light…Melissa only gets out triggered…she has no light….that's how I know my sister will kill Mandisa. To stay out longer elicited …without light… means she's killed some of the weak ones. I tried to put things in the pictures to see if anyone understood what I saw from INSIDE.

'But I noticed Hakim and when I realized why he was so sad….I saw how I could fix Hakim, Darius, and you…and I decided if you were so determined to save US…then I'm going to stay and love you all…by any means necessary. It has to be destiny…I don't believe in coincidences.

'We were all put together, making choices, and now…we will face the decisions we make…I can't keep letting Angel hold things down. She's just a baby though she's lived here with Mandisa the longest. A baby can't keep pretending to be a woman, Lionel. She's like our mom, but she's still just 4, the age when Daddy first hit US. Angel can't age like we can…I guess because she and Francois were first and together…neither of them can grow up."

"Oh, my God…" I thought aloud. Everything was starting to make sense. It was crazy…but it was really cool as hell hearing her say shit like that! At least I had the answers to Mandisa's motives…THIS was the girl we met, PAULA, and her motives were as pure as snow. She was trying to fix Hakim in her own crazy-ass way. I could see it all now. It made me look at this whole mental illness thing in a totally different way. "It's like trying to put a puzzle back together one piece at a time while someone kicks the table, right?"

"That sounds kind of right, Lionel…except… there are so many pieces to the puzzle. We don't know who's kicking the table, and…we have to put the pieces back together alone in the dark.

'I understood how Hakim feels trying to find anything that made him feel something other than the state that birthed ELYEUH…that means that Hakim is too weak to drive. ELYEUH overpowered the real Hakim long ago when he took over, and now he won't let Hakim out long enough to remember anything.

"It takes time to recover from all the blackouts. Some memories stay with the persona that was driving when things happened. There's so much I don't know or understand about US, Lionel…like I said…We're all in HERE…in the DARK…and Hakim is going through the same thing…but at least maybe now …He's not going to fuck with his family like this anymore, or Melissa is going break it off with him. She's more formidable than Angel and I now, thanks to Darius.

Melissa has jumped out, protecting Angel or me when we drive. Hakim was the boy I fell in love with, but she fell with Darius skating. I wasn't there…after I spilled my drink. I remember…I got upset…I didn't want anyone to see my legs. But Hakim made me feel so beautiful and exceptional from the beginning. He boosted my self-esteem, and it triggered my pride…now I get out more than Angel. Before…Angel was always driving or Melissa…We didn't love ourselves much. So Elyeuh has to want to get better. If he's not going to let Hakim run things, she'll break my heart…and I love my Robin…

"I love Darius as well for being so very loving and accepting of me and my shattered vision. The more people I learn to love with this broken heart of Mandisa's, the more Angel relaxes…The sadness…fades…so…I need you all too," Mandisa explained, staring down at me with a soft and solemn look.

It was like she was looking at herself in the mirror when she looked at me. Or maybe she was looking in my eyes for something. It wasn't scary like when Melissa did that to me. It was so sweet and warm…soft…golden and loving…like a mother…or The light from my dream! It led me to Maya…just like Mandisa! I didn't know what it meant. All of this was too much to take at once. One person couldn't really be that weak and powerful…right?

"Why wouldn't he talk to me, Lionel? Are you sure THAT was Hakim on the phone?" She questioned me, stroking my shoulder.

"Hakim…is just emotional now because he's scared. Them niggas tried to kill Cyrus, Sis. They shot him in the shoulder, his jaw's broken, they broke some ribs, and they put a cap in the back of his head," I emotionally explained as I pointed to the spot where Cyrus wore his ponytail.

She screamed and dropped her head on the countertop. I couldn't get her to calm down because I lost it when she broke down. When Mandisa cries…it's the saddest sight. Sometimes when she gets too emotional…and screams…it sounds like a little girl. Now I know why…It's that little girl in the tutu with the halo in that painting. Sometimes when she tries to talk, when she cries, she sounds like a sweet little girl and makes sad faces that make us all cry.

Finally, I pulled myself together and took a breath saying, "Mandisa, listen, the bullet missed. His hair redirected the shot, and it grazed the back of his head. They had to wire his jaw shut so it could heal. He's stable, but they're moving Cyrus to a hospital in Dallas to watch him closely. I know they were going to give him some good medicine for the pain! Broken ribs ain't no punk, and Cyrus took two bullets? He's probably on cloud nine and getting morphine shots in the ass, not feeling no pain!"

I chuckled, not telling her everything once I saw a smile. "Cyrus's gonna be alright, Sis. But he ain't gonna be smoking for a minute. I bet he's going to try to rip those braces off, though. You know they're going to try to force Cyrus to drink milkshakes and shit."

"Oui, Darius hates ice cream, and he doesn't really like cheese unless it's on a bacon burger, "Mandisa giggled, wiping her eyes nodding. "I think he is lactose intolerant."

"Nope, when we were kids, he used to love strawberry and chocolate ice cream, but he saw that Two Girls One Cup shitshow years ago, and it fucked Cyrus up," I died laughing.

Mandisa's eyes grew wide as she gagged, "I'll never get that out of my head now…Thanks a lot, Nigga! No wonder MY MAN hates ice cream! THAT SHIT…!"

I fell out laughing at Melissa as I recognized her cute ass tone, "Yeah, Cyrus has a weak stomach but tries to eat everything. Funny thing though, when I showed that shit to him and Hakim….Hakim was eating a sundae, and Cyrus lost it! Hakim just kept eating like he wasn't affected, Nasty-ass nigga!"

"HE would be the nigga to like that SHIT," Melissa giggled. "At least he cut those snakes off his head. I don't see how a bitch can like a nigga with no beard eating her out all the damn time…Friction feels good…He's lacking…."

I shook my head, trying to breathe as Melissa roasted my brother…I couldn't take it. Nobody talked shit about Hakim….other than Kaliah's wife when she was fucked up. I never heard another woman say shit about Hakim negatively. Of course, Mandisa would never say this shit…but Melissa was a BADDIE! SAVAGE! BOSS BITCH…but she had morals…and I think that's what turned us all on.

'She would jump out and start barking orders, and niggas got active. But she was actually adorable when she calmed down. But that meant she wasn't gonna be around long. So as soon as Melissa calmed down or started feeling another type of way…Someone else was there…I was beginning to figure out who I was talking to…it was in the eyes and different facial expressions.

"Hakim said he'll try to make it here before we leave for Shreveport to get Maya. But listen, Sis, Cyrus is in a horrible place mentally right now. So, he needs some time to get his head together. So, Hakim is going to stay with him until Cyrus's alright. But you don't need to be there like this…until he's cool. He can't be stage diving out of bed with broken ribs after you!

'Let's give him a few days, okay? Then we'll go see him, alright?" I told her, hoping that she didn't take it as an order.

She wiped her face and nodded, frowning, and said, "He was messed up and still trying to get to me. It scared me. It was as if he didn't care if he hurt himself. I'm glad, really relieved he's going to be alright. I just want to hear him crack a joke or do an impersonation again. I can give…him…some time to heal. If…that's what HE wants. I can wait."

"So, I guess that means that you forgive Cyrus?" I raised, grinning at her mischievously.

She stared at me a second, and her face grew shocked as her eyebrows rose higher. Then, she thought for a second and blinked her green eyes, saying, "I just want the questions I need to be answered, that's all. But I can wait until the nigga can talk, shit!"

She stood up, putting her hand on her right hip…Then she suddenly glanced in my direction, making me nervously ask, "Sis, you alright?

Mandisa smiled at me and said, "Yeah, I'm golden, Lionel. I mean, I love that chocolate motherfucker. So I can forgive him for taking a dip. But it ain't over!

'If he does some shit like that to me again, I'll break his dick in half. So next time, I'll skip his face and aim lower than his jaw. Come on, Lionel, a bitch can forgive, but she ain't gonna ever forget unless she's a damn fool.

'He's sweet, funny, I know he really loves me, but any nigga will jump into some easy pussy…if they don't fear losing shit…He's scared now…That bitch Mia threw her swamp pussy in his face, and she's no better than her raping spouse. So what the hell is she doing fucking young boys, with a whole husband, kids, stripping, and hoing on the side? The bitch sounds like the ho that has all of you so fucked up in the head. Do you all have some fascination with ignorant hos?

'That Nasty-ass nigga, Kaliah's bitch seems to have more of a hold over you niggas than you think. Mia's lucky her husband fucked her up before I got there. I can hold my own in a fair fight, but it was too many niggas in there. I'm not trying to fuck my way out of any situation like that! Hakim may be a bad motherfucker, but I can make a bitch cry if needed," Melissa laughed, going back to watch the movie.

She had a massive grin on her face with wide emerald eyes watching that shit. I followed her into the den, and she was all into that shit.

"That's what the fuck I'm talking about, Django! Whip the shit out of those crackers! Make them hate they invented that shit! Snap! Django that ass black and blue!" She snorted noisily while I observed from the entryway.

"Lionel, turn that damn TV down! It's almost 4 am!" G.D. screamed downstairs.

Melissa jumped up from the sofa and strutted over to the steps waving. When G.D. saw her, he smiled, waving, thinking it was Mandisa.... She playfully covered her lips, saying, "I'm sorry, Granddaddy, it was me, not Lionel...I will turn it down, okay? Don't be upset...I sat on the remote."

"Oh, okay, Baby! Try to keep it down. Sophie is working early so we can go to the casino tomorrow night," Granddad told Mandisa sweetly and limped back down the hall to bed.

My jaw dropped, and I walked over and snatched the remote from Melissa. She smiled at me sweetly and asked with huge green eyes, "What?! I know how to handle Paw-Paw Dunn. He loves me…Y'all niggas dozing over here…."

She snatched the remote from me and wiggled back to watch the movie. I moved over to the recliner closer to her and watched Melissa rather than the TV. Melissa was on one, and the longer she was out now, the more she reminded me of ELYEUH…I started to wonder if he could flip in and out like Melissa just did for G.D.?

I'm beginning to wonder about what Paula said about Melissa maybe hurting someone or Mandisa. She seemed to feed on anger and rage. But how could she switch up and get sweet suddenly? This shit was too much…I needed…a blunt…Naw…a nap…fuck it. I'm tired.

#

I heard the front door crack, and as I opened my eyes, Hakim came through the front door. His shirt and jeans were covered in Cyrus's blood! I had forgotten about everything until I saw him and his sad face when he saw me sit up. Mandisa had fallen asleep on the couch. Hakim glanced over, noticing us, and tried to look better but just quietly waved, taking off his coat. He hung it up and staggered slowly toward me as I stood up.

"She alright?" He asked nervously, checking his pockets and noticing his bloody shirt. Hakim frowned furiously and tore off his shirt, and threw it in the trash. But, unfortunately, his A-shirt was just as bloody underneath. He groaned as he exhaled and looked lost. "I'm trippin…I'll be…How is she? Don't worry about me, Bro? Is SHE still mad? She gonna leave me?"

"She took things…Good…I…guess?" I tried to explain but got confused. Afterward, I started to think I dreamed some of the shit I saw last night, still waking up. "Yeah…Mandisa…she's good…. But, when you say…SHE…Who YOU talking about, Willis?"

Hakim stared at me and glanced at Mandisa, whispering forcefully, "HER…All of her…I LOVE HER…I don't give a fuck what's wrong with her. That's my wife! I knew something was up when we met! She was made for me, and I don't care how crazy she is…I want ALL of HER…okay, Lionel…?

'I'm not choosing favorites like Cyrus!

"Cyrus's the one that is all up MELISSA'S ass and hurting PAULA with his little games. You don't know how deep this shit has gotten!

"My wife is afraid of ME because of ELYEUH, who is me, and she's got lots of niggas coming out of her like fireworks when she gets hurt or scared now. Cyrus DID that….making her take up for him when he should have found courage like I said.

"She's been spoiling his grown ass for months and talking shit about me with him. She told me that shit herself. I know that she just wants the best for us….. She's just pissed off at me… I love her…I'm not letting her go, Lionel…. Neither of US wants to hurt her. I fucked up…my EGO…all my training, and that running…It just made me worse…."

Hakim suddenly went upstairs in the middle of his thought. I followed him to the bedroom. He was limping around the room slowly and packing things into a bag on his bed. As I came into the room and sat on my bed, HE looked over and smiled with that strange look in his eyes from last night.

"How YOU holding up, BRO? Did you get ANY sleep?" I asked HIM as I scratched the parts between my cornrows.

"ME, yeah, I'm gravy, Little Bro," He answered, scowling and his eyebrow twitching violently. "I only SLEEP when HE's HAPPY. I nap when I'm tired out HERE. Hakim isn't going to be back for a while, Little Bro.

"AND…If Cyrus doesn't recover…IT'S A RAP!"

He started to take a step and exhaled, amused, "I'm gonna need my glasses, a knee brace, and all the lights in the waiting room gave me a headache. I've never been in pain or appeared weak before, so this is a first for us all. I dislodged Hakim's knee out of place again, but it's all good. He did that playing soccer, but I never felt the pain. This is different. I'm just glad WE saved HER.

"We got to HER before something dangerous happened…But I'm worried…If Tony touched her…He may have really fucked her up more…like THAT BITCH did US. All that rape and negative energy are why I didn't want HER to go like that! I KEEP Kaliah and Trisha away because when I am out…when they touch me, it makes me crueler and more violent!

'What if he touched her when she was like that, and it REALLY made Melissa angry? I think that's why she swung on Cyrus! I know Tony touched her…I could hear and feel it when it happened…that's how I hurt Hakim's leg, breaking the door. I could catch Melissa screaming at Tony for touching her!

"I thought the worse until I saw what was happening…Then I realized…I could hear HER from inside Mandisa's head…when I'M on the outside! I kind of lost it for a moment, trying to wrap my own understanding about what the hell was happening.

"I don't comprehend myself…so I know it's much more problematic with the shit she's been through with her father. There's no telling how many are inside of her. But when she's crying on the outside…I hear…the OTHERS….on the INSIDE, now! That's why I started trippin…When Cyrus left…I started hearing THAT BITCH getting louder and louder until she popped out!

"I'm always on the giving side of the fear…SHE scares the HELL out of me…those eyes…though…and…THAT BITCH is still…PAULA underneath all that mean…and it is so damn…tasty…

"I think…it started…when Cyrus and I…did…she was a virgin…and was fine…then…suddenly….Melissa… started. BITCH!"

"You try to fuck Paula, then Melissa is gonna drop you like a bad habit. She said you can't mess Paula up or

Angel...But if you hurt Paula...you gonna get dealt with....so what YOU gonna do...Ain't Paula the girl you asked to marry you, NIGGA?" I chuckled, watching his face drop.

"NO! THEY ALL are HER, and I'M going to marry THAT girl...fuck what Melissa says...she's just gonna have to learn to love me too...WE need PAULA to feel happiness," Elyeuh nervously chuckled with huge eyes scanning the floor.

You already know me. I'm the instigator. I'm the brother that runs his mouth. So, I fucked with Hakim until I made that nigga ELYEUH come out once before. I wanted to know why he kept running off on me. Come to find out...He's really pissed off and doesn't like to use violence. Hakim is the fighter, after all.

But Melissa scared Hakim and made Elyeuh fight tonight. That's why I didn't say shit! HE needed to get put in his place because he thought that none of us knew HE wasn't Hakim. I started to see the difference in anger after Hakim cut his hair. He couldn't hide his mood under headbands with a fade.

Cyrus kept warning me to leave him alone, but I couldn't do that...HE's my fucked up brother too, and I wanted to know what he had against me! He doesn't hate me. ELYEUH can't be around me because my brother knew if I knew I was there, I'd fuck with him. He was so ashamed that he didn't want to risk my finding out and gossiping. That nigga knew that Cyrus wouldn't snitch! But I wouldn't let him live that shit down if I knew Hakim was like that back when I was just 13.

ELYEUH's got the same anger and rage as Melissa, probably because the same type of experiences molded their personas? I don't know. Kaliah would get this. He texted me, telling me he was on his way. Now...I was starting to wonder if Kaliah could fix this shit? He never told me anything about his research in this field. He was more focused on making money with the medicine he grew. Seriously, Kaliah worked nonstop for nearly 4 years, keeping shit going to avoid going home to Ms. Trisha.

But Kaliah has the same rage issues...and he scares ELYEUH too. I feel sorry for them because these are all family in one way or another, and these personas appear to be each of them crying for help and understanding. Not understanding from us...they need the personalities to understand themselves and what happened when their mind got fucked up. It's like the actual person can't see who they are at all.

All I know is that with all the extra niggas inside the fam now…there's enough actors and entertainment for a reality show! I know niggas will watch just to see who snaps on who and for what!

Necks will snap every Friday night as Hakim and Cyrus try to protect his model wife, PAULA, from his mean ass brother, HIMSELF, aka Elyeuh. Melissa is sneaking and creeping with Cyrus behind Hakim's back. ELYEUH tries to set a trap to get PAULA all to himself?

Yo, season two…! Paula is pregnant, and ELYEUH is demanding a DNA test! Cyrus is quiet... because Melissa is the one showing…Who's the actual baby's mama AND which is the baby's daddy?

Yo…tell me that shit ain't stupid as hell, and niggas won't watch? I'll be rich…I may start filming all this shit. Get money! Hit 'EM UP like 2Pac! So MY BROTHER did get me a bad-ass camera for Christmas after all?!

I'm just clownin. You know I wouldn't put my fam on blast like that, but yo…if THEY ALL down…I'm on board! I need to be on TV! LMFAO!

THIS NIGGA got me the camera and my chain, so HE ain't all bad. Obviously, he cared about Cyrus, too. But Melissa had to put foot to ass to get him serious about how he felt to save Cyrus. He has been playing Cyrus like a simp for years, and I know Melissa didn't like that shit. Cyrus would never stand up to him, so …I get…it…Melissa is picking on Hakim because Cyrus won't say shit!

She knows who is sweating HER Sexual Chocolate! My sister is crazy as hell, but it is still cute as hell. Because it's Mandisa flipping out…anyone else…I'd be a little shocked…

Hahaha…naw…really…I can kick it with ALL of THEM, but Trisha's rapey-ass. She'd be like having ELYEUH and Pretty Tony together…Ewww…fuck that…!

#

"Where are they moving him?" I questioned my brother as he finished packing.

"The Dallas Institute for Rehabilitation just wants to keep a close eye on him. They need to watch his lungs for infections because of his ribs. His shoulder has to be in traction a while, but he's cool," Hakim said, rubbing his bouncing left eyebrow. I stuck out my lips, glaring.

"Nigga, why are you lying?" I requested, eyeing him skeptically. "I thought the games were over! I guess I'll go wake Mandisa up, and we'll go find out what's really going on for ourselves since you can't keep shit 100…ELYEUH? This ain't the time to be hiding shit from me. I'm the only friend you go, for now, Nigga."

"Not now, Lionel…I…can't…think…straight…I told you what I know…That's where I'm going…Shit's…really…NOT NOW…okay?" Hakim warned me nervously. "I don't want you all there because he hasn't opened his eyes since they got him out of the operating room.

'He's not alert, and they can't wake him up! They said it went well, but they had to pump his stomach. He drank too much liquor, was high on coke, and when he went into shock…his heart…stopped."

"Hakim, Cyrus died!?" I yelled, and Hakim floored me, slamming me off the bed.

"Shut the fuck up, Lionel! Don't say another word!" Hakim shouted, holding me down on the floor. Tears ran down his cheeks, and he gasped, dropping his head on my arm. "Cyrus's fine… He's not gonna die! That's my brother! He can't die…I can't lose…him."

I held Hakim crying, "He's gonna be alright, Hakim, hear me?! That's my brother, too. I ain't going to let you give up on him."

"Niggas, are y'all fighting again? Just when we thought you finally got your shit together!" G.D. hollered from the door.

Hakim glanced up at Granddaddy and started crying again. He crawled up off the floor and limped over to my bed, and sat down in tears. Grandma Sophie entered, probably hearing us thinking we were fighting too.

"What's the matter, Hakim? You ain't cried in years? Lionel, what did you do? I told you don't kick another man in the nuts! That's playing dirty ball, Lionel!" G.D. yelled down at me as I moved up off my back.

I glanced over at my grandparents and sighed, "Cyrus in the hospital, y'all. When he left last night, he got messed up by Pretty Tony and his boys at Gucci's."

Both of my grandparents stared at me in disbelief as I nodded. Granny began to cry as she grabbed Hakim. G.D. looked at Hakim, asking, "He's gonna be alright, right, Hakim?"

"I...don't know...I don't know!" Hakim yelled, dipping his head between his legs.

"How bad is he? Cyrus is not a little boy. He's as strong as an ox! A little ass-whipping ain't gonna keep him down too long," G.D. thought, staring down at me because Hakim was lost in tears.

"Naw, G.D., that nigga shot Cyrus in the head and broke three ribs," I clarified, frowning. I grabbed Hakim's A-shirt from the bedroom trashcan.

When G.D. saw all that blood, he sighed and patted the top of Hakim's head. Hakim trembled as he glanced at the shirt. I quickly threw it away. Hakim fell down from the bed to his knees, weeping hopelessly lost.

"Hakim, look at me!" G.D. demanded. Hakim raised his head but didn't want to look at anyone. His face was so long, his eyes were bloodshot red, and he looked like he was just a kid. "Cyrus is a tough boy, and he's going to be okay. You need to have more faith in your friend. I know it's hard to picture him as being as strong as you or Lionel. He doesn't like to fight like you two, but Cyrus has spirit.

'He has more spirit than anyone that I've ever met, and that's why he's going to be fine. So if you're that worried about your friend, then while you're on your knees…say a prayer for him. It can't hurt worse than those tears you're crying."

Grandma Sophie glanced up at me and grabbed my hand, then took G.D.'s. We locked hands around Hakim, and I sighed, "Blessings to the Highest, this family comes today asking for grace and mercy. We pray for forgiveness. Touch us…my brother, Hakim, myself, grandparents, sisters, and our injured brother, Darius.

'He's hurt and needs divine protection. Cover him with your loving energy and hold him near your precious gift of life. Keep him with us? We don't have many family members left. Please don't take him before his time? He's a good brother and means well no matter what he does wrong. I pray that you hear my words…Divine Spirit, Universe, Father God, All creation… be blessed, Amen...Ase…"

I opened my eyes, and everyone was staring at me. Sophie was smiling with tears in her eyes.

"Lionel, where did you learn to pray like that?" G.D. asked me with his eyes bugging.

"I don't know…I don't go to church, but I believe in a higher power…we are all small; something bigger made us. We don't have to give it a name for it to be a part of our purpose.

'It doesn't have to be outside of me either. I feel closer to God, knowing if he's in my heart, then he's a part of me…so I get what some Hindi people say…Namaste…If God's in all of us, so we can worship all versions of God just by loving one another…right?

'Mama used to go to church, but she didn't talk about Jesus. Instead, she said she loved how good God had been to her. I remember her saying that Jesus was just a way to keep us fighting and from finding God. It made sense to me. But I don't hate on anyone for what they believe. I can be me…and not be religious…and still be a man of God," I attempted to describe how I made it up.

I just threw out an intention with the family, but G.D. and Sophie took it as a prayer…and that's fine. Look at it this way….If our hearts are the microphone…when you pray, you're talking to God's speaker. Then in the silence, the heart tells the mind to chill when we meditate…we're listening for God's Response…that's what Kaliah told me.

Kaliah read the Bible a lot growing up, and he told me that even Jesus meditated in the wilderness to get clarification. All the visions and voices he saw and heard were during his meditative state! God was probably warning him of the niggas about to turn on him! We all associate talking snakes with fake homies… Imagine that! We've always had a way to see the future, past, and present…but we wouldn't shut up, relax, and listen long enough...to HEAR the word?

I don't know how to do that shit...yet...but best believe...I'm gonna be on it...

Everything Kaliah has been telling us for years has been on point. He warned me that you don't have to argue about beliefs when you know what you know. You can even help them renew their faith and maintain your own perspective if you do it all with love and no arrogance.

My approach is different than Hakim's long debates and yelling about what is wrong with religion. We once believed it too. First, you accept that shit, then evolve...I see people on the internet trying to save people from religion...Ain't that the same shit religious people say they do when converting people?

This country needs to loosen up its hold over people's minds before they have a Religious war on their hands for nothing...all that shit is more HIStory that is long gone. People need to mind their own business about people's personal beliefs...that's why that shit is called a PERSONAL BELIEF...If you kept it private, the public might not have a problem. But everyone wants a reason to feel one way or the other and fit in with folks.

Just don't fake the funk and be a good person. But, shit…
that's so hard for people, correct?

I don't care if you drink goat piss every day and dress in
poison ivy and say you praise, Kid Itchy…as long you keep
your itchy-ass off me…you can scratch your nuts…and
breathe over that way…opposite me. Kid Itchy might be a
really cool dude that just sees shit differently. I don't know
what he thinks, so as long as he ain't drinking or itching on
me, we straight. I will clown his ass…cuz…he knew Lionel
was a nut if he came near me…or he will learn once we meet.

This is my way of letting religion go without upsetting
my grandparents…and it still raises my vibe by making them
feel good too…See…I can learn new shit…huh?

I know Hakim felt me when he nodded and stood up.
Then, he gave Grandma Sophie a hug and went into the
bathroom.

"That was meaningful and sweet of you, Lionel. I know
Hakim thanks you for that. He's just too hurt to say so, but
one day you'll see…he won't be able to hide his feelings
about higher powers. I'm very proud of you," Grandma
Sophie told me, smiling. I gave them both a hug as I went
out into the hall headed downstairs to check on Mandisa.

"I'm telling you, Sophie...THAT boy is going to be something special one day. He's making good grades now, has a sweet girl, and once Lionel makes up his mind what he wants to do...Lionel's gonna be a hell of a man. That's MY baby!" G.D. snickered from the bedroom.

I smiled because I had never heard my Grandfather talk about me like that. It made me feel outstanding. I wasn't worried about Cyrus anymore...I was concerned about Hakim now. I started to think...Maybe I could be a doctor and find a cure for the shit happening to my family?

It's just a thought...I got lots of time to make up my mind. I'm really considering it, and I know Kaliah would teach me anything! Once things die down...I'm gonna talk to him seriously.

Who knows...I could be the first Nigga to cure this shit! That would be crazy...Hood Nigga Healer...LMFAO! I am a Scorpio...Kaliah...said elemental signs have natural abilities in their DNA every incarnation.

Since I'm water in this life, I must have some healing gifts...? I can't wait to see...This stuff gets me fascinated...History sucks...Give me science and the unusual any day. I'm always trying new things because I get

bored quickly too. Hakim and I have more in common than
he reckons.

# Chapter Ten: Xxx/King's Dead

### Hakim?

I kept scrubbing and washing, but Cyrus's blood was all over me wouldn't come off! My emotions kept shifting from fear, confusion, frustration, and finally anger. I grabbed the handle of the shower door and held my breath, shutting my eyes. I carefully got on my right knee. The left was swelling and too painful to put all my weight on. Fuckin...TONY GUCCIONE!

*(It's over! Breathe...We just need to breathe....)* I took a labored breath and tried to meditate beneath the water. As the warmth sprayed the top of my head...I concentrated only on           the           water,           not me...Peace...Calm...tranquility...DARKNESS....still...B LACK...Cyrus? "What am I missing?".... "Fun! What fun memories you got?".... "I don't know...none, I guess!".... "Then we need to go make some now!".....(Hakim?)

....More DARKNESS...(Hakim??) ....Blue skies...cool crisp air...breezes...so blue like the ocean...rolling waves...

I can see her now. There she is in her white sundress, with her toes in the sand, and she's looking at me with those eyes….so blue…her hair like the sunset behind her…The cold breeze!

The wind is so strong…so dark now… "I love you! I love you so much…I'll do anything to make you happy!... Both of you…Just don't leave me here alone!?... I need you…both! Mandisa….Cyrus…don't go!!....(HAKIM?!)

My eyes opened slowly, and Mandisa was standing at the bathroom door. Her eyes were gray like silver stars. I quickly climbed up and snatched a towel to dry off. I turned off the water, dried my head, face, and set on my glasses so I could get a better look at her face. My eyes were suddenly straining worse than ever. I wrapped myself quickly so I wouldn't make you know who suppose the worse. I took a step from the shower and remembered my knee as the pain reminded me why I hate fighting when I'm too emotional. Hakim used to fight without regard for pain because he didn't care if he got hurt. He only wanted to win. Me…I hate to lose, and I won't fight if Hakim starts it. But if a nigga knew I was pissed off and still tested me, then I'd introduce him to a quick nap.

I had never fought so many at once. No one had ever tried me before like that. Tony and his boys knew I always had something for them when I came, so they didn't fuck with me. They did that shit trying to send me a message, too. But they fucked up clapping my brother! Mandisa was the only thing that made me get Cyrus out of there and not fuck Tony off right there. I was more afraid of losing her respect and love than getting my revenge.

She made me realize that I have been acting like I don't need anyone. I took things too far, trying to pretend to not be jealous of Melissa and Cyrus's little alone time. I had not met her until now, but Lionel and Cyrus obviously had talked to her. I couldn't get Paula to speak to ME. She would go away, and Angel would make Hakim come out when she cried. Now that I know who I was meeting…It all makes sense. I knew there were different girls in there…but I couldn't make out what I saw and heard from one moment to the next.

Mandisa is the ONLY woman for US! I don't care! We will do anything for her. But now I knew Melissa never talked to me because SHE hates me, and PAULA doesn't love me either…They want Hakim, but I'm a part of HIM too…right? I thought I could prove to them all that I LOVED her when I got her from Dr. King. But Melissa said…I'm just like her dad?… If that shit is actual…It has to be the facts…Melissa is still Mandisa…she wouldn't lie to US about how she feels…like me…I can't lie to people I know. That's why I never wanted to be near family. Now I was getting everything Hakim wanted, and his life had no place for ME. But I'm not gonna go anywhere quickly. Hakim is my weak baby brother…see…I've always been here…I just keep getting stronger while he's sleeping. He's too afraid to drive and fuck up now that he knows Mandisa will dump us.

I don't want to lose her…for Hakim. He'll never be right if he loses his queen. I don't want that for him…he's me. He's already suicidal. He could kill us both one day…once he finds a method that will stick. I could take or leave a BITCH. THERE are lots out there…but I don't want Hakim to go insane-insane. I love this life. I HATE looking like an easy target. Hakim needs me to keep him strong enough to grow up. He's still a scared little kid.

I'm not saying that I'm incapable of feeling love…I'm just incapable of accepting any from women. I get the family shit…but I don't want a bitch on me unless she's gonna give me a baby! And I think Mandisa is the perfect Baby Mama for Elyeuh's seed. But I want PAULA, not Melissa or that little crybaby, ANGEL.

Paula is the softest, sweetest, and most intelligent beast I have ever smelled…When I get close enough for a taste…SHE runs from ME…Oh…I love me a shy BITCH! So, I'll play nice until she gives up the sugar to MASTER.

SHE told ME that SHE would never leave me! So Melissa can suck my crooked dick with Jody up her ass! Hmmm? Interesting…Idea!

"Did you sleep alright?" I summoned her as I kept drying myself. I halted, spotting the size of my knee. It looked like a melon now, with the redness, swelling, and pulsing bothered me the moment my eyes spotted it.

See…it doesn't work the same…being from the inside…driving. I don't feel Hakim's pain unless I focus on the injury too long. But with all of the anxious feelings, it's instant once I see a wound! I limped into the room to my drawer and took my leg brace to stabilize my knee. It didn't even hurt until I looked at it. I was uncomfortable walking until I saw the size and bruising.

"Not really. I had nightmares again," Mandisa replied, staring at my leg. Mandisa came closer, and she blushed as she realized I was still nude under the towel. "It looks so painful….Hakim, are you alright?"

"Don't worry about it. It's an old sports injury. I aggravated it last night playing Donnie Yen…Flash Point!" I laughed, putting on my underwear carefully. Mandisa held my arm so I could lift my right leg. She was making me too excited being so nurturing after talking crazy to me a while ago. I couldn't forget that shit. But I knew this was really HER. "I'll elevate it later and put it on ice. I have some pain pills if it gets too ugly….Don't worry about me. I'm worried about you, Queen."

"But you are limping, Hakim. Does it hurt badly?" She probed me with the saddest eyes.

"Naw…no! It's a weird feeling, not pain," I lied, putting on my pants quickly. I got my knee into the brace and walked around, showing her. "See, it's cool. I…just have to make sure I don't put too much weight on it in the wrong direction until the swelling goes down. It will pop back in when it moves more freely near the joint. I won't be running for a few weeks, maybe. But it's the holidays, icy out, so I'll be okay."

Mandisa knelt down, stroked my knee, and gazed up at me unhappily. Her face was so pitiful as she put her lips to my knee, saying, "What you and Lionel did last night were things you only see in movies, Hakim. Darius and I were very fortunate to have you both there to save us. I was so afraid, and you were so brave. I'm so sorry…if I said or did something bad to you…I didn't mean it…I was afraid…and angry…I wasn't ME. I understand if…I AM too much for anyone. Darius…"

"Come here, Queen?" I cried, grabbing her in my arms. "I told you. I'm not going to let anything happen to you or anyone in my family. You're all WE have left. Losing any of you will push us over the edge for good. I love you…I don't care how weird shit might get. As long as we're together…we'll all be alright. But you can't leave me…You promised me that you would never go, Mandisa. I need to know you won't kick me to the curb for another man if HE makes you mad! I would never dump you like that…we can talk over shit…Don't let HER push me away because HE isn't ready to love you. I know what I want, Queen!

'You make me stronger, Queen. I thought I was too late when I heard you screaming! That's why I was so pumped up. I BLACKOUT when I get afraid like that, and I know I hurt those niggas, but I don't care once I snap like that! All I cared about was you and getting my brothers out of there. Now all I can think about is waiting for his silly-ass to walk out of the hospital. Then we can all sit around and laugh through this shit. It can't end like this.

'It doesn't matter how long it takes to get my family back. I'll wait. But when Cyrus is ready to talk and chill, I will send word to Lionel to bring you. It's not a pretty sight, now. So try to enjoy the next few days and don't worry. I got this!

Your friend is coming to visit, go shopping, take her to meet Amani, and let me do all the worrying, alright?"

"Oui, Sweet Love…whatever you say," She replied, putting her head on my shoulder softly.

"Sweet Love? That's new…where did that come from? You know how much I love hearing you say my name, Queen," I teased her as I caressed her cheek.

"Hakim?" She playfully whispered, kissing my neck. I stared down at her, suddenly feeling much better. She always made me so excited when she said my name like she needed me. "I love you, Mon Cher."

"You better go home and get ready. Maya will be waiting for you and Lionel soon. I've got Cyrus, okay?" I reassured her as I kissed her forehead before her lips. Her eyes twinkled up at me, and I knew that it was Paula…When she got near me, it made me feel so happy. I wanted to give her anything to just stay and love me. But when I tried to do anything to show her how much I loved her…she ran…It hurt when I realized it wasn't her the first time…or any time I touched Mandisa. She was all I wanted, but ELYEUH scared her…my past made her run from me…no matter how much I tried to show her I would never hurt HER. Now Melissa…she wouldn't forgive me…I NEED Paula! FUCK!

BITCHES!!!! UGH!!! "I'm gonna finish getting ready here. I'll stick around and see you two off. You don't want to be late."

I observed her beautiful hips sway out of my bedroom, and I shivered. I just have to fix this shit! I looked in the safe and found what I was searching for. I had Cyrus's will, life insurance policy, and health insurance card copies inside my legal papers for the rest of the family. I put the life insurance papers back. I wouldn't need that. My brother, Lionel, took care of ensuring Cyrus would be okay with his prayer. Jah will answer that prayer, or there was going to be hell on Earth.

I'm not sorry for what I've done. That nigga asked for it, so I helped him find his way HOME. I don't give a FUCK…not ANYMORE…Melissa doesn't realize that in the process of pissing me off to fight…she fed me enough to actually get to the point that…

I'm tired of losing family to bullshit.…Anyone that fucks with MY FAMILY NOW…gotta get GHOSTED!

#

"Hakim, Nigga, you don't call me for shit! What's up, Baby bro number 1?" Les laughed, answering his phone. I glanced around the hospital parking lot as I stared at all the blood in the backseat getting more pissed off by the second. I thumped the ashes from my cigar and scratched my chin, frowning.

"Les, I know me and you don't always see eye to eye, but I need you to meet me at the Regional hospital on the Northwest side of town…ASAP. THIS is ELYEUH," I told him, staring at my blood-drenched fist and clothes. I took a deep drag and slowly exhaled, trying to avoid going home to get my gun!

"Fasho, Nigga! Lionel with you?" Les asked me.

"No, Lionel's at home with my girl. Les, don't tell anyone I called you, not even Lionel. This is BUSINESS…I SAID…THIS IS CHIEF…" I replied seriously.

"Alright, 15 minutes. I'm on the 20, as we speak. I been at the casinos and lost $15,000 in four hours. I'm pissed the FUCK off. But I'm near the 80 Hallsville exit, so I'll be that way, Nigga!" Les stated seriously. That was around as serious as Lester Woods was going to get on the phone. He wasn't about business until he was in my face, but he knew not to enrage me in either situation.

"Les! Don't call me nigga anymore, man! Not fucking cool!" I shouted, swaying my eyes at a vehicle leaving the parking lot in the night.

"My bad, Chief...I forgot you hate that shit, Black Panther," Les nervously chuckled, lowering his voice. He was silent a moment, and I let my eyes shift to my hand on the steering wheel. Cyrus was in surgery. They blocked the bleeding. But he went into shock, and there was no way of knowing if he would recover from the coma the bullet caused. They didn't want Cyrus to live after beating him 6 on one...AND... that was after the BITCHES shot him twice. Les's traffic talk broke my thoughts. "If you don't get in yo goddamn lane, Bitch, I'ma permanently get you a handicap sticker for that piece of shit! Da fuck you want with me, grandma? You need the cobwebs knocked off that fossil-ass pussy or what? Them teeth come out, or they real? ...Fuck that shit!... That hand ain't REAL?!

'No wonder you can't steer that battleship of a gravy boat, BITCH! You are not fine enough anyway! I love my Golden Girls like Sophia and Blanche...! But, SHIT, I'll take dumb-ass Rose right about now! DECAYING BITCH, you talk shit and hideous like Bea Arthur! My dick is dead, Old HO! AP-pr-E-ci-ATE you, BITCH, the cemetery is DAT way! Don't meet me there; beat me there, Granny Clampett!"

"Fucking, Lester... Woods..." I sighed under my breath, trying not to laugh. "15 minutes...look for SHUN. I'll be waiting."

"Alright, Chief...Where the fuck is Cyrus's crazy ass?" Les bade as I hung up the phone.

As I sat in my car, I took the sim card out of my burner and broke it—no need to use THAT number again. I had lots of prepaid phones for just such occasions. What I used Les for wasn't going to be healthy for anyone caught in the crossfire. I was done with Gucci's and Tony's trivial ass. He'd been raping bitches, selling drugs, and fucking up niggas since I was 12. I hoped his ass was still at the club and Mia's hot-ass too. It didn't matter...I know where they live. I fucked their daughter, Courtney.

For what they did to Cyrus, I would turn Gucci's into Syria with the lead shower I was about to rain down. My family soon would realize that ELYEUH is no bitch...like Melissa says behind my back and now to my fucking face. I want to fuck the shit out of her like that loud-mouthed ho inside of Trisha! But it's not out of hate...I want to fuck her out of admiration...I bet I can make her shut the fuck up...and she'll be all over my dick. But that's for another day. Right now....I'm determined to show THAT BITCH she ain't really Bout it-Bout it! ELYEUH is the ICE CREAM MAN... I'll kill as many birds with this one stone as possible to let it be known...I don't play about MINE!

I keep niggas out of my business because…I don't merely fuck bitches when I get out. This is a network I am building. It's not just about lust for ME. I'm very awake, BITCH! The girls asked to be hit…I never hit one that didn't beg me. I don't like violence. Martial arts trained me to practice self-discipline because my body is a weapon. The first time I got picked up by the cops for street fighting was when I was 13; they told me that I could be locked away for life if I harmed anyone because of my mental illness. So, I only scare the shit out of niggas, because if I get locked up again…The family falls apart. I was the breadwinner, the family hero, and the King of the Castle…so I needed subjects to protect OUR best interests above the systematic practices. Lester Woods was another pawn I utilized to keep the game in check.

Les hauled up next to Shun and got out. He plunged into the passenger seat and saw all the blood on my clothes, then saw it covering the seats. His green eyes grew wide as I stared at him. He shut the door and hit the locks, shaking his head. He was a little drunk, his red eyes, and I could smell the liquor. It didn't matter; I didn't really need Lester to do this shit. But he could contact the person that I knew would get the job done. I didn't keep the numbers of the people that worked for me…I let Lester hold my Black Book!

Lester has many friends in common with Hakim and ME. I knew he wasn't afraid to get his hands dirty, but I didn't need Les to do anything but make the call. If I sent Lester Woods, Tony would see him coming and make a run for it…like he did whenever he heard Les was in town. I knew that…shit…Lester never picked up the hint that Mia was warning her husband that her crazy ex was still gunning for him…because…Lester was still in love with Ms. Mia.

He's Courtney's father…not Tony! Lester told me that Mia was his first love, and Tony fucked her up…he started running hos and gave up on love…What he doesn't know is that he's Courtney's daddy. Mia didn't tell him that shit because she knew he was already fucking her sister.

Courtney told me everything…so don't…tell Cyrus…yet. I don't need Les to know that I fucked her either.

Les would be too easy….I needed…Angela Bradley. Yes…Angela…that same hot piece of ass that used to drive all of us crazy as kids. That girl had changed since she moved to Compton with her family. She couldn't cut it in college, and she got jumped into a real gang over there. Angela was still beautiful, but she was not the same sweet little bitch she used to be. She was rough, eccentric, and deadly as fuck!

One year in LA was all it took. She came back a totally different person. I had heard she was serving up niggas ass, bullets, and taking over trap houses all over East Texas only two months after her fine ass came home. Yes, it's true…She's a bad bitch, but she has one weakness…ME! Les knows where to find her all the time like clockwork. He was Angela's first, but ELYEUH is her EVERYTHING!

"Who is it?" Lester asked, staring at my hand, trembling on the steering wheel.

"First, we have to discuss business before pleasure. I just got my hands on a dispensary in Colorado that was about to go on the market. How would you like to own it?" I asked, staring at the lights ahead. It was nearly 2:45 am. We had plenty of time to catch them slipping.

"Y-you're for real? I've wanted to go into business with you for years!" Les laughed nervously.

"NO! Not go into business with US, man! I'm giving it to you as a gift. I drew up the papers in the glove box. All you have to do is put your name on the deed, permits and buy your product from us. You'll make enough for you and your entire family, but you'll be a very privileged customer. But, unfortunately, I can't put you on the team because of your criminal activities.

'I don't need the police, F.B.I., or the C.I.A. in OUR business…understand? But we do it this way; you'll be thrilled with minimal effort on your behalf," I explained, looking over at him seriously smiling. Les nodded, understanding.

"Hit me with a few figures? I know you did the math, Chief, right? What exactly am I spending and getting?" Les worried, and I thought for a moment calculating figures.

"I'm offering you our product at one-third of the asking price and a way to sell it legally. What we sell for $3600 a pound, you pay $1200. That's the old product price. Cyrus and Kaliah have created the 'Queen of Weed.' She'll sell for $6400, the lowest. Kaliah is going for full medical endorsement, and once testing is completed…we get those numbers and figures… demand will skyrocket by 42%. I'm talking $7,680,000 for sales the first year, then after medical approvals, $11.5 million we'll net annually.

'You sell HER, and you'll get a considerable discount, and a massive chunk of that will be yours because…we own all her seeds exclusively. All you have to do is sit back, count your money, and pay your taxes. The Queen will sell herself, Les.

'The 'Red Queen Kush' is Kaliah and Cyrus's masterpiece. Right now, they are growing over 2200 plants simply for the production of seeds. We're slowing production on all other colors and going strictly red in 2 years. So if anyone wants her…they have to get her from US and pay what WE ask if they want more," I disclosed to Les grinning. "You know this is strictly confidential info, no cap."

"Fuck yes! I'm in, Hakim! What you need?" Les laughed, resting backward, becoming enthused as hell.

He got US mixed up when he was ecstatic or anxious if I was gonna see red and fuck him up. I passed him a blunt of the gorgeous flower from the glovebox while pointing to the paperwork. I wasn't going to put Cyrus's blood on anything but the weed. You gonna get in on my FAMILY's shit…It's a BLOOD CONTRACT…So, Les was gonna smoke this blunt, and I purposely put Cyrus's blood on the tip and lit it. I took a deep puff, watched the blood bubble from the flame, and handed it to Les…I glared at him, pausing.

I was shocked Les had upgraded his sauce. His tastes in clothing were no longer flashy shirts that looked like Polynesians might show up and start fire spinning any moment. He took my advice and got some designer suits, and looked decent in Armani. If only he would stop trying to grow that red hair out in those cornrows! It's an abomination. I wonder if WE kept the locks would we look like this in Italian suits? But I'd instead get mine from the source. I'm dying to go to Japan, China, and even fuck up Bangkok with my boy Sai, now that he's back in Thailand…but I wonder… No, I'm FINE as fuck…LOL!

I take my CONTRACT SHIT seriously. If we have a deal, you better not break the rules, or it's your ass. Les burned that weed without reluctance, understanding what it meant. His green eyes lowered as he inhaled another hit…His face entirely relaxed, his eyes drooped, and his cheeks slowly grew crimson from the neck up…Lester rapidly gaped at the blunt in his trembling fingers a moment…he sluggishly hit it again.

"Fuck, Bro…why you wait til now to give me THIS shit? I'm feeling NO pain…GODDAMN, man! So THIS is the Queen?" Les very calmly raised, beaming bashfully, watching the blunt absolutely struck.

"Yep, right now, there are merely about 62 plants. However, the Queen is breeding, and she'll leave the streets grieving. But I need a favor, now, Les. I needed you relaxed enough to ring MY Pro-Ho for me. That's why I sent you on a flight.

'Angela Bradley….call her ….Pretty Tony and his punk- ass entourage capped Cyrus last night," I informed Les, sulking, exploring people heading inside the hospital, pondering the plan remorselessly.

"Nigga, What? Fuck That! We can go spray his pretty, raping, and shady fat ass right fucking now! I'll blow that bitch sky high, Chief!" Les abruptly sat forward, bellowing. "Where is HE?"

"Who, Cyrus or Pretty Tony?" I chuckled teasingly because I knew he was fucked up and ready to fly off the handle.

"Cyrus, Hakim! The fuck wrong is with your ass?" Les laughed, getting ampt hitting the dashboard. "I'm about to make Mia a widow, and the kids all bastards! ....But none of them is HIS any fuckin way…so no loss."

"Cyrus is upstairs, they're extracting the bullets, and he'll be out any minute. So…call Angela now!" I instructed Les, chuckling.

"Chief, please…Let me…off that bitch?!" Les groveled, so scarlet it made me smirk more.

"No offense, Lester, but you hang out with my brother. You stroll your ass up in there now, and you'll get swamped. But…Angela…is just what the doctor ordered. So she'll put on those pretty heels, let that hair down, sport a tight dress, and strut right into that shithole armed to the pussy.

'She'll saunter up to the bar, demand a spot as a dancer, and we both know the application process to twerk sumthin' at Gucci's?" I hinted to Les. Lester Woods wasn't a terrible dude, but he lacked finesse for particular situations. He had all the tools, but he couldn't calm down enough to reflect before he operated. That's why he was better off as…my Street Sweeper or Hitman. I gave Les the vision. Obviously, he caught on because his grin sprouted so vicious it made me relax. The last thing I wanted was for Lester Woods to fly up in there talking shit and dropping my name. Angela would be much more discreet and swift. "What's gonna happen, Les?"

"Angela's…gonna have to go in the back to the private room…and…." Les glanced over at me and shook his head. "Chief, you're fucking sick! I'll call baby girl right now! Shit…this is for you and Lionel…I'll take the shop and pay full price for the Queen. You throw in a pound of her RED FINE ASS when she's old enough for me to smoke, please?

Pretty-Motherfucker Dunn fucked wit the wrong family...Y'all All DUNN, Son!"

"Dunn Deal, Les," I attached as he put his phone on speaker.

"What's crackin, Lester?" I overheard Angela's cute tone pick up.

"Angela, what up, Crip-cakes?" Les hooted.

"Shit, it's Christmas, so you know the deal. Counting cash, Cuz...." She giggled. "You at home? What you up to?"

"Naw...no...Candygirl...I'm not at home. Actually, I'm calling for a big favor from...the Chief. You know he doesn't keep numbers any mo," Les told Angela and held his phone back.

"Chief? ELYEUH?! Where is HE? What does he need? Tell him...Mama got HIM...Lester...where is HE?" Angela started the motion. I stayed quiet and sat back smiling.

"Pretty Tony at Gucci's, you know the spot?" Les asked, grimacing and rolling his eyes.

"Yeah...the trash hole near Kilgore on the 20? Ain't that spot hot? I heard they just found his old lady near the chemical plant...." Angela included. "Are you with HIM now? Where are you...I'm on my way!"

"So he capped Mia? Hmm...Less work then," I thought quietly so she wouldn't hear my voice. It figured Tony would kill Mia. She was a witness too. Since he let us go and knew we wouldn't talk...That left HER as the only person to tell the police if Cyrus died. She would have ratted him out after that last ass whooping. She was done this time when she saw how she got Cyrus in her shit. Thus the universe begins to unfold as it must. I smiled to myself, elevating my eyebrows at the irony.

"Chief wants you to say night-night to Pretty Tony. But be your professional, La Fema Nikita, sexy fire-girl mode, and he wants you to make it look sexy for him...That op clapped Cyrus," Les replied, his face turning red, probably coveting a ride-along badly. He took the phone off speaker and kept it to his ear. I seized that moment to unwind. But no one loosens up like ELYEUH when he is enraged like this!

"Tell her ELYEUH says hello," I chuckled forcefully, spinning my eyes and jeering.

"Yeah, so go say bye-bye...and...ELYEUH says hello-...Damn...What...Bitch...? Calm down! No, I can't do that...he got business to take care of for now! His brother is in the hospital...yeah...LIKE I said...Cyrus! ..mhm... Naw, he ain't here, Bitch! He texted me! You didn't hear THAT NIGGA in my truck…! Shit, I don't know….He calls from a different number every goddamn time! Write his ass! Yeah, he got an email…you got a pen? It's…www…dot….

'BitchBait69@yahmama.com! I …don't ….fucking know! After you do the job, I'll start you a message board!" Les hooted, aiming to overhear through Angela's screams.

"Um…tell her…IF Samantha Reed is there at the bar…her to leave…." I added, gazing out the window and hitting the RED QUEEN. I needed to calm down before I went back around those nosey white people asking a million questions. I just wanted Cyrus to wake up so we could go home. I have hated hospitals since Dr. King showed up in Longview.

This is the second time I've been here this year. The first was to welcome my baby sister into the world…I can't lose my brother, Cyrus, here! He managed to tell me with his broken jaw that Sami tried to get him to leave through his tears. Djay told Lionel that Tony had snatched Mandisa from the bar. "Let Djay make it too once the bullets start raining. Split Pretty Tony, the boys, and Billy-B…like a pop-tart with a Tech 9 if she can stuff one…I want to hear about it on the news and appreciate a legend adores me."

"Yo, Angela, you let the Djay and little Samantha at the bar make it home. Have AB/VA cut the EYES outback. He knows where to look...Naw! I'm reading instructions on my phone from the text!... I told you HE ain't HERE!.... BYE, Crazy, Heffa!" Les screamed and hung up. "....Chief, that girl.... is crazy about you! What the fuck you do to Angela? I've fucked her a lot...she doesn't act like that wit nobody...but you."

"Nothing...I just kissed Angela once...a long time ago," I said, not lying but leaving too much out. Les glowered to himself as I passed him the blunt. "She was HIS loyal bitch, Les, and she set Cyrus up for that shit. She's a hood booger! A THOT, she ran through any nigga with money telling lies to get the dick Tony gave away, Fuck Tamia Sullivan!"

"That bitch was hollering and screaming.... 'Elyeuh! Oh my god! Where is he? What's his number?' ... Bitches don't look for niggas like that for kisses, Chief! I know that shit...." Les suddenly laughed. Poor Lester, I know that shit stings, but she would never leave Tony for him either. Les could have been her old man, but he wanted to run the streets. I bet if he knew Courtney was his daughter....He wouldn't be married and hating that shit...wrong...sister. "Tamia...she was just a hurt little girl...married to the wrong nigga. He fucked her up too, Chief. She was the first bitch them niggas got a hold of from round here."

I raised my eyebrow, not caring, and flashed out the window, moving my eyes. Poor, poor Tamia, right…that bitch was on borrowed time when she fucked Cyrus and got him jumped the first time. But Angela…I warned her that she would wear a collar if I got the pussy, but she didn't care. I got her when I was 14 after she moved back. I'm not sorry either. She begged for it when she saw me back then. Then she begged me to stop. So, I say to anyone out there. You mess with ELYEUH; you'll get fucked one way or the other in the end…HARD! LMFAO….BITCHES…!

#

"Good morning, East Texas! Tragic news in Longview and Kilgore as a local nightspot experienced an electrical fire after tragedy struck on Christmas night and burned down early this morning. Gucci Nights, the establishment incinerated, was owned by a local businessman, Tony Guccione Jr., later found dead was his wife, Tamia Guccione. Witnesses gave accounts of Tony and Tamia fighting violently many times at the nightspot publically.

"Authorities are saying it was a crime of passion due to their violent history of domestic abuse and Tony's sexual deviancy. Tamia Sullivan Guccione was discovered near a local chemical plant on the outskirts of Longview brutally beaten and shot twice. Her husband's body was found, along with his vehicle in the Ferguson Creek Reservoir, with what appeared to be a self-inflicted gunshot wound to the head. In addition, police and detectives found drugs, the alleged suicide weapon, and it seems that Mr. Guccione was under investigation for the disappearance of several young women around the East Texas area.

'Meanwhile, the fire broke out at their nightclub after a dispute where several employees fought over money, witnesses reported to the police. After shots were fired, ten not yet identified male suspects were pronounced dead on the scene. Witnesses say the fire started when employees tried to remove a safe from the establishment, and gunfire was exchanged, causing the lights to overheat, which caught fire inside a storeroom behind the old building.

'Many residents have commented that the nightspot was notorious for shady dealings, and they are not unhappy to see it gone. More on the story at 11. Coming up next on the news, Sports! This is KLTV News Channel 7, Longview, East Texas," The pretty sister reporter announced as I turned off the TV and lifted my eyebrows, grinning.

Bravo, Angela…I feel the love! That's how a bad bitch takes out the fucking trash…Make it nice and neat for Daddy…

I tossed the remote on the sofa next to me and rubbed my knee, sighing as Mandisa came rushing through the backdoor into the den. She stopped near the couch, looking gorgeous. Her golden top clung to her figure, her sexy tight pants held those legs like a second skin, and she had to wear those badass boots that go higher than her knees! Antoine's clothes fit her body, so right…everything she wore looked like it belonged on display. *(Ugh…a taste…would be…so nice…)*

"Hakim, turn on the news! Tony and Mia are dead?! It is everywhere!" She shrieked to me. Her face looked suddenly horrified. I clutched the remote very calmly and turned on the TV.

"Dallas lost to Miami in an upsetting fumble in the last 11 seconds of the game! Miami's defensive end, Oliver Vernon, intercepted the pass and runs it in for a last-second touchdown. Tony Romo was not a happy camper, to say the least," The male sportscaster announced.

"That's not news, Queen. The Cowboys always lose the moment the pressure is on. To Miami…? Wow! Gots to be more careful," I groaned, shaking my head.

"Hakim! That's not funny!" Mandisa thoughtfully mumbled…but almost giggled.

"Yes, it is…." I replied, laughing. "Don't tell me you're a Cowboys fan? I like Dallas, don't get me wrong, but naw…I can't…not a fan, Queen…But I see how everyone wants to believe they can make it…But not since the 90s…sorry."

"Hakim!" Mandisa giggled but put her hands on her sexy hips.

"My bad, Damn, Queen! Go…Romo…!? Let's extend his contract for another 10 years since he's so hot! Sheesh…! You Cowboy fans are so damn sensitive," I giggled, rolling my neck frowning, pretending to be like Cyrus's feminine alter-ego…LaQuiesha.

"What did you do?" Mandisa questioned me…her eyes shut slightly…and I threw my hands up.

"Nothing! I was at the hospital all night with Cyrus! I promise…this is the only place I've been since yesterday," I replied honestly? I was SPITTING straight facts. "Besides…Lionel had my fire, so what could I do?"

"That's right...I forgot...I'm so sorry! I thought that you-," Mandisa exhaled, hiding her face and relaxing. She jingled over and planted her sunshine on the sofa, and I played with her golden chains on her black boots. "This is insane...It's ironic?"

"I call it karma... Tony had more people to worry about than us. But, what goes around comes around, and thusly the universe unfolds as it must," I informed her as I grabbed a sip of grape juice. I patted my knee as the tingling and throbbing seemed to burn a bit higher than the leather on her boots. No one walks like HER...the others are too stiff. No...this girl has all the drip!

God, PAULA...I know it's YOU! You're so gentle and....smell so delicious. It's like taking a whiff of the freshest honeysuckle mixed with any fragrance she wears. It's always something floral. She is a golden sunflower in every way; also, it's her favorite.

Paula, my juicy mango! I'd love to munch and slurp all that fruit until nothing but the skin remained. Then I'd suck the color from the leftovers until the next taste. But, one look at those eyes and those gratifying features, and WE can't maintain. Those darkly painted gray eyes sparkling like the waviest ice, round plump lips painted... RED...*(Nommy noms)*…. And how dare you wear your hair down! Those golden curls look like waves of caramel-coated popcorn falling down her shoulders and trying to conceal a tiny portion of her face.

I playfully batted my lashes at her over my glasses, joking, "Don't you look all sexified in that golden wrapper? Girl! If I didn't have this bad knee!... I'd take you up them stairs…peel off that gold foil…and lick those chocolate kisses until you call me Big Daddy Longstroke!"

Paula began giggling at me as I emulated G.D., "Hakim, Stop!"

"Come give ya granddaddy a kiss, Man-DEE-SA," I enticed her, puckering my lips ridiculously. She snorted, moving her red tips over my aching knee softly. I gave her juicy lips a sweet taste, held her hand, and gave that treasure a squeeze. I don't care if she's wearing clothes…uh…that ass feels like it was made for my palms. So soft, but it resists the touch and fights back…oh…I love that shit! As I glanced at her ring about to see if I could get Paula to follow me back upstairs a moment, I heard a car horn outside! I know I had stone-face as I lost my mojo and hobbled up. It was Lester's crazy ass!

I limped outside to the curb.

"Commander, Merry Belated Christmas compliments of the ladies! I fetched a gift for you, Bro!" Les snickered, rolling the illegally-tinted windows entirely down on his shiny new custom-painted Midnight Blue, Model S, Tesla.

WE could afford to get a few of these…but Hakim is so frugal …smh…But…He won't be back…I just may make some purchases for the BOTH of US; while I'm up…Hmm? That is a car! If I spent my money…yeah…Chrome was everywhere, glistening with that paint capturing all the light with silver flakes. Yeah…I need all that…But, RED!

…I don't have anything personal against blue at all…We're not affiliated with the brotherhood of the Crips or Blood cliques…It's a personal preference for ME…I'm always angry or anxious, so red is the only color I sometimes see. It grabs my attention first when in motion while sharing Hakim's vision.

"Sup, Lester…in a Tes-la…THAT is a fly-ass Model S. I'm thinking about putting Shun away. A car like that would really get my engines revved up," I chuckled, admiring the way the morning sun reflected off the chrome in contrast to the black wheels in the slush.

"It's my Christ-Mas gift to me this year! You gotta enjoy money if you make it, Chief. You can't take it when you die, and the fam just gonna scrap over that shit!.... Oh yeah...

'Angela and the homies found something pretty on Tony they thought Cyrus might want back," Les murmured to me with a smile. He passed me the watch WE had given Cyrus for Christmas. I glared at the black band and put it in my pocket, nodding. "Right on time, Les."

That was the last piece of evidence I needed to be returned that could lead back here. I gave Les's hand dap as I glanced around the street.

"I get it, Hakim...! That was a good joke... You're a nut, man!" Les laughed as I spotted Lionel above, watching from the bedroom window. "Anything else you need, Chief! Holla at ya, boy. I got your back, Bro...umm... Tell Lionel to stop changing in the window!.... Nigga! Put on yo damn shirt!... Bony-ass! ....Po, Lionel,.... the only thang swoll on him is his head."

I chucked as Les drove away. I pretended not to see Lionel watching me from the open window, smoking, but he hollered down, "What the fuck you doing with Lester, Hakim?"

I glanced at Cyrus's watch from my pocket and said, "It's 10:30? Don't you have to get to Shreveport in less than an hour?!"

Lionel suddenly dashed out of the window, smiling from ear to ear.

My phone rang, and I slowly walked over to Shun and answered, "Hakim, I'm getting on a plane as we speak. Last one to Dallas. Yuh handle yuh business, Bro?"

"Not a problem, Kaliah. The goose is cooked," I replied, noticing the bloodstains on the backseat and frowning.

"Good, gud...lucky muthafucka! I could have dropped the son of a bitch myself for that shit," Kaliah responded, so pissed his accent was gone!

"Handled, Bro, you feeling alright?" I worried, rubbing my temples.

"Bitch-ass wife, Hakim! She knows I am done, but now she's calling more and more. I'm done! DUNN! Why is it when they have you they are never there...then when you're done they suddenly can't leave you alone? She has bitches and niggas every fucking where, but now she wants to change? FUCK THAT! I'm out this piece, Bro...I've put in too much time and energy trying to patch up a bitch that doesn't want to be repaired. There are limits to my genius…and I admit defeat," Kaliah groaned.

"Sir, you're going to have to turn off your phone," A lady said, interrupting Kaliah.

"Of course, eh, mi know…rules..fly all di time, Love," Kaliah replied, playing.

"Just turn it off before the Captain speaks," She changed her mind.

"Aaagh! Every fucking time! Didn't even try to flirt…I was just pleasant…what the fuck? Canna even look at another woman…they all turn me off… Why? Ugly women, pretty women. Little gals and female animals just want to fuck me too!?

'I'm not fucking anyone! My dick is on hiatus… the Flight attendant even looks like a bat to me! It's not har…it's me! The spell Trisha had on me must be too strong. I can't look at another woman without seeing HER. It's hopeless, Hakim!

'I'm cleansing…this has been the worse six months of my existence. Bro…no sex sucks…I think I'm going crazier…But I can't do it! I am seriously not with Trisha…I am afraid I will mess up another woman if I do her like my wife…. So I'm going to have to reprogram my sex drive…It's a process…and…I'm falling to pieces…Healing…it isn't pleasant…remember that shit…." Kaliah complained.

"Bro, you don't talk like this…you gonna be alright?" I chuckled, hearing the clarity.

"Might be my problem, Hakim…I'm tired, horny as fuck, my marriage is over, and bitches keep testing me! This shit with Cyrus was the last straw for me too! I need a nap or a good fight! Fuck! I may kill someone soon!" Kaliah laughed, trying to slow his voice down.

"I thought people got married to have fewer problems involving sex?" I teased him.

"Aye-aye, but mi canna fuck a woman dat always talk shit, Hakim. It's an immediate turn-off for mi, now! Dick just dies when the swears fly. Gotta go…the bat returns…." Kaliah chuckled. "About to hang it up…. right, now, Love."

"Yes, Sir, you have a beautiful smile…." She told Kaliah.

"Three hours, Dunn, and I land in Dallas….What yuh doing!? Nah…gratitude, Love," Kaliah groaned angrily and hung up.

"What you doing talking to Les, Hakim?" Lionel questioned me again as he shocked me handing me my bag.

"Les?... Oh, he found this and returned it to me to give back to Cyrus," I reported to Lionel as I withdrew Cyrus's Christmas gift from my pocket but couldn't look at it. "Pretty Tony thought he had a nice little reminder of our encounter last night. But instead, he got his shit burned down and his ass handed to him by some shady bitches....I learned."

"So, YOU clapped him, Elyeuh?" Lionel posed, frowning strangely.

"He tried to kill my brother, Lionel! Anyone that fucks with MY family has to go! This is Hakim's Code of Law...I'm making the rules for these BITCHES that think they can break the circle! The scales are constantly tipping when I put you on time out... Tony has been asking for that shit for years now! If it were YOU...He'd have been dead before I left that club. I couldn't finish him with Mandisa right there! But now Tony's gone, and no one's going to miss his ass!

'No one is going to take any of YOU away from me...NO ONE!" I conveyed to him as I got in the driver's seat.

"What about Courtney, Hakim? Tony's got kids and a family, too," Lionel reminded me. I tensed up.

"Lionel... Who do you think started the rumors that Cyrus was fucking Courtney and let Tony believe that shit? ...Mia!

'She lied on her own daughter to cover up her fucking around with Cyrus. But the real kicker is I fucked Courtney, Lionel! Tony never knew...I fucked her over a year ago, she had a damn heart condition, and she stopped breathing in the middle of shit.

'Cyrus went to see her in the hospital and found out that Mia was Courtney's mom. Mia didn't know that Cyrus and Courtney were cool...Courtney used to be in love with J-Rock! That's how Cyrus met Mia...She was fucking James, too! But Mia loved Cyrus, and Cyrus asked her to leave Tony. She didn't want to give up that lifestyle...But she got jealous, thinking Cyrus was fucking Courtney, and told Tony that shit. I know Mia did that shit...Courtney told me when we talked not too long ago.

'She went to college...no thanks from her mother...and fake-ass father. Tony tried to fuck up Cyrus over the wrong ho this time. He knows Mia's a ho, and he's not dumb. But Courtney's not even Tony's daughter, Lionel. She's got red hair and green eyes just like her father...Lester Woods, but he doesn't know. Les and Mia were together before Tony came here.

'So yeah, I'm going to Dallas to pick up my big brother at the airport and check on Cyrus. I started it…and now…I finished it," I warned Lionel putting on my seatbelt.

"What?!" Lionel demanded, shaking his head.

"She's not his daughter, Lionel. She knows she's Les's daughter…I don't really know IF Lester knows. But I don't think he does…He was always hanging around Gucci's watching out for Mia because he still loved that girl. You want to know another reason all this had to happen? It's all jacked up, but I just feel like I can tell you, and you'll believe me," I invited Lionel frowning.

"Just blow my brains out, Hakim," Lionel answered, dropping his head.

"Samantha Reed has been crazy since Pretty Tony and his boys ran a train on her ass at that club! Wonder why she came back to town and started working there…then trying to get ahold of Cyrus after so long?

'Yeah, she was crazy about me because I was the one that saved her ass from those niggas, but I was too late! Cyrus doesn't know why she was so obsessed with me. He thinks I fucked her. No! He knew that she wasn't a virgin when he got with her, and she already liked me. But he didn't understand why. I didn't want to tell the facts because I didn't want him trying to fight Tony over her back then!

'But look at how shit just kept coming back? Tony hurt that girl when she was 13, and she lost her mind. What we did as kids has nothing to do with her obsession because I never went past a hug with Sami. I couldn't touch Sami when I saw how crazy Cyrus was for her. But he still believes that I made her like that. So I let him imagine what he wants, but I still love him, but Cyrus secretly hates me over THAT mean bitch.

'I'm always…looking out for him because he's too sensitive about his BITCHES. One thing…I'm glad…Sami did try to save his ass. So she got a pass. But Tony and his BITCH can rot in their shallow graves, now…."

I pulled out of the driveway and hit the Interstate heading West toward Dallas to meet with my big brother, Kaliah. I had just enough time to greet him at the airport.

# ACT THREE

## OVERLY DEDICATED

# Chapter Eleven: Love/Paramedic!

## Lionel

Mandisa seemed fine in her model-sister mood. PAULA…I think that is what Melissa calls her. We formally met early this morning, and she told me everything she knew. Paula stayed quiet, sitting pretty in Cyrus's truck like a Baddie in her gold and black all dolled up. But she was miles away in thought. Her gray eyes twinkled in the sunlight, but I could tell she was heartbroken. It didn't matter which version of Mandisa we got out…THEY all loved Cyrus and ME!

It made me feel kind of extraordinary because I was a jerk to Mandisa at first. Then, she forgave me like nothing and loved me like I was her real brother. The one constant thing, Mandisa will let the past go when it comes to others, but she can't seem to get over her own. Hakim is precisely the same when it comes to that shit! Maybe that's why they were attracted to one another all along? If they need one another to fix what's broken, then it's no wonder THEY hate ELYEUH but love Hakim. If Hakim wants to keep Mandisa…any part of her…ELYEUH has to change or get the fuck gone!

MELISSA made it known that she would dump him and mess up any future plans my brother makes. So, either way, it goes…Elyeuh is fucked as long as Melissa is alive. This shit is crazy…but I can follow it like a soap opera. Granny Sophie watches The Young and the Restless….Nigga! Put us on that shit! The drama is so delicious that I'm drooling thinking of the fights alone! I'm gonna seriously start filming this shit for something! I'll get everyone's permission once I decide what to do with all the shit! I gotta have a way to make money too!

I know one damn thing for as much money as it takes to get on a plane, you would think the people that worked for airports could be more cheerful and shit. But this terrorist bullshit has everyone looking at anyone as a possible threat to security. I understand the need to keep weapons, drugs, and dangerous things off commercial flights with passengers. But I don't get why it is illegal for anyone to have a private airport, plane, and transport whatever….When the government does that shit with the military and pays for it all with tax dollars?

If we can pay for your activities…Then let us be great too, niggas! What I'm saying is…If we make enough money doing legal activities, then what we do with our money shouldn't bother you unless we cross a line. Instead, you're treating everyone like suspects to cover your own illegal actions and collect to make up for your losses. While the people fight over who's the bad guy and panics…you made off like a fat cat and buried all those hopes and dreams of generations in the ashes of a capitalist monument. All the while happily throwing more money to the military to go overseas to fight an imaginary war that had nothing to do with us…now we look like the bully to the world.

When you have a HIStory of being a bully…people walk lightly around you. But the more people that you pick on…the more you invite the possibility they all will team up and teach you a lesson. Especially when you're a boastful, arrogant, ignorant, musclebound jerk and owe everyone money…They don't forget shit…either…They teach us not to forget…but some shit we remember is a LIE, and the truth never shuts up until it's heard. That's the shit that I think about when I see stuff. I don't say it…but…I think a lot. I know the balance missing in myself now…and the world…it's insane!

The way I see it now, people have to master their emotions first, then their thoughts, finally. Then, we can control how we feel about thoughts we can't control. That's how we can restore most imbalance in ourselves. But, some things have to be faced and can't be buried, or…they crawl back out like the walking dead haunting our thoughts and confusing our emotions…some of us…become so terrified of being around others because they feel so profoundly.

I was talking to some dudes online that play games with me in Japan. This one guy Jamire knows he is a black dude in Tokyo, and he only leaves the house to go shopping. He's a complete recluse! I got his gamers tag just to make contact with a brother in Japan. I want to go there and see what's hood. But he is so scared to talk to strangers…the guy hasn't looked at my friend's invite. I'm gonna keep trying…something tells me to link up with people like this more…You know…the oddballs seem to be my tribe…like Kid Itchy…?

Most people would avoid niggas with problems like this, but I actually think…the way…they see shit…it's just totally different than me. So, I want to see what they see to maybe understand…Everyone ain't like me…but…if more people let everyone be and watched out for one another no matter what they looked like…It could heal most of these crazy people. You know they all lost their minds when the world showed them something they were not ready to see! I told you…I know a lot…but I only say the ratchet to keep my fam aware I'm 16. Kaliah might be the only brother I can really talk to like this. He'll be here soon! I'm ready to link up.

But with Cyrus fucked up, Elyeuh running wild now, Melissa ready to kick ass and take names, shit all I want to do is see Shamaya again. Everything happens for a reason, so yeah...thing's crazy around me, but...It got me here...waiting at a jacked-up airport, with rude clerks, but...She's close...and I can feel her! It's the only thing that will make me happy! I knew it the moment I saw her smile on Mandisa's phone.

#

I paced the airport near the baggage claim, glancing around, and scratched my head. It was nearly 12, but still no sign of Shamaya. I texted her a few times but got no reply. Her flight was supposed to arrive by 11:45. I checked the itinerary several times before Mandisa and I left Longview. We searched all over for Shamaya, but nothing, however...something told me to just let Mandisa lead things.

She seemed to be moving around like she knew where she was going. Mandisa went to the ladies' room near the gift shop. Nigga's was staring at us the entire time! Anyone that tried to get close knew I wasn't the one to be tested. I wasn't gonna let anyone near Mandisa or Maya once I found her!

I stepped inside the gift shop noticing the Hello Kitty merchandise and thought of Maya. I found myself grabbing a pink backpack. It was just like the one Maya always wore in my dream! I remember Maya always picking the yellow flowers in the park when we sat in the grass. Sometimes she wore flower clips on her pigtails. I snatched every different flower hair accessory I could find. Then as I went to pay for everything…I noticed all the candy. Why was the first thing I spotted was the Lemonheads? Maya used to call me 'Lemonhead Lionel.'

I turned away from the display and ran right into someone standing at the register.

"Damn it!" She gasped, dropping a box of candy on the floor. I quickly knelt down to help her get her things up.

"My bad, I should have been watching where I was going…I'm...sorry," I started and paused.

She glanced over at me as she clutched a plushie in her arm. Her brown eyes shimmered like amber copper when I saw her lovely shocked face. She was so beautiful! Shamaya's long black hair hung over her shoulders, falling down her back as long-ass blue and gold nails nervously pushed it behind her blue matching crystal earring. She had sparkling blue and gold gemstone clips holding her waves to one side 'Boss Bitch' all in bling everywhere! Shamaya wore make-up, lashes, and heels like a model on Instagram with sauce, unlike any woman I'd ever seen. As she smiled, her cheeks looked like rosy apples with dimples when her shiny lips curled up.

"Maya…It's really…you?" I sighed, unable to glimpse away as I unexpectedly needed to shout. I grabbed the candy from the floor, standing up while staring at her body as she stood, nodding. Shamaya Lockhart was a TOMBOY! She was a cute little chocolate doll in my memory. The woman standing in front of me could not be 15 and belonged in a music video! She was still so short, and that face was like Ashanti back in the day…but…Maya had some…body tucked in that blue bodysuit hugging all that ass! She wore bad-ass boots like Mandisa…nails…those vibes… Ooh! What the fuck?! She was a short coke bottle tucked in a denim bodysuit, bedazzled in drip, and dipped in Lionel's favorite flavor…. "Fuck…Bae…I know it ain't yo birthday until June, but…You deserve a bag to go with all that flex…I ain't even mad at ya."

She threw her arms around my waist and squeezed me. I was paralyzed by the sensations taking over me and couldn't believe she was really here with me. So many times, I thought I was crazy talking to myself or a picture wishing to hold her again…just like this…I thought I was dreaming for a moment. But when I felt the tears…I realized I was awake this time. I never cry in my dreams…I wake up…then I bawl. I never want anyone to see me crying, but I always do when I wake up from dreams about Maya. But this is no dream, and I'm terrified I'm gonna mess it up now.

I was so afraid I trembled when I touched her. Her head came to my chest, and I put my arms around her shoulders. Maya's hair was so soft that it made me smile. It was gorgeous like the Indian girls' that they used to make tracks and bundles. But that was all Maya's hair. Her eyes sparkled under blue eyeshadow as she smiled up at me with sweet pink lips.

"Look at you! So tall…skinny…How with as much as you eat, Lemonhead? You really aren't a kid anymore…I don't know what I was expecting," Maya giggled, grabbing my face, yanking me down, and staring at my hair closely. Damn, she had some muscles in her arms! Maya could have untied my boots if my feet weren't flat! That was when I noticed her bag near the checkout. It was huge, and she was lugging it around by herself? "It's so long now…I want to see what I can do with it."

Shamaya suddenly started scratching her long nails all over my scalp, and I jerked away timidly, snickering. I glanced back, and Shamaya's face was stuck in the cutest state of shock covering her lips.

"I'm so sorry...I know you're tender-headed...but I couldn't resist!" She giggled with her high voice. I squared up and quickly paid for her gifts. As I reached for her bag, Maya grabbed my arm. "You're not upset, are you, Lemonhead?"

"I've never been mad at you, Maya," I replied, shaking my head. I took her things and stole her hand. "Come on, Bae...we gotta find Mandisa."

"How is Cyrus doing? Has there been any news?" Maya worried as we walked outside the gift shop.

"Cyrus, he's not doing too-...." I stopped as I saw Mandisa coming from the restroom.

When Mandisa saw Maya, she lost it! She ran over, yelling, "Giggles! Look at you!"

"Uh-uh...Bestie! Look at you!" Shamaya screamed higher, grabbing her beautiful friend.

Yo, Mandisa and Maya look like two scoops of chocolate and butter pecan ice cream in a sexy dish next to one another.

They give a nigga those…oh my…vibes…I knew Mandisa had to have fine friends…but Shamaya has changed so much on the outside. She's still my nigga on the inside, and that is all that matters. But nigga…I love my family so much now! Two fine ass goddesses…and I know…the more they do together…oh shit! The more fine women are gonna wanna hang…ooh…This is gonna be heaven! I get it…I get…IT…Hakim…Bro…YOU ARE the Master. I owe my brother a lot more credit than given initially.

I had to look away because I had never seen Maya with a homegirl before. She was always surrounded by boys. But Maya and Mandisa vibed like two bad bitches that didn't care what anyone did around them as long as they didn't fuck with them. I loved their waves and was a happy surfer following them through the airport! When two baddies talking…you shut the fuck up…and listen…if you want the tea, Nigga! You know I was like a church mouse following them like a happy puppy. I was all ears and eyeing all that beauty and booty from a safe distance. I was the happiest nigga on earth that moment!

"You never wear your hair down, Giggle Pie! You look so sessy…Who you trying to pull, Bitch? Lionel…? Girl…he'd want you if you walked up in here wearing Key-Key's clothes…But probably not smelling like her old pussy," No...That's Melissa that said that shit! Yep, those eyes were green. Something must have pissed her off in the bathroom?

"Beyonce, you are terrible! You up in here looking like you got a recording artist about to risk it all just so you can start the next season of Love and Hip Hop!" Shamaya teased Melissa, wiggling up close and messing with her hair as she walked.

"Bitch...Love and Hip Hop...? We lit enough to get our own shit! No hate on the past, but we the Future like DMT and LSD. They scared of us and sleeping on the real since the 60s, but the energy we gonna bring can show these hos how to do shit right!" Melissa chuckled as she put a switch in her step, passing a group of businessmen. I had to ice grill the niggas once they got an eyeful. She seemed to be doing this shit to test me because she knew I was watching too. Hahhaha...very funny. "If Niggas wanna see anything I show off, they are gonna pay my asking price, and only a motherfucker I choose gets to putt off this green. Even a ring doesn't mean shit when the nigga gifting it is a BITCH. I refuse to put up with a NIGGA with no heart. Mister Elliot..eh eh eh ELYEUH...got me fucked up."

I tried to calm Melissa down as we got to Mercedez, but she was even angrier when she saw Cyrus's truck! She started pacing behind the car as I put Maya's bags away. I was amused by Maya, who seemed to no care at all about the way her friend was talking!

"Beyonce, you're bad...I'm going to tell, Mami," Shamaya teased Melissa giggling playfully.

Melissa's gaze locked on me, and she smiled viciously with glowing green eyes like jade. She looked back at Maya and said, "I'm just teaching Baby Brother a lesson, Sissy Pie. Lionel's a dog, but I just wanted him to know that I don't appreciate him ogling at US like the hos he fucks with on a routine. We are queens and merit more respect in society. Why do you think all the other men are looking with him following us, rubbernecking like a bobblehead?"

"Ah... you got me! I'm a man, so I'm gonna look. There ain't a nigga on Earth that can resist what you two got together. You know you fine as hell, Sis! Antoine's gay ass be looking at your behind. When he takes your measurements, he puts his head against it on purpose! I know he wants to close his eyes and get a hug...," I chuckled to lighten the mood. I grabbed Mandisa and squatted down, and held her. "Paula, you need to stop losing weight…Your hips are shrinking.…..What the fuck!?"

Mandisa fell forward, giggling, "Omg, Lionel! You sound just like Antoine! That is so good!"

I relaxed, realizing that Melissa was gone as I let go. Maya was giggling as I stood up, "Who's Paula?"

"Antoine is a fashion designer. I model for him, he makes all my clothes and calls me Paula all the time. He says I have Paula Patton's face and color, and he adores my figure and hips," Mandisa told Maya sweetly, blushing.

"You do have sexy curves, Beyonce! But you never dressed like this in Philidelphia. Getting you to put on tight clothes was like trying to strike a match underwater," Shamaya giggled and smacked Mandisa's butt.

"Oh, you like that?" Mandisa playfully giggled, strutting around the truck, making her jello pudding jiggle like water…oooh…I need my camera…and I know I'm gonna miss a moment if I go for it! That was PAULA? OH SHIT! No wonder Elyeuh…ooh. She had that saucy walk that oozed sexily, her attitude was so sweet and confident, but she had mad jokes too. She was the trophy wife Dr. King was trying to raise! She reached out her hand to me. "Give me the keys, and stop staring into space. Maya's right over there…talk to her!"

"Right! If you drive, then I can focus on talking to her. Good looking out, Sis," I replied, giving her the keys loving the vibe.

"Lemonhead, you're blushing! Omg! You like Beyonce?!" Maya screamed, making me blush harder. I ignored Maya and pretended to rush to open her door for her while Mandisa got in the front driver's seat. I sat next to her and shut the door, trying not to look too obvious… "Lionel…look at me…? Come on…you want to smoke one with me?"

"He's just embarrassed because he doesn't want you to know he looks at other women, Giggles. You look…He needs to know everything about you, and I'm happy you're here…But…I miss Darius!" Mandisa sighed as she started the truck. "I love Hakim so much…but I cannot lose Darius. I know he's not telling the truth. He doesn't want me there for another reason…and we're going to find out. It will be a long ride to Dallas, but Melissa can't always drive for US. I'm going to see HIM, Lionel…I'm sorry!"

"Beyonce, you're with Hakim?!" Maya yelled, grabbing her arm and climbing up into the front seat.

"No, I'm with Trey Songz, and we're engaged," Mandisa giggled as she showed Maya Hakim's ring. Maya's eyes exploded, and her face followed suddenly, looking at me. I nodded, confirming.

"Shit, Mandisa! You ain't lying with a ring like this! It looks like it was made from a piece of the iceberg that sank the Titanic," Shamaya laughed in astonishment staring at Mandisa's ring up close. "That's… tits!... It's three tits on a mama with one newborn…overkill! Someone dropped panties to get diamonds that twinkle like this…."

"Yo, Sis, you got on drawers?" I questioned, raising my eyebrows playfully. "Hakim has never wanted a girl the way he wanted Mandisa. I know that ring is worth more than he's ever spent on anything. It's insane…He loves her more than anything…."

"Aww…Hakim really has changed? He used to be so mean and distant…Hakim was always cute and nice around Cyrus but was quiet…unless there was shit to talk about that nobody wanted to hear," Shamaya sighed, playing with Mandisa's hand. "I always thought if Hakim had a girlfriend, he would be sweet. Lionel and Hakim needed a girl to soften them up…they were so hard when they moved here.

'Granny Sofie was always working, and Granddaddy said that I made Lionel listen. He was bad, and I realized he was just mad when I learned he had lost his Mama and Daddy. Hakim and Lionel have anger issues because nobody talks to them about that stuff inside the family unless it's negative. So they both lash out at anyone that says something bad about anyone in their family. They really care about each other but don't know how to say it. So they kept fighting, hoping to beat the love into each other. That's why I used to get Lemonhead away from the house. Hakim had Cyrus, but Lionel needed a friend that knew him."

"You knew all that about us from just hanging around, Maya?" I groaned, thinking back. She was so right about everything. "I used to be jealous…of Hakim…but naw…I fought the niggas talking shit about my family and me that didn't even take a second to get to know us. Everyone here seemed to have it against us for being alive. We didn't want to move here. Hakim kept saying that he hated it here and wanted to go home…There wasn't shit for us in Georgia or Chicago…Fuck! I never thought that…my brother was trying to say…he wanted to die back then! I kept fucking with him because I wanted him to do something besides sit around angry, reading, or staring into nowhere. Everyone called Hakim crazy, and I fought so many niggas when they found out he was my brother. I never denied Hakim, but it …messed me up…I knew he was going crazy…I saw it…and all I did was make it worse…I didn't know what to do! Nobody ever listens to me! Maya was the only one…."

Maya had to dive on me as I had a breakdown. I was already in tears recalling it all, but the more I remembered, the more it hurts…because I know…shit…Hakim felt all of this…He carried all the burden while I placed all the blame. I never had it as bad as I thought, and my brother kept trying to show me, but I never wanted to look through his fucked up eyes. I thought he was that selfish, mean, and hateful person purposely. Damn! Kung-Fu Kenny, you got me…my brother went through a lot of shit just to get me here to be happy. Even if it meant…he fucked up…with Mandisa…he wanted ME to have my queen!

"It is just like I told you, Lionel. Hakim is the sweet boy that I love. But I cannot help that I love Darius now. It felt necessary to heal Hakim and selfish, but they wanted this too. I can't take all the blame for this shit! I know Hakim said to stay away, but I'm not going to relax until I see Darius is alright.

'Hakim's not the only one that cares, and he had no right to tell us that we should stay away. We're ALL family, and

I'm tired of him trying to play DADDY to the rest of US. We're going!" PAULA demanded, staring at me in the rearview.

"Sis, I promised Hakim! You can't do that! He'll literally kill me...THAT NIGGA...you know...HIM!" I yelled, trying not to tip off Maya.

"HE won't touch you, Lionel, or he'll have to talk to me. He may be afraid of MELISSA, but HE wants me...so he'll listen, or I'll tell him where to go. I care but not what happens to HIM. If you're so worried...I can drop you both off at the house on the way there," PAULA told me, seriously pulling out of the parking lot!

"No! HE'LL kill me if I let you go there alone too! But...you don't know...Cyrus hasn't woken up yet. He's been out since he went into shock last night," I groaned, wiping my face.

"That is exactly the reason why I'm going. Something told me Hakim was faking earlier. He was too sweet, not Hakim. I need to see Darius. If I talk to him, he'll wake up...My intuition keeps telling me that Melissa messed up, and I need to let Darius know...I'm not mad at him anymore. But I am...PISSED off at FUTURE HUBBY," Mandisa, or whoever, said, taking the highway west toward Dallas.

Maya looked up at me, worried, asking, "Lionel, what's going on?"

"That's right, you don't know yet, Giggles. I'm engaged to Hakim, but I'm also in love with Cyrus. I feel this happened because Hakim didn't tell Darius he was proposing or about the ring. Why else would it upset him so that he left right after Hakim gave it to me? This game they've been playing for affection and bragging rights has to stop! I know he loves Darius, but he's up to something else, and it blew up in his face. If he thinks for one second that I'm going to keep playing the ignorant submissive child...he has me mistaken for ANGEL," PAULA declared, pressing the accelerator.

#

Three hours and 258 miles later, we were in Dallas, and Paula was not playing.

"Um, why are we at the University Hospital. Hakim said he was at the Rehabilitation Center?" I worried, staring at Paula's clear gray eyes as they shifted around the parking lot.

She smiled at me and said, "Do you believe they would move an unconscious patient to a Rehabilitation Center, Lionel? How can they work out someone that isn't awake? My parents are both doctors...I know better than that...lie...

'Darius is here, and I'll bet money he's in ICU or Post Operation for observation. I spent the first five years of my life in hospitals…Follow my lead…all you have to do is be quiet and look worried. So act like Hakim is going to kick your butt or Melissa. Whatever convinces them of what I say."

Mandisa got out of the truck, put on her coat, grabbed her bag, and took down her hair. She fixed herself in the mirror, and as she took a look at herself….I saw something happen! Her eyes suddenly turned blue like Amani's, and she smiled, putting on more jewelry until she looked like she was worth millions. Cyrus had Mandisa ready with all the shit he bought. That ring looked like it belonged on her finger once Mandisa had all the diamonds everywhere.

Suddenly she glanced at me and smiled, motioning Maya and me to follow. Mandisa, or whoever was, put on a hell of an act for the attendant. She walked right up to the information desk with the sweetest eyes and saddest face talking to everyone around.

"I'm searching for my fiance. His name is Darius Cyrus Jefferson Jr. He was brought here from Longview, Texas, this morning. He suffered from several gunshots…I just…Can you please tell me where he could be!? His family in New York can't be reached!"

Mandisa cried through her speech and had everyone on the phone trying to find Cyrus in a matter of moments. The clerk made several calls and finally located Cyrus and gave her the info.

"Merci, thank you so very much," Mandisa cried, wiping her tears. She grabbed my hand and pulled Maya and me along. Once we hit the hallway heading toward an elevator, Mandisa let go of my hand. Her walk slowed, and suddenly her shoulders straightened as the sauce returned right before my eyes. Her eyes twinkled like the ocean as her face became so soft and innocent, but that walk was dangerous! That was not PAULA or MELISSA…whoever SHE was…she was in Charge and had it going on like Mami! I mean…Damn…Paula has drip…but …SHE has the Goddess Goodness in her walk, and she even got Maya's attention. "16th floor…Hold on, Baby…I'm coming to find you…fuck all the drama…I need my chocolate back, now!"

I stared at the juice that girl suddenly had from just putting on all that ice. It was like Miss America was standing next to us on the elevator. I wanted to say something, but I didn't want to run her off! I covered Maya's lips in the elevator, and we were gonna let Mandisa handle Hakim. I did not want to be the first nigga he saw walking in. She said she had my back…so she's gonna play the front row on this one. Whoever we got was gonna get it if they pissed Mandisa off. So, I am really gonna shut the fuck up…now! Damn! I should have brought my camera! I thought we were gonna go home and maybe go skating or shopping. If I gotta fight Elyeuh today…At least Maya and Melissa are here with me. I don't know what's about to happen!

# Chapter Twelve: Flying Lotus/You'll Never Catch Me!!

## Osiris/Ausar/Cyrus

"Why is it so dark?" I asked, trying to see hearing an echo. It was so bleak that I couldn't make out where I was. I can hear water rushing off everywhere around me, I'm wet, and it feels like I'm sitting somewhere in the water?! But I can't move. I know I didn't piss in the bed! "Why can't I see?!"

"What do you want to see, Osiris?" I heard a rumbling voice echo back from behind me. Why did it feel like everything shook from the sound all around? The rattling actually gave me a headache! Or, I could already have a headache? I couldn't move…but I can talk…I remembered.

"Um…I'll take seeing my own black ass for $500, Alex?" I demanded. A faint light came on when I requested, illuminating inside a room that appeared to be an old movie theater. The screen was enormous, stretched as far as I could shift my eyes without moving my head. The walls were all gray, with wires running all up into to roof and behind.

I realized peeping down why it was cold! There was black water up to my neck! As the walls around pulsed tiny black droplets, barely noticeable, dripped down, making this massive BLACK pool all around me. I couldn't move much and panicked. Then, the water slowly began to creep higher up to my Adam's Apple! "What the fuck?!"

"The scales are infinitely tipping, Osiris….How long will you pretend to know yourself and walk willingly into your own undoing?" I heard a female voice ask.

"He is not ready for the light, and the darkness is not his destination…His heart…has been weighed…he shall return. Note that Ausar  shall return to death until he is spiritually awakened or measured for the afterlife…." The male voice sighed.

"What?!" I demanded, perplexed. The fear began to grow as I tried to remember what had happened. That nigga said I was going to return to death! The pool crept higher to my chin. "I don't want to die!"

"…Oh…?" The male voice asked as the room grew totally black. "If you don't want to die, then you have first to get rid of the fear that holds you captive in your seat. So why have you not yet moved, Osiris?"

"I can't move, Man! This water…is…." I held my breath as the water covered my nose.

"A metaphor of your own fear of death. The water cannot harm you, but your fear will paralyze you into believing your demise if you allow it to keep you stagnant...." The male voice bellowed to me. "Are you so afraid to die that you will not live, Osiris?"

I suddenly didn't know what to do as I was completely submerged in the darkness. The entire room was flooded, and there was no light...but no water! I stood up, staring around as my feet touched the floor.

"Lights? ...Can someone pay the damn bills around this bitch?!" I groaned, trying to make out anything in the darkness. Then, as I contacted something on a wall that felt like a doorknob, I turned it. A bright light, so white, blinded me and filled the room. I shielded my face. "Damn, my bad! Tell them other niggas that were on the mic to turn the effects down in the club!"

"Boy, stop being silly!" I heard a voice say from behind me. Someone grabbed my head and shook my face...I opened my eyes. She smiled into my eyes with her sweet face, and my heart stopped. "Still clowning around...Osiris...God!"

"Mama!?" I cried, staring at her brown cheeks and bright eyes. Finally, she nodded at me, dressed in her beautiful colorful dress. Her hair was wrapped up in a bright green scarf, but I could see her brown and red locks tied up beneath the fabric. I reached up suddenly, remembering something important. "My hair…Where's my hair? Who cut my crown?!"

"Darius…it's just hair! It will grow back…look at mine!" Mama told me, smiling as she unwrapped her headdress and let it fall down her back. "See…time heals all wounds…even Cancer. It's a physical disease. But this…you…me…our bond? That's spiritual, and the spirit never dies."

Mama smiled, shaking my head and playing with my cheeks. Then, as she released me, I touched my missing pride and frowned, thinking aloud, "I'm dead, aren't I? So that's why I'm dressed in all white like I'm going to Thug's Mansion with 2Pac?"

"No! You're still asleep! That's actually worse than being dead because if you were genuinely awake or even deceased, your soul could fly free. Being numb is like being a lucid dreamer that refuses to wake up. Such people like the comfort and security of no responsibility for their mistakes. So a belief is an excellent cover to hide the most significant truth we each have to accept in the end. We don't know what happens once we die. That fear alone is enough to cause many different results.

'Each man handles fear differently and interprets courage from experiences. So rather than honestly saying they don't know, they need a way to control that fear alone to every possible advantage…If people didn't fear death…they'd welcome it as natural and live life with purpose…There would be very little to profit from in the world. Less to manipulate men over…Osiris.

'Money is supposed to be a gateway to freedom…not a prison sentence. So many work hard for a taste of the independence you have…and you waste it being insecure about being judged. People think wealth makes things easier…no…it's worse when you are not mentally strong enough to endure poverty with grace. A humble man knows that money is earned with hard work and dedication. His knowledge is the greatest gift he gives. His money will only lead to more confusion without the proper guidance. To build a nation of wealth without love, education, and loyalty is a nation that will crumble from its own weight with time.

'Many have traded their freedom for the illusion that the money projects. The insecurity shows with the drugs, addictions, and greed as the pressure builds to keep the illusion while the body crumbles. When we project fake…our body becomes just as fake inside. You cannot maintain false illusions for long with so many eyes watching, no matter how much money…the universe…God…the soul…only answers the voice that speaks loudest. You keep talking fake…you get phony, take false, and become artificial…You talk real…that's precisely what comes to you when your heart means what you say.

'You are a King! A supreme being to attract so much abundance so young…It means the universe loves your heart, but you're rejecting your gold to give the world a counterfeit! What are you doing, Darius? Spending all that money on uselessness.

'You know that you can't buy true love! Everyone wants money, but few want to love! I struggled to raise you with very little, and I didn't hate my life! I made a choice to sacrifice to nurture you that way. Would you still see me the same if I worked as hard as your father? You see him as wrong because he wasn't there, but he sacrificed for you, too, Osiris. People that make the kind of money you've been blessed with must work so hard… there's no time for family.

'You've been given a wonderful opportunity to learn what many won't in a lifetime. The money would have been great, but the love meant so much more Osiris."

I held my mother's hands, feeling everything she said and recollecting things I had been doing for years. I started swaying her arms and made Mama wiggle with me. I twirled her around and leered, uttering, "What else do I do? Spending it is better than just lying on it like Hakim and Kaliah. You can't take it with you, right? Come on, Mama...? We in the club...groove with me?"

Mama spun around with me and snickered, "I'm pleased you still dance, Baby, but really? Why are you so afraid? You're not trying in school, and you know you're intelligent. Yet, you're holding yourself back...why?"

"I'm not, Hakim, Mama!" I groaned, spinning in a circle playfully with her on my heels.

"Anyone can see you're not your friend, Osiris!... But you're so caught up trying to not be compared to him you're acting just like him.

'How you respond, what you believe, and you even have the same taste in women. What's so great about being someone else outside if you're gonna be him on the inside?" Mami scolded me, grinning skeptically. "I don't know what you think you're doing…but I hope that you're serious…you two could kill that poor little girl. She's so fragile."

"Mandisa loved me, and I messed it up, huh?" I mumbled, shaking my head.

"She still loves you! Getting some sense knocked into your head might have saved your relationship. If you kept going the way you were, you would have seriously hurt her, and she'd never forgiven you. Then you'd be running again like your friend, pulling more girls, because you don't love yourselves. You can't buy a love that will last. You build a lasting love, then surround yourself with more people to love.

'That's the rule of the family. Build relationships, expand your horizons, and then grow numbers while protecting one another. Everyone is supposed to grow from one another, but if you're pretending to be someone else. You're learning from more illusions. You can't raise kids like that. Do you think that you're becoming the kind of man your grandfather or son could respect? If you can't say yes, then it's time for a change. Who's going to love you for who you are if you don't know who you are trying to be in the end?

'That girl doesn't need your money. She loves your tall, black, silly self despite your confusion and flaws. You have to stop all the doubt and meaningless competition over a woman you've already won. Next time this...won't be a dream."

"I'm sorry, Mama...I thought I was doing me. I didn't want to be like everyone else. It's bad enough I'm as dark as an outline, but I didn't want to be in Hakim's shadow. I want to do better...So, you like Mandisa?" I chucked at her, raising my eyebrows.

"Boy, you know how to pick them....But it doesn't matter what anyone feels about your choice! How do you feel about her?" Mama questioned me seriously as I dipped her. She giggled, pushing my hand, standing with her hands on her hips.

"Mandisa's beautiful, funny, sweet, and she really loves me. I've never known anyone like her, Mama," I replied, tearing her back with a smirk. I twirled her in a circle, and she grinned beautifully at me.

"I just want to know one thing, Darius?" She demanded, using a suspicious tone.

"What's that, Mama?" I wondered, snapping my fingers.

"How can you share your love with someone else? You're too jealous!" Mama giggled, making me pause.

"It's actually easy with Hakim, Mama. We've always been able to share…anything. I guess I keep losing focus on what really matters because I feel inferior to him. But I want to change that," I sighed, realizing it all. It was easy to share Mandisa once I relaxed and stopped trying to jump over Hakim. We had fun when we just sat around laughing, talking, and doing the usual shit.

"If you're so tight, how can you get resentful of him playing with your toys? Doesn't he share with you and let you have playtime?" Mama giggled, pushing my arm.

"Okay, now I know this is a dream! MY Mama doesn't talk like that!" I chuckled, seizing her hand again.

"Boy, please, I did it too! Where do you think you came from?" Mama snorted, blushing as she strolled a few steps with me.

"I miss you, Mama," I groaned as she teased my fingers. "I tried to grow your hair back, but I guess I broke my promise now."

"Boy, my hair is fine! You didn't break a promise to me. But you've been holding on to the pain and anger, trying to keep me alive in your hair. It was beautiful… But all that pride was misplaced in a physical manifestation of your love for me. Keep it deep down inside. It's not worth anything to you outside of yourself, Osiris…You can't show love with your hair…it's in your heart! Look at you now…so handsome…and free of the weight.

'Let me go and make a new promise that you're going to be a stronger man for yourself, Darius? Who knows what the Most-High has planned for your soul once it's truly elevated to his presence…." Mama expressed, hugging me close.

"Why haven't I dreamed of you before now, Mama?" I wondered unexpectedly.

"As long as you kept that hair, all that malice, and guilt…I couldn't be freed from your thoughts to touch your heart. Both are connected…you know…? You need help to break the chains so you can stop hauling the grief of loss. There is life after death on many levels people do not understand. I'll only tell you one secret…The rest you will learn if you keep searching…

'Holding on to the memories keeps souls alive to be transferred like any energy. Think about how deep a connection can get? Imagine being held here because your child cannot let you go. Someone would say that means you'd live on forever. Others would say that it's hell to have to keep coming back in the family until we teach these babies how to love and let go.

'Life and death are just cycles that we go through, like waking and sleeping. Most of the time, if you are not paying close enough attention…you can't tell one cycle from the other. Men are not born as gods…they do divine things when their hearts and minds are aligned with mankind's needs. Gods are not mere inventions of men…they are reborn repeatedly in the hearts of men who love the universe bringing balance to Earth. That's what I learned, Osiris.

'I couldn't tell anyone while I was alive…I was afraid no one would believe me, so I changed how I lived to reflect my beliefs. I couldn't be so wrong…I got you when they told me no…and your father stayed…when no one else would, Darius. I named you after the God Father Ausar, Osiris…because you were not supposed to be alive, and I was never intended to have a child. They tried to get me to terminate the pregnancy, and I refused because I knew you were a boy and extraordinary if I could get you here…then my purpose was done!

'Purpose is just something that makes all the pain and suffering worth it! You do what brings you natural joy daily…it doesn't have to be a career to give you purpose. Universal Love is a hell of a purpose for any man to accept. To love everyone no matter what they say or do…?

'I've never met someone on that level…but…I have a feeling that YOU will or already have… Let it go! You couldn't help what happened to me back then. You're stronger than you believe, and you can become so much stronger if you just stop, feel, think, then…change your mind if you know in your heart…you're wrong. It's okay to feel…but you must be balanced or remain lost enslaved in confusion," Mama warned me as she began to sparkle like colorful starlight before my eyes.

The room began to fade, and she grabbed my face with luminous hands as I watched the light fly free from all around taking her. The darkness consumed me as her light vanished from my sight.

#

"M..a…? Ma..?" I tried to say as the darkness and cold covered me like a flood. The shock hit me as I realized I was underwater in the dark again! It was so cold…I couldn't breathe….Mama…I don't want to die…I didn't mean it…Mandisa! I wanna make it all right…I can fix it…I can help…Oh…GOD! What was it that dude said before about the water…can't hurt…me…? "What the fuck!"

It was still bleak. I could move and breathe unexpectedly. But for some reason…I had the most terrible pain. I felt unsteady as my feet touched down, hoping that I was still near a seat in the theater. Luckily I was right in front of a chair as I landed.

My sitting resulted in a light started trying to ignite the screen. There were buzzing electric sounds like an old bug zapper overhead and trailing sparks moving through the powerlines. The fading from black to gray, then growing white pulsing behind my eyes. It gave me a strange feeling staring at the glow…but I couldn't look away suddenly ….It felt like the white light was trying…to pull me into the screen! But the flashing gave me a headache. So I held my head as the glare grew overshadowing …I couldn't move as I fell back in the seat…tears…too intense!

# Chapter Thirteen: Humble/The Ways

## Mandisa

"Room 1619, this is it. Don't say a word," I told Lionel quietly. Giggles was so worried she didn't say a word clinging to Lionel's waist like a little doll. "If Hakim trips, let him trip on me. I drove us here."

"Alright, Sis, you got the flo," Lionel whispered nervously, ducking down for some reason.

I opened the door, put my bag on my arm, and walked into the room. Hakim was sitting in a chair near Darius, fast asleep in bed. His face was swollen only a bit, but it was wrapped up. He had a cast on his left arm and looked so peaceful. Hakim glanced up, clutched his knee, and stood.

"Queen! No!!" He bellowed, and I stared him down thoughtfully as I switched my bag to my right arm in case I needed to throw a quick left. But Hakim was in tears the moment he saw me glancing over at Darius. "I told you to stay away! You don't need to see him like this! Mandisa! Why!??!"

On the sofa along the far wall, Hakim's friend was lying down. He was startled and sat up with a red face trying to wake up. He wiped his eyes and gawked at me as I stopped in front of Hakim and looked him over a moment.

"Kaliah, I presume?" I asked. His hands wiped his face, and he stood up towering over me, built like a football player! His bright gray eyes stared down at me his square jaw smiled. Whoa! This is…Kaliah…? He had the same light skin as mine and Mami's, short soft red curly hair, and he was so handsome that I immediately shifted my eyes back to Hakim to avoid making eye contact with THAT beautiful creature…

"Aye! Who yuh be?!" Kaliah questioned me as he moved in front of Hakim. His silver eyes glowed as he smiled more handsomely, showing his brilliant smile and folding his massive arms. Hakim pushed Kaliah over and frowned as he stared at my expression. Kaliah pushed Hakim and made him hobble on his leg. Kaliah suddenly panicked and lifted Hakim entirely from the ground and made him sit back in his chair. "Sit yuh stubborn ass down, Dunn! Mi up now, so what the fuck?"

Hakim stared at me and sighed, "Kaliah, Mandisa… Mandisa…Kaliah," Hakim introduced us formally from his seat but frowned, staring at me. "You can't stay here, Queen."

467

"I'm sorry, Hakim, did you say something? The last time we were in a hospital together you told me I was free! So yes, I'm here, and I'm staying. You best stay seated like your brother put you, or we'll need two beds and extra wires for your jaw, Nigga," I warned Hakim seriously as I glanced back at the door and signed Lionel and Maya. Hakim shook his head. I suddenly giggled as Kaliah got my attention taking my hand. "A pleasure to finally meet you, Kaliah. I'm glad you came. At least Hakim allowed you to come to check on HIS friend."

"Man-Di-Sa…Aye?" Kaliah requested, glancing at me thoughtfully with scanning eyes grinning. That man was as tall as Darius. He must have been at least 6'5, and he was intimidatingly handsome with his innocent looks, but his size was alarming. I could see the definition of his body through his clothes, and the way he smiled at me made my cheeks burn while he grasped my hand.

"Queen," Hakim called me, breaking my gaze from his beautiful brother's spell. "He's not awake…I'm sorry I lied to you, but I didn't want you to know…he might not make it!"

Kaliah gently stroked my hand, and I looked at him thoughtfully. He frowned and sighed, "It doesn't look good, Kween. His vitals are fine, but there is very little brain activity. Cyrus has not responded to any stimuli since he arrived. He's going to need to be alert so we can know the extent of the damage, but…nothing. If I were there…this would not have happened…I'm sorry. He's my black-ass brother, Kween."

Kaliah was a big teddy bear getting so emotional. I shook my head, disagreeing as I glanced over at Hakim, frowning. Kaliah suddenly startled me, noticing Lionel, "Lionel! Bro, yuh looking good! Dat glow all ova yuh…so golden!"

"I told you not to bring her here, Bro," Hakim grumbled from his seat, staring at Kaliah strangely.

"He didn't! I took the keys from Lionel, and I drove. I found the hospital and the room. You can't blame him for riding to ensure I was safe," I informed Hakim growing upset.

Hakim stood up with a frown and tried to make a move toward Lionel and pushed him back in the seat, yelling, "Sit your five dollar ass down before I make change…Hakim Jahlil Dunn!"

Hakim stared up at me and blinked with a blush in his cheeks, saying, "Queen, are YOU alright? This ain't like YOU at all…."

"No, I'm not alright! I'm angry, I'm…disappointed, hurt, and… I'm horny as FUCK right now!" I admitted. "I…mean...I'm hungry!"

Hakim smiled as his blush grew darker and said, "If that's why you came all this way…then we can just go get a roo-…."

"Uhh-uh, later, G.D. You got a messed up knee!" I taunted him, making Lionel chuckle. Hakim's eyes shot over to his brother, and I snatched his cheeks in my hands.

"Listen to me, Hakim, and hear MY words…Everyone here loves you, they love Darius, and you have NO right to keep any of us away from him because you feel guilty about your fuck ups. If this shit took him away from me, and I'm not allowed to say goodbye…I will kick your ass! I don't care who knows anymore…

'I'm in love with him, and I love you. Keep your anger in your chest, your hands off your brothers, and stop blaming yourself for all of this! Darius had a part in it too! He has to face the consequences of his own mistakes. He didn't deserve this, but maybe he's learned something. I'm about to find out," I said, letting Hakim's face go and raising my eyebrows.

"Damn, Beyonce," Maya giggled. "I've never heard anyone talk to Hakim like that, and he didn't fight back."

"He doesn't want none of this…This is the last damn party. One more fuck up from Hakim, and he's gonna be a free man," I told Maya. I glanced at Hakim as he sat back in his seat and nodded. "I want a deal…NIGGA…forget about whatever little plan you have…Get serious about THIS family…and…I'll drive more and let you have fun with ME. But if you FUCK anyone else…It's over…If it's a deal…stay in that seat, and don't test me."

I know what you're thinking. You're wrong. I'm not Melissa, but I'm not the young girl that Paula was…Things keep changing outside, and WE keep changing on the inside to balance what people see. It is what it is…so what you see is what you get. I'm still Paula, but I guess I'm much more aware of shit now.

I walked over to the hospital bed and looked over Darius. His head wrapped up tightly in bandages, the monitors were peeping, and my heart wanted to follow the steady pace but couldn't. He was fine, and I knew it. All the tubes, machines, and even the look of being far away didn't mean anything. I could feel him as I drew near his skin.

"Look at you…One minute, you're busting jokes, and now you're busted up? Over what, a little ring? I thought I told you that money doesn't mean anything if there is no love behind the gifts? Were you so worried that you couldn't talk to me, really?

'How can you say you love me if you don't trust me to set your mind at ease?" I whispered softly, attempting not to cry as my fingers stroked his swollen cheek. "You hurt me, betrayed my trust, and you pissed me off. So I hit you, and I'm sorry. I hurt you too, so you and I are even. I forgive you, okay? I still love you. I'll always love you, Darius…You're my Sexual Chocolate…remember?"

I leaned closer carefully, so I didn't touch his ribs and pressed my lips gently against his. As I let go of his cheeks, I let my fingertips trace his face to his neck and rested my hand over his heart. I felt a tear roll down my cheek, and I covered my face.

"M…a…Ma… I don't..wan..na..go…to…sch..oo..l," I heard weakly groan between gasps for air!

I opened my eyes and saw tiny tears roll down the side of Darius's face, and he slowly blinked…then rolled his eyes. He very slowly turned his head and stared up at me with swollen red eyes.

"Hey, Randy Watson..." I giggled, and he very slowly smiled as Hakim moved closer with wide eyes in disbelief.

"Bro? Fuck!" Hakim sighed, touching the top of Darius's head. I began to back away, and Darius grabbed my hand! His eyes were so sad as he raised my hand to his lips and kissed it. I smiled as my cheeks blushed and nodded.

"I love you, Silly-ass!" I told him as he nodded and wiped a tear from his cheek with his free hand. Maya and Lionel ran over to say hello.

I stepped away to the hall. I lost all my courage and broke down! I was so afraid that Darius was not going to wake up. I knew he was alive, but I wasn't sure what to expect. Something told me to just come and talk to him...Now that Darius was okay...the wave of relief hit me...but the fear still had a grip on my heart. It was so painful and frightening to think he could be dead...what would I do...if...

"Man-Di-Sa," I heard Kaliah call from the doorway. I nervously tried to wipe my face. "Where did you come from, Gal? Hakim talked to Cyrus all the time, and nothing. Then yuh come, Superwoman! Boom Magic? Cyrus comes back...Aye?"

"He can't… leave me yet! I want my man, a car, the house, and he promised me a baby…so he can't leave until I have it!" I cried, growing more emotional. Kaliah grabbed me and held me close, and I cried on his shoulder. He patted my back and put his head on top of mine.

"I know…Mi…know…it's scary as hell. You love someone so much, and they hurt yuh. But it terrifying to have to let dem go, aye? But Cyrus gonna be fine now yuh save him and him gonna be so happy," Kaliah told me, squeezing tighter.

Oh, my God! Let me go! What are you doing? I don't even know you…He smells fantastic, and his touch is calm yet secure.

Kaliah drew away, grinning attractively down at me with his beautiful eyes sparkling. I blushed. Now all I could sense was his cologne about, and when he touched me, I wanted to die or take off running. My heart was zipping speed to and fro, and he was still cuddling my hand, not wanting to let me go! And why was he smiling at me like he could read my mind?

"Come, come…Wi will go to walk off yuh tears? Yuh need to get some air, Man-di-sa, aye?" Kaliah summoned me as his eyes shifted to a dazzling blue suddenly.

"I shouldn't, Kaliah... I feel I should stay. What if Darius calls me?" I anxiously calculated my escape. Oh, no! I had enough men trying to get me out of my pants. Kaliah was sweet, but I was not interested! No matter...how...good he smells...or how completely mature Kaliah appears. Wait! Kaliah is the brother that's the doctor! He's the one that made all the money...and THIS is what Hakim... "I should stay close to Darius, Kaliah."

"Cyrus needs all the rest he can get so we can take him home. Yuh can take a walk wit Kaliah. Yuh need to get to know meh. Wi gonna be friends, Mandisa...Aye?" Kaliah insisted as he hauled me along the hall leisurely.

Kaliah was so powerful he didn't have to use any force to persuade me. The moment he took a step taking my hand, my feet pursued involuntarily! He wore a silk maroon vest, a white collared dress shirt like his dress slacks, and designer loafers. He had diamonds in his ears, and when Kaliah laughed enough for his teeth to flash...The most adorable dimples formed in his square chin near his full round pink lips. He had a tiny ring that sparkled golden above his fuzzy red left eyebrow...When he blushed, his red hair seemed to look brown darker as his skin flushed, and it made his eyes flicker and change shade like a mood ring.

But the one thing that caught my eye instantly about Kaliah was… the many scarcely visible… but clearly evident …tattoos! The man had colorful ink running everywhere beneath his clothing, from neck to wrists. With his beautiful golden skin tone…all the colored ink stood out like art on his skin, yet I hadn't seen anything but the outlines through his shirt!  He had so many tattoos it was insane…Obviously, Kaliah was the most attractive brother of the four, and suddenly I started to get the feeling… I should not have met THIS brother. Hakim was right to keep him away from me!

The moment Kaliah touched my hand, I began to feel very…calm. But I was so jumpy because he was so alluring. His voice was the only thing that threw me for a loop. For him to be such a massive guy in physique…Kaliah's voice…it's high pitched…unless he's talking slow and seriously…Then…his tone is intense and mellow…It's the complete opposite of what you envision a Jamaican man. Most Island men have vibrant deep accents. Kaliah's voice was hyper and excited…like a man swinging on a vine and just as fast… until he relaxed.

How in the hell did a soft curly red-headed, tatted-up bodybuilder that looks like Micheal Ealy…end up tugging me around a Dallas hospital like a clueless fan? I heaved back swiftly, and Kaliah stopped strolling and glanced over his shoulder. He slowly turned around and freed my hand uneasily. He looked at his expensive watch and reached in his breast pocket, putting on a pair of designer glasses that accentuated his dreamy eyes.

I gasped, eyeing him from a safe distance, "Ce que Je fais?" (What AM I doing??)

"Vous marchez avec, Kaliah," He chuckled, glancing with silver eyes at me back from his wrist. I froze, gazing at him sincerely. "I speak many languages. See? Yuh learning about mi already. So…like mi say, yuh walking and talking wit mi?"

"Alright, we're just walking and talking. But if you cross over a line like on the phone…I'll cut you," I giggled, clutching my bag nervously to my side. Really…staring at the man…I couldn't believe he was the same person I talked to on Christmas Eve. But unexpectedly…I began to see more than the surface. His Facebook posts, the sad poem…Oh, God! "Your wife!? Where is….Tisha?"

Kaliah's face suddenly grew relaxed, and he glanced around sensitively as if searching and decisively said, "We don't do dat here, Kween. Change the subject…I'm no longer discussing negative shit! You would know…Dunn Deal…?

Come…wi go see something positive…transmute dis shit quick?!"

Kaliah retook my hand and walked me toward the elevator. He stood in thought for a minute and groaned, "Hakim told me what happened last night. Are you really okay, Mandisa? Tony…He didn't touch you or hurt you in any way?"

"I believe I'm fine…Nothing…happened to me, but I was scared to death. Oh, and I lost an adorable sweater," I tensely giggled, viewing Kaliah frowning. He was so solemn when he was contemplating…He made the most spectacular faces with his expressive eyes and chiseled jaw and chin. His cheeks would relax, and it made his eyes seem to look so miserable and olive. "I'm okay, really….I was blessed…Hakim and Lionel heard me scream."

"Oh, eh, aye?" Kaliah grumbled, rubbing his neck pondering things.

"What's that mean?" I inquired, watching him. "I've never heard that expression before…you say…Aye?"

"It's my way of asking or confirming your thought you expressed without repeating…a possible lie…If you say so…Oh, eh…Aye…Aye…Eye…I…Oh, I see…I can see what you said, I heard you, but I think you may be confused.

Or…in anger…You have me fucked all the way up if you think I believe that…hahaha…

'Kaliah creates his own language, so the magic is specific. As long as the receptor overstands my intention, then the magic works….Aye?...You see?" Kaliah very articulately explained with a soft tone and slow intention. It was charming, and I felt I overstood where he was getting.

"Eye see…You put an accent on your Eye…so it's Aye…like if you were a vessel pilot taking to the Captain…Aye…Eye?" I giggled spiritedly. Kaliah smirked, dreamy, and abruptly glared at me curiously with his painful olive-green eyes. "Eye see why you're friends with them all. They imitate you in many ways."

"Aye…aye, Mandisa…Hakim be mi crazy little bro, Lionel, and Cyrus…shit dem all crazy as fuck! But mi love dem all like wi family, aye? Wi grew up together, seen so much change, and now…yuh the first woman dat Hakim lose it all over…mi overstand," Kaliah chuckled, holding the elevator door open. "Come come…wi go see di babies? It always makes Kaliah feel happy."

I got in the elevator but was confused as Kaliah followed me quietly. He leaned against the wall with his hands behind his back. Kaliah suddenly chuckled, "Mi pray to the universe for a sign. I'm a strong believer in the spiritual world, Mandisa. Everything mi do, mi ask the stars. Marriage is no joke to Kaliah, so it's a very significant spiritual connection for me. Been praying, meditating, and waiting for years to get an answer…should mi stay or go…aye?"

"Funny thing about praying for signs, Kaliah, you rarely know if it's a real sign or just a moment…I used to think there were no coincidences…now…I don't know," I murmured, trying to lift his spirits. He seemed so down.

"Nah! You'll know a REAL sign when it comes… When I see a REAL gift from the universe, my whole body feels it…I have to stop and take notice. Everything is scary, your heart races, you can feel the spiritual energy moving through you like ants marching or chills, and sometimes it stops in different parts of the body….telling me when to look. It's warm like the sun one moment…then suddenly freezing cold…makes your stomach quake…You'll know," Kaliah clarified with a gentle smile.

I giggled anxiously, unexpectedly intimidated by Kaliah's detailed description of things I often experienced recently. He was giving me such a vibe of admiration and respect when we talked. It wasn't flirting at all. His nature was just magnetic and kind. It made me feel very excited, and I wanted to run away from him the longer he stared at me. I knew Kaliah was only 21 years old from talking to Lionel and Hakim, but his relaxed demeanor said...Old soul...He's been here before, and Mami would go insane meeting this man...He was PERFECT!

"Your Facebook page is depressing, Kaliah," I thought, breaking the silence as the elevator stopped.

Kaliah waited for me to exit the elevator, and he retook my arm and walked with me nodding. He slowly strolled and chuckled, "Been through a lot lately, Mandisa. The only way to vent without resorting to violence, sometimes. Mi work all di time, and git bored...lonely...

'Facebook's okay, but I miss real interacting wit family. But I stay away cuz I know we all got shit going on...I get mad... Don't want to go back to jail...I've been a bad boy in the past...Aye?"

"Oh...Eye see...but you said that things are different?" I responded as we came upon the window to the Neo-Natal/Maternity ward.

Kaliah abruptly jerked away from me and slowly walked along with the window as if hypnotized in a trance. His eyes were so bright and blue as he glanced at the few newborn babies lying asleep. Kaliah put his hand to the glass, beautifully entertained. An attending nurse noticed him, and he nodded, indicating to the only black baby. She picked her up and held the baby girl closer so he could see her.

Her little pink hat fell off, and Kaliah flushed red, staring at her dark curly hair. His face suddenly grew intense as he stared at the precious baby. It made me miss Amani. I played with her before we left for the airport and made a video of Mami talking to her. I grabbed my phone and showed it to Kaliah as the nurse put the baby back.

When Kaliah saw Amani…his face lit up so brightly he squealed, "Look at dat! Beautiful Mum, gorgeous baby, and so sweet…a gal?"

I nodded, giggling at his reaction, "My baby sister, Amani. She's almost four months old."

"Aye…EYE, mi can see! Har look just like yuh, Mandisa! Big favor! Yuh Mum, too! Wow…Divinity!" Kaliah exhaled, blushing scarlet, staring at my phone in wonderment! "Eye-eyes blue like the ocean back home….How?"

"My father's white…Daddy has big blue eyes, and they look gray in different light…Like yours," I replied, tickled as Kaliah glanced up at me. He nodded with a puzzling gaze.

"I suppose I got my eyes from Mami, but people say they turn blue. I can never see it when it happens."

"Mi Mom a white woman, har crazy, but not so bad...Aye?" Kaliah chuckled, walking me back toward the elevator. I got quiet, not wanting to talk about Daddy. "Mi Mom, mi love har, she's mi crazy best friend. She's alway-always tryin to git mi leave Trisha. Mom hated har! Talks big shit about Trisha since they met. Maybe...one day...yuh meet mi Mom...Mandisa, Aye?"

As Kaliah offered me my phone, he held my hand and grinned magnificently. His blue eyes twinkled as he studied me a moment and turned, moving on. It was the strangest feeling...Kaliah's vibe made me feel perfectly normal and understood. I couldn't stay angry, sad, or worried about much. I was stuck like this with HIM near me! Holy shit! Now it made sense when Darius said that Kaliah could keep ELYEUH under control! That was Hakim in Darius's room, not Elyeuh...and Melissa couldn't get out! There was something to Big Brother that no one overstood, and Lionel said that he had anger issues, too.

"Who knows, Kaliah...." I managed to reply as a wave of realization crashed over me...

Kaliah reminded me of all his friends that he called "Brothers." He was sad under all those beautiful smiles and innocent like a child in ways. Heartbroken, really, as I thought back to the night before Christmas. That terrible poem on his page. Kaliah was so deep and injured…just like…my KITTEN! My sad, frightened little kitten with the beautiful eyes from my dream!

I was suddenly terrified! What did all this mean? Was THIS really a sign or coincidence? I've never met Kaliah before, I couldn't have, because he's been in Jamaica. But with the remembrance of that dream, I felt…infatuated. I tried not to look at Kaliah as we walked because I was mystified and terrified out of my mind. My heart was shuddering, my stomach rumbled noisily, and I nearly died as Kaliah smirked, blushing at me.

"Come, come, mi nah eat all night, bad nerves….yuh hungry, Kween?" Kaliah invited me.

"Oui! I'm starving!" I giggled as he pushed the elevator button…to the ground floor? "We can eat here in the cafeteria…Where are we going?"

"Mi saw a noodle shop across the street. Hakim will love it! Wi go and bring back food for everyone? Get a big bowl of soup for Cyrus. Him nah like milkshakes. Dem gonna try to get him to drink milk…He'll slap a bitch wit him gud black-ass pimp hand. Cyrus's pimp hand is strong, Boo-Boo! The weak arm's in the sling, Bitches…." Kaliah chuckled, producing a silky smooth voice, getting me to giggle.

We walked across the street, ordered to-go plates and bowls of soup, with dessert for everyone. I reached for my purse to get my wallet, and Kaliah grabbed my hand, shaking his head. He quickly squinted, noticing my ring, and leered.

"Dat…be one gorgeous diamond, Mandisa! DAMN, Woman! Custom-made eternity band, five karat diamond, set in platinum, gold inlay about 24 karats, ruby-diamond heartcuts, and each about a karat…eight total…Worth about one million dollars! Aye, sound about right?" Kaliah posed to me, examining Hakim's ring.

"Maybe…wait…What?! Oh my, God!" I gasped, realizing Kaliah may be correct.

"Oh, MI know…Worth every penny, too! You know THEY say a ring is supposed to be 3 months salary, Mandisa. It's supposed to represent a man's sacrifices to prove how much his love means to the woman. He's giving her more than a meager possession. It's supposed to represent how he values his own heart in giving away his life to her. The energy exchange from hard work, to money, to the diamond….Then…he passes that to his queen.

'Partner supposed to accept his heart and keep it precious while honoring the sacrifice. Build up the man that breaks down for you…." Kaliah revealed, laughing deep in thought. But his eyes grew sad, and he frowned. "I think I spent 500 thousand on Trisha's ring. She never wanted to wear it because she said I was just trying to show off. She didn't need a constant reminder that she had my heart. That was the second sign that I ignored. She didn't want my heart, no matter how pretty I made it for her or how much I sacrificed building my world around her….But..Anyone dat sees DAT ring…knows you got a man dat loves yuh more than life itself, Gal! Hakim never ceases to amaze me the older he gets. Thought him wah silly joking until Hakim tells Kaliah to spend real money on one woman, but him nah waan mi tah see yuh."

Kaliah was quiet as he grabbed the bags after paying for everyone's meal. When Kaliah was silent, it was as if he were a different person too concerned to speak. Even when he conversed, he was always in contemplation, but the silence seemed to make him someone else entirely. This Kaliah wasn't a cold person either, but he seemed bothered by strangers. Bearing all the sacks, he refused to let my hand go, and he would not let anyone get near without a determined thought after noticing his size then snubs.

#

We returned to 1619, and everyone was sitting around. The family was happy to see us with food. I sat on Darius's bed and helped him drink his soup. He was so delighted because they had brought him shakes. He could talk through his braces but couldn't open his jaws, making him drool a lot more and much funnier. Besides being swollen, having headaches, sore ribs, and an arm, he couldn't move…Oh, and no dreadlocks. Darius was Darius, and I was so happy to have him back.

I admit I was smothering him with so much affection that Lionel said Hakim might run and get shot. I slapped him for that shit.

"Queen?" Hakim sighed as he finished his noodles. He put down his chopsticks and slid his chair closer to me. I stared at him as he put his hand on my thigh. "Listen, I'm sorry I told you not to come. I was wrong. If you hadn't of showed up, Cyrus might still be out of there.

'Since you've arrived, the air seems lighter, and I can breathe easier. I was so worried about being here and what could happen next. I was selfish, thinking of only my feelings and no one else. Forgive me, please?"

"Oui, I forgive you, but…don't do that to me ever again. You pushed me away when you needed me. You treated me like a different person, and it scared me. I don't like HIM! He's a very mean person. I can take you BOTH now that you have that bad knee…Don't forget, Nigga," I replied, exhibiting my fist but pushing his forehead back.

"Oh yeah?" Hakim arrogantly chuckled, coming back to grab me. "Prove it, Queen…take me now…please?"

"You, Pervert!" I giggled, ribbing him in the cheek with my red fingertip. I startlingly glanced around, noticing people missing. "Where did Lionel and Maya go?"

"Day in Luv…They shooo in Luv!" Darius spat out, laughing through his braces as I teased his leg through the covers. "Ooooh, Baby! WA-it! KW-eeN!"

"Oh, God! Did I hurt you?" I worried, staring at his legs carefully now. "Is your leg hurt too?"

"Uh-uh, I wantsss…. DaT …assssh! Come ere!" Darius spat, trying to grab my butt with his one good arm. I cracked his leg as I exhaled in relief. "Man-dissha…wheelly?! Fluck…I shound…Ai-shian…"

"Too bad yuh look like Daffy Duck…black mothafucka," Kaliah chuckled, sitting down his cup. Hakim hid his face laughing inside his red tee shirt.

"Fluck you, Kaliah!" Darius tried to shout and grabbed his side.

Hakim choked as he coughed, laughing louder. Kaliah nervously stood up and came near. He checked Darius's side a moment. Darius rolled his eyes and smiled to himself a moment as I pushed Kaliah's hand.

"Don't upset him right now, Dr. Kaliah. I thought you knew better," I mumbled at Kaliah playfully, trying not to laugh. "Darius, bad boy, NO! You've got broken ribs, a wired jaw, that busted shoulder, and Hakim's got his sprained knee. Jah, help me! I guess I'm going to be hungry for a while."

"Damn!" Darius mumbled, trying to move his lips more. "I can't even taste the pussy like this!"

Kaliah died laughing as he pushed Hakim's shoulder, "Damn, Cyrus, Bro…yuh tongue in prison!"

"Don't make me laugh again, Kaliah…that…shit…ain't funny! Fluck you, Kaw-wahl!" Darius stuttered and burst into laughter. All of us were in tears.

"Nothing wrong wit Kaliah's tongue, Bro!" Kaliah chuckled as he stuck out his very long, pierced clapper. It reached down and curled under his chin backward!

"Holy shit…!" I mumbled, gazing away.

"Nah! Look-look, Man-Di-SA!" Kaliah screamed, getting my attention as he began to flick it in different directions, like lightning.

"Nasty asses! All of you!" I shouted, rolling my eyes humiliated. Hakim was dying of amusement. Darius laughed so hard he yanked the call light for the nurse. The sweet nurse came and poked her head inside the room. She looked at Darius with her bright brown eyes and a blond ponytail and put her hands on her hips in her pink scrubs, grinning.

"Look at you! How are you feeling, Mr. Jefferson?" She questioned, glancing around at all of us. Hakim and Kaliah were both faking to be innocent while I shifted the string out of the way.

"I'd be better if you let me go to the bathroom on my own! Take this thing out of my shit, pweesh!" Darius mumbled, glancing at the nurse.

"I'll see… what the doctor says," The nurse answered timidly, about to leave.

"Hey!" Hakim shouted to her raising his voice. "We have his doctor right here now. My brother wants to move around so take that shit out!?"

The nurse glanced around and asked, "Who's his doctor?"

Kaliah stood up and replied, "I am a licensed medical doctor with no public practice, private. Doctor Clark answers to me now. Take the catheter out, please, Mam?"

I raised my eyebrows, glanced at her, and got up out of the way. She went to get gloves and pulled Darius's curtain.

"Don't stare at it! I got one hand. You got two, so grab it!" Darius yelled, and we all laughed. I nearly fell on Kaliah as he came closer to me. He didn't get the joke yet. As Hakim and I covered our faces giggling. The nurse, poor white girl…she left the room as red as hellfire. "Oh, my god! That feels so much better! Queen, walk me to the potty?"

I smiled as I moved closer and paused his IV, and let Kaliah unhook it. I helped Darius slide off the bed and held him close as he limped up…and slowly stepped into the bathroom.

"Blackest ass in Texas!" Kaliah laughed, and Darius had to hold his side, trying not to laugh. Hakim was still crying.

I had to hold my breath as I closed the bathroom door and helped Darius sit. As I turned to leave him alone, Darius grabbed my hand.

"Wait...I don't really have to go...I want to say..sobbry..ugh! I hate dish jaw shit!" Darius sighed, moving his lips but struggling to speak clearly. "Man-Disha...I wuv you, and I'm sobbry..never gonna happen again. Hear me? I was ..stupid, mad, and wong...w..you know what I'm tying...Love you!"

"Darius, it's over, okay...? But you need to know something essential," I replied, staring down at him at his sad swollen eye and cheek. His skin was bruised, but he looked like my sweet Cocoa Puff. He slowly nodded. "Darius...Tony and Mia are both dead."

Darius wrinkled his eyebrows painfully, asking, "How?"

"Tony and his boys killed Mia, and Hakim had Lionel's friend Lester got rid of Tony somehow. I don't know the details, but many people are dead, and Gucci's got burned to the ground. But don't tell him I told you," I informed Darius. His face appeared disturbingly astonished, and he concurred again. "Hakim is not himself lately, and I'm worried. I think he snapped after everything happened. Kaliah may be keeping him calm…I don't know. We have to wait and see what happens from here on."

"Kween, Ha-keem…he'll be fine once he calms back down," Darius told me as a tear ran down his right cheek. "I heard what you shed about my jaw. I disserve dat…don't trip, okay? I wuv your little attitude now…ish so cute!.... Okay…I do have to go…you can weave!"

"Ugh! Nasty!" I giggled, slamming the door behind myself.

"You stayed in there with him while he used the bathroom?" Hakim demanded, snickering. I blushed and turned my eyes.

"He was having problems relaxing, so I talked to him until he could go," I giggled, still standing by the door. "I would do it for you too, Hakim!"

Hakim sank over, laughing in Kaliah's lap, bawling again. Kaliah stared up at me, dreamy-eyed, declaring, "Dat dere be REAL love."

"Stop it!" I growled at them, both utterly embarrassed.

"Seriously, nah, every woman sit wit har man in the toilet! Got to love him and his shit too! Yuh already put up wit enough bullshit!" Kaliah squealed, falling back shaking his head.

"You know what? This conversation is over!" I demanded, pointing at Kaliah.

"Baby! I CAN'T wipe my ass! Help!" Darius yelled through the door. I paused…and Hakim's head shot up straight. Kaliah grabbed Hakim's cranium and rocked it back and forth, waiting.

"Flush the toilet first, Darius!" I groaned as I opened the door. Hakim and Kaliah were clowning me so hard we could hear them laughing through the door. I helped Darius back in bed after I washed my hands.

"Long-ass claws, ooh! I don't see how women can wipe themselves with those things," Hakim chuckled, pushing Darius's arm. "Bro, did she scratch up your ass?"

"Hakim…Fuck you! From the blackish spot on my ass," Darius groaned, trying not to laugh aloud. "Hell no!"

Kaliah and Hakim had another laugh at our expense.

"You know what? If you need help, Hakim, you're on your own," I told him, folding my arms, frowning.

"Aww, Queen, come on…We're just teasing you. It's so cute! You love YOUR little Cyrus-Cyrus," Hakim said, pinching Darius's right cheek.

"Get the fuck off me, Hakim!" Darius said as Kaliah turned his IV back on. I sat back in my spot next to Darius's legs and pushed Hakim back. Kaliah checked the lines and glanced down at me. A beautiful smile grew across Kaliah's pink lips, and his eyes sparkled gray. "Ka-LI-AH, stop starting at my wife, NIGGA!"

Kaliah glared over at Hakim and grinned even more enormous and announced, "Told yuh when I filed for divorce that mi Dunn wit Trisha for good…aye?"

Hakim nodded and shook his head, saying, "Heard that before, Bro…Remember this past summer? Then the year before that? You always go back once you cool off, Kaliah."

Kaliah just nodded, smiling at the floor, and chuckled, "Aye, Hakim…Mi pray, meditate asking for a sign. Mi got MI sigh. Mi waan…Man-Di-Sa.."

I raised my eyebrows as I nearly died of laughter, "Nigga, you must be crazy!"

"Aye-aye! Mi crazy bout yuh, Gal!" Kaliah confessed, staring down at me thoughtfully. "Yuh call Cyrus, Randy

Watson, Sexual Chocolate?... Mi Prince Akeem, mi come to America to find mi Kween...U...Mandisa."

Hakim glared over at me and smiled viciously. He raised his eyebrow and groaned, "Is that...right, Kaliah?... I don't think she likes you, Bro."

Kaliah's eyes shifted blue suddenly, and he glanced at Hakim laughing, "Oh, eh, aye...? I think she does like me, Bro. You wait and see, Aye?"

I gasped as my stomach suddenly knotted up as Hakim suddenly glanced at Darius. Kaliah raised his eyebrow and offered me his hand asking, "Dr. Kaliah Morgan...an absolute pleasure to welcome you to the family, Mandisa. Unfortunately for Hakim and Cyrus, but blissfully providential for you...I'd like to formally place my intent out to woo you as well?"

"You're already married, Kaliah," I laughed, shaking my head not making eye contact with him.

Kaliah placed his hand on my shoulder, and the warmth from his touch made me unexpectedly get goosebumps. He moved closer and turned my cheek toward him with his finger. His blue eyes studied my face a moment, and Kaliah smiled dashingly, whispering, "No, Mandisa...I filed for divorce...when Hakim told me to start working on YOUR house…in Jamaica. No need to think about my ex-wife…building a palace for a REAL Queen. I was just waiting for the universe to bring me to you…We had a few close calls…but nah. This time…It's destiny, Goddess! Kaliah wants you, too."

"I swear…if you weren't my doctor…I'd choke your Iwish-wooking…Al B. Sure looking ass…." Darius threatened Kaliah while sitting up. I pushed him back down. "KWEEN, WHEELY? Don't tell me you really want his light-bright-looking ass?"

"I don't want you fighting over me. You're all family. Isn't the fact that we're in a hospital again enough to stop the petty fighting?" I grumbled. "A woman shouldn't have to choose when it comes to love…This feels so wrong."

Hakim sat forward and folded his arms over the back of his chair, laughing, "I thought you started THIS SHIT? That means it's only wrong if you say it's harmful, Mandisa. You know I want you. Cyrus isn't going anywhere…

'I knew with Kaliah running from Trisha…You're just his type too. I can't tell you what to do…But you promised me…You would never leave me as long as I obeyed. I'm here…."

"No rush now dat wi so close, Mandisa...all wi got is time... and... space, Love," Kaliah handsomely chuckled as he placed his lips on my hand and went to sit on the sofa. He leaned back and folded his arms behind his head, and he crossed his ankles. "Black-ass, yuh keep being a hater all yuh life gonna wind up wit more than broken jaw, and bulletholes...lose yuh, good woman. Be nice...Kaliah a patient-doctor...aye?"

"Kish my black-ash, Shamus G-Money!" Darius shouted. I had to grab him and make him lie down. "Sorrwy, Kween...He knows I can't stand his one shade from the clouds-colored ass!"

"You're all going to calm down so we can get out of here! Stop upsetting him, Kaliah...Hakim? We're going to be in Dallas a while, so we may as well relax and go with the flow," I reminded them.

"Whatever you say, Mandisa...You're the boss," Hakim replied, holding up his hands.

"That's right...I am the Queen...But this is getting out of hand," I giggled, shaking my head patting Darius's side.

I couldn't tell Hakim the truth about the way Kaliah made me feel...It was too soon. I really didn't know much about him at all. There was no way I could dream of being with three men at once, but Hakim seemed very willing to go along with anything I said as long as he was included. There's no way that he can be so cool with his brothers, and I'm not stupid. THAT NIGGA, Elyeuh was still in there trying to get out…He might be calm as long as Kaliah was around. We'd know the moment something started to feel strange or anything else made the news involving someone we knew.

## THE END

www.ingramcontent.com/pod-product-compliance
Lightning Source LLC
Chambersburg PA
CBHW070337170726
48291CB00001B/87